PRODIGAL

Prodigal

Published by The Conrad Press in the United Kingdom 2019

Tel: +44(0)1227 472 874
www.theconradpress.com
info@theconradpress.com

ISBN 978-1-911546-63-4

Typesetting and Cover Design by:
Charlotte Mouncey, www.bookstyle.co.uk

The Conrad Press logo was designed by Maria Priestley.

Printed and bound in Great Britain
by Clays Ltd, Elcograf S.p.A.

For Tessa

PRODIGAL

MICHAEL WATERHOUSE

1

2013

think I heard scuffling during the night. It was difficult to tell. The row the guards make tends to mask every other sound. Even the tick and twitch of insects is drowned out by them. They shout and laugh and let off long screeching yells. You'd think they were drunk at a parade, the Notting Hill Carnival or New Year's in Trafalgar Square. But they're not drunk. They're not allowed to drink. And they've probably never heard of Trafalgar Square, and I'm damn sure not Notting Hill. If anything, they're bored. I've often wondered how they can be bored and appear so jolly at the same time.

A few feet from me, Rashid shrinks away when he hears them. He is always afraid that their exuberance will be the prelude to violence.

From: spadge@tyzl.com
To: me@padgett.com
Sent: 8 June 2013 18:16:33
Subject: Hello parents

Despite the latest deaths, which you'll have heard about on the news, things have generally quietened down here. I don't feel I'm in as much danger as I was. I think more about the heat than the

possibility of being blown up or shot. During the day the tempera-
ture never sinks much below 35º (or ninety-five Fahrenheit, as you
insist on saying, Dad). You step out of the compound and it's like
someone has shoved a hair-dryer in your face. The heat is always
that close. You feel it on the surface of your skin. All the time.

They've been running old movies for the last few nights, keeping
the lads entertained. I saw 'Death in Venice' recently. V good.

I remember you mentioning it, but I'd no idea how brilliant
Dirk Bogarde was. He's dead now, isn't he? All that Mahler too.
I'm guessing it's one you both love. You should get it out on DVD.
I'm sure it's worth a second viewing. Or have you already seen it
dozens of times?

I'm well. Cold cleared up. Will contact when I can. Love to
you both, Steve.

'Cara!'

She was upstairs, in their converted attic, trying to rehearse.
Bach.

'Cara!'

'Alright!'

She had intended to give the whole morning to rehearsal,
followed by lunch with Edward, then Sainsbury's. It was now
scarcely 11.30. He was going to wreck her plan. He'd want
coffee, a chat. None of this would matter if she could return
to her work and slip right back in exactly where she'd left off,
but voice drill wasn't like square bashing. She would need to
warm up a second time, exercise, and in any case coffee often
clagged the chords so that further rehearsal became pointless.

'We've had an email from Stephen.'

She was half way down the stairs, pausing at the turn.

'Wonderful,' she said. 'When did it arrive?'

'I thought you'd want to read it.'

'I do, Edward. But it could have waited, couldn't it? Until lunchtime, I mean. I was working, darling.'

Edward made his way to the kitchen. He called back 'Coffee?' as he ran water into the kettle and plugged the cable into a wall socket next to an enamel bin labelled BREAD. He took down a fresh bag of coffee from the cupboard above.

'I can't work.'

'You've made that abundantly clear.'

'Have I?' Edward seemed genuinely puzzled. 'Is Tim coming down this weekend?'

'I thought I was going to read the email.'

'I printed it out. It's in my study.'

Cara was annoyed.

'No coffee for me,' she said, and she went to fetch the email.

'They're forecasting rain.'

15th June 2013

Dear Stephen

We have sunshine here, too, though it's scarcely ever very warm. Since the barometer bust last July, I've not had a clue exactly how warm, but I have just discovered how to change the temperature reading on my car dashboard from bloody centigrade to friendly fahrenheit. I can now confirm that it has been around sixty or sixty-two for the best part of a month, which is good for the fruit. They've had a largely dry time of it on the farms.

Some new people called Carlisle, Jon and Lavinia (she calls herself Vinny), came for drinks on Sunday. They seemed pleasant enough. He's an osteopath and she teaches somewhere. She said her subject was Resistant Materials. Do you know what they are? Presumably what we used to call Woodwork and Metalwork. Resistant Materials makes it sound as though they're stubborn, not quite behaving themselves.

Your mother is preparing for the B Minor Mass. I wait to hear about a Wigmore gig at Christmas. I suppose it's too much to hope that this government will bring you home for that. Take care. Affectionately, Dad.

Her stage name was Cara Loire. From the moment she'd thought of it, back in the Seventies, when she'd first met Edward, she'd loved it. They'd both loved it. She had been born Cara Laher and had never imagined that she'd have to change it to perform. But Equity claimed they already had a Cara Laher on the books. Cara had never heard of her. She was tempted to demand proof; it seemed so unlikely. Edward suggested she think of something French. At the time, they were eating French food, drinking French wine, reading French novels. Posters of Impressionist paintings from Athena hung on the walls of their flat. They listened to French records, as old as Rameau, but probably only as new as Poulenc, with Berlioz, Satie and Ravel sandwiched in between. A French name made sense. Loire was close enough to Laher. For months and months she could summon up the taste of a bloody good Vouvray every time she said it.

Of late Cara Loire had done rather better professionally than Edward Padgett. It was not a subject they discussed, but she knew he found it painful. At one time, he'd been in continuous demand. He'd never boasted about his success. He simply enjoyed it and for as long as Cara's chorus work kept coming in, the disparity between them was not a problem.

Then two things happened: his heart attack and her chance meeting with Karl Rouse. Word got around that Edward was not so well and some of the people who'd regularly cast him began to think it would be kind to let him rest for a while. When the phone did ring, it was more often than not for Cara, because Karl Rouse, the conductor, had taken it upon himself to tell everyone he knew that the great, unacknowledged soprano of the new century was Cara Loire. No one could have been more surprised than Cara.

Solo roles followed, concerts of her own. Rouse asked her to make a record with him, which Classic FM picked up and promoted. The CD sold thousands of copies. She couldn't recall how many.

She discovered audiences. As a member of a sixty-strong chorus, she'd not thought about the audience. They were appreciative, of course, and clapped and whooped enthusiastically, but they were an undifferentiated mass, and not there for her. Now, as a soloist, bathed in isolating light, she saw faces, smiling individuals, who belonged to her, if only for a moment. There was nothing quite like the completion of a performance. The hiatus before the applause was vivid in a way that nothing else in her life resembled or had resembled since she'd first fallen in love with a young Edward Padgett.

There were days when she felt bad about Edward. Her concerts meant evenings, sometimes nights, away from home. At first he'd gone with her, attended every one, put up with the hotel food she knew he was hating. Then he stopped, not altogether, but he began to come only to the occasional evening, judged by where she was singing rather than what it was.

She was aware that he would like her to be at home more often, to be together. She would have liked it too, but not at the expense of this late afternoon sunshine, this mellow unlooked-for renown. Why shouldn't she enjoy it? The boys were grown up. 'This is your time now,' her yoga teacher used to say at the start of the class. That was how she saw it.

17ᵗʰ July 2013

Hi Tim

It's unusual for me to write you, I know, but I've had a few thoughts I wanted to put down, and we're discouraged from spending time on our phones. I'm writing to you because I need to. I've got to tell you, bro, my leave in two months can't come fast enough. The situation here changes from day to day, week to week, and it's not generally as grim as I think it's painted in the papers back home. We do get things done, most of the people like us and they approve of the early signs of reconstruction which you can see happening all over this part of the country.

But – you probably heard it coming – the past few days have been difficult, to say the least. I was out with my company on a clear-out op and there were moments when I was shit scared and I thought we'd had it the last night. We were sleeping out in some smashed up compound, under the stars - not as great as it sounds, the ground was either concrete or broken stones. Anyway, it was okay overnight, and then, just before it got light, we were attacked on three sides. There was open ground around our compound, but beyond that scrubland. All the fire was coming from invisible positions in some trees.

The lads were half asleep, but I got them mustered and we returned fire. We were pinned down, no two ways about it. I called up air support and got a couple of rocket-fired grenades poked into the trees where we thought they were. There was thick black smoke blowing across, which led to a strange silence, but it didn't last long and as soon as the smoke cleared, the pop-pop started up again. Those single shots seem to echo around the place for ages.

In all I reckon they had us cooped up for over five hours. Thank God we managed to keep the rear flank open – they were trying to encircle us the whole time. A couple of my lot went down with heat exhaustion. We got them out, but it was close run.

I don't know, maybe it's because I have leave approaching, but I don't remember feeling so bad during contact. Don't let on to Mum and Dad. They're best not knowing. Love to you, your brother, S.

A heavy shower had wet the lawn, much needed after what had been a dry coolish summer, punctuated by storms. Closing the window, he could see droplets of rainwater trembling on the surface of the glass, clinging, as if their survival mattered.

He was trying to study the manuscript on his desk: *the St John Passion*, a work Bach had kept revising for a quarter of a century, almost until his death. In his mid-sixties, he couldn't leave it alone, kept tinkering, but adding very little. Nowadays, they usually performed the original.

Perhaps the later versions were the work of a disillusioned man. It had been all over for him by the time he was sixty. He was washed up, yesterday's man. His music had closed an era and taste had moved on. Edward had been amazed when he'd first read that Johann Sebastian Bach probably played no part in the musical education of Wolfgang Amadeus

Mozart. Mozart would have heard of Bach's name, but as the boy genius toured the courts and capitals of Europe with his father and sister, no one was playing Bach. He was, in every sense, passé.

There was still no word from the Wigmore.

Edward himself had sung in most of the capitals of the world, not perhaps in royal courts, but in cathedrals and churches, and those purpose-built auditoria in which diminutive spaceships floated in the ceiling and last notes lingered. He had worked with all the great conductors: Mackerras, Marriner, Haitink, Gardiner, Previn, Davis, and most recently, Rattle. They had asked for him. He'd counted them friends. They used to talk on the phone.

In the States, he'd sung for Clinton at the White House. Bach again: *Sheep May Safely Graze*. Four minutes of glory, alone on an impromptu stage under a hot light, the powerful of DC spread out around him in a semi-circle of respectful attention. The man himself, the president, spoke to him afterwards, impressed him. He seemed to know his Bach: the whole cantata, of which *Sheep* was a part, was something he said he frequently listened to. He also knew about Edward. He had three of his recordings, he told him: the Strauss songs, the Fauré and, like everyone else, his celebrated *St John Passion*. That, Clinton said, was a masterpiece. It must, surely, be his crowning achievement?

What had he said in reply? When did this man find time for Strauss and Fauré and Bach? Like it or not, he was running the world for God's sake. What was *his* masterpiece?

'Yes,' Edward must have said, and something to the effect: 'It's a piece I've loved for a long time. I was very pleased with it.'

Clinton smiled and moved on to another singer, a woman with a guitar. Edward was too far away to hear whether clever Bill had some of her recordings too.

He stood under a wide chandelier, which appeared to run down on ten feet of chain, and drank Mondavi merlot.

In that halo of light, he wasn't at all sure that this moment hadn't been his 'crowning achievement'. To perform in the most famous political residence on the planet, in front of the men (and a pinch of women) who ran the world, had been refracting, as though all the light in Washington had coursed through him and excited his veins in those four joyous minutes. BWV 208. It was such a pity Cara hadn't been with him.

Over ten years ago now, he realised: years in which Big Bill had come and gone, and Iraq had transmogrified into Croatia and Bosnia and then Iraq again. Plus ça change. At least, that's how it appeared to Edward, thumbing his way through a Sunday newspaper every week and sampling earnest, occasionally rebarbative, debate on late night radio.

Some of what he knew about the world and how it failed to change he learnt from Cara, who rarely slept more than five hours and spent a good deal of the night listening to the World Service through stringy headphones. She was always ahead with the news; she knew about the invasions and the resignations, the actors who had died, the bombs and scandals, hours before they reached Edward, and sometimes she passed on her knowledge in short by-the-way bulletins.

Certain things had changed, though. Over ten years ago, he didn't have a son in the army.

The rain continued. He watched it from his study. A violent wind gusted at the shrubs and trees, rolling them backwards and forwards. Wet waves were visible in the wind, coiled in genie-like clouds that circled and dispersed in slow motion. Occasionally, one hurled itself at the study window, slapping a shower of wet onto the glass pane, like an angry phantom hand.

Above him, the gutters were heavy with water. He was paying the penalty, of course, for not having cleared them of the dozens of leaves that now lay limp and clogged in the deep plastic channels that surrounded the house. He'd planned to unblock them the previous weekend, then forgot, and narrow drizzles now spilled over the edges and fell as plumb lines do straight down the back of the house.

After an hour, the rain eased, leaving behind it a strong, drying breeze. He stepped into the garden, in his old boat shoes and no socks.

The sycamore would have come down in the last forty-eight hours. Yesterday's storm being so ferocious, he hadn't been out in the garden, and because the damaged tree was concealed from view by two others of a similar size, he hadn't noticed that anything was wrong.

The stricken sycamore had broken away close to the ground, split from the other two trees it had grown up with. As it fell, it broke off branches from these other trees, and they in turn slowed it down, snagged its fall, delaying the moment when it came to rest on the wall that bordered one side of the garden. Surprisingly, it appeared to have settled without disturbing a single brick.

It was odd how healthy the flesh of the tree looked. Where branches had been torn from its sides, supple white wood gaped at him, fresh wounds that were uncomfortable to see. At the top, growing upwards, as it might be from the wall itself, a crowd of twigs and leaves continue to sway in the wind, the leaves predominantly yellow, a few green, unaware it seemed that this was no longer a living tree.

He resented the fact that his days were without form. He admitted it reluctantly, but it was true. Each morning he sat down to study the Bach manuscript, but it was desultory work and he was easily distracted. The longer he went without hearing from Derek, his agent, the more convinced he became that he'd lost the Wigmore concert and that preparation of the role was pointless.

At least, that was the way his thinking tended some of the time. But to give up the idea of the Wigmore altogether, in the absence of any other offers or even the rumour of a possibility, would be tantamount to announcing his retirement. He wasn't ready for that, and so the mornings, in the diary he imagined to be dividing up and allocating his time, were earmarked for rehearsal.

Cara, on the other hand, had no problem with her time and how to occupy it, and that, if he was honest, he also resented. It made him realise how effortless it had been when his own career had been in full swing, when the number of offers exceeded the weeks in the year, and he could pick and choose amongst the concerts, recordings, recitals, interviews for Radio 3, *Classical Music*, even the *Today* programme once, at the time of the White House invitation. Derek would ring up and say, 'They want you on *Night Waves* tomorrow night. Means being at BH around eight. I think you should do it.' And off he'd go. Ten minutes on air, another fifty quid in the bank, doubtless a few more in the audience at Saturday evening's performance, perhaps an extra CD sold. Derek called it 'profile', keeping him in the minds of the public and people in the business, providing a few more reasons to employ Edward Padgett.

Cara had all that now. She wasn't as complacent about it as he had been. She had, after all, the experience both of her own years of obscurity and Edward's 'fall from grace'. That was his phrase, not hers. She wouldn't have it and insisted on calling his shortage of work 'temporary' and not, as he preferred, the more sardonic 'terminal'. She liked to speak of 'luck'. The good luck she was enjoying had nothing to do with merit; she hadn't suddenly improved shortly before meeting Karl Rouse; nor, she imagined, would she have lost the whole of her talent when the warmth of public adulation began to cool and others, younger and fresher, began to take the parts for which she was currently the perfect fit. The wheel simply turned, and sometimes those who had all but disappeared, re-emerged to enjoy a last chapter of fame. Autumn sunshine. Look at that chat show host, Michael Parkinson.

He could just pick up the phone to Derek, and ask what the result of the casting interview had been. Derek was bound to know by now. It had been three weeks, and although it remained possible that no decision had yet been taken, it was much more likely that Derek was sitting on it, reluctant to convey gloomy news to Edward before there was at least the possibility of another, compensatory interview coming up. Edward had come to appreciate Derek's idea of kindness.

Wouldn't he rather know?

As a matter of fact, no. Derek was probably right.

The leaves were bad again this year, pitted and ragged-edged, black spot speckling them like cheetah ears. Edward bent down and picked up a few that had already fallen. He'd first noticed these signs of blight a decade or so ago, on a tree by the river. It was no longer there, blown down in the high winds of '97. He'd hoped that was the end of it because the blight didn't come back the following autumn or the one after. Since the millennium, however, it had returned every year, depositing its sooty spots on the leaves as if they might be the dark blotches of a plague.

He was no botanist, had little interest in the science of it, but he was sufficient of a record-keeper to know that the trees were deteriorating, and no one he consulted had a clue how to save them. He could expect another of the sycamores down this winter.

The wet grass brushed his feet and ankles. He crossed the lawn away from the river and headed towards the fence on the east side of the garden, which bordered a cornfield. He walked quietly, aware, in a sense, of what would happen.

He startled a deer, a young one. It sprang from behind a tall beech and had cleared the fence and run the length of the field before he'd scarcely registered it was there. He never ceased to be astonished by their power. Always on wet mornings after the rain had moved on, deer strayed onto his lawn, seeking out the tender grass, eating his saplings. They thought they were safe, immediately after the rain.

The garden was too big for him really. Cara had no interest in it, or perhaps, to be fair, no time for it. She knew all the names of the flowers, which Edward could never remember, but she wasn't keen on the garden as a project, the 'maintenance' as she put it. That fell to him, and the result was a garden that was, in part, well-trimmed and pleasing to the eye, and in part rampant. Fecund chaos.

He tried his best to conceal the chaos, to tuck it away. He planted new trees, which stood in front of the brambles that were greedily taking over one corner of their two acre plot. He kept the door on one of the sheds shut and opened it only when he was feeling brave. Inside were generations of kids' bicycles, flat-tyred, their chrome brown-speckled, the steering stiff. The last time he'd plucked up the courage to go in, he'd found a bird's nest in one of the boys' cycling helmets. There were three sky blue eggs in it.

When he leant on the fence, ten or perhaps a dozen pheasant chicks the colour of dried mud scattered into the air and flew towards the wood a mile or so off.

He still felt young.

J.S.Bach was in his fifties before he added the remaining movements that would complete the Mass in B Minor (BWV 232). He'd composed the *Kyrie* and the *Gloria* back in the early 1730s, a time when he thought himself ill-treated by the civic authorities in Leipzig. He'd dedicated these two movements to Friedrich August II, the new Elector of Saxony, in the hope that he'd get some sort of court position out of it, which he calculated would shut up his detractors at home. But Friedrich didn't play.

She snoozed on the train, occasionally aware of the rehearsal room to come and bright light glancing off her music stand.

The rehearsal for soloists was due to start at ten, in a large house on Duke Street, close to Selfridges. Cara had taken the seven-thirty from Petersfield, which put her at Paddington soon after nine. She'd slept most of the way and so had only the tube journey to go over her rôle. Not that she really needed to. She'd spent the last four weeks closeted in the attic, studying the part as if it were holy writ.

It was sunny as she surfaced at Marble Arch and she walked quickly down Oxford Street. She was ahead of herself and had time to browse in the windows of Selfridges and to gulp down a styrofoam cup of hot, tasteless coffee from a stall at the junction with Duke Street.

She opened the door of the first floor room feeling excited, but slightly regretting her mildly scalded mouth.

Most of the others she knew: George (bass), William (tenor), Martina (contralto) and Fiona, her fellow soprano. Fiona ran up to her before she'd had a chance to take her coat off.

'We're still on for lunch, aren't we? I do hope so. I've found this wonderful new place. RIBA. Do you know it? In Portland Place? They have a fantastic restaurant and the beauty of it is no one knows it's there.'

'Fine.'

'We'll go there and find it packed to the gills, of course, but it was very quiet the other day.'

The rehearsal went well. For Cara, it focused on the *Christe eleison* and *Laudamus te* passages. Their conductor, a German called Jakob, knew exactly what he wanted, which helped. It frustrated her when conductors insisted on taking them over the same ground – 'Okay, from thirty-eight again' – without ever identifying properly what was wrong with the last attempt. She responded much better when the direction was sharp.

'Very good, Cara,' said Jakob, which he succeeded in making sound like *sehr gut*.

She loved it. If she were honest, there was nothing she'd rather do on a crisp August morning than take the early train to London and make her way to a rehearsal in a room flooded with sunlight, where instead of 'marking it', she could sing out and sense the thrill of her voice filling the dusty air. *Laudamus te, benedicimus te, adoramus te, glorificamus te.* She could always tell when she was at her best. She caught the eye of the accompanist and he allowed himself the hint of a smile. Eric was never loose with his praise; a smile, however understated, meant *you're doing brilliantly, darling.*

By ten to one they'd had enough, and Jakob was content. He didn't hang around to chat. He confirmed the date of the next rehearsal, sorted his notes and music into a briefcase and sprinted for the door. He was a man in demand, always working towards at least three performances. He was due at Abbey Road by two.

Fiona and Cara found themselves strolling down Oxford Street in a mild euphoria. The B Minor Mass was a turning point, a landmark in religious music. At Christmas, it would be magnificent, a joyous start to the holiday.

'You know Jakob's shagging Martina,' Fiona said as they walked.

'No!'

'That's why he hurries away after rehearsal. I'm sure he thinks that if he stays, he'll let his guard down and give something away.'

'Does his partner know?'

'That woman he has tucked away in Berlin? I don't suppose she has a clue, darling. But how would I know? I only learnt about it when I got to Duke Street this morning. George told me. He saw them together in some restaurant in Bayswater. Jakob made some excuse about discussing difficulties Martina was having with the contralto part. Can you believe it? She was wearing next to nothing, according to George.'

'He doesn't look the shagging type.'

'Not given you the once-over then?'

'I'm twice his age.'

'We'll have to watch what we say when Marty's around. It'll all go back in pillow talk.'

They entered the foyer of the Royal Institute of British Architects and Fiona checked with the man at the desk that there were likely to be places in the restaurant.

'He says it's practically empty. '

Fiona led the way up the wide sweep of staircase to the first floor. They passed the Members' Lounge, where various young men in grey and white and black were drinking sparkling water, and found the restaurant beyond two oak-thick columns. They were escorted to a table for two by a window overlooking the institute's inner courtyard and handed a list of drinks.

'Go on,' said Fiona. 'It's only Vermeer.'

Their plan was to eat and then go to the Vermeer exhibition at the Academy. Fiona, it seemed, did not regard this as too serious an engagement.

'I'll have a large Pinot Grigio.'

'The same for me, please.'

They both ordered scallops. Then Cara chose a salad with wild rocket and parmesan, and Fiona opted for a steak.

'How's Edward?' she asked.

'He's fine.'

Whenever her fellow singers asked after Edward, Cara had an awkward sense of talking about an older man. Perhaps it was because they were all so young. Fiona couldn't be more than early thirties. She had no children, wasn't with anyone, as far as Cara knew, and she lived in Clapham, which meant that she had little in common with two fifty-somethings with grown-up sons and a cottage in the country.

'He's hoping for a gig at the Wigmore, in December.'

The word 'gig' did not come naturally. Why had she used it? No doubt because their difference in age, not being as young as Fiona, made her uncomfortable. Gigs were what the Rolling Stones did, not classically trained tenors like Edward. He'd have laughed.

'Hoping?'

'Well, they called three people to interview and he hasn't heard yet. They're taking a long time to get back as a matter of fact, which is always disconcerting, I think.'

'Is he doing much these days?'

It was heartbreaking to listen to Fiona. She didn't intend to be insulting or condescending, but the very nature of her questions made her so. This was what Edward complained of, relegation to the ranks of 'also rans', the formerly successful. Cara hated it. She could deal with Edward's pessimism: it was a function of his personality nowadays not to be confident about the future. Fiona, on the other hand, if she had any sensitivity at all, should know better.

'He has a fair bit of work,' she lied, 'but he has to consider his health now, after the heart attack, so we try to ensure he doesn't take on too much.'

They raised their glasses and toasted each other. As Fiona sipped her wine, Cara could see in her eyes, hovering above the rim, that she didn't believe her. In a freelance world, you couldn't help but be aware of the ruses and cover stories people commonly used to conceal the unattractive truth that they were out of work.

Fortunately, their food arrived.

'We chose well,' Cara said brightly.

'You should get Edward to contact Harry Miles. That producer I told you about. He mentioned Edward's name only the other day.'

'Are you two going out?'

'No. Don't change the subject, Cara. I'm serious. Harry was saying how he'd like to do some recordings with older singers. I don't mean people you've never heard of, but names like Edward Padgett, really great voices of the last generation. He wants them to re-work the pieces they're famous for. Edward would love that, wouldn't he?'

Had she misjudged Fiona? Here she was, patently unconvinced by Cara's suggestion that Edward now chose to work less, and trying to offer constructive help, and of a kind that showed respect for Edward's history. If there hadn't been a laden table between them, with glasses and crockery, she might just have leaned over and hugged her.

'I'll mention it to him.'

'Do. I'll give you Harry's e-mail.'

As they walked around the Academy, Cara was surprised by how few paintings there were in the exhibition. She read the biographical notes as she studied each picture, and tried to make sense of how work of this calibre, so simple and yet so intense, could be almost entirely ignored in Vermeer's lifetime and for two hundred years after his death.

'Didn't shag around enough,' Fiona remarked.

To Fiona, shagging was the secret history of art.

Now there is drowsy silence. Are my ears blocked? Can I hear all there is to hear? My other senses function well enough. I feel pain, in my knee. I thirst, a persistent dryness to my tongue and throat that will not allow me to forget that I'm desperate to drink.

Even in this darkness, I make out specks of light, through which dust falls.

But I can hear nothing. The shuffling of rodents, the twitch of insects, the shrill disorder of the guards: they've all knocked it off. At least for these few minutes.

In the silence, I can feel my fear spill over.

As he turned the Golf onto the patch of gravel in front of the house, Tim was struck by the silence, the tranquillity of his parents' home. In London, he would scarcely have heard the crunch of tiny stones under his tyres, but here it was the sound of arrival, perhaps the only sound of movement in a still landscape. The wind had dropped, the rain eased, the birds were quietly recovering from the stormy weather of the last few days. A moment ago, he'd seen a young doe in the distance, just outside the trees at the edge of the road. She'd paused and raised her head and, as he passed, she stepped slowly into the wood, fleetingly alarmed.

There weren't many signs of life. No lights were on, despite a dull day, and more significantly there was no music. He tried ringing the doorbell. He could hardly remember a time when there wasn't something or other playing. It was one of the defining features, of the house and of his parents' life together. Sometimes, there might be two different pieces playing in two different rooms, or a CD jockeying for position with a human voice practising scales. Depending on where you stood, the house could be in perfect harmony or bewildering discord.

He raised the lion's head knocker and rapped it sharply three times against the scooped, worn cup of greenish bronze. No one could fail to hear it.

When the door opened, it was his father standing inside, greeting him.

'Sorry, Tim. I must have dropped off. Your mother's shopping. Forgot some vital ingredient for that feast she's preparing for you. Come in, come in.'

He was relieved by his father's casualness. He hadn't visited them for three months or more. He handed over a 2012 Sancerre.

'Very nice,' Edward said.

'No music?'

'A temporary hitch, nothing to worry about. Music will be restored to the soundtrack of the house in a matter of minutes. There was merely a brief interval while I had forty winks. Drink?'

They walked into the sitting room, where Edward had an old-fashioned mahogany drinks cabinet, with a fold-down door that triggered an interior light and became a shelf when it was opened. Inside he kept a dozen bottles and divers glasses, which multiplied in the mirror at the back. He switched on the radio, then turned to Tim.

'Whisky? Gin? Beer? Or will you have the ubiquitous glass of white wine, which everybody seems to want now? None of my generation drink gin these days, including me. Why is that? Very sad. Shall we open your bottle? No, I think I'll keep it for lunch.'

Edward poured while waiting for an answer. Tim took the glass held out to him and went over to the french window to look at the garden. His father had raised the volume of Radio 3 and he thought he recognised Khachaturian.

'Expecting quite a good crop of eaters this year,' Edward said. 'I'll let you have a bag when they're ready.'

'Thanks.'

'Lot of blight, though, and I had a sycamore down the other night. You can't see it from here. It's just behind those other two.'

'The river's very high.'

'You noticed that.'

'Couldn't very well not.'

'No, I suppose not.'

'And how are you, Dad?' Tim asked. 'How's work?'

'I'm extremely well, thank you, Tim.'

Tim sensed avoidance. It was natural for his father to talk about the weather and the garden – he always had – not so much with regard to growing things, but as signs of the changing seasons. He'd always encouraged them, when he and Steve were kids, to notice the differences between the seasons, to mark down in their memories what each one looked like, its characteristic features and whether the events of nature were late or early or about what they should be.

But he'd said a little too much on the subject this time, a sentence or two more than was necessary or informative.

'Stephen will be home soon.'

'I know,' Tim said. 'Can't wait.'

'Is he okay, do you think?'

'Seems so.'

Edward smiled and raised his glass, implying 'Cheers!'

'As a matter of fact, your mother and I are continually astonished how well we are. We look at our friends and they're all dropping like flies. Cancers, slipped discs, what they call 'late on-set diabetes'. Breast cancer's popular at the moment.'

'You did have a heart attack, as I recall.'

'All in the past, Tim, all in the past.'

'And the work? Have you got anything on?'

'Oh, the work. I feel quite nostalgic about it. This and that, to answer your question. Bits and pieces. Waiting to hear about a couple of things. As a matter of fact, there's a producer in London who wants to do a retrospective of my work. Should be fun.'

'Sounds very exciting.'

Tim somehow knew this was not the truth. If his father wasn't lying, as such, he was embellishing, turning into something agreed and planned an idea that was only, as yet, a possibility. It was exactly what so many of his colleagues in the department did, to enhance their standing, give an impression of professional expertise. It was not what he expected from his father.

His mother swept into the room, a large bunch of flowers, lilies, wrapped in pale green paper, filling her arms. She threw them onto a table and embraced him.

'I brought you…'

'Yes, I saw them, darling. How kind of you.'

'They probably need to be put in water. I bought them on the way down. They seemed a bit dry to me.'

'Yes. Of course. I'll deal with them. But, first, let me take a look at my son. You look so well, Tim. I hope it's not an illusion. Hard work must suit you.'

'I've been running.'

'Running? Did you hear that, Edward? We have two fit sons.'

'Nothing compared with Steve.'

'Nonsense. Now, you stay here and talk to your father. I have to attend to lunch. Could you get me a glass of that, Edward. Whatever you're drinking.'

She picked up the lilies and headed for the kitchen. He noticed that she left the carnations where he'd put them down in the hall.

'Won't be a moment,' Edward said. 'Just sort your mother out that drink. I'll put your wine in the fridge. Sit down. Make yourself comfortable.'

The register of their voices, the polite intimations, were a form of estrangement. Over the last couple of years he'd noticed how his parents had taken to speaking to him in a particular way, a new way, that was both kindly and distant. Now that he was, as they saw it, an adult, they had adjusted their tone, which turned him from boy into man, from resident into guest and, he feared, from the child they loved and were responsible for from day to day into a friend, a special friend of course, but someone who was no longer a participant in the life of their house.

He stared out over the garden, a fine rain falling on the grass and the apple trees and sycamores. He could scarcely remember it as the place where he and Steve had played cricket and drop-kicked a plastic rugby ball back and forth over their mother's washing line. It seemed an entire world away.

He found himself wandering through to the kitchen, where Cara had her hands full of potato peelings and Edward was saying something about the need to build up the banks of the river.

Cara emptied the peelings into a swing bin and went to wash her hands at the sink.

'He's obsessed, your father. There was a time when all he wanted was to talk about Bach. These days it's the weather.'

'Global warming,' Tim said. It seemed the obvious response.

'Well, perhaps, but it doesn't come across that way. There's not much global about it. You'd think we had our own micro-climate here.'

She spoke as if Edward were not present in the room.

'I simply make the point,' Edward came back, 'that the rainfall is increasing. We have more flooding in the fields. The road through the village is under water more often each winter.'

'It's always been prone to flood.'

'Of course, we know that. But it's getting worse.'

'I don't know that you're right. Do you make a note of it when it happens? I think you're exaggerating.'

This was mannered bickering, nothing that either of them could not handle. In the old days, when Tim had hidden in his room, to avoid witnessing the conflict in close-up, real arguments had raged through the family home. They'd usually involved Steve, if not directly, then as the subject of the blood-letting. They shouted as though they hated each other, even though they knew that their differences were about love, the difficulty of loving their elder son and of managing that love.

'I shall start to keep a record,' said Edward. 'Then you'll see.'

Now they aired their differences in a kind of parody of argument, as though they lacked the energy for the real thing, and found it easier to treat every contention ironically.

At lunch, they ate largely in silence, with intervals of conversation that were long enough to convince the three of them that they were enjoying themselves and short enough to hear the crunch of their teeth on roasted crackling.

'You've heard your father's news? About the CD?'

'Nothing's definite,' Edward added.

'Yes, Dad mentioned. It sounds great.'

'The producer is someone my friend Fiona knows. Have you met Fiona?'

'I couldn't remember his name, darling.'

'Harry Miles.'

'Ha-rry Miles. Of course.'

'No, I don't think I've met Fiona.'

'Very pretty, bubbly girl. Not that much older than you. I'll introduce you at the concert. You will be coming?'

'I hope so.'

'Do we know anything about Harry Miles?' Edward asked.

For the first time in many minutes, Cara turned away from her son and looked at her husband.

'He's been around for years, darling. He doesn't really do our kind of stuff. He's more your classical classics man.'

'Is that what I've become?'

Tim laughed to conceal his father's awkwardness.

'Must be at the top of the profession,' he said. 'A classical classic.'

Edward raised his glass to thank him.

'It's all down to how carefully you select the grapes.'

After coffee, Cara noticed it had stopped raining and suggested a walk around the garden. The grass was sodden and tipped with rainwater. Their shoes darkened as they crossed the lawn to the sycamores. The stricken tree leaned heavily on the garden wall.

'There it is,' Edward said. 'Look at that black spot. All over the leaves. I'm worried the other two are going to go the same way.'

He stretched over the brambles to reach a broken branch of the sycamore. He tore it away from the trunk and dragged it backwards through the bramble thatch. The flesh of the tree had begun to dry out, but otherwise it looked healthy enough. It ought to be possible, Tim thought, to put trees back upright if they're not rotten and soft.

'Can't you get someone to look at them?' Tim asked.

'Assess the risk, you mean? I don't know how easy that is. You can't really tell if a tree's about to fall, can you?'

'Well, I can't, but I'm sure there are people who can.'

The telephone was ringing in the house. Edward let it ring, but then decided to go and answer it. Tim watched him stride up the lawn and while his mother droned on about the comforts of a relationship, it passed through his mind that his father was not unfit. He walked quickly, confidently, not as a man debilitated by a heart condition.

Was he anxious about who might be phoning?

'I know it's none of my business,' Cara said, 'but you must appreciate I do worry. It's been a long time since you had someone, a very long time.'

'I haven't met a girl I fancy. It's as simple as that.'

'But London must be full of attractive women.'

'I'm sure it is, but I don't seem to meet any of them, or at least ones that are attractive to me.'

'Do you think you might be a little too choosy?'

'Perhaps.'

'I know you're going to like Fiona.'

Edward was running towards them.

'I'd really rather not talk about it, Mum. Just let me sort my own life out.'

He almost fell, recovered, slowed to a fast walk. Tim felt a kind of terror course through him, like 'flu, and he realised that it had nothing to do with the possibility of his father tripping over.

Edward was breathless.

'That was Stephen's C.O. Apparently, he's gone missing.'

'What!'

'My God!'

'Is he injured?'

'He didn't have many details. He's going to ring back later. When he's got more information. They think he's been taken hostage.'

2

That evening they sat around in a stupor, uncertain what to do. Cara cooked them scrambled eggs and, for distraction, they watched a re-run of *The Maltese Falcon* on TCM. Tim had made up his mind not to return to London, and texted colleagues in the department to warn them that he wouldn't be in until Tuesday.

Occasionally, one or other of them contributed a thought.

'He's probably hiding out,' Edward said. 'He'll find his way back when it's dark.'

'He'll be terrified,' Cara said. 'Supposing he's alone? My poor darling.'

'He's not a child, Mum.'

'He's my child, Tim. I don't know what might be happening to him. It doesn't bear thinking about.'

'Steve's got a good head on his shoulders. He's well trained. He'll not be easily caught out.'

He wouldn't admit it to Cara and Tim, but Edward realised how little confidence he had in what he was saying. How straightforward it had been until now. They had been concerned during Stephen's brief spell in Iraq, glad when he rang or emailed to say he was okay, relieved when he returned home on leave without injury. Perhaps that had given them all a belief that he would survive. The deaths in the papers, the soldiers massacred by suicide bombs or fatally wounded in a firefight, were upsetting and caused them a few hours, even a day sometimes, of anxiety, but they failed to dent the belief, a deep inner belief that Steve would not be one of the victims. He might suffer, but he would return.

News came in the morning that, on Saturday, Steve had been leading a night patrol on the streets of a small town. Around eight in the evening. He was reported missing in the early hours.

Nothing had been heard of him since.

'What do we do?' Edward said into the phone.

'Sit tight, Mr Padgett. The army is doing all it can, here and in London. He hasn't been missing long and I've every confidence we'll have him back at base with us soon.'

'I hope so.'

'We're keeping a tight ship, by the way. Best not to involve the media.'

'I see.'

'I'll keep you informed of any developments.'

Tim thought his father looked like a man in his dying hours, as he put the phone down. He sat heavily, placed his hands on the arms of the chair.

'That was Mike Jeffreys, Stephen's CO. A lieutenant-colonel.'

'I bet he was looking for that translator,' Cara said.

'Translator?'

'The guy who was grabbed a few weeks ago. You remember. Stephen was concerned about him.'

It went through Edward's mind that at least Mike Jeffreys had not rung to report Stephen's death. So far as they knew, he was alive.

'Did they think there was any way in which we could help?'
'It seems that we have to wait, Tim, wait to hear,' Cara said.
'No, I'll have to go out there,' Edward said.
'You can't!'
'Dad, all the FCO advice says it's too dangerous. I've read it.'
'Really?'
'Look it up if you don't believe me.'

Edward did. He scrolled through the Foreign and Commonwealth Office site. The advice was exactly as Tim had said: avoid all or all but essential travel to Afghanistan. *There is a high threat from terrorism and specific methods of attack are evolving and increasing in sophistication.*

He asked himself why he'd never looked at this website before, why, out of simple concern for Stephen, he hadn't tried to quantify the danger he was in. There were, he now learnt, 'frequent attacks' against British forces, political and civilian targets, and those working in the re-construction and humanitarian fields. The country was littered with unexploded bombs and land mines. This was the truth. The very different picture painted by Stephen's blueys and emails, he realised, had never pretended to be accurate; they were attempts to reassure, to curb the parental neurosis that anyone with a child serving on a frontline suffered.

It appeared that nowhere was safe. Hotels, restaurants, the markets: all off-limits to military and embassy staff. If you were considering travel outside Kabul, the FCO said, *take permanent armed protection and armoured vehicles*, and if that was not sufficient deterrent, if you were still mad enough to think of going out there, the site pointed out that private security was, in any case, only available to embassies and diplomatic missions.

'I'm sure I could go,' he told Cara. 'Take my chances. The army would presumably help.'

He could hear the doubt in his voice.

'You'd be dead in a couple of days,' Tim said. 'Or stuck in an army camp and unable to move.'

Edward was still at his computer, staring at the discouraging screen. Cara put a hand on his shoulder.

'The message is pretty clear, my love. They don't want you to go, anyone to go. Think of your heart, darling. And if you ended up kidnapped, it would all be far far worse.'

'Then, what in hell do we do? He's our son. We can't just abandon him. This god-awful website just goes to prove it. It's bloody dangerous out there. What do we do, Cara?'

She leant forward and kissed his cheek.

'We pray, my darling. We pray, and we trust the army, and we believe what you said last night, that Stephen has been trained to deal with situations like this. He'll find a way to cope, and he'll survive. We have to believe that.'

He stood up and when he took her in his arms, he could feel the tension still bracing her body, the stress that belied the comfort she offered.

'I know, I know. That's right,' he said. 'But at the same time I can't just sit around and do nothing. I'll go up to town tomorrow, see the MOD. Tim can come with me.'

If I'd given it any thought whatsoever, I wouldn't have gone there. I was, after all, responsible for ten men: Corporal Lucie, three privates and half a dozen local police recruits. Apart from the stupidity of the plan, it was breaking regulations to leave a patrol without an officer, especially at night. I guess it was a bit of the younger Steve re-surfacing.

In my mind, I'd thought it wouldn't take long. We could drive to Rashid's house in less than ten minutes. All I intended to do was to ask his wife if she'd heard anything about him. To be honest, I was expecting her to say no, and I'd already decided that I'd try to buck her up with the 'no news is good news' line, which I sort of believed. The chances were that for as long as no one announced his death, he was probably held somewhere.

What I'd entirely failed to consider was the possibility, the likelihood, that the house was being watched. Had I worked through the logic of my own argument, that Rashid was valuable alive, as hostage, as leverage, I would have realised that monitoring the movements of his family would follow. As it was, I drove an armoured car almost to the front door and hopped out as unconcerned as I would be visiting my parents in Hampshire for Sunday lunch.

Slightly against my better judgement, I told Lucie and the others to go on ahead. My thinking was that if Rashid's family were aggravated by my last visit, they'd hardly want another bunch of army and police turning up mob-handed and unannounced. As it turned out, I needn't have worried.

I knocked at the door and waited for an answer. There was a dog barking inside the house, towards the back. I knew straightaway that the place was empty. The windows at the front were shuttered and there was something about the dog's bark, the way it echoed, the impression it gave that the dog had been on its own for some time and had done a good deal of barking into vacant space.

I walked around the side of the house. I knew it was a risk to leave my vehicle unattended, but I was only going to be a few minutes. What light there was from residences nearby failed to penetrate the alley. I switched on my torch and threw the beam across the side wall. It was pitted with holes from various skirmishes and slabs of plaster had fallen off, leaving patches of exposed concrete. Threads of plant had begun to grow in the holes.

I glanced at my watch. I didn't want to overrun the patrol and start questions buzzing back at base.

Was I scared? I don't think so. Naïve, I think. Actually, I was more puzzled than anything. I couldn't imagine where the family had gone. It wasn't safe for anyone to travel far, and if Rashid had the chance to make contact, he would try his home first.

There was another possibility, and that was that a member of the family, perhaps the family as a whole, had been threatened. Collaborators and their relatives were frequently intimidated or assaulted, even murdered. If they had been led to believe they were in physical danger, official advice about the safety of travel would count for nothing. The family would have packed up and headed for the hills without a moment's hesitation. Rashid might have told them to. He might have got through on his mobile and told them to get the hell out.

I shone the torch into the back yard. The flash of light drove the dog frantic. I could hear it throwing itself against a door. The last thing I wanted to do was attract the interest of neighbours, so I switched the torch off.

The barking suddenly ceased. The silence was shocking. I felt the heat in my face. It was as if a hair drier had just been thrust under my helmet. Sweat ran into my eyes. I looked back to the street and the army Land Rover parked at the front. Time was running out. There was still a chance we could return to the compound and no one would be the wiser, except for the lads on duty at the gate, who would probably give me the nod.

The silence was broken by rapid firing: Kalashnikovs, I was certain, and slightly later what I assumed was returned fire from our lads. I was about to run out – I needed to join them – when two men appeared at the end of the alley. Bearded, black beards, armed. I saw them, dimly, just for a moment, hovering around the front of the vehicle. They walked back alongside it, out of sight, giving it the once-over. They appeared not to have any light with them.

Had they spotted me? The chances were they'd seen my torch splashing light over the house.

The gunfire stopped.

I crouched down, tried to squeeze my body as close to the wall as I could. The two men re-emerged at the end of the alley. At this distance, it was impossible even to guess who they were, except to say that they were probably local militia. I kept still and tried not to think about the heat and the almost irresistible urge to get my helmet off and let some air onto my face and head. My skin was wet.

One of them started up the alley. He'd raised his gun and I kept thinking: he's seen me, he must be able to see me down here, he's looking straight at me.

Behind him now were two other men. So, there were three of them, at least. As far as I could tell, they were identical. In their flat caps, their beards, their long cloaks, their guns, they were uniform. They were even the same average-looking height.

The man in the alley took a couple more hesitant steps towards me. The barrel of his gun led straight to my head. He was being extremely cautious, like a dog that's sniffed something he doesn't trust.

He called out, flung his free arm in the air, beckoning. A second man came up to him and tried to peer into the dark alley. They moved forward, maybe a metre, maybe more, talking agitatedly.

I couldn't move. I thought about my gun and just knew I'd be dead before I touched it. The cramp in my calves was agony. I must have been squatting by the wall for ten minutes by now, and I was desperate to ease the pressure. It felt like I was seconds away from crying out.

The first man yelled into the darkness. I couldn't make it out, and I wouldn't have understood what he was saying even if I could.

And yet, I did know. He was bluffing. 'We know you're in there! Come out, and you won't get hurt!'

Like fuck!

As abruptly as they'd appeared, they went. The two in the alley turned, joined the third man, and then I could no longer see them.

I waited, eased myself down into a sitting position, stretched out my legs. The ache in my calves intensified for a few moments, then began to fade. I thought about taking my helmet off, just for a second or two, but decided against it.

That formidable silence again. There were insects close to me, busy, magnified by the alley's walls. But behind them, behind their rhythmic twitch, out there, was a deep silence. It was the interval between symphonic movements, the sound of anticipation. Of fear.

Gradually, taking care to move as slowly as I could, so that all my wretched belts and buckles, the sodding flaps and bits of kit hanging on me, my torch and radio and gun, made little or no noise, I stood up. I tried to make out any movement around or beyond my armoured car, the slightest human hint. There was none.

I decided not to risk the torch and started to make my way

towards the street. I hated the crunch of my boots on the alley's concrete floor. Each step seemed to echo and linger. Inside, I was pleading with my body to be quiet.

It felt like an age before I reached the street. It was empty. Corporal Lucie and the others were nowhere to be seen, presumably pinned down with the police lads further into town. I took a walk around the vehicle, had a quick look underneath. Nothing. No signs of damage. Nothing had been attached to it. Everything was in order.

I had no time to reach for my weapon or shout out. An arm was round my throat and I immediately lost my balance. I went down like a bowling pin. My helmet was ripped off and some sort of sack was pulled over my head. I felt my legs being tied together.

They lifted me up, carried me a like a corpse. The pain in my throat and neck was now agony, and I struggled to breathe in the heat. The sack pressed against my face and every time I took a breath, the sackcloth clung to my nose and mouth. I felt like my head would burst. The heat felt hot as fire.

It happened so quickly. Even in the quiet of the street, I had no sense of their approach.

I was pushed into a vehicle. They couldn't have cared less whether I was injured in the process. My head collided with the roof as they pushed me down and threw me onto the back seat. I caught my face on the edge of the door. From the other side of the vehicle someone else started to pull at my arms, dragging me onto some kind of bench seat.

My legs were pushed up under me so that they could close the doors. I tried to shout, to get their attention, so that I could at least move myself, but either they couldn't hear me through the sack or they were too stressed to listen. A pain tore through my calf and I thought I would pass out. The engine fired up and the car or whatever it was jumped forward. I rolled on the bench and dropped to the floor.

A man called Kerrell had agreed to see them. Adam Kerrell. He described himself as a Deputy Secretary, whatever that might be. If they'd care to turn up at 11.15, he'd be able to give them half an hour. It wasn't ungenerous, Edward decided, though what Adam Kerrell would say at the end of their thirty minutes if they weren't satisfied with his answers, he couldn't begin to guess. Perhaps he would close the meeting with a gentle phrase like 'Well, I think that's it for today', as a psychotherapist might, faced with a distraught client.

The building was far less austere inside than out. Tim and Edward sat on a worn oak bench in a long corridor that was restless with people going to and from meetings, some of them in uniforms. It smelt of polish and cleaning fluids. When Edward looked up, he was surprised by the number of cobwebs hanging in the ceiling, traps for unwary insects.

'How long have we been here?' he asked Tim.

'Twenty minutes. It's only just gone quarter past.'

'Yes. We were early. It's alright. I'm not impatient.'

In the car, coming up the M3, they had run out of conversation just before the exit for Bracknell, and hadn't found anything to talk about since. It was inevitable. The only subject was Stephen, and there were only so many things that could be said and, perhaps more significantly, only so many *times* they could be said. They both knew what the other was thinking and feeling. Sadness. An immense, imaginative, enveloping vision of a lonely man in a circumstance beyond his control or interpretation, hoping it would come good.

He remembered, years ago, driving through the village at night and seeing a young man standing on a pavement, alone in a black duffel coat. Edward was listening to Handel, a CD of Handel's *Concerti Grossi*, recorded at the Moyzes Hall in Bratislava. The music had put him into a buoyant mood. As the car glided through the night, he'd been conducting the whole of the concerto in G Minor (op.6, no.6), flinging his free arm about, stabbing out the tempo on the steering wheel.

At first, he'd seen the solitary figure at the side of the road and thought what a sad young man he was. That was moments before he recognized his own son. Handel made him glad to be alive that evening, and there was Stephen, perhaps nineteen years old, motionless and staring, as if life was passing him by.

There had been something about his face, caught in the headlights, that frightened Edward. It was the look of a man who was haunted; he was pale, his eyes dark and sunken down, his black coat buttoned to the neck. Edward pulled up, no more than twenty yards on and called back through the opened window of the passenger door.

Stephen had run off, and Edward couldn't be sure whether it was because he'd been spotted or a coincidence.

He was tempted to swing the car around and follow him, search for him amongst the maze of similar roads that divided up the housing estate on the edge of the village.

Instead, he stepped out of the car and walked back to where Stephen had been standing. A beer bottle lay smashed in the gutter and next to it a cigarette butt was still smoking. It had been thrown away, not crushed.

'Mr Padgett?'

Adam Kerrell, the deputy secretary, had appeared from a door behind them.

'Yes,' said Edward. 'This is my younger son, Timothy.'

'How do you do? Would you like to follow me?'

They walked into a small room with a table and four chairs. Adam Kerrell directed them to take a seat.

'Not my office, I'm afraid. I share that. And I apologise for this poky little spot. Meeting rooms seem to be at a premium these days. You have to beg for one.'

The deputy secretary laughed, briefly, then checked himself.

'I was very sorry to hear that Lieutenant Padgett had gone missing.'

'It's been a terrible shock.'

'Of course. Only to be expected. We are doing all we possibly can to find him. A reconnaissance patrol went out only this morning.'

'And?'

'No luck, I'm afraid. But have no doubt, Mr Padgett, we will find him. We have experience in these things and we know what we're looking for.'

Tim chipped in.

'What is that, exactly?'

Adam Kerrell leaned back and crossed his legs. He appeared to weigh up Tim's question.

'Lieutenant Padgett,' he paused. 'Stephen, I should say, is not, as you appreciate, I'm sure, the first soldier to have gone missing. What we've discovered is that there's a pattern that is common to most of these kidnappings.'

'Is that what's happened, then? He's been taken hostage?'

Edward wanted to snatch up this fact and hold it in his fist. Mr Kerrell shook his head.

'We believe he may have been snatched in the street and driven away in a car. But it's true we do not know that's what occurred. I'm sorry. That was premature of me. We don't know that Stephen has been kidnapped. I am of the opinion that is what has happened, but I can't confirm it.'

'So is this silence part of your pattern?' Tim asked.

Kerrell was irritated.

'Yes,' he said, 'it is. It usually takes a few days for the full story to emerge.'

'And then?'

'Well, then experience suggests that there will be a limited number of options for his kidnappers – if, as I say, that is what has happened to him. They don't tend, for example, to travel very far.'

'Do you expect them to contact you?'

'Hard to say. We'd expect some kind of contact, yes.'

It was easy for him, Edward concluded. His collected tone, his assumption that Stephen's case was unremarkable and would be resolved in the same way that dozens of others had been: he was rehearsed in reassurance. Edward felt like someone reporting a routine burglary, and with a similar sense of despair that not enough would be done about it.

'I was thinking I might go out there myself.'

'We wouldn't advise that, Mr Padgett.'

The answer had come back straightaway, not a moment's hesitation. It probably wasn't the first time he'd said it. The deputy secretary, the department no doubt, did not want to leave any room for ambiguity or misunderstanding. Individual initiative, in matters of this kind, was firmly discouraged.

'I know that's the FCO line,' Edward said. 'But I thought, with Stephen being an army officer, I might get some cooperation. It's very difficult just sitting here, waiting for news. I want to help find him.'

'Naturally. We're doing all we can, as I say, and best kept quiet, don't you think? We don't want the press crawling all over us.'

Adam Kerrell stood up. He walked around the table and called into the corridor: 'Vicky!'

'I'm awfully sorry. Where are our manners? You've not been offered anything to drink. Tea? Coffee?'

Edward asked if he might have coffee, with milk. Tim shook his head.

'We'll be in touch.' Kerrell hovered at the door. 'As soon as we hear anything, and you can be absolutely certain, Mr Padgett, Tim, that will be very soon.'

Edward made to get up.

'Don't trouble,' Kerrell said. 'I have another meeting to go to, but take your time. No rush. Enjoy your coffee. As best you can. Department's stuff's not the best, I'm afraid. Very good to meet you.'

The deputy secretary stepped out into the corridor and shut the door behind him. In all, the meeting had lasted a little under fifteen minutes.

She turned off the radio, and rolled over in bed. One phone call – how long had it been? Five minutes? – that's all it had taken to destroy her equilibrium, her peace of mind, her sense that there was order in the world, a protective force that kept her first-born, her Stephen, from harm.

It wasn't that she wanted to cry. The sadness and anxiety were beyond that. Instead, for the last two days, she'd had headaches, usually first thing in the morning, followed by a kind of torpor that made it hard to sleep and equally difficult to get up from bed.

She propped up the pillows and stared out of the bedroom window into a wet garden, not really taking in anything that was there. It was as if her thoughts, what she allowed into her imagination, were somehow trapped between the actual house and garden that surrounded her and a scarcely realised vision of Stephen, somewhere, alone, frightened, hoping to live.

My poor son. Be safe. Be well.

That morning Cara had decided that she must try to lead a normal life, as normal as her preoccupation with Stephen would allow. Edward had gone off to London, and she didn't expect to see him much before five. She would have breakfast: a boiled egg, orange juice, coffee.

She poured out the juice and measured out a scoop of ground coffee, and realised she couldn't face any of it.

She went to sit in the study. Edward's manuscript of the *Christmas Oratorio* lay in front of her, unopened. She felt his presence at this desk. His pens and books and bills, the stapler and nail scissors he used, pamphlets from mail-order companies selling wine or shirts: all scattered across the green leather top. She was sitting in his chair. It swivelled, giving her a view of the french windows and the garden beyond, always a distraction for her restless husband.

Cara unlocked the wide drawer in the middle of the desk

and pulled it open. It was where Edward kept Stephen's blueys and the print-outs he always made of his son's e-mails. They were arranged in date order, the most recent at the top. She hesitated to look at them, afraid that hearing Stephen's voice might be overwhelming. But she'd opened the drawer with that intention, and one or more of them might give her a clue to what had happened, why he'd gone missing.

From: spadge@tyzl.com
To: me@loire.com
Sent: 27 May 2013 18:10:16
Subject: hi

Darling Mum
   How are you? I'm well, you'll be glad to hear. Difficult week, and the heat is so intense at times that some of the lads keel over. Not me so far. The compensation, though, is the occasional magnificent sunset. The other day I saw an armoured car driving off towards this vast ball of sun and the sight of the silhouetted dark vehicle appearing to melt into the shimmering orange fire was amazing. Some days it's so beautiful here that I forget we're in the middle of a war. They've been showing Carry On movies. Not your sort of thing at all, but they make us all laugh, which we need at the moment. All my love, S xxx

He'd adored *Carry On*, especially as a little boy. He used to love what he called 'the funny voices', Kenneth Williams, Charles Hawtrey and the rest. Years before his voice broke, he'd imitate Sid James's dirty cackle, which, once she'd gathered what he was doing, always made her smile. Even then, he'd recognized something anarchic in that laugh, something not respectable, drawn to the inappropriate as he was.

She picked up the second e-mail. It was addressed to Edward and she suspected she'd never seen it. Edward did that sometimes, held back a message from Stephen if he felt it might upset her or start her worrying.

To: me@padgett.com
Sent: 24 July 2013 17:52:52
Subject: brief note

Dear Dad

I've nearly used up my time on the net, so this is brief. We have had the Jack at half mast since Sunday. It's not been a good week. Yesterday I attended a service at the airfield for one of my corporals and two privates. The honorific prayers were a bit much to take, but what else can be said in these circumstances? They probably help us carry on. I watched them lifting the coffins onto the plane and I don't honestly know what I felt. It was like a strange mixture of pride and sadness and pointlessness. Sorry, Dad. Had to tell someone.

I'm fine. Love to Mum and you, Stephen.

Neither of these was the one she was looking for, the email in which he talked about his translator being taken hostage. She eventually found it in another part of the drawer, hidden from the chronology by a stack of white envelopes and a jar of paperclips. Was it an accident or had Edward put it to one side because he, too, thought it was significant?

21ˢᵗ August

Dear Dad

I don't usually write you if I have shocking news. On the whole, I think it's better you don't hear. (You must see enough on TV.) But last Sunday something happened that has really knocked my confidence about what we're doing out here.

It's getting to be so difficult to persuade people like translators to work with us because as soon as it's public knowledge, one or other of the death squads targets them, and often their families as well. Last Sunday afternoon the guy who's worked with us for the past three months, was dragged into a car on his way home. It wasn't as if he was on the street either. He'd taken a taxi, lots of people around, but then a grey car apparently pulled up alongside and he was dragged out of one car into the other. We only know because the decent old bloke whose taxi it was told us what had happened. We've heard nothing since and it's been three days. His family must be going through hell. He was a sweet guy, probably about thirty or so. All he was doing was translating for us.

There's no end to the hatred out here.

I'm okay, so don't worry.

Love as always, Steve.

She had no idea in which town Stephen had been leading his night patrol. She certainly didn't know whether it was the same town that the translator had lived in. But, deep down, she believed it, and she believed, too, that Stephen's disappearance was connected with this message. She folded it over and placed it back in the drawer, exactly where it had been, apart and dignified, and at that moment, as she did so, she knew that whatever effort she made, she was going to cry.

They pulled the sack from my head and pushed me through a doorway into a dark room. I had no sense of its size or whether there were things like furniture that might trip me up as I stumbled around the space. The soreness in my throat still hurt, and I'd bruised my forehead and the upper part of my arm in the car.

I fell forward. God knows what I'd tripped over. Perhaps I'd just stumbled on myself, misjudged my step. I felt the unforgiving hardness of the concrete floor as my knees struck it. Cautiously, I crawled forward. I held my hands out in front of me, one sweeping the air slowly from side to side, hoping to locate any heavy or sharp obstructions before they located me, the other testing the floor for stones, glass, anything capable of inflicting an injury on me.

I heard men chatting and laughing outside. I had no idea of time. How long had it been since I was grabbed? In the car it was as if we'd travelled no distance at all, but it was possible I had passed out when I hit my head. It was just intuition, but I suspected we were still in the city, in one of the suburbs. We could be less than an hour away from our compound.

As soon as they found the Land Rover, they would institute a search, house to house at first, trying to establish whether anyone had seen or heard anything in the night. Assuming that drew a blank, which I was sure it would, they'd widen the search, bring in air surveillance, put out a message to all police patrols. They wouldn't give up. I felt certain. They wouldn't just wait.

My left hand slid away from me, bits of grit picking holes in the skin of the palm. I collapsed on my side.

'Hello.'

I lost all my resilience in that fall. For the time being at least. It drained out of me in an instant. So I wasn't at all sure what I'd heard. It was a human voice, but coming from where? I felt so tired I couldn't work it out. I couldn't be bothered.

'Hello there. Who is that?'

The voice I now realised was only a few feet away. I made the effort and dragged myself in its direction.

'Hello,' I said into the dark.

'Who are you, please?'

'Talk to me.'

I wanted to hear his voice. It sounded gentle, friendly. I wanted to hear it.

'What is your name, please?'

'Padgett. Stephen Padgett. What is yours?'

'Lieutenant Padgett?'

'Yes. Who's that? Who are you?'

'It's Rashid, sir.'

'Rashid!'

'Yes, sir.'

I thought I must be within reach of him. I held out my hand and found his leg.

'Thank God, Rashid. You're alive.'

'But you, Lieutenant Padgett, sir, why are you here?'

'Me? Good question.'

I pulled myself up onto my elbows and shuffled in what I guessed was the direction of a wall. I had only a few feet to go, but tiredness nearly overwhelmed me. I could scarcely think straight.

I threw myself against the wall as I reached it.

'How long have you been here, Rashid?'

'I don't really know, sir. A month?'

'They picked you up off the street? Same as me. Know who they are?'

'No, not exactly, sir. I know the kind of men.'

'I was at your house.'

I could sense his alarm.

'How is my family?'

'I'm afraid I've no idea. There was no one there, or at least there were no lights and no one answered the door. I went round the back, and that's when they jumped me. Your dog seemed okay. Could your wife and children have gone away?'

'I don't know, sir. There has been no communication.'

'No. Of course.'

There was no fresh air in the room, not that I could detect. The heat stayed close to my face. I suddenly realized there was daylight outside. I could feel its warmth on my cheeks, falling from a slim window in the ceiling. Sweat was running on my forehead. I must have travelled much further than I thought.

The exertion of crossing the floor made me perspire all over. I sat still, trying to regain some composure, letting my heart rate and breathing slow a little, my body cool.

'Why were you at my house, sir?'

'I was hoping to get word of you. It was stupid. I got separated from my patrol, broke the basic rule. I thought I could pop into your house, ask your wife if she'd heard from you and back at base inside an hour. Fucking idiot!'

'You wanted to know about me?'

I could hear the puzzlement in Rashid's voice.

'Yes. Is that so strange? I was worried about you. What's wrong with that!'

'Nothing, sir. I am grateful.'

'Nonsense. You've been excellent at your job, Rashid. Your work's good, and it was bloody brave of you.'

'I try to do what is right, sir.'

'Yes, well, it's still bloody brave in my view.'

'Thank you, sir.'

I thought of Dad at that moment. What would he think to hear that? To hear Rashid calling his son 'sir'? What would he make of that? Sir! The reprobate Stephen was now a Sir.

Back at his flat, Tim whisked some eggs to make himself an omelette. The meeting at the MOD had gone much as he'd expected: the tailored concern of the mandarin not fully concealing a departmental preference to avoid engagement with army families.

He found he had no expectations, no vision of how events might turn out. He didn't know what to think. He was scared. This was the one catastrophe they'd feared might happen. Of course, as a family, they'd joshed each other into imagining that Steve was safe and sensible, but you couldn't just ignore the real dangers that being there imposed.

And then there was the man himself, the grand narrative of his big brother's life, Stephen's legend. Wasn't it always going to lead to disaster? Wasn't that what they all, even Steve, believed? Hadn't they persuaded themselves that it was just a matter of time.

For Tim, the first warning he'd had was on a visit to France, their last family holiday together. Although he wasn't getting on too well with their parents, Steve had agreed to go, attracted by the warmth of Provence and, in particular, the prospect of the three course meals in French restaurants, free.

They'd hired the same villa they'd been to twice before. In August the air was dense with the sweetness of lavender. They had an infinity pool; the water spilled over the edge in a cascade. Ahead to the horizon were fields of grey and mauve bushes, and the spindly vines of their neighbour's rosé.

The sun shone continuously for nineteen days, bar one when they had the most violent thunderstorm the boys had ever seen and half of Marseilles was flooded up to their knees.

They lay around on loungers, soaking up heat. He and Steve had their CD Walkmen, their parents books, and from time to time they swam in the pool. If you chose breaststroke and kept your head above water, it felt like you were drifting towards a purple garden, a view so sun-baked and painted and heady with scent that he could think of nowhere else he'd rather be.

When it was cooler, in the early evening, they played pétan-que on a patch of stony ground at the back of the villa. They brought with them shiny steel boules, which Edward had bought in an antiques market in Brighton, and between throws, as the boules came to rest, they had cold drinks, rosé for the parents, small bottles of Kronenbourg for him and Steve. They played for an hour, after which Edward would start to prepare a barbecue, or they would hop in the Volvo to the village a few kilometres down the road, where there were three restaurants arranged around the square, all good, all with terraces of tables covered in starched, white tablecloths and open to the gentle, night air.

They rowed, naturally, sometimes about petty things, like the washing up he and Steve were supposed to do, or laying the table for breakfast and lunch. Sometimes, it would be because Edward wanted to go out for the day, to visit an abbey he'd found in his guide book or a vineyard he'd heard about; on those occasions, everyone was against him, even Cara.

Despite the shouting, the rows seemed good natured. Everyone kind of knew they'd blow over. Edward caught Steve smoking once, out by the pool, late at night, but he promised not to tell Cara.

Tim, though, knew that something was wrong. One afternoon Steve slipped away, and when he came back, five or six hours later, his face and chest and thighs were badly sunburnt. He was in a lot of pain, and the burn made his skin sting whenever he tried to cool it with water or 'After Sun'. He'd crashed out on the beach, he said, without any sun lotion.

'How come you crashed out?' Tim asked.

'Cognac.'

It was all he said.

Cara's anxiety was older. At the age of five (strictly, four years and five months) Stephen had changed. He'd gone to school in September, a green apple in his pocket from a tree in the garden, and he'd discovered that he wasn't alone in being good-looking and clever and funny and advanced for his years, and all the other things Cara had caressed him into believing.

Far from alone.

So he'd decided that his new distinguishing feature would be 'difficult'. That would set him apart. He threw the apple across the classroom.

The following Christmas , during the school's nativity play, he showed his bare bottom to the audience, which made some of them laugh. Mrs Payne was furious and told Cara so.

There were incidents on most days: talking at the back of class, fighting in the playground, cheeking teachers. He was popular with boys his own age. They looked up to him, turned him into a leader, and then quickly disappeared into the shadows when trouble gathered around him.

A boy had started screaming during the lunch break and the duty teacher had discovered that Stephen had him pinned against the school fence. He was holding a stick with a nail through it up to the boy's face.

Stephen said that he wasn't going to do anything with the stick. He'd just picked it up, he said.

It was all Edward could do to stop himself striking his son. Instead, at Cara's suggestion, he took him for a long walk through a dripping wood and tried to instil in him the idea that cruelty and bullying were wrong and demeaning. Stephen managed to nod in the right places and there was a moment when Edward thought he was crying, but it might have been rain on his face.

Within days, they were asked in to the school again, ostensibly because Mrs Payne wanted their help in trying to understand and manage Stephen. In reality, it was a telling-off.

'And what was it this time?' Edward asked wearily.

Unlike their meeting three days earlier, Mrs Payne was not alone. She was the senior member of a triumvirate, flanked on one side by her deputy head and on the other by Stephen's form teacher.

The head hesitated, turned briefly to her deputy, then set down the charge.

'Stephen was caught looking defiant in Assembly.'

Edward was on the point of laughing. It went through his mind that they must, all five of them, surely agree that this was absurd.

'What was he doing exactly?'

'He was, as I say, defiant,' Mrs Payne explained. 'He was witnessed.'

'I see.'

'Are you sure it was a defiant look?' Cara asked.

'Quite sure.'

'He couldn't perhaps have been sleepy, or even bored?'

It was unclear whether sleepiness or boredom in Assembly would be an even greater crime than defiance, but one of these possibilities affronted Mrs Payne. She turned again to her deputy, at a loss for words, but conveying in her manner that she regarded Edward and Cara as intractable, possibly as intractable as their son.

'There's no doubt that it was defiance,' the deputy said.

'He used to be delightful when he was little,' Cara said.

'We see no evidence of that here.'

Cara asked the committee what they proposed to do.

'The issue,' Mrs Payne said, more loudly than she needed to, 'is Stephen's lack of conformity. He simply does not do anything he's asked to. Can I ask you: is he obedient at home?'

'Up to a point,' Edward said.

'Is that satisfactory?'

'Not entirely. But he's a boy. None of them are obedient all the time, are they? That's what boys are like.'

'We have other boys here who pose no problem.'

'Well, Stephen's different.'

'Indeed.'

Cara was becoming impatient.

'What would you like us to do, Mrs Payne?'

Mrs Payne embarked on another brief visual consultation of her colleagues, at the end of which she nodded.

'We think you should seek advice from your GP.'

'What kind of advice?' Cara asked

'From the psychological services. He can be visited here by an educational psychologist and your GP can arrange for you both to see a psychologist in private. With Stephen, of course.'

'Do you think he's disturbed then?'

Mrs Payne chose her words.

'We think there may be some family issues to be resolved. Around parenting, the home environment, boundaries, that sort of thing.'

'What about Tim?' Cara asked. 'Is he involved in this?'

The deputy head intervened.

'Tim is, thankfully, quite normal in our view.'

'Well, thank God for that, eh?' Edward was unable to keep the sarcasm from colouring his voice.

'We'll obviously have to give this some thought,' said Cara.

Although they agreed, between leaving Mrs Payne's office and reaching their car, that they would look for another school for both boys, they argued, as they drove home, about what should be done. Edward took the view that the Head Teacher was entirely to blame. Stephen, he maintained, had liked the school until Sheila Payne arrived two years ago and made it plain that she regarded boys as deviants.

'Then how does Tim manage as well as he does?'

Edward sighed and changed into a lower gear.

'Because she's wrong,' he said. 'However prejudiced she is, she can't stop clever boys like Tim, who are willing to toe the line, from succeeding. But Stephen's a free spirit, isn't he? He doesn't like academic study and the only way he'll do it is if there's a teacher who likes him, encourages him and enthuses him. That's why he's good at maths.'

'He has an aptitude.'

'Of course, but Hilary, or whatever she's called, is the only teacher who tries to foster that.'

They drove in silence for several minutes. Edward was, if anything, relieved. Being summoned to the school on such a flimsy pretext had focused his thoughts. In the weeks and months leading up to this meeting, when they'd dealt with repeated complaints about Stephen's lateness and his behaviour in class, and short, repetitive notes about his lack of effort, he'd remained ambivalent, uncertain how much responsibility lay with the school and how much with Stephen. 'Looking defiant in Assembly' had made that crystal clear.

'So you don't think we should contact the GP?' Cara said.

They both knew the argument was pointless, but neither of them could quite let it go.

'We could do.'

'You obviously think it's unnecessary.'

'I just think that any child psychologist will shift the blame away from the school and away from Stephen.'

'On to us, you mean?'

'Yes.'

'Which is where it belongs.'

'No, it doesn't. I don't believe that.'

'Just look at him, Edward. He's not simply badly behaved at school. We, or rather I, because you're away so much, I have a hell of a time with him at home. He lies.'

'All boys lie.'

'Not the way Stephen does.'

'So some of the blame attaches to Stephen himself.'

'No, Edward, no. Somewhere along the line we've gone wrong. I don't know what it is, but he's not the child he used to be and the main influence he's grown up with is us.'

'We brought Tim up in exactly the same way. We don't have the same problem with him.'

'Perhaps Stephen required a more thoughtful kind of nurturing.'

'So nature does play a part. You're saying Steve is intrinsically different from Tim.'

'I don't know,' Cara said. 'But I'm sure we could have done more. I'm sure we could have made Stephen happier.'

That stung. In the past, an accusation like that, even when it included Cara, would have led to a furious row. Edward balked at the idea. It left him defenceless, left him no room for manoeuvre or improvement. He, or they, she was saying, had made their own child's life unhappy.

But this time he avoided confrontation. He avoided it not least because he knew that she didn't altogether believe it. They had given Stephen what they could: affection, what time they had available, holidays abroad as a family, praise, security. She knew that as well as he did. Why wasn't it enough? Those were the building blocks of good parenting, weren't they? They'd both felt their own childhoods had lacked some of those things, so they'd made damn sure they provided them for Stephen and Timothy.

'We let him get away with too much,' Cara said.

Edward had learnt what little he knew of the incident from Tim. As a boy of six, Tim had been fond of a girl in his class called Holly. Holly lived on the other side of the village. Edward had often given Tim a lift to her house, but Holly's mother was a nurse and worked irregular hours, so it was usually more convenient for Holly to come to Tim's.

Stephen kept his distance as a rule. Being that much older, he hadn't a lot of time for girls and, although he disapproved of Holly and of his brother's friendship with her, he left them to it. Generally.

In Edward's memory, it was all associated with the 'caught looking defiant in Assembly' episode, in other words a day when Stephen was already in trouble at school and no matter how much Edward and Cara had reassured him that this most recent recrimination was absurd, he continued to see himself as an offender, in 'the naughty corner' again.

God knows what got into his head! Tim and Holly had just left school, following afternoon prayers, and were making their way home. Edward had agreed that they could walk because it was a fine day and it would only take them ten minutes. Their route did, admittedly, take them through a small wood, but it was a useful short-cut, quickly traversed. They should have been away from the main road and the pavement where they were always visible for a matter of two or three minutes only.

Stephen attacked Holly as she crossed a little bridge in the wood, which ran over a dried-up stream. The bridge was an old railway sleeper, too narrow and insecure for more than one person to be on it at a time. Holly had gone first, Tim behind. As she stepped off, Stephen jumped her. He threw her to the ground and began slashing at her bare legs with a stick he'd found. His brother ran up behind him and attempted to push him away. Stephen turned on him and pushed him so hard in the face that blood burst from his nose and his mouth started to swell.

He went at Holly for several minutes. She screamed and kicked at him, but she couldn't defend herself. What had been scratches were now cuts. There was blood over her legs, and it ran down into her white socks. She was crying and screaming and shouting 'Help!'.

Tim tried again to stop Stephen. He grabbed the arm with the stick, hoping to snatch it away. Stephen punched him in the eye and pushed him over and hit him twice with the stick across the head. Then he ran off.

Eventually, people walking past, on the pavement close to the wood, heard the children calling out. They peered through the trees and then went to help.

I think I heard scuffling again last night. It didn't last long and it was intermittent. No, not intermittent. That's the wrong word. It was staccato. Whatever the animal was, it must have made short bursts of movement, leaps. Then it checked itself, afraid it had done too much, made too much noise. In the dark it sounded large, like a rat perhaps. The dark magnifies, so it could have been a mouse or possibly a vole, quite small. I can't say I was worried either way. They don't do any harm, the rats and the mice and the voles, and they leave us alone.

We had a dog in here once. That frightened me. It was intended to. We were scarcely awake and the door flew open and I woke up and rubbed my eyes and standing in the door was one of the guards. He was holding back a black Alsatian. He'd got him by the collar and the dog was barking and growling and showing its teeth.

We just sat there, paralysed. There was nothing we could do. I knew it was a stunt, to intimidate us when we were half asleep, but there was always the possibility the guard would let go of the dog or lose his grip, and then what? We didn't know what it was trained to do. Neither of us would have stood a chance against it. We had nothing to fend him off.

So we just sat, very still, and hoped that the less we moved, the more likely it was that the Alsatian would calm down. I was too frightened to risk a glance at Rashid, but I could sense his cowering on the other side of the room. I could sense that he was doing everything in his power not to squeal or shriek or produce any kind of sound that might provoke the dog to break free and attack us. That was what they wanted, of course. The dog and the guard, both. They wanted Rashid to whimper and piss himself. They wanted him to wallow in his fear.

I thought about saying something, shouting at the guard, telling him and his Alsatian to fuck off, to show them we weren't as afraid as they'd like to think. I suppose I wanted to protect Rashid, to make him feel a bit better about himself and his fear.

But it wouldn't have done any good. The guards understand 'fuck off' well enough, but it makes them laugh. It doesn't anger them. It doesn't make them back down. They just laugh.

The dog was on two legs, reared up, gagging on the taut collar. Saliva dribbled from its mouth. Its eyes seemed to be filled with shiny light and hatred. But that's nonsense, isn't it? Dogs don't do hatred. They can be hungry and desperate. They can be trained out of a natural wariness of humans and made to attack them. But they don't hate them.

Eventually, the guard laughed and yanked the dog back into the outer office and shut our door. I felt a cold perspiration sliding down my neck and back. The bolt shot across the door, and the Alsatian's barking slowly eased to an occasional growl.

I looked over to Rashid.

'Ideal way to start the day, don't you think?'

He was still too scared to speak.

'Like a cold shower. Gets you moving.'

Rashid shuffled on his arse, away from the dark corner. I caught his face for a moment in the slice of light that fell into the room from the ceiling. He looked exhausted.

But that was another day.

My face has healed, just by my ear, where I caught the edge of the car door as I was thrown onto the rear seat. But I am troubled by my left knee. The skin is rough like sandpaper and torn in places. There are other grazes and the odd cuts. They stripped me and tied me to a chair, wrists behind the back of the chair, ankles to the front chairlegs, and then they beat my legs and feet with a leather strap. They paid particular attention to my left knee. I don't know why. It stung at first, like a wasp, but then the skin turned red and broke, and I began to scream.

They no longer ask any questions on these occasions, and they give no reason for hurting us. I've come to the conclusion it's nothing more than intimidation. The guards take it in turn. I don't think it gives them any pleasure. If it does, they don't show it. They pick up the rope or strap or prod and go to work. It's mundane.

Mundane violence. No one enjoys it, so let's get it done and out of the way as quickly as possible.

My fear is that my knee will become infected. The floor is filthy and, as I say, there are vermin at night, sometimes in the day as well. I thought about dabbing the wound with a little water from my bottle. I thought I could tear my shirt and make a rag, dip it in the bottle. I thought about it for a long time. I pictured the pale green cotton darkening as it soaked up the water. I watched myself fingering the wound with it, cleaning it. I felt I could imagine my knee healing, the rough cuts closing and forming scabs.

The problem is that my bottle of water is precious. It is never enough to satisfy my thirst. I am always thirsty. My throat aches with it so much my eyes and forehead begin to ache too. Every drop of water in the bottle has the power to stave off pain. That's why it can't be sacrificed. Any of it.

She lost weight. With that came a kind of blurring of the senses, a loss of agility. For weeks, she spoke of Stephen as a dead man, a dead son, gone from her, and some of her friends, when they spoke on the phone, thought that she was reconciled to it, adapting to a life without him. But that was not it. They were wrong. Her stoicism, if living with apparent self-control could be described in that way, was the temporary effect of shock. When she came out of it, it was as if from an operation, and the long labour of waiting began.

She hadn't planned to at all, but having opened the Chinese chest in the hall and seen them piled high in their yellow, cardboard, Kodak cases, she couldn't help herself. She picked three of the earliest videos and carried them into the sitting room. Edward, who would probably have advised against watching old footage of Stephen when he was young, was out, meeting a friend in London. She felt an odd thrill about what she was about to do and that Edward couldn't protect her.

The quality was poor. The pictures had a soft, almost bloated appearance, as if everyone had gained a few pounds. The camera work was pretty ropey too, far too many occasions when she'd forgotten to switch it off and the tape played interminable sequences of bookshelves or the three of them eating at their old dining room table. Quite suddenly, the picture would swing violently about, glimpsing blasts of light at a window and the blurred, bright colours of toys and furry animals scattered about the floor.

Then the image held, steady and focussed, as intended, and Stephen, aged two, looked uncertainly at her. He was actually less than two, maybe eighteen months, because there was no sign of Timothy. He had a nappy and a green shirt and bare feet.

Cara turned up the volume a couple of points and heard the familiar music, *Oklahoma*, the Fred Zinnemann film. The camera tilted to reveal a television in a far-off corner and another video playing. Video of video, Stephen in the foreground, *The Surrey with the Fringe on the Top* in the vague distance.

Stephen turned away from her to watch. Then he ran, lolloped the length of the room and stopped in front of the television screen. He squealed at it appreciatively and swung round to the camera with a big smile on his face that showed every one of the smattering of teeth he had. He jabbed his hand at the horse and carriage and screamed again. Then he ran back to Cara.

She heard her own voice, more nasal than it usually was, the camera pressing hard against her eye and nose.

'Do you like this song, Stephen?'

Stephen nodded excitedly, and made a long reply in a string of unintelligible sounds, which were sentences to him.

'Are you going to be a singer like Mummy and Daddy?'

'No!' he said, with an extremely serious look, as if he'd understood the question.

Cara watched all this and considered whether Edward was right about not re-visiting the past, at least not when she was in a vulnerable state. She was falling in love again, with her little boy, forgiving him all the offensive and cruel things he had yet to do, hugging her to him and kissing his wide, inclined forehead just below the quiff of blond hair that sprang up however hard she brushed.

He was funny, affectionate, perfect.

Edward opened the door to his study, but was unable to walk in. Had he had another recording scheduled, or he'd been booked to make a guest appearance on some arts programme on Radio 3, there would have been plenty to do, plenty to listen to and study and practise. But there was nothing. *Nothing in The Diary.* Work would provide a distraction. He could absorb himself in the prospect of performance, in the detail of the music, each phrase, its notation and intonation, the feel of it. Then, then, he might be rid of the one abiding, penetrative, irresistible image that occupied every waking thought, day and night, and that was of his son, Stephen, dead.

What did they call it in psychological circles? Catastrophic thinking: that was it, the ineluctable ratcheting up of every setback from a problem to a crisis to a catastrophe. It took a matter of seconds and, in the hands of an expert, the mind of an expert, the vivid eloquence of the final, most feared consequence was like raw adrenolin, distilled and taken as drops on the tongue, a mind-wrecking tincture.

The worst of it was that there seemed to be no way back. The psychologists! The psychologists said that you could train your mind to spot 'wrong' thinking, catch it in its infancy, and persuade it from taking the irrational, disastrous course. They underestimated its power, in Edward's view, the energy of it. Catastrophic thinking could not be persuaded to give up its possessions, its dominions, easily. It had to be exorcised, like true demons.

For relief, he walked in the garden and watched the river slip by.

It was actually a meander of the river that ran across the end of their lawn, and it was deep, sufficient in the summer for tourists to row shallow-bottomed dinghies from the boathouse in the village, past Edward's property and up to the medieval manor, which the National Trust was restoring. They could get there and back in three hours, a convenient hire. People took a picnic. He'd had to erect a notice at the edge of the grass to deter picnickers from using his garden.

The river looked high again. He wasn't in the habit of measuring it, but there were ancient tree roots that projected out from the bank and he swore that, before today, the water had not risen above them. There had been three days of rain, of course, and flooding further downstream.

Their house lay in the middle parts of the river, where it slowed down and took a long circuitous look at itself, snaking across the floodplain. On their bank there were trees, sycamore and birch; they stood in clumps, and in the intervals between them there was a broad view over a meadow to grey hills. Edward sometimes spent hours at the river's edge, beyond calls from the house, the ring of the phone, beyond reach.

This was where he came now when he felt overwhelmed by thoughts of Stephen.

Years ago, he'd built a low bench, three planks roughly nailed together. In the past, he and one or other of the boys, sometimes both, would sit and watch the brown river. He'd always thought it was his equivalent of teaching them to fish. He hadn't the slightest idea how to cast a line, in salt water, fresh water, bays, streams or rivers, anywhere. You learnt such skills at your father's knee, and Edward's father had been as clueless about fishing as he had been about carpentry and car mechanics. Instead, what Edward had offered Stephen and Timothy was the calm of contemplation, the drowsy mesmerism of flowing water. It hadn't appealed much when they were young and restless, but they'd quite liked it as just-turned teenagers. It was useful to have a shared activity that didn't require them to speak or look at each other. Elsewhere, parents felt obliged to ask questions. On the riverbank, questions didn't seem necessary.

Occasionally, a fish would jump and startle them.

Now, he retreated here for some peace of mind. The trouble was that it was always easier to fear the worst, to admit the possibility of loss, to imagine those monstrous, vile videos in which a figure in a black hood knelt over a freshly cut grave.

They came to mind so quickly, so vividly. To be brave, you had to shut them out. You had to try not to think at all. But that seemed like a betrayal, and that was a feeling he'd had about Stephen for far too long.

He'd always found Tim the easier of the two. Who wouldn't? When he went to university, he'd looked forward to him coming home at least once a term and for most of the vacation. But that hadn't happened. Once there, Tim saw no reason to leave and during vacations he travelled abroad or worked in one of the Oxford pubs or went to stay in the family homes of his new friends.

At first, Edward had put it down to novelty, the excitement of change. Compared with a city, compared with the stimulation of so many intelligent young minds flung together, a cottage by a river, deep in the Hampshire countryside, hadn't much to offer.

Then Cara said, 'It's me.'

His instinct was to dismiss it.

'Haven't you noticed? Over the years? He doesn't like me.'

No, he hadn't noticed. Had he been blind? What had there been to notice? He'd thought the difficulties, such as they were, had centred on Stephen. Had he missed something? There'd not been any open quarrelling, not between Tim and Cara. On the contrary, they seemed to be close, affectionate, rather like each other in fact.

'You talk about it in the present tense, as if it still goes on.'

'I'm sorry. That *was* part of the problem.'

He suspected she'd meant it, though. It was not a mistake. She defined it as a problem of the present because the estrangement continued. Tim's was a mature resentment. It confirmed

73

the division lines within the family: Cara & Stephen, Edward & Tim.

As he walked back to the house, he caught phrases of Bach, as if on the wind, traceable to the study window. He must have left the radio on. Two oboes d'amore, alone - it might be in a forest - and the merest hint of organ, keys scarcely touched, then a single voice, a curious fatalism about it. *Qui sedes ad dextram Patris Miserere nobis.*

He went inside and laid out a snack lunch for them: crackers, Cornish Yarg, vine tomatoes, a baguette with French butter. He considered white wine and decided to resist. He'd probably had enough. In the fridge was an unopened bottle of sparkling mineral water from the Highlands. He lifted it out with a feeling of pathetic virtue.

It didn't last. The table laid, he went back and took out the half-drunk white Rioja that stood in the shelf of the fridge door.

Have mercy on us!

'Rashid.'

I always call his name quietly. Rashid is often asleep, and the longer he can blot out the truth of our situation the better. He is convinced he will die. He says he knows what the guards are like. He knows these people, he says, and what their eventual orders will be. It's only a matter of time, he says, and if he is without hope, he must sleep to quell his fears.

It makes sense to me. Rashid is a rational man. At least, for a man without hope, he is. He thinks things through. But he is without hope.

'Rashid.'

If I raise my voice above a whisper, a guard will come in and shut me up. They've been told to. They have been told that they must discourage our talking whenever they can. But we talk all the same and risk the shouting and the beatings and the days without food. Without talking, I'd have given up long ago. Sometimes, I'm even glad to be shouted at by the guard. I used to feel the same when Dad shouted at me. It's communication of a sort after all.

Rashid must be asleep, as I suspected. He sleeps silently. When the guards finally separate around two in the morning, I can hear the shuffling of a rat, or the drill of insects, but I scarcely ever catch Rashid's breathing. It's as if he's trained himself to be imperceptible, someone who never intrudes, whose purpose is to be invisible. Perhaps that's why he's been so successful as an interpreter. Isn't that the goal of all translators and interpreters, to be so good at their job that language is converted, promptly and inconspicuously, back and forth, the two foreigners so closely in touch with each other's thoughts that they don't even notice the punctilious, bald Rashid seated next to them? They don't hear his words, his pauses for breath. They think they are conversing unaided, and that is what Rashid would want them to think. If that is what they think, he has accomplished his task.

There are times when the guards shutter off the thin window in the ceiling. They mean to disorientate us, to create artificial night. But darkness during the day has a different quality. It is not merely a matter of sound, though that may contribute to the sense of difference. It is more subtle than the obvious distinctions and distractions of day and night. The darkness of day is warmer and noisier, it's true, but it has an intensity that darkness at night lacks. We always know, Rashid and I, when day becomes night and night becomes day. The rule of darkness they occasionally impose has failed to confuse us. When it should be daylight and the darkness continues, we know it. We sense the intrusion, the wrong.

It is like that now. I suspect there is only one guard on duty outside the door. The other two will be at lunch or prayer. On his own, a guard reads the newspaper or watches the shoebox sized television that hangs from the ceiling. I know this from the glimpses I get of the outer office when the door is unlocked and we are marched to the washroom. Sometimes, I hear one of them on the phone to a friend or his family, or a superior. I've persuaded myself that I can tell when the call is to family. Obviously, I understand nothing of their language, but they change their tone when they are speaking to family, all of them, and they laugh less. At least, this is my belief.

We have a game, Rashid and I, which we play twice a day, once in the morning, once in the afternoon. We imagine how someone we know or used to know – it can be anyone we miss – is spending his or her time, at that very moment. If we play twice, it means we have one go each. Usually, I imagine events involving Holly, as if we were still together. But recently, I have tried to conjure up an hour or so in Mum's life. I'm sure Rashid must feel he knows my mother by now and would recognize her on the street. I don't suppose anything I've told him bears any resemblance to what is actually going on in her life. I describe her rehearsing in her attic – a room I haven't seen in donkey's years – and she's writing e-mails, going to meetings with flamboyant men in expensive suits (conductors, I'm guessing), picking up a salmon and wild rocket sandwich from Prêt-à-Manger in Oxford Street. She's neatly dressed in a narrow black skirt that stops just above the knee, and a grey, close-fitting jacket, which she takes off as soon as she arrives at rehearsals. I tell Rashid that her job is creatively rewarding, but marred by the anxiety of being freelance and the occasional attack of stage fright. Then, by association, if we play the next morning, Mum will be at a party, perhaps after a performance, or she'll be driving Dad to a concert. In my stories, she smiles in the evenings, and laughs. She feels confident, free.

I have kept myself from speculating about whether she misses me. There's no point. It throws me off-balance. If Rashid asks, I laugh and say 'Why not? Of course!'

When Rashid plays the game, he often chooses his grandmother, and imagines an hour in her difficult life. She is old now, ninety-two I think he said the first time, and she is lame, the result of an operation on her hip that went badly wrong. She rarely walks, Rashid tells me, and when she does, she is stooped. Her eyes follow the ground, and she drags her leg like a dog determined not to let go of a dead chicken. As he describes his grandmother, trapped in her chair in her tiny flat, asleep with a book on her lap, Rashid always weaves in the story of her past. She taught him to read, and she read to him at night. She read English books in translation, books like Treasure Island and Robinson Crusoe and the short stories about Sherlock Holmes. She fed him a fantasy of the Pacific: white sands and coral reefs and clear turquoise water, palm trees he would one day climb. She drew a picture of dirty London, always fogbound, criminals and cut-throats lurking in the city's alleyways. After she'd read one of the Holmes stories, she would tell Rashid about her own visit to London, in 1947, the only time she'd been there. The city, she said, was black from bombing. There were so many half-buildings, chimneys cut down to stubs, houses with their kitchens gaping at the foggy sky, their sitting rooms and bathrooms on the outside, revealed like an opened doll's house. But she also said that St Paul's still stood, with its high dome, and the Houses of Parliament brooded over the River Thames. The King and Queen had been in residence at Buckingham Palace, and there were bright bulbs of light around the entrance to the Ritz hotel.

She had come away happy. One day Rashid should go there too.

Part of her craved the past, the nurturing part, the part that wanted them to be living together again, Dad and Mum and the two boys in their respective bedrooms. Sometimes, Stephen's disappearance had set her hankering after that, tumbling through a nostalgia for a time she knew to be more constructed than real, when Timothy and Stephen played soccer on the lawn and billiards in the old garage.

Despite what she might say to Edward, she felt that, on the whole, she had been a good mother. She'd cared for those boys, given them virtually every hour of the day when they were too young for school, then making sure she was in the playground each afternoon by three, well before they exited the Hall, detonating the energy and joy suppressed by end-of-school prayers.

They raced to her, arms conductor-wide, and flung themselves into her embrace. That had been affirmation. No child comes willingly to a mother who is hard or cruel or indifferent. They ran in a state of enchantment, knowing that they were not only loved but desired. Cara, through her smiling eyes and kisses and hugs, warm and enveloping as their nightly bath, gave them the idea that her life was empty without them, that the hours between breakfast and their meeting again in the playground were a time of yearning. They would think they fulfilled her.

Was this a false memory? She didn't believe so, but sometimes the past did seem impenetrable or vague, the earlier periods of family life obscured by the later. She found herself trying to imagine Stephen at six, what he was really like, when he wasn't hurtling across a playground. The sixteen year old somehow got in the way, and she found herself thumbing through photo albums in the ground floor bathroom, trying to remind herself.

That morning, returning from Sainsbury's, the road was flooded, along the stretch between the two bridges, where it dipped and ran between fields. The fields were frequently waterlogged. They sat slightly below the riverbank and the thick, claggy soil beneath the grass was slow to drain. After a heavy downpour, even when the river didn't spill over, water would lie in the fields for a day or two, forcing any livestock there might be to move to the higher ground at either end.

Cara took the car forward, gingerly. Ahead of her a Land Rover had sped through the flood without difficulty, but her much lower Volvo had far less clearance. With the Land Rover gone, there appeared to be nobody to assist if she got into trouble. The last thing she wanted to spend the day doing was hanging around in the cold, waiting for a tow-truck to come and pull her out.

The front wheels seemed to sink as she edged into the water. She changed down to first and, very tentatively, urged the car on with the accelerator. Slow, but sure. That's what Edward always advised. The river slewed around her. It squelched and gurgled as the Volvo pushed its way through. She saw that the water had breached the driver's door and the well by her feet was now wet.

She pressed on, sensing that beneath her, under the wheels, the surface of the road was slippery with mud and water. At the half-way point, the car appeared to judder. She thought it would stall, so she throttled the engine and at the moment it seemed about to die, it lurched forward. As she began to rise out of the flood and onto the second bridge, she was suddenly frightened by how fast her breathing had become.

She was aware of music in another room. The St John Passion, towards the end, *Allda kreuzigten sie ihn.* Wherever it was playing, she thought, the volume must be turned right up.

'Have you been drinking?' she called out.

Something about the length of time it was taking him to reply made her panic.

She found Edward asleep at his desk, the Bach manuscript on the floor by his feet. It must have slipped out of his hands as he dozed off. She picked it up, closed the book and slid it between other 'parts' on the shelf above the desk.

For a moment, seeing her husband slumped forward, his forehead on one arm, the other hanging loosely beside the chair, she couldn't help but be reminded of that day two years ago when she'd come on Edward at another table, in the kitchen. He was unconscious, having some minutes before convulsed and fallen forwards amongst the cheese and ham and plates and bread he'd laid out for lunch. His shirt was torn open, his face an inhuman grey. She ran across the room to the phone.

They'd saved him, but with not much time to spare, they said. 'Acute myocardial infarction' didn't sound as life-threatening as a heart attack. On the contrary, it had the sound of something treatable. She listened patiently as a young doctor told her how there would have been a blockage of the blood flow, resulting in the death of cells in the heart. Had he complained of chest pain lately, or breathlessness? He had, of course, and she'd poo-pooed it, assuming it was yet another of Edward's phantom illnesses. They always occurred when he wasn't working, when he was panicking that he was washed-up and that no one would ask him to sing again.

'He must take it quietly for a few months,' the young doctor had said. 'The damage that has been done is irreversible. He'll be fine, but he needs to rethink his diet and reduce his cholesterol. Take it easy, at least for a while.'

She didn't say it, but taking it easy was the problem. Edward was fine when he was active. It was only when he had time to imagine, to dwell on things, that he began to think he was ill. What had Voltaire said was the answer to suicidal thoughts? *Keep busy.*

She had ignored his lunchtime bulletins for weeks, she realised. 'I just don't feel right' was the phrase he used, and if she allowed him to say more, didn't shut him up with conversation of her own or, more crudely, signs of impatience, he would expand, detail the most recent symptoms: shortness of breath, pain in the middle of his chest or sometimes his arm. He thought he was sweating more than usual and he felt restless.

'Go for a long walk,' she'd said. 'You know it always make you feel better.'

Dutifully, Edward would go off, three or four miles through the woods or along the river. When he got back, an hour or so later, he'd kiss her gently on her forehead, or the nape of her neck, and tell her how wise she was. He felt cared for, he said. Fancy a drink?

That morning, though, the day it happened, he'd complained of dizziness, which was new. He didn't appear to be ill. She'd not noticed anything peculiar as he made them toast and prepared a jug of coffee. She'd assumed it would pass. Like everything else.

Did he seem quieter than usual?

She'd taken the car, to visit a friend who lived in a village about ten miles away. That had left him stranded. He told her afterwards that when the pain came on, when the pressure built up and he feared his chest might burst, when he was convinced he was going to die, it would have been too late to make use of the car. He wouldn't have trusted himself to drive it.

That wasn't the point. She knew it. The point was that she should have read the warning signs and stayed at home.

She was more gentle with him now, at least when she remembered to be.

'You fell asleep, darling.'

She lifted his hanging arm and placed it on the desk as he came round.

'What?'

'You dozed off. I thought you said you found Bach stimulating.'

He laughed a little.

'Must have dozed off. Not like me. Lunch is ready.'

'You're forgiven. I think you might have been drinking…?'

'Just a little. Glass or two. Want one?'

'No. Thanks.'

He followed her into the kitchen, where she'd left the shopping bags.

'You don't think you might be drinking too much at the moment?'

'Not really.'

She carried a plastic bottle of milk to the fridge.

'The music's a bit loud.'

'Do you think so?'

She stopped what she was doing, put down the spreadable butter and the packet of vine-ripened tomatoes.

'What's wrong, Edward?'

'Nothing that hearing our son has been safely returned to his regiment won't cure.'

He smiled and appeared to dance across the room towards her.

'Don't you feel the same?'

'Yes, but there's no point saying it. We're doing all we can.' She paused. 'Is it just Stephen?'

'Absolutely, darling.'

'Edward, I haven't been married to you for thirty years without knowing exactly when you're in a mood or something's wrong. What is it? And don't put on that act of being jolly for me. It won't work. Are you just worried about Stephen?'

'Yes, of course.'

'Then, shut up about it, will you. Put on a different face and cheer up. Let's not eat here. Take me out to lunch.'

They settled on The Rock. It was an unimaginative choice, but they knew they would have a table to themselves, even at short notice, and the food was reliably good. Cara asked for a tomato, mozzarella and pesto Panini; Edward took the bacon and brie sandwich on granary bread. For continuity, he decided to stick with white Rioja.

'I've just realised what it is.'

Edward nodded, unsure what to expect.

'Derek rang, didn't he?'

She might have jumped to the wrong conclusion initially, but she got there in the end. Edward never failed to be impressed by her apparently effortless deduction. He realised she must have been sifting through a pile of possibilities on the journey to the pub, but no one would have guessed. She kept up a light, multi-topic chit-chat as they drove, serial trivia that belied the idea that she was thinking at all.

'I didn't get the Wigmore.'

'Oh, what a surprise! And there was I wondering why, after weeks of silence, they were still considering you. They probably made the decision the day of the interview. Why didn't Derek tell you? Was he doing his usual thing of waiting for something else to come up before imparting the bad news?'

Cara was angry, not with the conductor, certainly not with Edward, but she disliked the way in which Derek hung on to information that was, rightfully, Edward's. It was not, in her view, how agents should behave.

'If he was,' Edward said, 'nothing has come up.'

'Who got the Evangelist?'

'James Archer.'

'Good voice.'

'Half my age.'

'That's beside the point. Anyway, he's not. James must be forty-five.'

'He'll pull a bigger crowd.'

'Possibly. I doubt it.'

Her annoyance made her drink more quickly. Her glass was now empty. She would, as a rule, ask Edward to fetch her another, but she decided to do it herself this time.

'We should have had a bottle,' she remarked. 'Cheaper.'

As she stood at the bar, trying to catch the eye of the young woman with black jeans and green hair, it occurred to her that Edward might have already drunk several glasses. She'd been away from the house for over three hours and if Derek had rung soon after she left, Edward might well have hit 'the sauce', as he liked to call it, by ten o'clock. She decided to order small measures, instead of those colossal, balloon-like glasses, with nearly half a pint in them, which they loved to lure you into buying, as if it were the publican's treat.

Their food arrived, inevitably accompanied by the two bowls of chips they'd said they'd rather not have.

Her bad temper was focused on what Edward would do, now that the part he'd been pinning his hopes on had been given away elsewhere. She suspected that his resilience to disappointment was weakening. His old, rusted metal might puncture, if exposed to harsh conditions for much longer.

It was not that they needed the money. Edward's investments, made when he could do no wrong and every week glittered with performance (*The Clinton Years* as he called them, somewhat sardonically), together with a newer surplus income that Cara herself had generated, meant that they had no financial worries. The mortgage was paid. They enjoyed good food and wine. They had foreign holidays, some of them, like Peru, quite ambitious. If she wanted to sum up their situation, if it was appropriate to, at a party, she'd say

'Well, we no longer have to panic when the dishwasher breaks down'.

Edward, though, had wrapped up his entire self-worth in the part of the Evangelist.

After lunch, they decided to walk back to the house. They took the bridleway that led through the pheasant wood and up to a low grassy ridge that overlooked the village.

They were walking through an avenue of old oaks, their trunks swollen by dark knurls from which newer, finger-slim growths separated. Earlier, the sky had been so bright it had made them squint, but here the light was dappled, sprinkled through brown and yellow leaves, and alongside them there was an almost constant rustle of pheasants shuffling about in the undergrowth, imagining themselves undetected.

'I'm not fashionable any more. You put my name on a bill and it draws no one. I have to face up to it. The number of people who know me is getting smaller and smaller.'

The path broadened out, so that they could walk next to each other, and then turned a corner, which took them past Blake's Hut, a single-roomed, single storey structure, with logs piled high outside the door. In eighteen years, neither Edward nor Cara had ever seen Blake. The only proof that he existed was that the log pile would slowly reduce each winter.

A chain saw whined in the distance.

'Whenever you have a period like this,' she said, 'you behave in exactly the same way. You can have rave reviews for your last performance, but as soon as the phone doesn't ring for a few weeks, it's finished. You're a has-been. *Caput mortuum.*'

'And if I'm right?'

'But you never are, are you? You're not getting as much

work as you used to, but it comes in, enough of it comes in. The Harry Miles thing, the retrospective, could come off. And you're fifty-eight years old, for God's sake!'

'That's my point.'

'No, your point is that at fifty-eight, you're done for. That's not what I believe. It's not what your agent believes. The only hard fact you have to face up to is that your opportunities will dry up slowly, not suddenly.'

'Ever the optimist. I hope you're right.'

'And you're ever the pessimist. Does it ever occur to you that you're horribly self-obsessed? I don't want to talk about your bloody career any more. I have enough to worry about.'

They crossed a stream by means of a two-plank bridge with scaffolding poles for a handrail. Beyond the wood, the path crossed open fields, rolls of hay still lying about, and without the protection of the trees they felt a cool breeze on their faces. Ahead of them were tree-topped hills and other fields, some with sheep grazing in them. A dog was barking somewhere. For such a light wind, the clouds were moving surprisingly swiftly.

'You let yourself worry about trivial things when the worst crisis we've ever had to deal with has just hit us,' she said.

'I try to force myself not to think about him.'

'Why can't you force yourself not to worry about your work?'

'It's not the same. Worrying about work is manageable. It makes me gloomy. I stomp about the house, but it's not a disaster. If I allow myself to imagine, even for a moment, what might happen to Stephen, I think I could go mad, so instead I keep reminding myself that he's cautious and sensible, keeps his eyes and mind alert. All that. And I try to empty my mind of him. Does that sound callous? It's the only way I can persuade myself he's safe.'

Safe was hardly the word Cara would have used, but she knew that what Edward meant was that Stephen wasn't dead. It was how she coped too, resting all her faith in army training and the instinct for self-preservation. Every reported death, every execution of a hostage, ate away at that faith, but the core was strong.

'Yes, he will be,' said Cara, and she let him hold her arm as she stepped up onto the cross-plank of an old wooden stile.

'They were accompanying local police on a routine walkabout, designed for show frankly, keeping up a presence.'

It was Stephen's CO, Mike Jeffreys.

'At 0200, they were ambushed, almost certainly by a local militia. Three of Stephen's men were killed outright, as were two of the policemen. One man made it back to base, a Corporal Alan Lucie. He reported seeing Lt. Padgett, Stephen, bundled into a car and driven away at high speed. We think he's been taken hostage in the mountains south of here. Probably with a local chap called Rashid, who we used as a translator.'

Edward pressed his mobile closer to his ear to catch every word.

'Now that we have the story straight about how he came to be...' The lieutenant-colonel paused. 'Taken. We can get a better idea of where he is.'

'How so?' Edward asked.

'These events tend to follow a pattern.'

Patterns again. Edward didn't believe it.

'And what pattern do you expect this to follow, Colonel?

He tried not to sound sarcastic.

'Too early to say. Look, I have a few other calls to make, Mr Padgett, but I'll be back to you, obviously, as soon as I know anything. Do keep this under your hat, won't you? You don't want the press crawling all over your doorstep.'

The line died.

The new people in the village, Jon and Vinny, had invited them to Sunday lunch. They were asked for 12.30 and they arrived on time, which seemed to surprise Vinny when she answered the door.

'Oh,' she said, and she ran her fingers through her hair, as if she still needed time to have a shower. 'Come in. Let me take your coats. Jon's out in the garden.'

'Not gardening, I hope?' Edward said.

'No, no. He's fetching logs for the fire.'

He'd meant it as a joke.

When Jon appeared, slightly short of breath from carrying a heavy basket of wood, he was equally disorientated.

'You're very prompt. Must be the musical training.'

'I hope you don't mind,' Cara volunteered. 'It took rather less time to walk here than we'd anticipated.'

'We're practically neighbours,' Vinny said. 'What would you like to drink?'

'White wine, if that's okay.'

'The same for me.'

Vinny left them in the sitting room, and Jon followed her into the kitchen.

'Why are they so put out that we turned up exactly when they asked us to?'

Cara smiled and tapped Edward gently on the knee.

'It's got nothing to do with that, darling. They're anxious about the conversation we're about to have. They want to ask about Stephen and they're not sure how to go about it.'

Cara had been the one who dealt with people's questions right from the start. Without speaking about it, they had tacitly agreed that 'outside enquiries', as Edward called them, were better handled by her. He, too, would have begun by being patient, but quite quickly he'd have lost his temper and started shouting, demanding to know what business it was of theirs how they were coping or whether their son lived or died. He could only see prying where Cara saw understandable interest. She had the knack of putting people at their ease and deflecting the turn of the conversation in such a way that they went away satisfied whilst Cara didn't get upset.

Their drinks arrived and were placed on the table between them.

'Cheers!'

Vinny had her glass up by her shoulders. She smiled and, as she sipped her glass, she squeezed her eyes as if to say it was the most delicious wine she'd ever tasted.

Cara could see she was edging her way towards a sensitive question.

'It must be so difficult,' she said. 'Where do they think he is now?'

Edward replied.

'No one knows. They think he's been kidnapped. If he escapes, he'll probably head into the hills, trying to avoid people. He would stay clear of towns, I imagine. But we just don't know.'

'The hills, the countryside, it's all very dangerous, isn't it?'

As soon as she'd said it, Vinny regretted it. She realised she might have strayed over a line, put doubt in Edward's and Cara's minds where before they had had hope.

'I didn't mean to suggest...'

Cara stepped in.

'I hope this won't sound rude, but to be honest I don't think there's anything you can suggest that we haven't, at one time or another, already thought. We know there's a strong possibility Stephen's dead. We know that he could have got away from where he was held and ten minutes later, or ten hours or ten days, he's dead. We don't have any illusions, Vinny, so you don't have to be embarrassed when you happen to say something that implies the worst. We've lived with a kind of bereavement for weeks now.'

Edward looked at Cara. She was right. They had not spoken as bluntly to each other as Cara now spoke to the Carlisles, but they had both entertained these thoughts and each knew what the other was thinking and going through. He realised, perhaps for the first time since Stephen had gone missing, that despite the rows they'd had, despite their differences about what, or sometimes whom, to believe, it had brought them together.

'I think you're incredibly brave,' Vinny said. 'The way you cope with the uncertainty.'

'Yes,' said Jon. 'Very brave.'

Edward raised his half drunk wine.

'This helps.'

Jon immediately stepped across and refilled his glass.

'We don't have any choice,' Cara said.

'Nonetheless.'

'No, we don't have any choice. We can't just give up and go into full mourning, can we? We haven't been informed that he's dead, so for us, he must be alive. Yes, he's in danger. Yes, we're worried that he won't make it safely out of there. But he has a chance and for as long as we don't know anything to the contrary, that chance is a good chance. He's well trained. He's intelligent and resourceful. Why shouldn't he make it back? Stranger things have happened. As long as there isn't some bastard standing over him ready to stab a rifle butt in his face or shoot him in the head, there's hope. That's something, isn't it?'

She'd said too much. As she'd been speaking, Edward had placed his hand, carefully, on her arm, hoping to calm her down, hinting that she might want to stop, but the visceral storm had been gathering, and the more it agitated the less she was able to slow down or stop.

'I'm sorry,' she said.

As they made their way to the lunch table, she wiped her eyes with a tissue. It was sufficient.

My eyes are stinging and wet. I expect it's sweat, but it might be blood, probably is. The blindfold is soaked in whatever it is.

Wrists tied behind the chair, ankles to the legs.

The first time he hit, it came out of nowhere. No warning. A thinnish wooden stick, I'd guess. A schoolmaster's cane perhaps? Across the back of my neck. Then to my face, immediately. He scarcely had time to draw back from the first and strike again.

I screamed.

It split my forehead open. A trickle running, descending from my hairline...

I scream again.

My thighs leap with very pain. I can't keep my legs still. They're trembling. Bouncing.

...snags in my left eyebrow, drips into my left eye, another snakes left temple...

Please! What do you want? Please! Don't!

They whip my thighs again, my shins, to stop my legs shaking. They don't. It doesn't.

...my head fallen, it slides into my ear. Blood in the ear.

Naked arms. Thrashed. Both. Twelve strokes.

I can't see.

There is nowhere he will not hit me. He wants me to be in pain in every part of my body.

I can't see him. Can't see it coming. The first is the hot burst of my skin.

Then pain.

And blood.

Have mercy.

3

October 2013

We have now been here for forty-seven days. There have been no further beatings. My forehead has scabbed over. The bruises on my arms and legs ache and disturb my sleep, but it's my knee and my neck that give me the most trouble. All of this could be worse. I feel no bitterness.

My phone was torn from me during the skirmish outside Rashid's house. Surprisingly, I have hung on to my watch, which appears to keep accurate time and I score up each day on the wall above my head before falling asleep at night. I use a coin they failed to find to scratch a short vertical line. On the fifth and tenth days, I score crosswise, so that I can quickly count up each hatch of five. It's such a cliché. I feel like Edmond Dantès, the Count of Monte Cristo, in the Château d'If. Robert Donat played him in an old black and white movie. Except that our conditions on the whole are better than his. We have tolerable food. We are permitted a shower once a week, so we have relatively clean hair and fingernails. On the debit side, we do have rats, our water is sometimes contaminated and we have to defecate in a bucket at one end of the room.

I'm not sure how to describe this room we live in without reducing it to a list of its features. It means so much more than a few bald points. It is not only our environment but our being, a part of us.

The room is large, perhaps ten metres by five. Ceiling to floor, it must be six. I can't imagine what it was last used for. The walls are covered in a rough plaster, painted grey, but it was clearly never a prison. There are broken chairs and tables stacked in one corner that suggest it might have been a classroom or some kind of meeting place. The chairs have wooden backs and seats, the legs being steel. The seats are cracked and provide no comfort. I tried sitting on one and found it strangely harder than the chaises longues we have created out of newspapers and scraps of cardboard we found lying around.

In the ceiling there are three brown, twined flexes. Two have naked bulbs hanging from them. The third ends in an empty socket. Only one of these bulbs functions, and the rota of light and dark is, as I say, unpredictable. Today is a Day of Light, which is why I can pick out and describe the features of the room. In principle, after forty-seven days, I should be able to recall every detail with my eyes closed, but things shift and small things disappear through the gate of memory. On a Day of Light, there is only a fraction of light, a sliver from a window on the sloping ceiling above the tables and chairs. To call it a window is to flatter it. A 'slit' would be a better word, much like an arrow slit in a castle, wide enough to let an arrow pass, but too narrow to peer through with both eyes. The window is, in any case, at a forty-five degree angle, following the line of the eave. Although it provides, at most, a glimpse of blue sky, the light falling into the room is welcome and it sometimes catches Rashid's face and that makes me glad.

Apart from our stinking bucket, there is nothing else. We have no source of heat and on cold nights we shiver and try to wrap ourselves in the newspapers from which our day loungers are made. We have complained about the lack of heat, but our complaints have met with the same deafness as our request for a fan. They make their tepid apologies, but nothing changes.

Rashid is asleep now, as he so often is. My left knee hurts, my neck, my arms. I feel desperate loneliness. And fear.

We are fed once, at noon. If we are lucky, the food is hot and will include meat, very poor quality and heavily spiced chicken as a rule. They drench it in a watery gravy. There are no vegetables, as yet, but we are given enough coarse bread, which mixed with the thin gravy seems nourishing.

They leave us our bowls for the rest of the day and collect them when it starts to get dark. This is a blessing. There are times when I am too hot or too miserable to eat, and I am grateful for a second chance later in the afternoon, by which time my mood has often changed.

Water is brought to us every four to five hours, usually in half litre plastic bottles. The water is not what the label says it is. The bottles are secondhand. The seals on the caps have been broken and whatever it is we drink I know it is not purified mineral water. It's come straight out of a tap. If the broken seal didn't give it away, the taste and colour would. It has a pale greenish tinge and a tanginess to it, which lingers in the mouth long after you've swallowed. So far I've avoided being poisoned, but I suspect it's only a matter of time. Since I have been here, Rashid has had two bouts of stomach cramps and diarrhoea. I feel for him as he goes through the indignity of sitting on the grey aluminium bucket every couple of hours, and we politely ignore the horrendous stench.

There is a sense of anticipation about the hour before noon. It's like waiting for the phone to ring. It's not merely that we have the prospect of lunch (a disruption to the routine for which we are pathetically grateful) but because I imagine it being a time when decisions are made. I'm confident that one day a guard will unlock our door and a senior official will walk in and announce that we are free to go. He will be impatient and find it difficult to understand why we are so slow to grasp what he is saying, so slow to act.

I imagine that decision, the decision to free us, will take place in the morning. It feels like a morning decision, the kind of decision that is taken in the morning, the result of a two hour meeting that began at eight or eight-thirty. I don't know why I am so convinced of this, but I just don't believe that decisions about whether or not to release hostages are made in the afternoons.

We have asked for books and newspapers, also paper and something to write with. A particularly nasty conversation with Rashid, which began as a discussion, turned into a debate and ended in vicious and futile taunts, has persuaded us that we need other forms of entertainment. I'm not sure what I would write if I could, probably a diary of my time here, but I thirst for some reading matter almost as much as I long for sex.

We have our loungers, of course, but they have only old news, stuff that's forgotten, in a language I can't penetrate.

The guards have no doubt been told not to let us have newspapers. One of them hinted this was the case. They don't want us to be aware of the outside world. For all we know, there may be a running commentary on our disappearances, perhaps some indication of who it is that has taken us hostage. They wouldn't want us to see that. To a man, the guards have refused to answer when we've asked about the organisation they work for.

But books. They could give us books. Rashid is desperate enough to have volunteered to read aloud to me, translating as he goes. My hope, of course, is that they can drum up an English novel or two. I don't care how crappy or poorly written they are. I just crave the written word. I fantasise about it. If I'm given a book, I shall ration my reading. Depending on the length of it, I'll allow myself nine or ten pages a day. I shall read it twice, three times, maybe more. It would be so easy to finish the entire thing in a day, but I don't want to be greedy or wasteful. The pleasures we have must be measured out, a spoonful at a time.

I would spend more time in the shower, but the place they laughingly call the bathroom is too disgusting to want to stay there any longer than is absolutely necessary. The bracket on which the shower handle used to rest has broken, so the hose hangs loose and the shower head lies on the floor when not in use. This wouldn't matter if it weren't for the weight of it, which is gradually pulling the taps away from the wall. No one has made any attempt to repair it and my fear is that if the whole lot collapses, that'll be it and we'll be without a shower. The thought is unbearable when I am in the room, at a distance, and untroubling every time I take a shower. I switch it on and as the water, which is invariably cold, begins to fall out of the shower head, it disturbs the cockroaches. They scurry round behind the back wall of the cubicle. They sound like a thousand eggshells being stirred and mashed. I don't know any other sound it compares with. It is far worse than the rats at night or the insects in the ceiling, and it grows, as if more and more of the loathsome things are on the move. I smell them before I see them. It's a smell like a putrid gas which you're sure will harm your internal organs if you inhale it. Then they appear, two or three at a time, at the edges of the shower tray. They move at different speeds, some shooting across the floor and vanishing through cracks, others lingering, creeping very slowly, stopping altogether for seconds at a time. They shine and twitch their antennae. However bad the light is, on any day, they shine, a grey-black shell, wet and glossy and repellent.

Even though I am disgusted, I have to watch. It's not fear. They are strangely compelling. They make no attempt to climb into the tray or to approach me. I find myself 'paused', as a 'play' button might be paused. The water drizzles from the shower head, but I have ceased to wash. It's as if I am bewitched by them.

The moment doesn't last. A noise erupts in the corridor outside or a sudden, rogue spoke of water spits across the floor and sends them scuttling for darkness. Their smell is slow to fade and above the spurt of the shower, I can hear their stir and mash.

'My mother and my brother don't speak to each other.'

Rashid is lying down. He is probably asleep, or dozing. I watch him move. The rustle of newspaper around him is surprisingly noisy. He drags himself up and sits propped against the wall.

'Not really. I mean they make arrangements. They talk politely to each other. But it's trivial stuff. In the old days, they'd row. Not now.'

'That's very sad, sir.'

'Is it?'

Rashid is not sure where I am taking the conversation. Is it a passing comment that requires little more than a nod? Or am I embarking on more serious matter, a confession? I'm not sure myself, and he waits for me to say more.

'Tim can't forgive my mother, you see. He can't forgive her for having an affair. He's never proved that she did, but he's convinced himself, do you see? Do you know what his evidence was?'

Rashid realises I am looking at him now, that I expect a

99

response. The light is poor. I can't make out what his face is saying. Eventually, he moves his head slightly.

'Tim saw Mum kissing another man after one of her concerts.'

Rashid hesitates. Then he says:

'That's what you do, right? In your country? You congratulate your artists, and their friends come up to them afterwards and say 'Wonderful, darling' and they kiss. Right, sir?'

'Yes, that's exactly right, Rashid. That's what they do. But Tim doesn't see it that way. He says that it wasn't that sort of kiss.'

I feel as though I'm drunk on a mixture of anger and resentment and something I can only call sorrow. I can't think of another word to describe it.

'He thinks she was having it off with the guy who's the conductor, and the kiss, Tim says, was definitely passionate. He's never confronted my mother. He told me, but I'm not going to challenge her about it. I didn't see the kiss. I wasn't there. So I said to Tim: if you're that bothered about it, ask her. But he won't. He just lets it fester. He feels more and more bitter towards her and does nothing about it.'

'It will destroy their relationship.'

I can hear Rashid's thoughts. He's thinking of his own family and making a wild transfer across cultures, imagining that Tim is his son, imagining that his own wife might have been unfaithful. It unsettles him. He wants me to tell him the truth.

'Do you think she was having sex with this man, the conductor?'

'I've no idea, but that's not the point, Rashid. You see, the reason Tim's so uptight about it is because he blames my mother for everything that's gone wrong in our family. He's a complicated guy, my little brother, and he's bright. He went to Oxford University.'

'That is very good.'

'Right. He's a talented guy. But I think he's got this one wrong. I told you both my parents are singers, didn't I? My father's career's not been going that well recently, whereas my mum's has, so Tim sees that as a kind of double betrayal. Hitting a man when he's down sort of thing. Do you see?'

Rashid looks confused.

'I know that it doesn't make much sense, but that's why I reckon he's wrong, you see. He thinks my mother's to blame for my father's lack of success. It's nonsense. But Tim sees Mum kissing the guy and he gets it into his head that she's having an affair with him because he's some great conductor and my father's career is in the doldrums.'

'That would be cruel indeed, sir.'

'Exactly, and I don't think it's true. And another thing is that Tim blames Mum for everything that went wrong in my life.'

Do I want to go any further with this? I can't tell whether Rashid is fascinated or bored to death. He sits quite still, the newspapers settled around him.

'Does this interest you, Rashid?'

'I am most intrigued, sir. Please continue.'

'Okay. You sure?'

'We must pass the time.'

Isn't that the truth? Here I am, baring my soul, and it might be the dullest, most self-indulgent monologue in all history, but at least it passes the time, soaks up seconds by the hundred. I suspect Rashid would be grateful if I talked all afternoon.

'He's wrong about that too. Mum's not responsible for how I was.'

'Were you all that bad, sir?'

'I don't know. I suppose it depends what you're comparing

me with. I didn't kidnap people and hold them hostage. I didn't torture anyone.'

They taught us how to slaughter a chicken and a rabbit. They said it was one of the survival skills we'd need when we go on exercise on the moor. We learnt how to use cotton wool from a tampon as kindling and how to navigate in the dark with a torch the size of your thumb. We were, as they put it, standing on our own two feet for the first time.

It's odd. I felt a sense that I belonged right from the start, strange as it was to see a fully grown NCO shower his cock and bollocks stark naked in front of the thirty of us. Apparently, we didn't know how to shower properly before joining the army. He also demonstrated a clean shave and ironing a shirt to army requirements. It was like being back at school: no school of mine, mind, but we were all kids learning from the master. I was twenty-two. I think the corporal teaching us was probably my age, but it didn't seem to matter. He was the instructor, the man with the expertise, and early on it made absolute sense to me that if I took on board the skills, the standards, just knuckled down, I'd get through the training and make something of myself.

For six weeks I vomited after every cross-country run. I thought the bones in my arms would shatter if I had to do another press-up. I got so exhausted and cold and drenched I cried, my clothes soaked in sweat or mud or downpour, my feet shredded. Putting on boots every morning was agony after a while.

I thought I was losing my mind. There was too much to take in. Thought made impossible. That's what they wanted, of course. If you can't think, you can only obey.

That's how it was, at first, before officer training.

I stared at the corporal and the chicken he was stroking, calming it, reassuring it there was nothing to be alarmed about. It was raining, I remember. We were in a clearing, surrounded by beech trees. Drips fell from the leaves onto the corporal's cap and the chicken's feathers.

He bent down and picked up a three-foot staff, the one he tucked under his arm during drill on the parade ground. He gently lowered the bird to the grass and placed it face down with the staff across its neck. Then he stamped on the staff with both feet and snapped off the chicken's head.

We were suddenly silent.

He snatched up the headless body by its feet. He was smiling, and we all watched, riveted by the thrashing of the chicken as, in death, it struggled to fly away, to be free of the corporal's grip. When the writhing had almost stopped, occasional twitches, he laid out the body on the grass and took up the head.

'You can have some fun with this,' he said.

He'd forced his hand up the bird's neck and was operating the head like a glove puppet. The chicken stared and nodded and pecked the air, and we laughed.

We have not really got to know our guards. They have decided against revealing their names and although we recognize them now by their faces, their reluctance to engage with us has inevitably meant that they tend to merge into a single 'type'. There is one exception to this and, for the sake of convenience, I'll call him Guard One, because he was the first I met. He stands apart because he does make the occasional remark, enough to differentiate him from the barked orders and screams of recrimination that we get from the others. Guard One has even risked a smile.

Rashid tells me that Guard One's remarks are usually to do with the temperature in our room, a football match he's seen on TV or the long hours he has been forced to work. He apologises frequently for not providing us with a fan. The problem, he says, is his boss.

The other day, when he brought us our meals on a metal tray, he advised us not to eat the chicken.

'What's wrong with it?' Rashid asked.

'Smells bad.'

'Have you tasted it?'

'Of course.' He sounded indignant. 'We eat the same as you, you know.'

This conversation is relayed to me by Rashid in a hesitant, more broken English than I am used to hearing from him. He appears anxious to impress on Guard One that his English is not fluent.

It surprises me that the guards are obliged to eat the same meals as we do. Guard One notices my look of disbelief and he nods energetically. He goes on to say that the guards are in much the same difficult situation as we are, and I hear the irony in Rashid's English as he translates this preposterous thought. The guard smiles, as if to imply that we should find at least a grain of comfort in this shared experience.

Once Guard One has left, I feel free to release the repressed laughter that has built up over the last five minutes.

'What is he talking about?'

Rashid shrugs.

'He's mad,' Rashid says. 'They all are.'

All the same, it is interesting that the guards share our meagre diet. Presumably, they are given more than we are, but it is no doubt a source of resentment and in that I believe there is hope.

If they lack the unity and incentive to do a thorough job, they may become careless. We may be able to push our friendly guard to say more than he should about the plans for our detention and the layout of the prison.

'Have you ever tried to escape, Rashid?'

'Once.'

'Why didn't it work?'

'I'd asked if I could be permitted some exercise and fresh air. There's a small garden at the back of the house. They let me walk round it and I noticed there was a door in the garden wall, and it was open. So, the following week, when they allowed me another chance to get out, I went straight to the door and checked that it was still unlocked. I was sure it would exit onto the street. I reasoned that if there were people around, there was a limit to what the guards could do and I could slip away in the crowds.'

'What happened?'

'I should have realised from the silence. No car horns, no traffic, no voices or music. I waited until the guard turned away, then I opened the door and walked out. But there were no streets, no people, just a dusty square with an abandoned football pitch at one end. There's nothing out there, sir. We are in the middle of nowhere.'

'You had nowhere to run?'

'I stood in that square for what seemed like ages. I suppose it was less than two minutes. I looked around, but you're right, there was nowhere to run. Just scrub in every direction. There were some outbuildings and I thought about hiding in one of them, but they were the obvious place to look. Anyway, by then, the guards had appeared. They just stood there, looking at me and laughing. They didn't even bother to point their guns at me. They didn't even shout, and you know how much they love shouting.'

'Were you punished?'

'They beat my feet until they were raw. I couldn't walk for a week. One of them said if I tried it again, he'd make sure I didn't walk for the rest of my life.'

'Nice.'

'As you say, sir.'

'Look, Rashid, if we're going to be cooped up like this for months, you can't keep calling me 'sir'. It's Steve. My name's Steve.'

'Thank you, Lieutenant Padgett, sir.'

I wait for him to hear the irony.

'So you haven't made another attempt?'

'What is there to try? Where could you go? Without a vehicle, Steve, there is no hope.'

Walks were important to us, as a family I mean, at least when I was very young. The four of us would set out on a Saturday afternoon, backpacks stuffed with spare jumpers, cagoules in case the rain came on, chocolate bars and fizzy drinks, and a packet of ham sandwiches Mum had prepared.

I went reluctantly at first, but Dad knew just what to do to turn that around. He went out early in the morning and walked the circuit we were due to take, planting little gifts along the way, in trees and hedges, under the step of a stile. Then he'd tell us, Tim and me, that we were going on a Treasure Hunt.

'Can you imagine, Rashid? He went to all that effort. The word 'walk' was never mentioned. Suddenly I was excited, couldn't wait to go.'

Often we'd take the route to their favourite pub, The Rock. We'd follow the bridleway that went through a wood and opened out in a field above our village.

'Well, what about it?' he'd say to us.

That was our cue to start hunting. We'd peer into the hedge-rows and scan the lower branches of the oak trees. There was always something waiting to be found: a lollypop, a glove puppet, a bright red superball. I thought of it as a wonderland. Aged five, it never occurred to me he'd been out earlier and left all these treasures for us.

We got wise to some of the hiding places he favoured. Blake's Hut usually had half a dozen prizes tucked in between the logs stacked outside.

'I wonder if Mr Blake was aware that my father regularly turned his winter fuel into an Aladdin's Cave. No one ever saw him, you see, Mr Blake. I don't even know how we knew his name.'

There was a bridge that invariably delivered. It had been put together using two railway sleepers and scaffolding. Dad could never resist stuffing packets of balloons or liquorice allsorts into the poles. It was just as much fun finding them, even when we knew where to look.

'But then I got greedy, Rashid.'

'How so?'

'I stopped wanting the treasure.'

'Surely every little boy wants treasure, Steve.'

'Not me. I decided the prizes weren't good enough. They weren't big enough or expensive enough to make it worth the effort of walking.'

'So you missed out? That is a great shame.'

'No. Everyone missed out. I burst the bubble. Once I said I wasn't going walking any longer, they stopped the treasure hunts. I killed them stone dead.'

Rashid does not understand. His experience fights against what he's being told. In his life, something must be better than nothing. Rejecting the little in the vain hope that something bigger might come along makes no sense to him. None.

'I can still picture that walk, Rashid. The pheasant wood and the English oaks. Blake's Hut. Above all, Blake's Hut and the pile of logs.'

'You miss this walk, Steve. I can tell.'

'It means something, Rashid. It means a lot. But I don't know what it is.'

I wouldn't admit it for a long time. Teenagers like a drink. All my friends drank. We got pissed, talked too loudly. Sometimes one of us threw up in the streets of Petersfield or down the stairwell of a bus. So what? Not particularly pleasant, but that's what boys do. Lads.

But the difference was that the others, my friends, drank when we were together. We'd go out on a Friday and Saturday night, maybe three or four nights together, get tanked up, and it was great. Fun. We told each other stories about being drunk. I was so wasted Thursday night. We found it very funny that we all got so drunk. You should have seen us down Portsmouth Way, planked we were. I think the more we told each other these stories, the more drunk we got, drunk on past drink.

But, as I say, that was in public.

Then there was France.

They took me up the far end of the beach, where the shoreline curved round to a headland and there were flat rocks overlooking the sea. They had a couple of bottles of brandy with them, and we sat out on the flat rocks and drank the brandy and smoked joints. They talked to themselves mostly, and I stared out to sea.

Occasionally, they'd shoot a remark at me, and I'd shake my head to show I didn't understand, and they'd laugh and hand me the brandy.

It was a hot, cloudless day. Even though their French didn't mean much to me, as I got drunk, I felt as though it did, as if I had some super intelligence that translated it all without me having to learn the language. I was so happy. I felt like we were friends. I started to laugh when they did, and they found that very funny and they laughed a bit more.

I guess we must have finished both bottles.

When I woke up, they'd gone. The sunburn on my stomach and thighs was enough to tell me I'd been asleep for several hours. The rocks burnt my feet as I made my way back to the beach. I still felt happy.

You always do, and it's not just the first few times. Drink makes you very happy for a very long time before it's too late and it takes you over.

'Opal, eight-zero, Arthur.'

I was trying to call up air support.

'Opal, eight-zero, Arthur. Over!'

Nothing. The radio comms were down.

The incoming was fierce. They'd been firing at us for a good half hour. I could hear the cracks getting louder as they started to get closer to us.

We were fifteen men, held down in five Jackals, which were well armed, strong vehicles, get you up a hill of scree any day, but in fifty degrees, with American ammo and a wind of sand, our weapons were jamming.

I started to crawl around my vehicle. Lucie was in the Jackal behind mine, and he had a phone that might get us through to our base. Without air support, I could see us being done for.

A mortar exploded not twenty feet from me and showered dust and grit over us. Fortunately, no one was hurt. I could feel the sweat go cold on the back of my neck.

I struggled on my belly over the sand and stones, ribbons of sweat falling over my eyes, the dust making me cough and spit. I got to Lucie's vehicle and tucked myself in on the safe side.

'They're mostly on mopeds,' Corporal Lucie said. 'Shoot and off.'

'Give me your phone,' I said.

'It's useless, sir. They're too mobile. Fast and furious, if you get me. We can't see them.'

'They'll take up positions soon enough.'

Zip-zip. Bullets past our heads, the Jackal shuddered on impact.

'For fuck's sake!' Lucie shouted.

Jets of water fountained out of the cans fastened to the vehicle's flank. I felt their wet warmth as some of them targeted my face, washing the sand from my eyes and mouth.

'It'll be the fuel next if we don't move, sir.'

'I'm going to call,' I said.

I snatched the phone.

'Opal, eight-zero, Arthur.'

I got through to a landline and spelt out our coordinates.

How in hell had we ended up in this crisis? We'd set out on what was supposed to be a short reconnaissance patrol, nine or ten miles from base. Our job was a friendly, to visit one of the villages and hoover up the locals' chat and what their opinions were. *Testing the atmospherics* is what we call it. We only took the Jackals because the route in was said to be a bit dodgy.

We chatted to the village elders, who hadn't much to say. As usual, they had their grievances, but were courteous enough. We were just starting on our way back when the 4X4 gearing on one of the Jackals snapped, and it refused to move. We put it on a tow and were making reasonable, if slow, progress.

The crackle of fire hit us as soon as we found ourselves on open ground.

Pop-pop-pop-pop-pop.

We were on the edge of the green zone farmlands, a narrow strip of cultivated land running through the desert floor of the valley. Dozens of civilians had their homes there, and the fire was coming from right in amongst them.

'Stand by! Incoming! RPG.'

'There it is!' I yelled above the roar of the rocket-grenade. 'See the smoke? In the treeline.'

I grabbed the phone again and shouted out new coordinates when they picked up.

'Jammed!' Lucie was screaming at his machine gun. 'Fuckin' American ammo.'

I knew what I was doing, what needed to be done, but the responsibility for fifteen men and the steady approach of the enemy got to me. I felt the adrenaline streaming through me, a current in my veins.

There were two planes above us. They dropped a clutch of explosives in the stand of trees three hundred metres to our right. Massive clouds of dust and debris mounted skywards. As they cleared, I could make out fallen trees and men scattering.

The firing continued all the same. We did our best to return it, but the lads were exhausted, frustrated by their weapons and fading in the heat.

Another RPG came in from nowhere and flung over one of the Jackals.

I could sense my guts were going to go, let me down in a big way.

The scream came from my left.

'Man down! Man down!'

As I leapt down, I bawled at Lucie 'Move! We have to get out.' Then I ran to the Jackal on its side.

Lance Corporal Tyson was lying on his back, his legs swung awkwardly under him. A private, Maschler, stood over him, stupefied by the blood pooling on Tyson's thigh.

'Get First Aid!' I yelled at him.

Maschler ran behind the Jackal, glad to be told what to do. I knelt down and took Tyson's hand and squeezed it. He was in traumatic pain, scarcely able to remain conscious. His blood shone in the sunlight like the metal of a new car.

Maschler pitched up, and I grabbed the kit from him.

'You're going to be fine, Tyson. We'll get you out now.'

I bound the tourniquet around his thigh and yanked it tight. His eyes pleaded with me to stop, but I kept tightening. Then I pulled out a syringe and morphine.

'This'll fix you, Lance Corporal.'

He would get through, live, but I wasn't so sure about his legs. I banged the morphine into him, and gave him a second shot to make sure, and he went out. I told Maschler to take an arm and between us we lifted Tyson's limp body to standing. The incoming was zipping past our heads. We got behind the Jackal as fast as we could, and struggled over to Lucie.

'That vehicle's dead, sir,' he said. 'Tow up the other?'

'No, leave it,' I said. 'Let's get the fuck out of here.'

Rashid stares at me, as if to say 'And...?'

'It was a fucking terrible day. What more can I say?'

'Did Mr Tyson make it to safety?' Rashid asks.

'Yes, he did. We all did. Bloody miracle!'

'And Mr Tyson's leg, was that okay?'

'He lost both his legs, Rashid. He'd been hit in one and the other got crushed when the Jackal tipped over. They had to take both of them off.'

'That is a very sad story, Steve.'

Rashid turns over, curls himself up in his newspaper lounger. He cannot cope with the outcome. It should have been better. Lance Corporal Tyson should have survived intact. That's Rashid's view. He doesn't say a word, but expresses all with his body.

I have to identify things in my memory which are certain and do not change. That is the only way I have found to cope with fear. It's not that I am caving in to Rashid's pessimism. I still believe that the guards, and whoever is above them and gives them orders, will not in the end want to kill me. I remain confident that there will come a day when I shall walk out of this place, a free man. But there are things other than death to be afraid of. They have given Rashid multiple beatings. Why not me? Why only two? This is a fear that will not go away. It is abiding. Most of the time it exists at a low level, like a virus, but it can become acute, my heart racing, when the bolt on the door shoots open or there are heavy boots in the corridor. In those moments, I fear fear itself, and wonder whether my heart will stand these daily assaults on its equilibrium. I have been frightened I might have a heart attack. It's in my genes. My father had one. Presumably, that was some combination of stress and disease. It's interesting how much more afraid I am here in this cell than I was in battle or on night patrol. This seems, rightly or wrongly, much more personal. The beatings are about robbing you of your identity, stripping you of your self-esteem. I can see it in Rashid's face, bit by bit. He cowers, even in his sleep.

Fear. What is it? I sometimes think it's never been the same twice. Never repeats itself. I feel my chest tighten, like a belt's around it. No, not a belt. Like a boot planted on my breasts, flattening me. I can breathe in, just about, but not out. I can't exhale. The boot is too heavy.

Or it might be I cannot close my eyes. If I close my eyes, some-one, a guard, will burst through the door and do me serious harm. With a stick or a knife or a length of leather. If I can only stay awake, be vigilant, I can keep him out. He will keep to his side of the door, slump in his chair, watch TV and smoke cigarettes. He won't bother me.

I don't know what's worse: fear you recognize or fear that's new. The first is like a recurrent nightmare, the second a rat in the night, scuffling by your ear.

I long to talk to Rashid about it, but he's so racked, I daren't add to his terrors. You must suffer alone.

Deal with it!

I try to count, rhythmically.

Music has kept me sane. I don't know that I'd have chosen it, but it's Bach. If I wasn't here - I mean if I was back in normal life, not struggling to fend off madness - I'd have said that I didn't know much Bach, any in fact. I grew up hating it. Bach was all over the house all the time. If Dad or Mum wasn't rehearsing, there'd be Bach on the radio or a Bach record on the hi-fi. You hear of parents going mad because their teenage kids are playing rock music at deafening volume. It wasn't like that in our home. Tim and I had to block our ears to keep out the Bach.

I say I don't know much Bach, but I must. It must have seeped in through every pore. I think it's the Double Concerto, one of them, and I seem to know every note of it. It's like I was wearing head-phones. There are two violins mimicking each other, two equal parts, sprightly, like horses dancing down a bridlepath. They nod at each other. I can hear the strings. I mean I can hear the gut or whatever it is, the material of the strings, and the horsehair bow stroking them. Is that why I thought of horses? No, it's the sprightliness, the high-spirited momentum. Dad always played this piece, I'm sure, for its pure joy.

What is it about this music? I've never particularly liked it, but now it represents all that I want to hang on to, all the steadiness of civilised life, the values, everything that seems about to disappear. For as long as I sit here, my back to a concrete wall, sweating, pain shooting through my knee, Bach is all my comfort. Perhaps I've unknowingly nurtured a secret love of Johann Sebastian. It seems to be part of my nature.

The track has changed. We're into something much slower and more dignified. The fast stuff was fun. This has a melancholy to it, as though it's straining to be better than it is. It's beautiful, though, quite beautiful. I have to close my eyes to enjoy it.

When I do, when I allow my eyelids to take me into darkness, I am transported home to Hampshire. Perhaps that's why I do it. Bach is a kind of time machine that enables me to flee from here into the past, into childhood with my mother and father, and the house by the river, and autumn and the start of the apples. He's out there on the lawn, as he invariably was, picking up the windfalls, one by one. He inspects them for bruises and maggots, and the good ones are placed in the blue duffle bag he releases from his shoulder. It's probably raining, but it doesn't bother him.

Why was it always conflict? Why couldn't I get on with him better? There came a point when he couldn't utter a single word to me without it turning into a row. I don't see it now, but at the time, I found everything about him incredibly irritating: his singing, the importance he gave music, his obsession with the garden and the trees, his wine drinking, even the way he chewed his food.

That's pretty normal. Most young men want to shout at their fathers, all that Freud stuff. But I took it further. They could not, would not understand that I was different to Tim. From the start. Right from the moment Tim was crawling around the sitting room floor and entertaining them with cheerful wauling, they could not see us as individuals, with separate paths to travel. I suppose it was because the two of them were so similar: singers, French lovers, Bach. They must have thought that since they were intelligent, well educated, successful, it was just common sense that their two boys would be too. Stephen and Timothy. Ste-phen. Tim-o-thy. Crap names. Timothy's particularly crap. It's just wet. Tim Padgett just about holds up. Padgett's a decent enough name. Good, hard sounds.

He kept going on about singing at The White House. He couldn't let it go, and every time he talked about it, he'd mention the chandeliers. Of all the things to remember, a thousand guests in the audience, Bill and Hillary on the top table, and he picks out the light on the glass of the chandeliers.

I had to get out. If they hadn't pushed me, I'd have gone anyway. It had got to the point where I was suffocating in that house. It was so obviously theirs, their way of life, and there was no room, no time in the day, for mine. If I'd have stayed, something would have crumpled up inside. That's what I believe. For sure, I could have handled it better, but then so could they. It was a cheap trick taking me to the pub to kick me out. He knew we couldn't argue in there, not in front of the other customers.

I feel cruel now, thinking about it. At the time I didn't care much about their feelings. I reckoned I wasn't anything like as difficult as they made out, and if they kept bad-mouthing me to their friends, as they did, I would punish them. If they hadn't a clue where I was, if they started to worry about me, perhaps they'd miss me and begin to value me a bit more.

When I left, I didn't imagine I'd be away for more than a couple of nights. I thought they'd be in such a panic they'd be desperate to have me back. But then I realised after about three days that it wasn't too hard being away and I was enjoying the freedom.

It's quiet as a grave. The guards are asleep. Even the insects sleep.

I can't. My knee aches.

Something about Rashid's breathing tells me he's also awake. He's much quieter when he sleeps.

'Do you fear death, Rashid?'

It's a cruel question, I know. And Rashid is shocked by it. He prevaricates.

'It depends what you mean. Do you mean the condition of death or the process of dying?'

'You can take your pick.'

This is not the answer Rashid wants. He shuffles on his arse. The room is so silent I can hear the sound of the grit moving under him, dragged over the surface of the concrete floor.

'I do not fear death. I do not think I have sinned that much. No more than an ordinary man does. I don't think I will be punished for what I have done in my life. Unless it is...'

'Unless?'

'Unless it is for not protecting my family.'

'You did your best, Rashid. You had no choice.'

'I chose to be a translator. I chose to work with the British.'

'You believed you were doing that for the good of your country, didn't you? The good of your people?'

'I did believe that, Steve, yes.'

'Then you'll go to a better place.'

'I hope so.'

'Couldn't be worse than this one.'

Rashid laughs, but only for a second or two. He is unable, or unwilling, to tear himself away from his deep-set belief that his death is only a matter of days away. He finds my jokes in poor taste, and he says so.

I look around our bare room. We have asked repeatedly for some kind of fan to relieve the close, stifling air in which we live. We sit still, as motionless as we can, to minimise our sweating. In the day we wear only our underpants and a shirt. The shirt is a gesture towards decency, one that we both know is ridiculous. I think we are afraid of losing our self-respect and keeping on our shirts in some way preserves our dignity, particularly when the guards burst in and shout at us. Occasionally, though, we relax the rule, like gentlemen permitted to remove their jackets after dinner.

When I don't have conversations going on in my head, pattering away like a loop of tape, it's scenes from films or bits of music or both. Right now, if I close my eyes, I see von Aschenbach on that beach in Venice. He's lying in a deckchair, wearing a crumpled white linen suit, and black make-up trickles down his face. He's dying, and Mahler just grows and grows and grows.

I'd like to read the book. *Death in Venice*, I mean, having seen the film, I mean. I wonder how faithful to it the film was. It's difficult to imagine the story without Mahler.

My father tried to get me to read. He read to me at night, when he wasn't away performing or on tour. He'd pick books he thought boys ought to enjoy. Treasure Island was one. I don't really remember the others. He gave up in the end. I just wasn't interested.

But I changed. That's the thing my parents were so bad at appreciating. People develop in different ways and at different times. I don't think I picked up a book voluntarily until I was twenty-three, but then it clicked. I read all the books I could get hold of in the army. Thrillers. Sci-fi. Dickens. The Catcher in the Rye. I read Friedrich Engels's The Condition of the Working Class in England. All about Manchester. It was a weird mix of stuff.

There's no chance of getting Thomas Mann here. Even as I think of it, the idea seems ridiculous. Earlier today they brought us the 'reading matter' we'd been asking for. Guard One dumped a stack of newspapers on the floor next to Rashid. He put on a big smile to go with it, as though he'd just served up a banquet. When he turned to me, the smile had gone, and he dropped me a single copy of Time magazine. It's a couple of months old, but it's something in the English language, which I haven't seen or read for months. I'm going to ask Rashid to translate the newspapers aloud to me, and when we're done with them, we can replace the shredded and filthy loungers we have. I feel pathetically grateful.

I'll hold back a while from looking at Time. Part of me is desperate, thirsting to grab it and suck up the words. I can't make up my mind whether, when it's in my hands, I'll greedily speed through the pages, not taking much in, enjoying the quantity of it, the thousands of words, or will I feast on the first article, the novelty of a single sentence in English pinning me to a single page, a single paragraph?

All that waits for me. I want to delay the moment of gratification, leave it to one side, like the final sweet mouthful of my mother's apple crumble. What makes the moment so rich is the certainty of the pleasure to come. I just know it won't disappoint.

Rashid has no interest in playing my game. He reads avidly, his eyes straining in the poor light. He doesn't look up or laugh or grunt, and since I have yet to ask him, he doesn't offer to read aloud or translate. He keeps it all to himself, the news of the world.

I feel myself drifting off in the afternoon heat. Today is warm without being suffocating, almost tolerable. If I close my eyes again, I am back in Venice, the city, before the First World War. It's an earlier part of the film, when the band plays at dinner in the hotel, and they move around the restaurant. There is a sense of menace and foreboding about them, as if they alone were the agents of the typhoid, spreading it from table to table, song by song.

It's odd. I saw this film for the first time in the compound, a matter of weeks ago, but as I imagine it now, I am in the sitting room in Hampshire, and we're watching it together. I suppose that's what we used to do. When I was a kid, in the late eighties, early nineties, if Dad wasn't out, we'd spend Saturday night watching a movie, a video. I remember seeing *Braveheart* like that. Everything seemed cosy when we watched as a family. It's as if it guaranteed a couple of hours of peace. I wasn't afraid of a row bursting out, the endless shouting that seemed to go on most of the time. I felt close to the others.

Is that what all these movie scenes and music are about? Am I trying to put myself back in contact with them, with Mum and

Dad and Tim?

'How do you catch a rabbit?'

    Rashid looks up. He shrugs.

    'Stand behind a tree and make a noise like a lettuce.'

It's five o'clock in England, a Saturday afternoon in early Spring. Rashid and I are playing our game, unusually in the evening, and I have put Holly in Battersea Park, walking in the shadow of the pagoda, heading for the river. The sun is already declining to her left and the pagoda burns in its furious light. The trees have yet to leaf. It's a dry day, with warmth lingering in the air, like the memory of a song someone sang years ago.

    People are leaving the park. There is a tinge of melancholy to their leaving, which Holly feels.

    'What is she wearing, Steve?' Rashid asks.

    What is she wearing? Can I see that? I want to be accurate, clothe her in things that I know she owns, but it's like University Challenge. Put on the spot, I can't think of a single item in her wardrobe.

    'Jeans?'

    Thank you, Rashid. Of course, she is wearing jeans. She always wears jeans. Black jeans with a silver belt, to be precise. She has a burgundy velvet top, which hangs loosely at the waist. And she has light suede boots, laced, the colour of fawns, and rounded in the toe.

    I suddenly panic that perhaps Holly would never put together that combination. Do they work? I have no idea. I know that I am always impressed and feel a sort of pride when we're out together. She looks great, invariably. Would she wear brown boots and black trousers?

'Has she reached the river yet?' Rashid demands. 'Is it the River Thames?'

'She's in London, Rashid. What else could it be?'

'You didn't say she was in London.'

He has never heard of Battersea Park and its pagoda.

The river looks very high to me, or to her rather. It's swollen with rain from the last few days, and the speed of the water is something she hasn't often seen. There's debris in it: a large wooden panel, a fence panel, soaked dark. Towards the north, on the Chelsea bank, she can see a shopping trolley, its nose submerged in silt, the handle wedged into a pier of the bridge.

Holly stares at the debris and the swift water and a passing tourist launch. Is she missing me? She waves and there are people out on deck who wave back.

'Step onto the boat.'

What? But Rashid is right. I can do anything in this scene. She can step onto the launch. She can fly across the river to it, if I choose. Except that I am challenged by the facts. Do pleasure boats travel this far west? Have I made a mistake?

'Does it matter, Steve?'

Right again, Rashid.

On the launch, I walk the length of the upper deck and nod to the passengers. Some of them have come out to view the sunset and the park with its sunburnt pagoda. They have been told to look out for Battersea Power Station, as was. Others are outside because that is where they can smoke.

I glance at the shore. Holly has gone. She must have walked off, or flown off, a while ago. I can see a good stretch of the Embankment and into the park beyond the pagoda. There's no sign of her.

Then she is beside me, on the upper deck. She is wearing a black fleece, Berghaus, zipped to the neck. Where did she find it? The game has got out of hand.

'Going to the cinema this evening. South Bank.'

She is beautiful. She holds her head at exactly the same angle she held it when we first got back together and I kissed her. Is she expecting a kiss now? I can sense my head leaning towards her. Even in this cell-like room, in Rashid's presence, I can't resist inclining a little, towards her beautiful face and her half-opened lips.

'I'm going with your brother.'

'Tim?'

If I lean much more, I'll fall. The slow trajectory I'm following assumes that at some point I'll collide with her lips, meet hers with mine, or else I'll teeter over the rail.

Behind her is the rushing grey water of the Thames, pulling back below the steel banister that stops us from toppling off the deck into the river.

'Has she seen a lot of your brother while you've been away?'

It's a pertinent, perhaps unkind, question, but Rashid means no harm. He doesn't entertain the idea of infidelity.

'We've seen a couple of things,' Holly says. 'Now that you're not here, I've got no one to go with. Everyone hates subtitles. I blackmail him into going. I tell him it's an act of loyalty to you.'

The moment has passed. She has altered her stance and her lovely, long white neck has withdrawn into the fleece. I am looking across to the park now. The sun has burnt the tops of the trees golden. A woman in a red leotard is sprinting along the pavement. She takes short pulls on her water bottle as she runs. Her hair is gathered back in a tail, which bounces.

Even before I turn back, I know that Holly has gone, and this time I'm powerless to recover her.

'I owe everything to the army, Rashid.'

'Do you, Steve?'

'I do. Everything. They put me back together when I was falling apart.'

'It is a marvellous thing, isn't it, the British Army?'

Is there irony in what Rashid says? It seems inconceivable that there would be. He respects the institution of the army too much to suggest that it might be imperfect, and yet there is something in his inflection, masked by his particular syntax, that demurs, makes fun of my gratitude. Perhaps he asks himself now whether the army is to blame for his predicament here.

Fair enough.

For me, though, it was a lifeline. I see myself alone on those rocks in France, sodden with cognac, the tide sweeping in. I am stumbling my way back. I lose my footing on the wet rock and graze my thigh on a sharp edge as I go down. It all seems hopeless. I can't get off the rocks in time before the tide cuts off the route to the shoreline. I might just as well give up, let myself slip under. The sea will cool my burning skin and I'll drift off.

The tide is cold when it reaches me, shakes me awake, and I'm trying to keep my head above water. I stand up and wade across the rocks, waist deep, struggling to get a foothold. But it takes only minutes and I am back on the beach. What seemed impossible has proved laughably easy. A split second decision has saved me.

I laugh out loud.

It was like that when I joined the army. I'd been sinking into a bottle, and some tiny spark of self-respect, still remaining, soaked in booze, lit up and I found my way back.

The song ends with na-na-na-na.

> *Everybody's talking at me*
> *Can't hear a word they're saying*
> *Only the echoes of my mind*

They used it in *Midnight Cowboy*. Jon Voigt, in a cowboy suit with a brand new hat, rolls into New York City on a greyhound bus and a bright, sunny day, and he thinks the world's his oyster. He thinks women will flock to him and he'll make his fortune. Within a few weeks, he's sitting freezing in a doss of a flat with a limping bum called Rizzo (Dustin Hoffman) as his only friend. The Great Scheme has gone to hell in a handcart.

New York is either bright and shiny or dark and sleazy. I can't get it, the song, out of my head.

Everybody's talking. Twig. Rashid. Dad, Mum & Tim. Col. Jeffreys. The guards out there, smoking, drinking their burnt coffee I can smell it.

What do they all say?

They SAY 'You're not worth it!'

Yes, I am!

Liar!

As a boy, yes, I admit it. I lied. Well, I didn't tell the full story. I omitted certain details. Sometimes I fibbed outright. Alright, yes, lied. But.

Not worth it?

Today will be different, we've been led to believe. Guard One has said that we are to expect a visitor. He didn't say when or who it will be, but he smiled and raised his eyebrows, which seems to imply that the visitor is important and commands his respect.

'Better be on our best behaviour, Rashid.'

'I'll put on my blue suit,' he says.

'And I shall wear the taffeta.'

Rashid laughs. The smile has gone from Guard One's face. He doesn't understand our talk and imagines that we have insulted him. In his hands he holds two bottles of water, which he'd intended to give us, but he's been slighted, or so he thinks, and he leaves the room and takes the water with him. It is a childish gesture, which makes us suffer and gains him nothing. All the guards behave in this way at one time or another. They are petty and vindictive. Guard One is, on the whole, much better, but he, like his colleagues, is quick to take offence. They're like a street gang, looking for the remark that will let them pick a fight.

'Touchy this morning,' I say, after he's gone.

'It cost us a drink.'

'No such thing as a free joke.'

'You won't be so resigned about it in a few hours, Steve. When you're dying for water, and your throat's sticking together, you'll regret it. I'm telling you. They don't like sarcasm.'

'I thought he'd got a bit more to him, that one. He seems jolly enough most of the time, doesn't he? I thought he'd find our little exchange quite amusing.'

'You have too high expectations, my friend. These men are simple folk. They're from tiny villages, where they don't have any education. They think humour goes against their religion. They only appear different because they carry guns.'

I vaguely wonder what our visitor will be like. Educated? Sophisticated? Another village boy? I feel nothing about the

126

prospect of his arrival other than a mild curiosity such as I used to feel turning over a terracotta pot in my father's garden and discovering an earwig.

I guess I must have dropped off to sleep for a moment. I could be back then, about to leave the squat, but it is here, and it is now, and I am frightened. I am sure I heard the echoing, abnormal sound of a steel door slamming shut in the dark silence. There is some moonlight falling tonight. It falls through the arrow slit of our window. If I can get in the way of it, I can read my watch.

I'm anxious to make as little noise as possible. The last thing I want is a guard bursting in and demanding to know what's going on. I can, however, crawl with a minimum of disturbance. My body snags grit across the concrete, but that's a noise audible to me; it does not escape the room.

There it is!

I heard a scream, and seconds later I hear another. The screams stop me in my tracks. I know it is Rashid who is screaming, Rashid who is being tortured on the floor above.

I shuffle quickly to the moonlight. It is half past three, the middle of the night, when all should be quiet, when there should be peace, broken only by the drill of insects and the scuffle of rodents. The silence should not be broken by human screams and doors banging in their frames. It is against nature.

Frightened? Is that the word? Children are frightened. It's a soft word. What occupies me, holds me in its vice, mind and body, is terror. Ter-ror. It has 'tear' in it, and 'roar'. It rages through my head and makes my body shake.

I don't feel. It has me.

Will I be next?

I am like a rodent, shuffling across the floor. I have crawled the length of the room, to establish what time it is and now that I know, it is meaningless. How long is it since they came for Rashid? Two, three hours? Or was it just twenty minutes ago? I cannot tell. I heard the bolt shoot across and the room was briefly lit up before two silhouetted figures filled the doorlight and started to shout at both of us. Rashid was asleep, I'm pretty sure. They grabbed his arms and didn't allow him time to stand. They dragged him out. I saw his legs scrabbling, trying to grip the floor long enough to get upright.

He is screaming again, in long bursts which don't seem to end. I'm sure I'm mistaken, but they sound nearer, as if he were outside this door. Can't be. I think it's more that with each time he screams, I imagine him more vividly. It's me, in my imagination, who's getting closer to him. I am almost in the cell with him, in the attic or the garage or wherever it is that they whip the soles of feet and pull fingernails from the quick. If I allow it, I begin to feel the burn and the raw openness and the crazed tears that are beyond expectation or hope.

I must.

It's making me fragile, this imagining, vulnerable to a fear I've not been through for a long time, the fear that I might come apart, not in the sense that a belt from a machine gun can shred your body and leave you in separated parts, but that I might lose my mind and never recover it.

Drink could do that. I remember lonely nights sitting alone on a mattress in the squat, full of drink, and the sense of a growing and powerful agitation, brimming behind my eyes, and knowing beyond a shadow of a doubt that when it came I would not be able to control it. There was no point in telling myself to be calm, though I did, because it would overwhelm me, burst the floodgates, rush in and spread out in every direction like bad water. I could only hope that I would pass out before my thoughts turned crazy and I did something destructive.

That's how I feel now, listening to each scream, each individual spasm of terror and pain. I can't help but pretend I am Rashid, wondering how I would cope with the pain, the fear of it and the actuality. The fact that they keep coming back for more. I've had some severe pain in my life. A broken arm. Appendicitis. But that one beating I had, that was new. I'd never faced pain that was deliberately inflicted, that comes at you in a frenzy and a raised bat. I am unable to move. My hands are tied behind the chair, my ankles buckled to the chair legs.

They must let him go soon. It's been.

4

2003

He'd decided to take Stephen out for a drink at The Rock. He knew there was something craven about choosing a public place to tell him, a place that would force him to behave reasonably, but he had somehow to ensure that Stephen understood the seriousness of what was being said to him. So many of their quarrels were fierce, brief and terminated by Stephen yelling 'You're fucking stupid! I despair of you!', or something of the sort, and walking out.

They arrived separately. Edward was first to get there and he ordered himself a pint. When Stephen turned up ten minutes later, he was obviously stoned. Fortunately, it being a Monday, there weren't many people to see him.

'Just water for me, thanks, Dad.'

They sat in the bay window, at a large oval table covered in placemats, in the middle a vase of fake daffodils.

'I suppose it's about me screaming at Mum again.'

Stephen would have guessed that they weren't meeting for the sheer pleasure of it. It must be fully two years since he'd suggested a drink without first planning an agenda and Stephen would have given thought to which of the many failings his parents identified in him was the current and most pressing concern. He clearly hadn't anticipated ejection from the house, though. What had preoccupied Edward for the last fortnight simply hadn't occurred to him.

'Your mother and I...'

'Yeh, I know, Dad. I know what you're going to say and I'm sorry, okay? If she were here, I'd say it to her face. I don't know why I do it.'

'I'm afraid, Stephen, sorry isn't going to be enough this time.'

'What do you want, then? Community service?'

Edward took a mouthful of beer and swallowed. It intrigued him that even at this moment of high tension between them, high noon, his mind registered how good the beer was, its coolness, the hints of caramel as it went down.

'There's no pleasant way to put this.'

He glanced up, expecting that some flicker of alarm might pass across his son's face. But there was none, nothing to indicate that Stephen realised, for once, that he was in serious trouble. If anything, he looked bored. The drug did that, of course. Whatever it was, it was blurring his alertness, attenuating that refined instinct we all have for enemy action, that suggestion of threat.

When Stephen did look up, it was because of his surprise. He didn't understand why his father had paused, mid-statement.

'What is it, Dad?'

The voice of the innocent, the child's words in a man's dark voice. It nearly made Edward turn back, but he'd been deluded in that way before.

'I'm afraid we can't live with you any more, Stephen. It just isn't working out.'

'You want me to leave?'

'That's it.'

Was he angry or shocked? It was hard to tell. The point

131

had gone home, though, and Stephen was reacting, physically. Edward's beer glass shook on the table.

'You've offended your mother too many times. You've stolen money, stolen our things.'

'One thing!'

'No, I'm sorry.' Edward struggled to keep his temper. 'You have stolen several things. You may call it borrowing when you take things and pawn them and promise us we'll get them back, but in my book it's stealing. You didn't ask before you took them and we've never got them back.'

'It was one bloody thing!'

'Keep your voice down.'

'Oh, is that why we're here? To keep our voices down! You think you can bring me to a sodding pub and tell me you're throwing me out and I won't shout about it.'

'You don't have to go immediately.'

'No?'

'No.'

'Well, that's fucking sweet. Real good of you, Dad. How long do I have, a month?'

Edward hesitated.

'Yes,' he said. 'About a month.'

'How did I know that, I wonder. You're so fucking predictable, it's corny. You want it to be so official, don't you? Like a letter, a notice to quit, sacking somebody. That's what they'd say in a letter, isn't it, a month?'

'You're out of your head!'

Stephen laughed, spilling some of his water on to his tee shirt.

'Better than off your head, eh, Dad?'

He left, walking out of the pub, slamming the purportedly fifteenth century oak door behind him.

People in the pub stared at Edward. Were they accusing him of something, blaming him? Or did they have no other thought than their objection to the noise he and Stephen had created, the disruption to their quiet lunchtime pints and gins and tonic and their spritzers.

For a brief moment, Edward thought he might cry.

When he returned from The Rock, Cara was on the phone in the kitchen. She took several minutes to finish the call.

'Sorry. That was Karl. He wants me to play the Blessed Virgin Mary, would you believe? They're doing *L'Enfance du Christ* in Manchester. I said I'm too old, but he's insisting.'

'Good,' Edward said. 'You'll be great in it.'

She could tell he wasn't thinking about the BVM or her age or, for that matter, Karl Rouse telephoning on a Monday morning with yet another job offer. His face was pale and he held on to the back of one of the kitchen chairs as if it were the bar of a zimmer frame.

'How did he take it?' she asked.

'Stormily.'

'As you'd expect.'

Edward sat down and pushed to one side yesterday's *Observer* magazines and newpapers so that he could lean his elbows on the table and rest his head in his hands. He said nothing for a while, then massaged his face gently until he felt ready to speak.

'Is he here?'

'I think he's left us.'

'Oh, really?'

She felt reluctant to share in Edward's anxiety.

'He came back here. Admittedly only for a few minutes. He said hi. I'm sure he'll be back in the morning.'

'Did he take anything with him?'

'I don't know. Karl rang just as he was going out.'

'I suspect if you go up to his room, you'll find he's taken half his clothes and his backpack.'

She noticed that he didn't volunteer to go and look himself. That meant he was confident that he was right.

Thinking about it afterwards, Cara couldn't have said whether, as she climbed the stairs, she expected to find Stephen's bedroom vacated or not. As a rule, it was a room she avoided. She frequently asked Stephen, occasionally pleaded with him, to clear it up, but he saw no point in doing so. He abandoned his clothes where they presumably fell off him. There were always at least three or four large tumblers half-filled with water, together with Rizla papers and rolling tobacco, bits of food on the carpet, crumbs from pizzas, crisps, biscuits, the bread he'd made a sandwich with. It was, for anyone unpractised in picking a route through the leads and plugs and television zappers, an obstacle course. If she raised it with him, he began by saying that a clean bedroom was not important in his view, and ended with him telling her to 'fuck off, you silly bitch!'.

She put the light on, two pearl candles in a wall-mounted wheatsheaf painted gold. One of the bulbs had gone and the light from the other was weak and left half the room in darkness. She stepped carefully across the carpet, finding places to put her feet between the distortion pedals and the socks and ee-shirts and DVD boxes, until she could get hold of the string that raised the window blind. Light flooded the room. She imagined everything in it, blinking at the unfamiliarity of it.

She knew immediately that what Edward had feared was true. It was usual for Stephen to leave all the drawers in his chest of drawers hanging open, as if a burglar had just riffled through them. The fact that they were closed was a telltale sign. Cara tugged at one of the smaller drawers at the top. Careless as he was, Stephen continued to give particular functions to his various cupboards and drawers. This one should have contained socks. It was empty. The drawer to the left was for pants. They had all been removed, save a pair with slack elastic in the waistband, which he'd for months refused to wear, but for some reason never succeeded in throwing out. Cara's instinct was to get rid of them, do what her indolent son had failed to do, but when she lifted them out of the drawer, she found that she wanted to hold on to them, just for a moment perhaps, and it was then that she realised she was on the verge of crying, and she knew that if she started to cry, it would be a long time before she stopped. She put the pants back, left the room quickly.

She had taken in more than she'd thought. His rucksack had gone, as Edward predicted, and so had his leather shoes and his trainers, the towel he tended to leave on the radiator, his deodorant spray and the speakers for his CD Walkman, this last confirming that he planned to be away for at least a few hours. Stephen maintained he couldn't live without his music, a compulsion he attributed to his parents' shared passion. Cara had never been quite able to see the connection; nor had Edward.

The following morning, in the kitchen, she started telephoning, first the houses of his four close friends, including a girl, Twig, who'd been going out with him for the last few months. Two of the four answered, and hadn't seen him. There was no reply from the others. Cara hunted through the scraps of paper lying around the kitchen for any other numbers he might have scribbled down. He'd told them very little about Twig, but he'd mentioned her place of work and Cara tried frantically to remember the name of it.

'Edward!' She called out to him in the study. 'Edward!'

Standing in the hall, she could hear the louder parts of the Bach he was listening to.

'Edward!'

St John Passion. He was learning it. The recording was only a couple of days away. CTS in Wembley. She wondered how he found the self-discipline to concentrate.

'Coming!'

The music stopped.

He seemed to run out of the room, like a young puppy called to have its lead put on. It made her smile.

'Sorry to disturb you,' she said. 'I wanted to ask you if you could remember the place where Twig works.'

His face was blank, no sign of recognition.

'Twig is Stephen's girlfriend. He mentioned an office somewhere. I've been racking my brains and I can't get the name.'

'Mackenzie. It's a solicitor's firm in Petersfield. No idea what she does there. I only remember it because I was thinking the other day that we ought to update our wills and someone, can't remember who, recommended Mackenzie. Coincidence.'

'I'm going to ring.'

'What on earth for?'

'To ask Twig if she knows where Stephen is.'

'She won't tell you if she does.'

'How do you know? She might.'

Edward had turned to go back to the study.

'I don't. I'm guessing.'

The CD resumed where it had left off.

'How can you take all this so calmly, Edward?'

He wasn't, of course. She knew him well enough to know when he was avoiding an issue. He was absorbing all thought and feeling in his other passion. Understanding the part of the Evangelist, immersing his whole being in it, entailed a kind of suffering. Eventually, people would hear that suffering in his voice, his interpretation, but however authentic it might sound, it was artifice and, to that extent, easier to bear than the real thing.

He had smiled and closed the door and turned up the volume, not impolitely, indeed with that trace of affection he invariably conveyed to her when they parted, no matter how briefly or how near to each other they would continue to be. It was a simple, friendly gesture, which meant 'I must get on'.

Cara returned to the kitchen and considered phoning Mackenzie's. She hesitated because of what Edward had said. Perhaps he was right. In the first throes of a relationship, one that presumably excited her, she might not want to betray Stephen to his parents, no matter how worried they evidently were. He would have told her some lie that made Edward and Cara look especially bad.

But she did ring. She couldn't help herself.

An authoritative voice, male, answered and to begin wi

he was unaware of anyone with the name of Twig working in his office.

'Are you sure it's Petersfield? We have other branches.'

'Quite sure.'

Cara sensed that he was consulting others around him. Several muffled and indecipherable comments were made before he came back to her and removed his hand from the mouthpiece.

'Apparently, Twig is a nickname, Mrs Padgett. She's known here by her real name, which is Holly Hawthorn. I think that's rather prettier than Twig, don't you?'

He was pompous. Cara began to feel her patience slipping.

'Is she there, please?'

'No, I regret to say she's not. She should be, but she didn't turn up this morning. Presumably hung over from the weekend. It's not the first time.'

This man, whoever he was, surprised Cara. He was so indiscreet. She began to wonder whether he would speak about all his staff with the same frankness, and to a complete stranger.

She thanked him and rang off.

Ahead of her, through the window, was the lawn running down to the river. Edward had abandoned his work and was collecting apples in a plastic bag, windfalls, which he seemed to treat with the care and amazement he might have shown to a sudden shower of frogs. He stared at each one as he picked it up and revolved it in his hand before dropping it into a bag from Tesco.

That evening, their states of mind were quite different, Cara holding on to the hope that she would hear the sound of Stephen entering his key in the latch, while Edward was resigned, not so much that he could relax, but having accepted that Stephen's anger would keep him away for two or three nights. He said as much to Cara, but it did little to reassure or calm her, and she went to fetch a bottle of wine from the cellar, a job she usually left to him.

He suggested they watch a video, an old film. She wanted to talk.

'I couldn't think of anyone else to contact. You know that's the girl he injured, Tim's friend?'

'I'd forgotten her name. The likelihood is he will have spoken to all the people he expects us to know and told them not to say anything.'

'Darling, he's not that organised. He's too stoned to be that efficient.'

'You'd be surprised.'

'No, I wouldn't. I don't think you realise how much he's deteriorated in the last few months.'

'I know.'

'No, you don't, Edward. You're always far too optimistic about Stephen. He's a mess and the main reason I'm worried about him going off is that I don't think he's capable of looking after himself.'

'He'll be fine.'

Wrong though she thought Edward was, she tolerated him. His assertion, he believed, would make it so and that was how he'd coped over the years with crises and reversals. She was not critical. His approach had helped him, indeed them, through a number of exigencies, and who could say that it wasn't a better attitude than her own blend of hope and anxiety?

She wanted to hug him. She wanted to go across to hi

armchair, kneel in front of him and drag him forward into her arms. It would be clumsy. She entirely accepted that, as all such gestures involving people over fifty and padded furniture inevitably were, but it was what she felt impelled to do.

She didn't. Edward sat on the other side of the ingle, thumbing through the *Radio Times* with evidently increasing apathy, and the moment passed, leaving in its place a curious distance, which she didn't fully understand. It was perhaps because she didn't share his confidence, his prediction that Stephen's fury would wear off and his desire for warmth and proper food would bring him home.

The irony wasn't lost on her, on either of them. She, of course, more than Edward, had decided the three of them could no longer live together. Edward would have let matters coast along for several months more, if it had been left to him. She'd forced him to speak to Stephen. What had she been thinking? Had she expected Stephen to bow down meekly, stay his allotted month and quietly move into a small flat not far away? Say he had done that, had she imagined that she wouldn't miss him, wouldn't pine for him, despite everything?

Acknowledging this parody of the plan she'd devised felt like a defeat, a pathetic failure. As they sat there, by the fire, their finished supper plates on a laminated tray, crumbs of scrambled egg hardening on the discarded knives and forks, there was nothing, nothing, she wouldn't give for the phone to ring and Stephen's voice to say those unambiguous words of consolation, 'I'm alright, Mum'. He had only to spare her thirty seconds, twenty, ten, and she'd be satisfied, would go to bed with at least some prospect of sleeping.

But the phone remained silent.

Edward was on his feet, at the wall-mounted cupboard where they kept their DVDs. He browsed the titles, pulling out the occasional box to remind himself of stars' names, plot lines, the director.

'I think I should contact the police,' she said.

'Far too early for that. What about *Manhattan*? The Gershwin is beautifully used.'

'I want to register that he's missing.'

'They'll laugh.'

'Laugh? Why? Are they allowed to laugh?'

He didn't answer, and her thoughts turned to the film, the start of it, the moment when, after the legal notices and warnings, and after the quaintly nostalgic lion of Metro Goldwyn Mayer's old-fashioned insignia, the New York skyline appeared in dull monochrome and the illuminated Manhattan sign turned slowly on and off and Woody Allen began his first words of voice-over. She unwound a little, allowing her to laugh occasionally and to feel the warmth of Gershwin's clarinet rise through her. She would put her faith in Edward's apparent calm and indifference, and trust that he had a superior knowledge of what was to happen next.

Now, he couldn't drive Stephen from his mind. Perhaps it had been 'Steffan', the name rather than the man, which had torn down the thin veil he'd hung to protect himself from racking anxiety.

Steffan Huntingdon called them to order. They were to rehearse-record for two hours. There would then be a break of twenty minutes for coffee, followed by a second, slightly shorter session before lunch.

Edward pictured Stephen in the pub, The Rock, the day he'd asked him to leave: a sallow, tired face.

The opening to the *Passion*, no matter how often he heard it, chilled him. The sparse instrumentation, the dread prescience, the implication that the music itself knows of the horrific events ahead. Even Stephen, when forced to listen to the prelude, had conceded that it would be a useful addition to any soundtrack for a horror movie.

The choir came in.

Herr! Herr! Herr! Unser Herrscher! They were loud, multiple; they meant business. *Lord! Our Redeemer!*

So, the first chorus was underway, no going back. He tried to concentrate. Once the choir's initial foray was over, nine minutes of the opening paragraph as it were, it was his turn, a thin reed of a moment, alone with cello continuo, taking Jesus into the Garden.

Steffan was tapping his baton.

'Back to sixteen, back to sixteen. A little more sinister, please.'

Cara frequently reminded him that they had been soft in their parenting, tolerating Stephen's smoking and swearing, encouraging him to have his friends round to the house, presumably for yet more of the same. On occasion, she or Edward would talk to Stephen about the reports they'd read or heard, reports from respected scientific bodies that said that the kind of stuff he was smoking could cause long-term damage. Stephen listened, or appeared to listen, and then ignored. For a week or so, he might move his activities into the garden, but that was usually worse. Edward would then find empty mineral water bottles, pierced by a straw-like pipe three quarters of the way down, scattered over the lawn, a cold dew speckling the clear plastic. He insisted that Stephen clear them up, but it would be two days before it was done.

And now? Well, now he'd happily clear up a thousand discarded bottles, as long as Stephen came back home safe. Time was running out, wasn't it? He'd said, predicted as a matter of fact, that Stephen would return in three or four days. Three had gone and there was no sign of him, no word. His close friends didn't seem to know where he was either. Two of them, Andy and Rob, had called at the cottage to speak to him. They appeared shocked when Cara explained that he'd run off.

'We'll let you know if we hear anything,' Rob had promised.

Unless, of course, it was a double bluff, designed to persuade Edward and Cara that they would never discover Stephen through his friends.

A red light went on above the studio exit. They were about to record. An engineer entered from the gallery and ran across to Edward's rostrum. He adjusted the microphone in front of him and explained that Edward's voice had sounded 'a bit off-mic'. They'd decided it was easier to move the mic than Edward, the suggestion being that he was known to be inflexible. He rather resented that.

He sang, he suspected, as he had never sung before. Every performance, the singers and the players in the orchestra, seemed to be individually excellent and perfectly in unison. It all sounded so very good. He felt, as JSB had no doubt intended, on a spiritual high. Even Steffan was pleased. He tapped his baton, made them do various sections again, but he plainly took pleasure in each new take. He must know,

Edward thought, that this was going to be one of the great Bach recordings of the decade.

There were, as always, technical problems that ruined moments of absolute perfection. They would, on occasion, be clapping after the completion of a passage, celebrating the achievement of everyone involved, when a voice from the gallery would intervene to say that a buzz or crackle had been detected. *Could we go again?* It was easy to forgive your fellow singer or violinist for not hitting a note cleanly, much harder to accept that a cadenza of near-faultless execution was spoilt, lost to the world, because of a defect in the machinery.

In his mind, Edward was shaking his fists.

Their son had held them in a kind of vice of love and hate, of laughter and anger, for as long as Edward could remember. He couldn't think of a time when there hadn't been some cause for concern. It might have started with complaints from un-indulgent teachers, but soon there were objections from other quarters too, from the parents of Stephen's friends, who accused him of bullying and swearing, and from the self-regarding guardians of public facilities like swimming pools, where Stephen was said to be 'a disruptive influence'. He'd been caught bullying and swearing in those places too. 'Disruption' was a catch-all term for multiple offences. It meant: Don't Come Back.

Gradually, and without there having been a month or even a year when Edward and Cara could have observed a change, Stephen had come to see himself as others saw him. He began to understand, to take deep inside him the idea that he was bad. Edward couldn't say what Stephen had made of it exactly, whether he'd relished the notoriety of it, the singling-out and the exclusions, or whether it had made him sad. Had it planted within him the conviction that he could never succeed on the terms set by others, by the majority, that he would have to make his way in the world along alternative routes, in the shadows of the highway?

In its simplest form, he knew that he was different and that, for an immature mind, was justification enough for any deviancy, any behaviour that did not conform. At home, it could be petty or monumental. He refused to clear away after a meal, to go shopping in the village. He left plates and glasses by the television. If he ate a bag of crisps or a bar of chocolate, he abandoned the wrapper where it fell from his hand. Edward and Cara raged about it. From time to time, Edward pulled himself up short and said, 'Who cares? What does it matter? None of these things are important!' Except that he knew, at a visceral and unsettling level, that these minor (what should he call them?) failings connected in a direct way to Stephen's more significant attitudes, his determination to pursue his own life exactly how he wished and, where that interest conflicted with that of others, he planned to win, however ruthlessly, however much hurt it caused.

That was the person it was difficult to love. He and Cara believed in loving the sinner and hating the sin and all that, but they each recognized that there were times when the two appeared indivisible, joined at the hip.

Steffan had dismissed them to the canteen. He found himself queuing behind Fiona, the soprano. She told him what a triumph the morning had been. She'd not known a recording session like it. Edward, she said, had been superb.

'Thank you,' he said. 'That's very kind.'

'No, I mean it. Five stars. I can see the review now.'

'You were very good too,' he said, and regretted that his praise sounded a shade muted.

She was pretty, Fiona, and always complimentary. That was, likely as not, one of the reasons she'd progressed so quickly. People liked to be flattered, even phlegmatic agents and lionised conductors. They were happy to promote rising talent of such obvious discernment.

'Martin was saying you have a recital coming up,' she said.

'If God spares me. Purcell Room. End of the month.'

'I'll try to make it.'

'Usual stuff. Nothing you haven't heard before. Some of the recitative from this. Probably bore you to death.'

'I'd be coming to hear you, Edward.'

He sipped his black coffee, tried not to wince when he discovered how hot it was, and eyed her over the thin rim of the plastic cup.

They didn't seem particularly interested in Cara at the police station. She'd taken the trouble to write up details of his height, weight, colour of hair and eyes, his age, distinguishing features (a slightly deviated septum) and the clothes he was last seen in. When she finally attracted the attention of the duty officer, she placed a photograph of Stephen in front of him, together with the sheet of information in a transparent, plastic sleeve, and explained why she'd come.

'How long ago?' the desk officer said.

'It's three days now.'

The officer laid down his pen.

'We generally find they're most of them back around the seventy-two to ninety-six mark. It's quite common.'

'You mean I should just wait?'

'Yes, madam, that's exactly what I mean. Your son is nineteen years old. Strictly, he can do what he likes. He's entitled to go where he wants, when he wants. Try not to worry, and I'm sure he'll be knocking on your door in a day or two.'

'Will you file those details I gave you, and the photograph?'

'Of course. We'll keep a record of your visit. If he's not back by the weekend, drop by again and we'll see what we can do. Hang on to the photo until then.'

It was a bit like being in a state of shock, she decided. Not that the police sergeant had been rude; on the contrary, he'd smiled and been sympathetic in a manner he'd no doubt honed over the years. She couldn't complain exactly. He'd been reassuring. She didn't question that what he said was true and most teenage absconders did return in a few days, but she felt she'd detected a tiredness in his voice, as if he knew before she'd completed her story that her anxiety was groundless, as if he knew the inevitable outcome.

Supposing Stephen was an exception to the rule?

She found herself wandering down the high street without a clear idea of what to do next. She'd anticipated spending at least an hour at the police station and the morning had, consequently, become vacant.

Outside the village post office and stores, she tripped, momentarily, not so much that she fell over, but losing her footing on the mat of wet red leaves that concealed broken pavement. She would have walked on, but she paused to look at the postcards pinned up in the stores' window. There were the usual ads for local builders and plumbers and gardeners, a couple of 'Y' reg cars for sale and a notice about a boot fair, but what caught her attention was a photograph of a black cat. It was a head shot and it made the animal look both thin and beautiful, a shine to its fur and bright green, unclouded eyes. Under the picture was a name: Armstrong. Armstrong, it appeared, had been missing for ten days. The postcard invited anyone seeing him to contact a local number. 'A reward of £100 is offered,' it added.

She stepped into the shop and asked a young woman she'd not seen before if she might speak to the owner. The young woman, who couldn't have been more than twenty and looked to Cara as if she might be from Malaysia or Thailand, somewhere in that part of south-east Asia, explained in a soft voice that the owner lived in Winchester, but that her husband was the manager. Would she like to see him?

Cara nodded and the young woman called out in her own language. She was a newish bride, Cara thought, and she wondered how she'd come to marry Ahmed, who had lived in the village for years and shown no interest, so far as she knew, in marriage. She hadn't realised, before now, that he was the manager and not the owner of the stores.

'Good morning, Mrs Padgett,' Ahmed greeted her enthusiastically. 'How may I help today?'

'I see you have a wife now, Ahmed.'

'Yes, indeed. I am very fortunate. Thank you, Mrs Padgett. My wife's name is difficult to say in English, so we agree that she is Phee.'

'I understand. How do you do, Phee?'

The young woman smiled and appeared to lower herself, as if to bow.

'Ahmed.' Cara felt embarrassed by the introduction. 'I wanted to ask you if I might put a notice in your window.'

'Of course, Mrs Padgett.'

'The thing is, I have a photograph, but I don't have a post-card. I should have written it all out at home. Silly, really.'

'Perhaps you would like to come back another time?'

'No, I'd like to do it now, if you don't mind. You see, I don't know when I can call again.'

'You are very busy, Mrs Padgett. With your singing.'

'Yes, that's right, Ahmed. Very busy.'

Cara was conscious that had she been on the receiving end of what she was saying, it wouldn't have made much sense to her, but she pressed on.

'Can I buy a postcard then?'

Ahmed plucked a pack of six from a shelf behind him and handed them to her.

'I can't buy one?'

'No, I'm very sorry. This is how we sell them.'

'And a pen?'

'Do you want to buy a pen or would you like me to lend you mine?'

'That would be very kind, Ahmed.'

She was at a loss for words. Ahmed and his wife were wait-ing for her to write her message, and they clearly expected her to do it quickly. After all, how complicated could a notice in a shop window be? The postcard looked so blank. In a way, it seemed a pity to spoil it with writing, especially in cheap biro.

'I probably need a few minutes,' she explained. 'To work out the right thing to say.'

'Of course, Mrs Padgett.' Ahmed beckoned to Phee to come away from the pay-point and go with him into the back of the shop.

As she thought about the postcard, she could hear Ahmed dictating numbers to his young wife. Stock-checking, probably.

Cara realised that what was holding her back was that, up until now, she hadn't attempted to put into words anything about Stephen's disappearance, about what had happened or about her feelings. Writing it down, like telling the police, confirmed it and it was something that she would rather not confirm.

In the end, she settled for a conventional phrasing. Immediately under the photograph, she wrote HAVE YOU SEEN THIS MAN? In large capitals, and under that she wrote *Stephen Padgett is nineteen and has been missing for...* She was about to put *four days*, to accommodate that day and the next, but the postcard might have to remain in the window for some time. It would be misleading to put *four*. She wrote down *several* instead.

She decided against adding details of his weight and height, and the photograph would communicate what he looked like far better than any description. At the bottom of the card, she added *If you have seen Stephen or know anything about where he is, please contact Edward and Cara Padgett on 01730 483128.*

Ahmed sensed the moment to approach. Cara handed him the card and Stephen's photo. He read the wording.

'This is very bad news, Mrs Padgett,' he said. 'I am very sorry. Has he been gone long?'

'Three days.'

'That is not so very long, then. Perhaps he will return soon.'

'I hope so, Ahmed.'

'Would you like to buy one week or more than one week?'

150

It wasn't a question that had crossed her mind, though it was clearly something he routinely asked.

'One week,' she said, trying not to think about the necessity to display it for longer. 'For the moment.'

'I'm sure that will be more than enough, Mrs Padgett.'

'You did what!' Edward said. He'd not long returned from the studio, and was up to his elbows in grey, tepid water, washing a saucepan, but when she told him about the postcard, he instinctively swung round, sprinkling her apple green jumper.

'I had to do something.'

'It'll be all over the village by now.'

'That was my intention. The more people who know the better. That way we may find out something.'

'He's nineteen, Cara.'

'All the same.'

'No, no, it's not all the same. Because he's nineteen, he can pretty well do what he pleases. If he chooses to leave home, he can. We don't have any rights here. That's what you don't get, isn't it? We can't *demand* that he comes back.'

Cara stood very still. He couldn't tell whether she was about to shout back at him or collapse in tears.

'I simply worry about him. I want to know he's alright.'

'I know.'

'You've put greasy water all over my jumper. I'll have to wash it now.'

There was something pathetic, he felt, about the way in which she left the room. It was as if the energy had drained from her, leaving her shoulders limp, her breathing heavy. She had none of her usual briskness, none of her impatience.

He regretted shouting at her. Did it matter if the village knew that Stephen had run away? Probably not. The worst that could happen was that everyone he now met would commiserate and offer him cups of tea. Doubtless, they'd all seen it coming anyway. They would have seen Stephen slouching into the pub or crashed out on the common. It didn't take much to put two and two together. Cara had only made public the unspoken expectation of dozens of their neighbours, who had witnessed his behaviour over the past two years or so. Cara knew that. But she'd thought they would want to help.

So, why had he objected? He suspected it was a fear that they would gloat. But why? Did he imagine his fellow villagers to be essentially cruel? They weren't, of course. What they wanted was, on one hand, conformity and, on the other, non-conformity, of a youthful and spirited, but unthreatening kind. Losing all your money gambling and getting drunk on cider at a point-to-point was alright. Passing out from too many drugs was not. Holding radical views whilst an undergraduate at Cambridge was a good sign. Dropping out of 'A' levels, with nothing much planned for afterwards, was not. Edward had dreaded every summer, the time that exam results were announced, when he'd go into the village and everyone he met would be bound to ask how the boys had done. He'd start by telling them about Timothy's routinely high achievements and then try to pass off Stephen's failures as a joke. Sometimes that had worked, but at the end of Stephen's last school year, they'd wanted to know more. Was he going to university? Why not? Grades not good enough? What did he get, as a matter of interest?

A matter of interest. It was nothing of the sort. This was *schadenfreude.* The people who pressed him most closely for information were the very people who, in response and with an affected modesty Edward found particularly nauseating, told him that their sons and daughters had done better than could ever have been expected of them and were ascending to heaven with PhDs next October, or something of the sort.

It was, then, a rarefied cruelty, confined to the subject of children and moralistic in the tradition of league tables. Edward realised that behind the fear of embarrassment, of admitting yet another of Stephen's 'failings', he wanted to protect his son from the disapproval of the village. If he couldn't deny that Stephen had stormed off from the family home, he would like it to remain a private loss, a family crisis.

'What's your French like?' Karl Rouse asked.

'Not bad. We've spent a good deal of time in France, holidays and so on.'

They were sitting opposite each other in a small French restaurant called Chez Bonville, which was tucked away in St Martin's Court, a dog-leg of an alley running between Charing Cross Road and St Martin's Lane. Karl knew it. He met everyone there, he said. He adored the starched white tablecloths and the clean, tall, patternless wine glasses. Difficult to find, he said, unless you're prepared to pay.

Karl, Cara inferred, was not, or only up to a point.

'Burgundy?' he asked. 'They have a very good Saint Véran.'

'Lovely.'

He ordered the wine and they studied the menu. She had been surprised by his invitation. As a rule, if you were being considered for a role, you either went to an audition or you were picked on the strength of your reputation. In that event, you might meet the conductor for a quick coffee the week before rehearsals started. No one offered you a free lunch, especially at a smart restaurant in central London.

'There was a bit of debate about whether to sing it in French or English,' Karl explained. 'I never had any doubts myself. It always sounds clunky to me in English, don't you think?'

'Why should anyone want to hear it in any other language than the one it was written in?'

'Precisely.'

Was she being creepy? His 'Precisely' had the tone of someone who thinks you've stated the painfully obvious. Perhaps she had concurred a little too enthusiastically.

'Cheers!' He raised his glass and clattered it against hers. 'Here's to *L'Enfance*. Is it a work you know?'

'I know *The Shepherds' Farewell*, of course.'

'Magnificent, isn't it?'

'But not really the rest.'

'I think you'll make a perfect BVM. The potted shrimp is good.'

She had a sense, for a moment, of being a young girl escorted by a bon viveur, taken out, perhaps for the first time, to a posh eatery and guided gently through the menus, courses recommended, wines chosen for her. Did he imagine she wasn't used to eating out?

'The problem is that no one has cracked the translation. Back in the eighties there was a television production, on ITV of all places, and they had the same old ding-dong about English or French. Anyway, the producers got Anthony Burgess to write a singable English version. Burgess was very keen to do it in English, but in the end his translation was used as subtitles and they sang in French.'

'On ITV?'

'9pm, just after Christmas, in French. Incredible when you consider today's ITV. I remember it.'

'Was it good?'

'Not bad. If you read Burgess's autobiography, he says it was sentimental, but the interesting thing that I read in a life of Burgess is that, according to his agent, he was deeply moved by it, especially by your part, Mary. Apparently, he kept saying 'What must it be like to be a mother!' Talk about sentimental.'

Why was he telling her this? She was impressed, it was true, by his knowledge of the piece and its past. If he was seeking to convince her that his preparation was thorough, it was working, but she could have been persuaded by less.

'I'm boring you.'

'No, not at all. It's fascinating. I hadn't realised the English-French thing was so hotly disputed.'

'Look, it's nonsense probably. How's your food?'

'Good. Very nice. And yours?'

She wasn't sure if he had looked directly at her, briefly. She felt unsettled by him, as she always did in the presence of big personalities. He seemed too much at ease with the world, as if life existed for his convenience and comfort. He must have his problems, though, mustn't he? Surely, no one breezed through life without a constant agenda of difficulties to be resolved. That's what life was, problem solving.

'You have children, of course?'

'Yes, two. Boys. Actually, one of them's not really a child.

He's nineteen.'

'One's children always remain one's children,' Karl said. 'What does he do?'

'Stephen?' She hesitated. 'He's just finished school.'

'I take it that since you say he's finished school and not started anything else, he's having one of those ineffable 'gap' years.'

'Yes, yes, that's right.'

Part of her wanted to tell him. His air of authority, the impression he gave of having things under control, made her feel that he might know what to do. He might have an idea, about finding Stephen, that would never occur to her, or to Edward.

'My wife left me several years ago. I see my son every now and again.'

'That's a pity.'

'As a matter of fact, it suits us both.'

Edward would never forgive her for letting on, confiding in him, which was probably right. She had, after all, only met Karl Rouse half an hour ago, and for the sake of her career, it was probably unwise to disclose that her private life was in turmoil.

'When are you hoping to start rehearsals?'

'Week after next. Didn't your agent tell you?'

He sliced neatly through the thin end of his steak and paused to take a mouthful of wine. He was attractive, Cara decided, but not in a conventional way. Despite his good taste – the food he had recommended was, as he'd advised her, delicious – his clothes were unironed and loose-fitting. It was as if he valued what he saw and digested, and cared less about how he was seen and digested by others. She pictured him flinging his arms about, hair flying, as he conducted from the podium.

'Have you been conducting long?' she asked.

It was a risky question. Some people in the business, especially conductors, expected you to have learnt their entire career histories before meeting them, either because they were famous or because they saw it as intelligent preparation.

'Only twenty years,' Karl said, not obviously offended. He continued to eat, allowing his reply to sink in. Then he raised his eyes and, as if they were a well-rehearsed duet, they laughed.

'What the fuck do you think you're playing at?'

Edward was not altogether awake when the phone rang. He picked it up, half expecting it to be a wrong number, and certainly not prepared for the discharge of abuse his son let fly at him.

'A fucking postcard in the post office. With my fucking photo on it!'

'Actually, it was your mother who placed it.'

He wished he hadn't said that. It sounded craven, and he knew that had he been more alert, he wouldn't have done.

'You don't get it, do you, Dad? I've left. I'm nineteen. I've a perfect right to do what I fucking like and I've left your shithouse for good. Is that clear?'

'Crystal.'

'And you can tell that fucking bitch of a wife of yours to mind her own fucking business.'

'Don't talk about your mother…'

He'd gone, cut off with a thumb pressed on a red hyphen. You didn't even have to slam phones down nowadays. A line could be silently and finally severed by the touch of a button.

He turned to Cara, who had woken and struggled into a seated position. She propped-up her pillows, her face filled with expectation.

'That was Stephen.'

'You amaze me,' said Cara. 'I thought it was only used car salesmen who said the word 'fucking' every three seconds.'

'Perhaps that's what he'll end up as.'

'Optimist.'

'He was annoyed by your notice in the village stores.'

'I could tell. Well, I suppose it's had one good effect. At least, we know he's alive and not so debilitated by hunger that he can't rave at us down the phone.'

'I'm sure he'll get over his new-found fame.'

They were consoling each other with stoical humour, pretending a kind of aloofness or resignation that accepted Stephen's maledictory behaviour for what it was. Edward, in particular, wanted to sustain the tone, keep up the belief that Stephen would be back with them in a couple of days.

'I thought I detected a little homesickness.'

Cara laughed.

They had both voiced a worry about what money he might have with him. Cara had discovered eighty pounds missing from her purse, but that wouldn't last long.

'He must be scrounging off friends,' she said.

'I don't suppose his friends have much either.'

That left stealing.

The loudspeaker on the wall above him crackled and spat, like a frying pan on high heat. It was an unidentifiable shade between yellow and green with a metal mesh, and could not have been replaced in a quarter of a century. Over it came the noise of the auditorium, the muted creak and brush and susurration of an audience moving down aisles and across rows to find their seats and study the evening's programme.

The house would be full. All the tickets had gone over a week ago and when Timothy had announced that the school debate he was due to take part in had been cancelled and he would, after all, come, Edward had had to plead with the box office for an extra 'comp'.

His palms felt sweaty, a light moisture which seemed to get worse whatever he did. He gripped the cold arms of his chair, wiped his hands on his trousers, but it was pointless. This was personal, his own symptom of stage nerves. Other people he knew had headaches, felt sick, couldn't sit still. For Edward, nervousness was focused entirely on his hands. He ought to be used to it by now – nothing had changed over the years – but it nagged at him every time. It was as if stress found out the particular weakness that was the least bearable.

The five minute bell went, and an assistant stage manager appeared at his door to call him to the stage. As he walked the featureless, tube-lit corridor to the wings, he asked himself how different it would be if he were being escorted to his execution. There was always the thought before a concert that he would do anything on earth – clean a high street loo, try to rid an attic of squirrels – rather than step onto a platform and sing in public. The ASM nodded encouragingly and urged him forward to the stage, gently pushing him by the elbow.

He heard the oboe first, then a violin tuning, and then a moment's silence was broken by applause. Allan, the pianist and leader of the quartet, must have entered from the other side and detonated the clapping and whistling. He was well-known, Allan, much adored on the London circuit. He would bow, which for Allan meant the slightest incline of the head, and take his seat behind the enormous Steinway.

Another silence. His turn. Walking on stage was a cross between a failed prison break and a surprise party. At first, he could see nothing. The glare from the lights was infinite, everywhere he looked, a transcendental brightness, behind which was the roar of the crowd, a thick wall of clapping hands, coloured by intermittent steely whistles.

He bowed deeply, turned to Allan and bowed again. The violinist's bow was already raised, the oboe in position. They were ready for the 'off'.

The frightening possibility, that he might open his mouth and nothing would emerge, had never left him. All his recitals began in this way, in fear, and it was only the success of two or three pieces which allowed him to start to relax and enjoy the performance. Why did they do it? Singers, musicians, actors: each and every one paralysed, neurotic with trepidation, before doing the very thing they affected to believe was their lifeblood, their reason for being.

He caught sight of Cara straightaway, smiling from the second row. Tim sat next to her, looking for all the world as if this was the most intolerably boring event he had ever been asked to attend. Thoroughly sixteen.

He opened on familiar ground, and against the concert organiser's wishes. Edward had insisted that he be allowed to sing the penultimate passage of the Evangelist's recitative from *St John's Passion*, 'Die Jüden aber, dieweil es der Rüstag war'.

'It's the bit where Jesus' side is pierced and his body's taken down,' Edward explained.

Nicholas, who had responsibility for planning a concert that would pull in a good audience, looked annoyed.

'I know which bit it is, Edward. But it's not material for a recital.'

Edward argued that his Bach work was what he was best known for and that his audience would expect to hear him sing at least some religious music.

'Why can't you do *Sheep May Safely Graze?* More popular. Easier on the ear.'

That had been the compromise. Edward would be permitted his 'Die Jüden aber' in return for a crowd-pleaser, 'Was mir behagt, ist nur die muntre Jagd', especially the bit about sheep.

It was short, the Evangelist's piece, less than two minutes, scarcely begun and it was over. He spotted Fiona, as he sang, some way back in an aisle seat, her eyes closed, apparently transported. It struck a false note.

As he sang, he thought about J.S.B. The first version of the *Passion* had been performed less than a year after his arrival in Leipzig. He was still in his thirties and in charge of the music of half a dozen churches. Surrounded by children, he was, as his wife would have attested, at the height of his creativity and Leipzig, the cradle of northern Protestantism, was the place to be. For Edward, there was something very stimulating about that, knowing that the man whose music he was singing was successful, prolific, conscious perhaps that every note sharpened the mind or touched the soul.

The recital went well. They particularly liked the Schumann and the Richard Strauss, and the sheep song won him a standing ovation, which should have irked him, but he decided instead to enjoy it. He bowed from the waist and, as he rose, turned to Allan and his colleague musicians and clapped briefly in thanks.

In the bar afterwards, a light perspiration ran across his forehead from standing in hot lights for an hour, but his hands were dry. Various people came up to embrace him, scattering their encomiums. 'Brilliant.' 'That's the best I've ever heard you sing.' 'It was nothing short of thrilling, darling.'

Derek, his agent, appeared at his shoulder, holding out champagne.

'Whatever they say, Edward, you were really very good.'

Edward grazed his glass against Derek's, acknowledging in that small gesture that Derek played no small part in his success. It was Derek who made it his business to know what of importance was going on well ahead of time and to propose Edward as the ideal solution to any 'tenor problem'; it was Derek too who whittled down the invitations, sifting them in such a way that his client would remain prominent but big-hearted, a star who was, as Derek himself put it, 'close to his fan base'.

Cara threw her arms round Edward's neck, kissed him hard on the lips and whispered 'Fantastic'. She and Timothy had struggled through the crush at the bar, not sure where to find him.

'Did you like the Bach?' he asked.

'Which?'

Edward raised an eyebrow, as if to say 'You can't be serious'.

'Of course,' Cara said. 'I always love the Bach. You know that.'

'And you, young man?'

'It was good.'

162

'Really?'

'Yeh, no, you were good, Dad. Where's Steve?' Cara answered.

'He couldn't make it.'

She hadn't told him, despite their agreement. There had been no opportunity for Edward to meet Tim before the recital, so he'd left everything to Cara. Tim's train had been due in at Paddington at 6.30. Cara would meet him. They would have just enough time to scoot across London to the South Bank and be in their seats for Edward's entrance. Cara, they'd decided, should talk about Stephen's disappearance on the tube.

She was aware of his annoyance.

'It was just too noisy and public. We can tell him on the way home.'

'Doesn't he have to go back to school?'

'He's been given a long weekend exeat.'

They spoke as quietly as they could, but their voices were necessarily raised to overcome the clamour of an excited bar. Timothy began to realise that their conversation concerned him.

'What are you two talking about?'

'Nothing,' said Edward.

'Explain afterwards.'

Cara smiled and put a hand on her son's shoulder.

'I'm going to get a beer,' he said, shrugging her off.

'Coca-cola!' Edward called after him, but he'd vanished in the throng.

He would have liked to say something to Cara, about her reluctance to discuss anything serious with Timothy, and her belief that important subjects were better left to him to deal with, especially if they involved giving bad news.

But he was prevented from talking further by a new wave of enthusiastic supporters, who seemed to sweep towards him in a single phalanx from the far end of the bar. All had their particular moments from the concert that they wanted to recall, moments of pleasure or poignancy or sheer joy and exhilaration.

'I felt like leaping from my seat,' one said.

Then Fiona's face emerged from the crowd.

'At times it was deeply moving, Edward,' she said, confidingly.

He wanted her to go away, to avoid the discomfort, which he resented feeling. After all, Fiona and Cara knew each other. What was the problem? He was angry with himself for not being able to dismiss her, to say to Cara 'Here's Fiona.' and move on. Instead, he had a cloying sense of attachment, hers to him, as if they had a shared past, as if they knew each other terribly well.

By the time they'd found the Volvo and pulled out of the underground car park, they were, the three of them, exhausted and, in Edward's case, drunk. They drove slowly and in silence through south London, the streets clogged with post-theatre traffic and the cacophony of young people drifting between pubs and clubs, black VWs and customised Fords palpitant with drum and bass. Edward found himself mesmerised by the fusion of jogtrot, apathetic music and the slow glow and fade of red brake lights.

'Will Steve be at home?' Tim asked from the back seat.

'Probably not,' Cara said.

She'd just joined the M3. She put her foot down and sat back in the tall seat, glad to have escaped the suburban crawl onto a clear stretch of motorway.

'Stephen has left home,' Edward said. He'd known it would fall to him to tell Timothy the truth and he'd searched around for a gentler, more euphemistic way to express it, but in the end it had sounded like a public announcement, a news bulletin.

'Why?' Tim asked. 'Where's he gone?'

'We don't know.'

Tim leaned forward out of his seat belt. Edward sensed the urgent proximity of his face.

'Have you tried to find him, spoken to his friends? What about that girl, what's she called, Twig? Have you told the police?'

The questions fell over each other, rattling together like billiard balls.

'Tim, darling.' She spoke as she glanced in the wing mirror and pulled out to overtake. 'We have done everything we can. None of his friends seem to know where he is and Twig has gone missing too. I suspect she's with him.'

'He's alright. That's the main thing.'

'How do you know, Dad?'

'He rang. He was very angry. He kept saying he was nineteen and could do what he liked.'

'So why didn't he leave in a normal way? Why didn't he say he was going to move out in a few weeks, plan it all? I don't get it.'

Edward glanced at Cara, but she kept her eyes fixed on the road and refused to acknowledge him. There was no answer that Timothy would accept, and he wasn't about to explain how they had decided that they could no longer live with Stephen.

Fortunately, Tim was too geed up to notice that he hadn't had a reply. He lay back in his seat, thinking it through.

'Why didn't you tell me earlier?'

Edward hesitated.

'Didn't want to worry you, darling,' Cara said.

'I've got a right to know! He's my brother.'

'We were going to tell you eventually. We have. Tonight.'

'He'll come back, ol' son. I think he just needed a break from us. He's that sort of age.'

They drove on without further discussion, Tim having run out of questions, Edward glad that he wasn't expected to account for what had happened and what they did. He was surprised Tim hadn't wanted to know what they were planning to do next. Perhaps he'd realised, even at sixteen, that there wasn't much they could do.

The miles slid by. The M3 gave way to minor roads and then lanes. Finally, in fine rain and deep darkness, no lights having been left on, they found themselves stumbling out of the car and into the cottage a few minutes after midnight.

Tim stared in horror at the postcard in the window of the village stores. What on earth had his mother been thinking? Of course, Steve would have been angry about it. Who wants his ugly mug displayed for everyone in the village to see? It was like Steve was a naughty puppy, who'd strayed off the home turf. He would not have put it past her to have offered a reward.

He read the card again. HAVE YOU SEEN THIS MAN? They'd all answer yes, wouldn't they? Of course they'd seen him, hundreds of times over the years. He was part of the furniture. No one would notice if he was around or not. The photograph was, in any case, long out of date. Steve had refused to have his picture taken lately, so she would have had to find something of him in an album. Tim recognized the one in the window from a holiday in France eighteen months ago. He had a tanned face and short hair and a sky blue tee shirt that got left behind on a beach a few days after the photo. It wasn't a true likeness at all, in fact. If you didn't know Steve of old, how he'd changed over the years, you could clock the photo and walk straight past him two minutes later.

A hand appeared in the store window. It was female, with soft brown skin, several gold rings, vivid crimson nail paint and a bangle that jigged about on her wrist. Long fingers removed the card above Steve's and the hand disappeared. Then, it returned and the fingers gripped Steve's notice, gripped the photograph, his face, the fingers masking Steve's eyes, and extracted it from the plastic display panel. It was gone.

Tim felt an absurd sense of shock, absurd because he'd spent the last few minutes convincing himself of what a misguided and embarrassing decision it had been to put the card there in the first place. But now he realised that, at some level, it was a lifeline to Steve, the only active thing that was being done to find him.

His mother must have paid for a week, the kind of meanness he'd come to expect from her.

In the shop, he found the young woman who'd taken the card in the act of placing it in a drawer. He asked her if she was going to throw it away.

'We usually keep them for a few days,' she replied, 'in case people change their minds and want another week.'

'Can I do that?' Tim asked. 'Change my mind, I mean?'

'You'd like another week?'

She was new, this woman. Ahmed had had another woman working with him when he'd last been in the shop, much older.

'You must be Mrs Padgett's other son?' she said. 'Stephen's brother?'

'Yeh. I'm Tim.'

'Very nice to meet you, Tim.'

She extended the hand he was familiar with, her long fingers with their red nails slightly relaxed, not tensed. He took it, briefly.

'Hello,' he said.

'I am Ahmed's wife, by the way. You must call me Phee. That will be one pound.'

He felt awkward, having momentarily forgotten what it was he was meant to be buying. The way she said 'one pound' sounded so impersonal, and yet the last few minutes had been intimate, hadn't they?

'I am very sorry your brother has not turned up. I know your mother hoped it would be a matter of days, which is why she thought one week would be sufficient.'

He fetched his wallet out of his pocket, produced a fiver, and pushed it towards her across the counter. She thanked him and asked him whether there was anything else he'd like.

He said no and fled, the colour rising in his face.

Tim had returned to school, reluctantly.

'Keep me informed,' he said as he got on the train.

Afterwards, Cara was restless. She paced around the house, tidying up newspapers and throwing away junk mail, putting off her work, putting off decision-making. She listened to Edward singing in his study and it irked her that he was so detached, so self-disciplined that he could apparently forget about Stephen for an hour or two and concentrate entirely on his next performance.

After lunch, she climbed the narrow stair at the top of the house and in the room they had recently agreed should be hers, for her privacy and for her singing, she tried to think her way into the part of the Blessed Virgin Mary. She could hear the words in her head, the clear and plangent call of a mother desperate to protect her child. She could hear, but she couldn't sing. She opened her mouth and it wasn't there. It was as if she summoned her voice from deep down in her diaphragm and it would not come, hidden in a sort of mute protest.

An hour passed, during which she stared out of the attic window at the high leafless branches swaying in the wind and rain. She tried to study the score. She'd played Mary before, in Vivaldi's *Stabat Mater*, a similar lament, a cry from the heart, but it had none of the dramatic progress of Berlioz's story, none of the cumulative despair Mary feels as she hurries into Egypt with Joseph and the baby, fearful that at any moment either Herod's troops will catch them up or they'll collapse from exhaustion in the desert. This Mary was something she ought to be able to get her teeth into, a woman in crisis.

But not today.

She thought about going for a walk, but the rain had come on hard. The gutters were overflowing, probably clogged with matted leaves, and the rain bounced high as it struck the paved terrace outside the kitchen. The day looked raw and cold. There couldn't be more than two hours of light left.

Another night.

She wondered whether Stephen would continue to stay

away if he knew the effect it was having on her. Judging by the phone call he'd made two weeks earlier, the only conclusion she could reach was that yes, he would. But there must be part of him that regretted what he was doing, regretted the loss of comfort, the ease of having meals prepared for him, his clothes washed, free electricity, a place to entertain his friends.

The rain was battering the house now and it was nearly dark outside. She fetched a coat from under the stairs.

'I'm going out!' she shouted to Edward, not caring much whether or not he heard.

'What for?' Edward called back. 'It's absolutely foul out there.'

'Need to clear my head.'

She slammed the front door and ran to the car, partly to avoid getting soaked, partly to deny Edward the chance to come after her and protest. He would have tried to dissuade her and he might have succeeded.

She drove too quickly for the narrow lanes and the wet road surface. She liked the thrill of being very slightly out of control. She could afford it. In a collision, Volvos generally came off better.

The lights of the car brought up curving, spiky hedges and grey metal farm gates. Black trees hung over the lane and a cluster of cows gathered in deep mud around a trough. They all had about them an exposed quality, as if rarely seen. The lanes were deserted, the night inky and cloudy: people didn't venture out unless they had to. Cara braked suddenly and swung the Volvo round a tight corner. She sensed the drift in the rear of the car, the tail loose on a skin of rainwater.

Her windscreen wipers were at double speed, thwacking

the rim of the window. She could no longer make out the rain, not as distinct downpouring lines of rain. Instead, there was a puddle or film that sat for a second on the windscreen, then was swept away, then was there again. She could see half of what she ought to be able to see to drive safely. God help her if there were any oncoming vehicles.

The rain seemed to assail her. It limited her sight, would drench her if she stepped outside the car, and it beat so hard on the roof that she found herself irrationally frightened that it might find a way through, might, through sheer attrition, drill holes through the Volvo's steel.

Then she saw her: merely a figure at first, then a girl in a short cream dress, soaked through so that the dress clung to her body and made her appear half naked. Her bare legs shone with wet in the headlights. She had on heeled shoes, totally inappropriate in the muddy lane. She walked towards the lights, but as Cara slowed down, she backed up against a gate, as if to let the Volvo pass.

Cara drew up and stopped. The girl's face streamed, her long hair heavy with water. She was shivering as Cara lowered her window.

'Can I give you a lift?'

The girl could barely speak.

'Was…the other way.'

Cara was already leaning across the gearstick to unlock the passenger door.

'Never mind. Get in. I'll take you.'

As she leaned back, Cara noticed bruises on the girl's legs and there seemed to be a small cut on her forehead.

'Get in, get in, quickly. You're wet through. Here, take my

coat.'

Cara struggled out of her padded jacket and pressed it on the girl, cloaking her, pulling it around her shoulders. She adjusted the heating to twenty-eight and turned the fan up to full. Warm air blew into the car. The girl shook uncontrollably.

Cara let the Volvo roll forward a few yards, down the hill, then reversed up to the field gate. She changed into first and pulled back into the lane. The back wheels spun wildly in the mud.

'What were you doing walking in those clothes? On a night like this?'

The girl had her hands in her hair, wringing out water.

'Wanted…' She stumbled over her words, trying to stop herself shivering. 'Get home.'

'Were you hurt? Did you fall over? You look like you've been hurt.'

'…alright,' she said. 'Thank you.'

Cara was surprised by her politeness. It seemed unnecessary, under the circumstances.

'Where's home? Where can I take you?'

She drove slowly, expecting that at any minute they would come to a house or a driveway to which the girl had been heading.

'I'm…'

Was she about to reveal her name?

'…very grateful, Mrs Padgett.'

Cara was astonished. This girl knew her, in some sense, at least knew her name, but as far as she could tell, Cara had never met her before. Perhaps her drabbled state disguised her.

'I'm sorry…' Cara began to say.

'I'm Twig.'

'Twig?'

It was Cara's turn to struggle for words.

'Well, I'm glad to meet you.'

She felt foolish saying it, but what else could she say? She couldn't very well ignore the fact that she'd introduced herself.

'Are you feeling any warmer?'

'Beginning to,' Twig said, and she made an effort to smile.

All that Cara wanted to do was to fire questions at her about Stephen. Had she been with him? Did she know where he was? Was he alright? Could she go to him? But it was possible that Twig hadn't been with Stephen, that she was as ignorant as the rest of his friends.

She tried to focus on the girl's need for help.

'Can you direct me?'

She said it gently, without any hint of order or reproach.

'I was hoping,' Twig said, 'I could come to your house.'

Cara liked that idea. That way she could interrogate her, get Edward involved.

'Of course,' she said. 'But won't your parents be worried?'

'It's only my mum. She's probably out at work. I'd like to clean up before I see her, if that's alright.'

They drove in silence, a silence that is in terms of words, conversation, but it was broken by coughing and the uneven breathing of someone slowly recovering from exposure to cold. Twig sneezed and produced a handful of tissues from a pocket. Cara wondered if she'd caught a chill, and then realised that Twig was crying. As she turned the Volvo into the driveway, Cara said:

'It'll be alright. Let's get you inside.'

She parked and went to help her, putting her arm around her not because it would warm her or protect her from the rain, but to comfort her, make her feel safe.

Edward must have seen the sweep of the headlights through the kitchen window. He stood at the front door, looking out at them, puzzled. He was slow to grasp what was going on and did nothing for several minutes.

'Is there a fire?' Cara called through the rain.

He seemed to hesitate.

'Yes, yes. In the sitting room. Who is she?'

Why did he ask her that? Wasn't it a question better put to Twig herself, once she was in the house? Cara was annoyed with him. He should know better, behave better.

She let Twig go inside first.

'This is Twig, Stephen's girlfriend. She needs a bath and dry clothes. She's wet through.'

'Of course. I'll go and run the bath.'

It was the sensible thing for him to do, far preferable that he help in a practical way than hang around the girl, desperate to ask her questions, but afraid to do so. Water was now running in the bathroom above them.

'I'll find you some jeans and a shirt.'

Cara steered Twig up the stairs and put her in the spare room while she went to fetch dry clothes. Twig had scarcely uttered a word since entering the house. She was cold and wet and exhausted, no doubt about it, but there was probably confusion worked into the mix as well. She'd never been to Stephen's home before, not that Cara was aware of anyway, and whatever had happened in the last few days would be vying with the quiet and dependable comfort of the Padgett home.

This was where Stephen was brought up. It was another insight into who he was.

She found, when she returned, a thin young woman with pale skin standing and shivering in her bra and pants. Her drenched dress lay in a lump on the carpet, alongside a pair of red high-heeled shoes.

'That bath must be ready now,' Cara said quickly. 'Edward's stopped running the water.'

'You're very kind.'

Was she used to kindness, Cara wondered. Or was that something she'd been denied? She couldn't help suspecting that these consolations were new to her.

She laid out the jeans and shirt. They would hang like sacks or prisoners' uniform on Twig's slight frame, but they were the most suitable things she could provide. No teenage girl would want to wear the dresses or skirts of a near-fifty year old.

While Twig had her bath, Cara remembered socks and left a thick woollen pair on the bed with the other clothes. She went downstairs, found Edward, and described how she'd come across the girl in the lane, alone.

'What was she doing there?'

'I've not found out yet. She could hardly speak. She said something about 'going home'. Then she changed her mind, I think, and decided she wanted to come here.'

'Why?'

'Not a clue.'

'Good job you went out.'

He could have no idea what her state of mind had been when she left the house and set off in the Volvo. He'd been wrapped up in his own affairs, his singing, the next performance, oblivious to her agitation, her instinct that unless she took some sort of action, a dreadful thing would happen to Stephen. It was the bargain she struck with providence; if she took seriously the messages of her instinct, providence would protect the people she loved.

It had brought her Twig.

She stood in the sitting room, her back to the log fire, a mug of Edward's Assam warming her hands. She was drowned in denim and cotton, scarcely strong enough, it seemed, to hold herself up against the weight of Cara's wardrobe. Her feet, which she would have wanted to look sexy in her red stilettos, were mittened in grey climbers' socks. For all that, and now that her hair was drying, she was good-looking, Cara thought, pretty.

'You'll be wanting some kind of explanation.'

'We...'

Cara interrupted.

'In your own time. Have your tea.'

The silence that followed was not surprising. Twig probably didn't know where to start and she would be glad of the extra time to think. For Cara, though, and doubtless for Edward too, the anticipation was almost unbearable. Discovering Twig, in the wet and the mud, had convinced her that she was a step nearer to finding Stephen. This skinny girl had the most precious knowledge and was all that stood between Cara and holding her son in her arms again.

'Why were you there?' she asked. She could wait no longer.

Twig sat down, as if to plan what she'd say.

'He chucked me out,' she said.

Edward jumped in, unable to stop himself.

'What do you mean, 'chucked you out'? Of where?'

'He said he couldn't be with me anymore and I had to leave. He said I'd be better off without him.'

'Where was this?' Edward asked.

'In the house, the squat. I argued with him, but he got mad at me.'

She was crying, bent forward, pressing her face into her hands. Cara moved across the room to her and started to stroke her shoulders. She leaned down and kissed Twig's damp hair.

'It's okay, sweetheart. We understand.'

Edward was on his feet.

'How can you say that, Cara! You may understand, but I certainly don't. I don't understand a single thing about this. Where is Stephen? Where's this squat?'

'Calm down, Edward. You won't achieve anything by shouting. The poor girl's been through a hell of a lot tonight. We have to be gentle.'

'Okay, okay.'

Cara took both of Twig's hands in hers and held them for a moment before speaking.

'We need, Edward and I need, to find Stephen, don't we? To talk to him about this. And we need your help to do that. I have the feeling you think Stephen has been in touch with us and told us where he lives. But he hasn't.'

Twig looked up, clearly surprised.

'He hasn't,' Cara reiterated. 'And so we'd like you to tell us where this squat is, or better still, take us there.'

'Not tonight.'

'Perhaps not tonight, but tomorrow then.'

The rain didn't abate, not through the night, nor in the morning. If anything, there was more of it and the wind, which had picked up shortly before dawn, blew it against the windows of the house and forced it between the hung tiles on the west flank.

'There's a leak down here.'

Cara was calling to Edward from the kitchen. She'd come to make tea for Twig and found that the ceiling was dripping. She pulled out a bucket from the under the sink and lined it up to catch the water as it fell.

'Edward!'

He appeared a few minutes later, concern making him frown.

'I'm sure it's just the wind,' she said. 'It'll dry out when it changes direction.'

Edward nodded and adjusted the position of the bucket, which annoyed her. She knew that he liked to think that he dealt with problems like leaks, but that made it no less irritating. The drips had been successfully captured by the bucket where it was.

'Are you coming with us?' he asked.

'Of course.'

He took his Barbour from the rail under the stairs and went to start the car in the garage. Cara, meanwhile, took a mug of sweet tea to Twig.

'He's not answering his phone,' Twig said. 'I've rung three times.'

'No, well he's never picked up when I've tried.'

'What do you think it means?'

She clutched the mug in two hands, like a child, and held

it close to her mouth, allowing the steam to warm her face.

'I imagine it means just what he said to you yesterday. He thinks you're better off without him.'

'It's not true.'

'Drink your tea and we'll go and see if we can find him.'

Cara watched her as she made herself ready. This thin girl – she could weigh no more than seven stones – was Stephen's partner. Stephen was nineteen, jobless, without any stated ambition that Cara was aware of. How old was she? Seventeen? Not more. Timothy's age. It was a thorough mess.

'You two all set?'

Edward, in the stairwell, impatient.

'Be there in a minute,' Cara called back.

She lent Twig a coat and a pair of trainers, on the large size, but better than the high heels in which she'd been stumbling around the lanes.

Twig seemed to hesitate before leaving the room.

'Will I be coming back here?' she asked. 'Only I ought to take my clothes with me if not.'

Cara realised she hadn't given it a second thought.

'Assume you'll be here for a couple of days. In any case, I can always bring your things over to your home.'

In the car, Twig explained that they would need to drive towards Petersfield and once they were on the outskirts, she'd give them further directions. It was quite complicated, she said.

She slept most of the way. Edward had insisted that they leave by nine, but when Cara knocked on the door of the spare room at twenty to, it was clear Twig was still deeply asleep. The experience of wandering around on country roads, in the dark and rain, had left her so exhausted she would need days of rest to recover.

'How on earth did she get from somewhere outside Petersfield to a mile or so from us?'

Edward whispered, anxious not to wake her.

'She must have got a lift. Hitched perhaps.'

'She was lucky not to get herself killed.'

Cara detected, in that exaggeration, a concern for the girl that surprised her. It wasn't that she thought Edward indifferent to what Twig had been through, but his impatience, the previous night and again as they were leaving the house, had made her assume that he was preoccupied with Stephen and could not, therefore, give much thought to her predicament. That was clearly wrong, though. He was worried about her.

Perhaps he thought his son was to blame and that it was his duty to protect her.

The drive to Petersfield was not long and as they began to see signs for the town centre, Cara turned in her seat and gave Twig a gentle prod.

'Oh, you turn here!' she said, panicky. 'Sorry. I went off.'

She wiped sleep from her eyes.

'Yes, it's down here, and there's a road on the left. Here, here. The next one.'

Edward followed her instructions and drove into what appeared to be a private road, flanked by tall Victorian villas.

'Are you sure?' he asked.

'Yeh. I recognize it.'

The large houses had well-kept gardens and expensive cars in the driveways. Speed bumps prevented them from hurrying and the rain made the well-laid tarmac ahead shine.

'It's this one, Mr Padgett.'

She said it quietly, as if she might be identifying a grave in a cemetery. When they pulled up to the kerb, Cara was suddenly aware of their silence, the rain pounding above them.

'There's an umbrella in the boot,' Edward said, and he stepped out into the weather, running down the side of the car. Despite the rain, Cara heard the distinctive sound of the metal tube sliding up the handle and the canopy snapping taut.

Twig's was the first door he threw open. He took her by the arm and stood her under the umbrella while he opened Cara's door and stepped back to give her room. In this way, a trio, the two women protected from the rain by a reproduction of Renoir's *Les Parapluies*, Edward havering at the edge, catching drops on his shoulders from the tips of the umbrella struts, they walked slowly down a narrow concrete path between patches of overgrown lawn.

The house was much like the others nearby, pale yellow brick rising to impressive gables and a deep pitched roof. It was double-fronted, two large bay windows in strong sashes flanking the front door, high ceilinged reception rooms behind them. But in other ways this house was different. The paintwork had flaked and fallen off, leaving areas of exposed wood on the sills and door panels, some of which looked as though they had gone rotten. Roof tiles lay scattered over the grass, where they had landed days, weeks, possibly months before. A sulo bin had been overturned, its lid flung open, cardboard pizza cases spilling out of it.

The windows were without curtains. Cara peered in at one of the bays. Inside was a large room with bare floorboards and a body in a sleeping bag at the far end. She didn't think it was

Stephen.

'Shall we knock?'

Edward had asked Cara the question, but he now turned to Twig, who produced a Yale key and unlocked the door. She looked scared as she went in and Cara wondered whether Stephen had been more aggressive than Twig had implied.

She didn't know what to expect as they stepped into the hall. The house smelt alright, she thought, nothing better than alright, but the kind of synthesis of cooking odours you might come across in any student accommodation: pizzas, of course, plus curry and chip fat. Strangely, it wasn't unpleasant. It reminded Cara of her own college days.

The guy in the sleeping bag didn't stir when they opened the door. The room had looked bare enough through the window, but it was in fact devoid of any furniture at all. With a high ceiling, large windows and a Victorian fireplace the height of a man, the emptiness conspired to dwarf the anonymous sleeping squatter on the floorboards. It was an Alice in Wonderland effect: he might have been a child.

'Hello!' Edward called out in the hall. 'Anyone about?'

'We're here to see Stephen,' Cara added.

Twig showed no initiative. Cara sensed her hanging back, almost cowering behind her.

'Where did you sleep, Twig?' Cara asked her.

'Here.'

The squeak of their shoes reverberated as they walked the length of the hall and started to climb the stairs. It was a clear, isolated sound, unmistakeably wooden. Without carpets, it was striking just how much wood there was in the house: floorboards, skirting boards, wide panelled doors, picture rails, stair treads, banisters, built-in cupboards, window frames and sills. The house creaked with wood.

'How does a place like this get left empty?' Edward said, as much to himself as the others.

'It was re-possessed three months ago.'

Edward and Cara looked at each other, surprised by Twig's prompt explanation.

'So you thought you'd move in?'

'It wasn't my idea,' she said, defensively.

They found a kitchen at the top of the stairs. A frying pan, congealed with burnt bits of food that could have been anything, leaned in the sink, along with unwashed plates and mugs with deep dark brown staining. The hob, Cara noted, hadn't been cleaned in weeks. It was splashed and encrusted, and she suddenly realised that a very low blue flame was alight around one of the rings.

'Too stoned to notice,' Edward remarked, as he watched Cara go to switch it off.

Their voices were now attracting attention and two faces, both male, appeared at a bedroom door further down the landing. Before they could see Twig, they started shouting.

'What the fuck are you doing in our house?'

'How d'you get in?'

Twig stepped forward to calm them down.

'Oh, it's you, Twig. These your parents come to have a look?'

'No, they're Steve's.'

'Look, sorry, man. No offence. Just that we had a lot of our stuff nicked last week, yeh? And so we're not exactly welcoming people who walk in off the street unannounced.'

'Do you know where Stephen is?' Cara asked.

'Steve,' Twig corrected her, as if the two young men wouldn't understand. 'He was here last night. Has he gone?'

Cara studied them as they attempted to think what might have happened to Stephen. They had obviously not long woken, probably disturbed by their arrival. One, the taller, did most of the talking. The other, a younger man, a boy really, stared out of his dark room with sunken eyes. His face was thin. Cara suspected he couldn't be bothered to feed himself properly.

'Yeh, Steve,' the taller said. 'He must have headed, last night, I guess. Might have been this morning.'

'Know where he's gone?' Twig asked.

'Gone?'

'Yes. Did he say where he was headed?'

'No, not really.'

Cara could see Edward becoming increasingly impatient. She stepped in.

'What do you mean 'not really'?' she said, softly. 'Did he give you even a vague idea?'

'Not really.'

'For God's sake!' Edward was shouting. He'd taken a step forwards. 'Did he mention anywhere? Anywhere at all?'

'Hey, it's cool.'

The taller one stepped back into his room, unwilling to confront Edward, no doubt feeling vulernable, bare-chested, in dirty white shorts. The dark-eyed one retreated too and disappeared from view.

Edward tried to moderate his tone.

'I just wondered if he'd mentioned a name, a place, names of friends.'

'Yeh, well, he didn't, okay? He's not the guy to do that, Steve. He goes his own way, yeh?'

'Do you think he'll ring?' Edward asked. 'Could you say we were here, with Twig.'

It was the shorter one, the invisible one, who shouted back.

'We don't have phones, man. They got ripped off, remember? With the other stuff. Bastards!'

The taller, in shorts, came out of the bedroom and stepped past the three of them. He crossed the landing to the bathroom and they heard the bar of the lock shunt into place.

It was pointless, Cara decided. Neither of these young men had anything useful to tell them. Either Stephen had slipped away, leaving no details of where he was going, or he'd briefed everyone in the house to say nothing if people came calling.

'What do you think?' Edward said.

'He doesn't want to see me,' Twig answered.

Cara was struck by how disappointed Edward looked. Had he expected to find Stephen? She herself had had no real confidence that they would. It seemed entirely probable that having got rid of Twig, he would realise that he needed to move on. Was Edward so naïve? She would have said, as a general rule, no. His face was tired and his left eye was twitching, always a sign with him that he was anxious and hadn't slept. Perhaps he'd wound himself up to a point at which all he had left was blind hope.

'What about the chap downstairs?' he asked. 'Should we wake him?'

'I don't know who he is,' Twig said quickly. 'I think he's new. Probably arrived last night.'

'Are people constantly coming and going, then?'

'I suppose.'

They were hurrying to get back into the car when the taller one, still in his shorts, came running out and seemed to fling himself onto the Volvo. Cara pressed a button and her window slid down into the passenger door.

'I just remembered,' he said, 'Steve said he wasn't feeling too well. That's why he had to leave. That's what he said. I'm sick, he said. I gotta go.'

'Was that last night?' Cara asked.

'Yeh, must have been.'

'How late?'

'Oh, now you're asking. I don't know, lady. Time's not a big thing for me.'

He'd started to shiver and the rain ran down his chest. He was turning to go, when Cara called after him.

'Thanks.'

He looked back briefly and smiled.

5

October 2013

What do I turn to? There was so much divinity in our child-hood, wasn't there, Tim? There was so much worship and celebration. But no God. The house was full of masses and passions and fugues and cantatas. *Jesu, Joy of Man's Desiring*. The Christmas Oratorio. Bach. Always and everywhere.

Neither of them believed in God. What was it Dad said? Bound to be pompous. 'The construct of religion was essential to the civilisation of man.' It didn't make him go to church, though, unless it was to perform or for the occasional Evensong when he was in a place with a good choir. He and Mum said they didn't need a god. If they had need of help, of consolation, they turned to their music and it was, they claimed, nine times out of ten there.

So we had no faith, and treated people with faith with caution.

What do I turn to? I need some sort of faith. Rashid's screams have driven Bach out of my mind. I try to hear it, try to start a sequence of notes, but they won't come, like Dad's old stylus sawing away in the outer groove, unable to move or create music. I can hear the scratchy diamond grinding the black vinyl, monot-onously, a mundane torture.

I could use a drink.

It's cold now. I've been so preoccupied I've failed to notice how the temperature has plummeted. A moment ago I was sweating, not I suspect because of heat but out of fear, nerve-shaken terror.

The sweat has run cold, and I am forced to wrap myself in newspaper from the floor to stop shaking. The newspaper reeks of mouse droppings and human sweat, and they are so old now that they tear easily when I try to arrange them around me.

There is silence. The doors upstairs have ceased to slam and Rashid has not screamed for several minutes. I don't know what is happening. Has he given them what they wanted? Is that possible? Is he unconscious, or dead? When I realised it was silent outside, I was so grateful and relieved, but now I'm worrying. Silence is, in some ways, more ominous, more charged with dire possibility than the awful screams a moment ago. This is like a refusal to answer your most urgent question. What's going on? I'm tempted to shout out. What's happening to Rashid? You must tell me. Is he okay?

The silence has an intensity. When you try to detect within it the slightest sound, a fragment that might confirm or deny that Rashid is alive, it makes you shiver. With its pregnancy.

It is an imperfect silence, of course. The machine noises of insects are constant as a computer hum.

There are hints of wind beyond the walls, which would explain the cold.

They contain the possibility of rain, a sound I have been longing for since I arrived, for its touch of humanity.

Rashid is bloody and exhausted when he returns. He is dragged into the room by two guards. Each has one of Rashid's arms around his neck. His body is limp between them, his head hanging so that I can't see his face. There is blood in his hair and on his shirt. His legs make no attempt to keep up with the guards, and as his feet slide over the floor behind him, I can see that they are bloody too.

We dragged Lance Corporal Tyson like that, his legs mashed.

He is dropped near me. They do not lower him gently, but unhook his arms and let gravity do the rest. He does nothing to protect himself and it must hurt as he hits the hard concrete. The pain is minor in comparison with what he has been through and he makes no complaint. He is, in any case, scarcely conscious.

'Rashid.'

I try to make my voice as gentle and soft as I can whilst trying to rouse him and get his attention.

'Rashid!'

The guards have gone, but I don't want to frighten him further. He may not realise that he's back in the room with me.

'Are you okay?'

It is an inane question. I am embarrassed to ask it, but I have somehow to express my concern and sympathy, and Rashid needs to know that there is one person in the building who loves him and does not want to hurt him. Without that, we despair.

He turns his head towards me.

'Lieutenant Padgett, sir.'

The words are indistinct, out of date. There is blood around his mouth, crusty and black, and his right eye has swollen and shut up. I move my arm under his shoulders and very slowly draw him closer to me.

His body is so broken that he cannot find a position that is comfortable for more than a few minutes. He shifts and turns in my arms, and I try to ignore the stink of his blood and sweat and shit. After all he's suffered, I'm surprised that it is the warmth of his body that impresses me. His body temperature is, I would guess, normal. I hug him to my side and, in the silence, I think I can hear him crying.

Eventually, after what seems to be an hour or more, he sleeps.

189

Please. Let this stop! I can't do much more. I don't have the courage for two.

The hope.

Enough light has fallen through the slit for me to know it's dawn. The door bursts open and Guard One is standing there, barking orders at us. They are, shockingly, in English.

'Up! Get up! Exercise.'

He throws on the light that hangs in the ceiling and I find myself blinking and trying to shield my eyes.

'We can't,' I start to say. 'He can't walk. You know that.'

'Exercise!'

Rashid must have slipped away from me as he slept. He is curled up in a foetal ball and doesn't appear to be awake, despite the guard's shouts.

Guard One has taken a step forward and I can tell that he is planning to kick Rashid, so I stretch out my arm to stop him. I must have moved too quickly, given him the idea I was going to attack him, because he turns and puts his boot into me instead. I catch it on my injured knee and I scream with the pain. It is agony, and I feel certain that he has fractured the kneecap. This is the first time for weeks that I have been on the receiving end of such casual brutality and it's Guard One, our almost-friend, who's the perpetrator. I don't understand what's changed. Why is he treating us like this?

'Exercise!'

The pain begins to subside, and I crawl across the floor to Rashid and try to rouse him. He comes to, but he is clearly in a great deal of distress from his multiple wounds.

I turn to Guard One, try to explain.

'He's injured. You know he was tortured? He can't walk.'

I point to Rashid's torn feet, then to my own, unharmed.

Guard One seems angry. He moves towards Rashid and I sense again that he's going to kick him. Without thinking, I roll over between Rashid's broken body and the guard's black boot. I wait in fear for the kick to the middle of my back that I am sure will shatter my spine.

But it doesn't. There is no kick.

I let a couple of minutes go past, still not convinced he won't hit out, and then I slowly start to help Rashid stand up. I can't begin to imagine the suffering that it causes him. His feet are raw, the rough, gritty surface of the floor merciless. I am all but carrying him. The weight of him pulls heavily on my shoulders.

'We can do this, Rashid.'

His face is close to mine. When I speak, it is scarcely above a whisper and I have no idea whether he has heard me or understood.

We make our first tentative steps towards the door. Guard One moves out of our way and we are allowed to enter the outer office. From there we can reach the corridor, which leads to the garden at the back of the house. Whether Rashid can make it that far is another matter. I am effectively taking three quarters of his weight on my back. He pushes forward with one foot and expends all his energy in that single effort. He then pulls up his other leg to join the first. Occasionally, he loses his balance and his feet slide under him and he yells out, so close to my face that I have to turn away.

A second guard is growing impatient at the end of the corridor. It's in his eyes. He holds the handle of the door into the garden, waiting to open it for us. He expected us to reach him several minutes ago. He feels he is being made a fool of, being made to wait, holding onto a door handle like a servant.

He barks out something at us, which I can't understand. It

probably means 'Hurry up!' or 'Get on with it!', no doubt embroidered with insults and whatever vile words he can throw in.

Eventually, we get there. To my surprise, the guard bends down and hands me a pair of trainers. Not mine. Too large. Methodically, I slip one foot inside, then the other. The shoes feel odd and misshapen and unfamiliar.

The guard pulls back the bolts, unlocks the door and opens it. We step out, cautiously.

I can't believe it. I'm almost in tears. I wasn't expecting to feel so much. This is the first time in weeks that I have seen daylight and felt the warmth of the winter sun on my skin. I am close to dropping Rashid, the urge to show my joy, to dance or run about, is so strong. I seem to be floating, my knee miraculously healed.

The garden is an even square. A concrete pavement with large pink flagstones encloses a patch of rough grass. I help Rashid to step off the path onto the grass, but the coarseness of it aggravates the injuries to his feet and increases his pain, so we return to the paving stones.

'We've made it, Rashid,' I whisper to him. 'We're winning. They didn't think you could do it. But you have. We're exercising!'

He has yet to speak to me this morning. His will is focused on keeping upright and tolerating his pain. He can't afford to waste any of it on speaking to me. I am more and more conscious of his weight. Each step that we take he seems to get heavier. I am confident that I can carry him once around the garden, but I am doubtful that I can do much more than that.

There is a bird singing. I've yet to spot where. It might well be on the far side of the roof of the building. We do not hear birds from our room. I convinced myself that the place was so foul it drove them off. Only the most repellent forms of animal life, like the rats and cockroaches, want to keep us company in our fetid den. A beautiful bird, as I imagine it to be, capable of such exquisite song, would keep away. Why sing to the damned? They won't appreciate it.

But this one has returned to remind me that hope remains alive, to bring me a message from the outside world that goodness and beauty continue there even if they are absent from life in here.

I can manage this weight. I keep telling myself. After all, Rashid is light as a bird himself. He can't be more than 5'7', and he can't ever have been anything other than thin. In fact, he's lost so much during his confinement that his bones push through his skin. I can count his ribs and, if I had to, I could produce a very accurate anatomical drawing of his face, the line of his jaw and cheekbones, his denture, the hollows that are his eyes.

I take Rashid's hand and draw his arm further around my shoulders. The adjustment feels like a huge relief, an unburdening, and the muscles that had begun to ache now relax.

'We're getting there, Rashid,' I whisper in his ear. 'I think we've won.'

The morning is still early and the sun is soft on my face, clean light, unlike the dense, infected heat of high summer. I want to smile and laugh, but I hold back, not wishing to provoke the guards any more than we have already. It's clear from the expressions on their faces that they hadn't anticipated that we would manage to walk around the garden. They know Rashid's condition. They have seen his feet and his battered head. They'd assumed he'd collapse and call out and crawl back to the room. They hate the fact that we are triumphant, even though we are careful to be quiet about it. They hate our victory, our determination, the love we share, the one helping the other.

I find it surprising to admit, but I am happy in this moment. I know now that I can carry this tortured, suffering man for as long as it takes. I know that birds sing close to the house of horror and I know that one day we, Rashid and I, will walk free from here.

Conversations run. Inevitably, I suppose, I think about the past and wish that I could have done things differently or better. I feel a great sadness about it all. At times, I am unable to move. I feel a burden of tiredness that is so heavy I can't get from under it. It usually comes with a mild headache.

I try to relax my neck, moving it from side to side, backwards and forwards, then in slow, semi-circular scoops. I've picked up a tip in the army. You can exercise your neck by making the letters of the alphabet. You raise your head diagonally bottom left to top right, and then down to bottom right. Insert a cross-bar and there you have it: the letter A. A vertical line up, plus two clockwise loops, one above the other, gives you B. Etcetera. Etcetera.

It occupies time, but I find it impossible to free up the tension. I tell myself it's due to the heat and the lack of sleep, but I know its causes are deeper.

The army has changed me. No doubt about it. I am less indulgent of my feelings and much more conscious of a duty to others. But I suspect I had begun to change before joining up. Although looking back, it seems like a decision made in a jiffy, becoming a soldier was a symptom, a characteristic of the new person I was turning into, the person I wanted to be.

I didn't deserve to become that person.

I should never have let her go in the first place. How could that have happened? How could I have let her go? She said she loved me. We were together. In the house. We had the front room, over-looking the overgrown grass. It was something to hang on to after all the shit. I'd walked out on my parents after that ballistic row. He'd turned me out, so I hated him. And her. Bastards, both of them. I couldn't stand living with them any longer, so I went.

She was all I had. She had gorgeous legs, slim and long and pale, and she wore a short cream dress and heels to show them off. I wanted her so badly sometimes. I could have screamed it out. We made love in that front room twice, sometimes three times a day. There were no curtains. People must have seen us, people walking in the street. I couldn't have cared if they did. I was so obsessed with her. She was all I thought about. I thought about different ways of fucking her, different techniques, different positions. I wanted to drown in her body, to forget everything else and disappear into her. Sex was a kind of oblivion.

'You pervert!' She used to say if I suggested something new. But she'd laugh as well.

'Why not?' I'd say.

She could never think of a reason. I don't know whether she enjoyed the novelty of it or she was afraid I'd drop her if she didn't go along with it. I don't suppose I cared. As long as she did what I wanted, I was content. The more she agreed to sex, the more I thought I was in love with her.

'How much?'

'What do you mean?'

'How much do you love me, stupid?'

This was not how I wanted to see us. It was about intensity, wasn't it? You couldn't count it up, compare it to a number. I tried

195

to drag her down to the mattress. I ran my hands up the backs of her thighs and started to pull down her panties.

'No, Steve, no. How much?

'What does it matter?'

'It matters.'

'Let's make love.'

I came into her from behind, pressing myself tight up against her cold arse. I was fascinated by the rise and fall of her back, the curve of her lower spine and the swell of her buttocks, the way her hair fell away to either side of her neck, her groans and tiny cries.

Afterwards, I could have lain there, on the bed, for the rest of the night. It was cool, and we were naked alongside each other. I could hear the rain outside. There was light from the street, rain falling through the pale yellow, and sweeps of headlights from passing cars stroked the ceiling. I lit a cigarette and the smoke drifted in the amber. Somewhere else in the house there were voices, just chatting, meandering and inconsequential talk, coming and going. It made me happy. I was happy to hear other people living in the house while we lay naked and close and dozing.

But sex was never enough, was it? I had to have the drink as well. So I was pulling on the neck of a bottle when Twig said:

'I'm pregnant.'

She said it so suddenly, so crudely I thought at the time. She made it vulgar, spoilt it. So I didn't react the way I know she wanted me to, loving and comforting, perhaps even delighted. I just said:

'How long?'

I stood up and pulled on my jeans and a shirt. It wasn't as if I didn't know how I should be behaving. I'd just made up my mind I wasn't going to. I knew I should turn to her and take her in my arms, say reassuring things about how it would be alright and that

I'd support her. But I didn't. Instead, I got up, got dressed and then turned on her.

'You won't be wanting me around then.'

'Steve!'

'I won't be any good as a father, you know that.'

'What are you talking about?'

'You could get rid of it.'

'What!'

'You'd be better off without me. I don't want a kid. I'm a depressive. I don't know what I might do.'

I turned on her, like that. Twenty minutes before we'd been making love, but all I could think of was getting her out of the house, finishing it, being rid of her.

'Go on, get out! I want you out.'

'Steve!'

She started to cry, and that made it worse somehow. I knew her tears should bring out my sympathy, and draw me to her, hug her, but it didn't work and I felt angry, as if I suspected she was putting it on. I grabbed her legs and tugged her naked across the mattress.

'Come on. You can't stay. You got to go.'

I misjudged what I was doing and swung her legs against a table by the bed, and that just irritated me even more. I kicked her, not hard, probably aiming to miss, but I caught her ankle and she cried out.

'For fuck's sake, shut up! Do you want to tell everyone we're rowing?'

'I can't believe you're treating me this way, Steve.' She was crying as she pulled on her cream dress and forced her feet into her red high-heeled shoes. 'I love you. Why are you doing this?'

'Yeh. Well, maybe I'm not the person you thought I was. I told you. You're better off without me.'

I didn't wait for her. I left the room and went upstairs. I should have cared for her, but I didn't. I let her go out in the rain.

I let her go out in the rain.

I'd said it out loud. Rashid had heard. It woke him up.

'Steve?'

I didn't answer.

'Is there rain, Steve?'

'No, Rashid, there's no rain. I was dreaming. I was back in the past. Dreaming of rain. In England.'

I'm hearing Bach. Again. But without the comfort. All the astringency and heartache of solo violin, the strings struck not stroked. He used to listen to this in moments of anguish, when something had gone wrong and he needed privacy to sort it out.

There were nights, after perhaps three or four months of training, when I asked myself if I'd made a disastrous mistake. It was the only time in my life when I smoked a lot. There were strict rules about smoking in the barrack, so on evenings when I wasn't on duty, I'd take a stroll, eight or eight-thirty, and light up.

It was summer I remember. June. The evenings were soft, the possibility of rain hung behind the breeze on my face, the smoke circling away.

I struggled to think, to assemble thoughts. The routine of exercise had all but broken me down and turned me into an automaton. Right away, sir. We'll get to it, sir. ASAP. Those snatched moments, alone with a cigarette, gave me a chance to escape that and try to think again, about me, about what I'd got into, and I realized it wasn't just that thinking was hard to do, but that I was reluctant to. It was easier not to think and to accept. If I'm honest, I'd spent too much time thinking, feeling, pooling my resentments. They were still there: bitterness about the past, a sense that I'd been deprived of happiness.

Sonaten und Partiten für violine solo. BWV 1001-1006. 1720. I can see it sitting on his desk. A stark white cover. A close-up profile of the bridge of a violin and BACH in fat black capitals. If it was playing, I'd know not to go into his study. He'd lose his rag if I did. Whatever was rattling him, he'd find something to shout at me about.

You know what the army has gradually done? Day by day, it's reinforced the idea that I can't any longer blame everyone in the world except me. I have to shoulder some responsibility.

But it's so hard, isn't it, to give up the story you've been telling yourself all your life? Here I was, smoking of an evening, a hundred days into the military, and asking myself to overturn the work of twenty years. In all that time I'd thought I'd made sense of my life. There wasn't much to recommend it. I wouldn't wish it on anyone. Some might call it a catalogue of misery. But it was *my* misery, if you like, and it was coherent. One event, one crisis, following after another.

The fags gave a shape to my strolls. I'd perhaps have five or six, then back inside. Sometimes I'd be dying for a drink. No! Not really. The thought of a large whisky slid across my mind occasionally, but I knew that drink, like resentment, was part of the old story, the one I'd made up about the past, in which I was always the victim. Convenient to be the victim, of course, but it never made me feel safe.

God, I think what surprised me, as the hundred days became two hundred, was that I liked the discipline. I'd had it in my head, as a teenager, that home was all about discipline. Constant friction and punishment. But that wasn't discipline. The confrontations at home were random, the punishments arbitrary, the result of a lack of discipline. They took place in the absence of any structure or rules. Home was a kind of lenient anarchy.

If there's a chance again, I'll walk into his study, hit the Pause button on Bach's violin, and forgive him.

And I'll ask if he forgives me.

It's the army that's made me feel safe, safe to do that.

The great man we have been anticipating eventually arrives around midday. We can always tell when the sun is at its highest. A fierce light shoots down through the slit window and spots the same small area of the floor, where an old dark stain stands out from the concrete monotony. No attempt has been made to remove it. The room is never cleaned. We suspect it is blood.

He waits in the doorway, pausing as if he might be expecting us to stand up or applaud. It is as much as we can do to look up at him and acknowledge his presence. He wears a karakul hat and an expensive-looking chapan, far too warm for the day. He is tanned, dark, and otherwise like the others.

He casts an eye around the room. God knows what he's thinking! Does he think these are appalling conditions and no one should be kept in such a place? Or does it appear luxurious to him, far too good for us? His face gives nothing away, and he turns around and crosses the outer office.

Two of the guards have clearly been given instructions that Rashid and I should follow him. There is a certain amount of shouting, barked orders and the like, and they throw their arms about, sweeping us out of the room. It is unusually warm and my shirt clings to my sweat-greased back. I know that I smell. I haven't been allowed a shower for over a week. And I have a headache that won't go away.

I take Rashid's arm around my shoulders and we are led to a room I haven't seen before. It's smaller than the one we occupy. A table stands in the centre and along one wall is a stack of steel and canvas chairs. Guard One separates out one of the chairs and places it for our visitor behind the table. He then nods to us and we understand that we should take a chair each and sit on the opposite side.

'I realise that you know nothing about where you are or why you have been detained.'

His English is good. He speaks with an almost unaccented voice, which suggests that he developed his skills in the language abroad. It appals me that because he is educated, I immediately warm to him.

'The reasons for your detention are not important. I have come here because I think it is right that you should hear that we are discussing the possibility of your release. It will not be for several days, of course, and there are many arrangements to make, but I think this is good news for you.'

He waits for us to respond.

'Very good news,' I say. 'Does that mean you've got what you want?'

'That is not important.'

The visitor smiles, reassuringly.

Rashid struggles to speak.

'Would you be able, sir, to send a message to my family?' he asks. 'I would be most grateful.'

'I shall try.'

There seems to be nothing further to say. The visitor smacks his hands on the table and stands up. It is not clear to me why this welcome, but brief information could not have been given to us in our room. I can only think that he wanted the meeting to be official. Or perhaps he couldn't stand the stench we've created.

'We shan't meet again,' he says, and he extends his hand to me, but not to Rashid.

Back in our concrete cage, neither of us can quite believe what we have been told. It has, in a sense, happened too quickly. I don't think I'd ever thought through how we would be freed, even in my most optimistic moments, but it was a given that there would be some sort of lead-up, even if it were only a change of mood, slightly improved meals, hints of kindness from the guards. This is too sudden.

'Do you believe it?' Rashid asks me.

'That we'll be released? I've no reason not to. Why should he bother to come here and tell us a pack of lies?'

Rashid shrugs.

'I have heard of such things happening. They do it to break you. They build you up to think you're going to be free, then it turns out to be untrue, and it starts to drive you mad.'

'Why did you ask him to tell your family then?'

Rashid studies my face. I can't tell what he is looking for. Does he think I'm angry with him?

'Because it might be true, Steve,' he says. 'I might be too cynical. I might be wrong.'

Rashid has never entertained much hope, of course. He expects to die, here in the room, so it's natural that he is wary of unexpected promises that he'll soon be allowed to go. I'm tempted to say that with that sort of attitude, you can't lose. If nothing happens, it simply confirms what he's always said. If he's released, it won't matter that he's wrong because it will be a wonderful surprise, all the more intense for being contrary to his expectations. I wish, in some ways, I could share his attitude. It is, if you like, a safe way to look at things, the win-win position.

But I need to believe in the visitor, that it's true he is negotiating our freedom. It's what I always said would one day happen and without that hope, what is the point of opening your eyes in the morning?

I was drinking more than was good for me, I know that now, but I was having a good time. More often than not, the alcohol made me pass out, but I did get angry occasionally and shout at Twig. She would keep asking me the same question. *How much do you love me, Steve?* What was I meant to say? Should I have got out my ruler and said *this much.* If I'd been kind, a tad more sensitive, I would have recognized her fear. She was pregnant and afraid of being left to handle it on her own. That's exactly what I did. I abandoned her.

After she left, when I'd let her go out in the rain, I got drunk. I knew the two guys upstairs, Ralph and Jag, kept a bottle of Teachers in their bedroom. They'd gone out and left their door unlocked.

For hours I sat in the darkness, drinking neat whisky. I liked the rough burn of it as it slid down my throat. I liked the rising sensation through my body, the door opening in my head. It felt good.

I was confident that I knew what would happen. She'd said I could find her at her mother's, her parting words, rain streaming off her face. But I didn't think she'd have the guts to go home, not with a baby beginning to show. My guess was she'd head for my parents' house. They'd interrogate her, gently at first, but making it absolutely clear that the tariff for B&B with Edward and Cara was information about their son's whereabouts. Cough it up with the chicken bones.

So I had to go. After a while.

I finished the whisky. I thought about throwing the few things I had into my rucksack and leaving right then, but I was so pissed I couldn't move my legs. They felt like they were railways sleepers laid out in parallel, heavy as hell. I'd go in the morning. They wouldn't arrive too early. I just needed to be out when they did.

The conspicuousness of it, the downright drunken display, still amazes me. How could they not see it? I tried to hide it, of course. I hid the cans and the bottles in the drawer under my bed and the sunken tray on top of my wardrobe, and I did most of my drinking late at night after they'd gone to bed. But even so. In the morning, by the time I got up, one of them would probably be away in London and the other rehearsing with a 'Do Not Disturb' notice on the door. I'd get up and with luck we wouldn't meet until late afternoon or early evening, by when I'd usually got over most of my hangover.

Even so.

There were times when I'd get home from the pub and start drinking again in my room, and I'd be throwing up in the bathroom at three in the morning, right next door to them. They must have heard. Maybe they thought it was usual teenage behaviour. They'd be pretty drunk themselves, on their wine, and perhaps they decided it had happened once too often to be worth making an issue of it any more.

Even so.

It wasn't just the hit. The taste was what I craved as much as the alcohol. Whichever booze you choose, it has a taste, an interior flavour like nothing else. There's nothing can imitate it. Addiction is all about the lack of substitutes. There are no effective substitutes for tobacco or sex or heroin, and if I'd succeeded in kicking the drink for the buzz, my mouth would still have been screaming for the taste of it. There was no way I could do without it for a single day, not then. I might postpone it for a few hours, to avoid discovery or just to test myself, but I always knew that ring was waiting to be pulled. There was a pleasure in holding off. Delayed gratification, like denying myself *Time* magazine here. Not everyone can do it, but I could. I always said that meant I wasn't a real drunk. Real drunks, who hung around the bus station in the centre of town, had two distinguishing features: they drank cheap sherry on good days and cider on bad, and they needed a constant fix. Not like me then.

I called them from a red phone box. It had been raining that day too. Somehow I managed to wait for it to clear. Then I went out and found the phone. I was cold. I had no coat. I stood in the old iron and glass cubicle and shivered while I tried to remember the number to dial. I was hoping it would be Dad who answered.

I'd been drinking all afternoon. Whisky. Not my usual stuff, but one of the guys upstairs had left some lying around again and it was just too easy. I sat on the mattress in the double room at the front of the house and worked my way down the bottle. It was good quality, and it looked so beautiful in the glass. Once the rain eased and a cold sun poured in at the window, I could see specks of light flitting about in the amber liquid. There was something cosy and reassuring about it.

I don't know when exactly that changed. I began to feel ve isolated and lonely. There was no one else around and I'd no i if they'd be coming back later. We kept ourselves to ourselves in that house, all of us junkies of one kind or another. I remember picking up the whisky bottle and looking at it. Three quarters of it had gone. I remember I screwed the cap on, and I tightened it so hard the threads tore. I suppose it was a way of saying to myself: no more!

Then I began to feel really bad: shivering, but frightened as well. I thought something terrible was going to happen to me. I decided I had to get away from the house. The house, I was sure, was tied up with it. If bad things were on the way, they'd happen here, in the house.

I was stumbling about, trying to steady myself enough to leave the room. If I could just get out of the room, I'd be nearer the front door and the street outside. I kept hitting my arms, then my shoulders, against the doorframe. It seemed to be in the way and unavoidable. It was like I was rocking from side to side on the threshold, unable to move forward. It seemed to require a supreme effort, a monumental act of will to propel myself into the hallway. I clung to the wall, running my hand over the bumpy wallpaper. I was so conscious of the colour of it, the feel of it, the ribbed pale green surface. If I held on to it and followed it as far as it went, I would find the front door.

The house was huge, above me and behind me, a vast echoing mansion it felt like. I knew it was speaking to me, urging me to stay in that seductive baritone voice it had. But I knew that was wrong. It was trying to allay my fears, but in reality it wanted to keep me prisoner, possibly to kill me.

I escaped through the heavy front door. How I opened it I don't ﾑow. How I found the phone box I don't know. It must have been ﾑrinted somewhere in my memory.

I stumbled to my knees. The pavement was wet, dark brown shiny wet and my hands felt cold as I pushed down and slid myself up the dribbling side wall of the red phone box.

This door was heavy too. I thought I would never open it. I had to use both hands and, as I pulled, I could still hear the voice of the house.

I shivered inside and dialled. I remember it like it was yesterday. I screamed into the phone.

'Help me, Dad! Please help me!'

He said something. I don't remember what, and I was afraid he wasn't listening, so I shouted again.

'You need to come and get me, Dad.'

I was crying into the phone and pleading with him and I couldn't hear anything he was saying.

Some days confinement gets to you more than others. During the light hours it's always stifling, stinking, maddening, but there are some days when I feel desperate for fresh air and open spaces, when I think I could throw myself against a wall and burst through it like a bulldozer. When it gets to you like that, you can't sit still. I roam around the room, punching my left hand with my right. I talk to myself. Rashid might just as well not be there. 'I've got to get out of here, got to get out-of-here.' My hands stray over the walls. What do I think I'll find? A handle? That I'll pull down and the wall will swing away, allowing me to step out into a busy street or a daisy strewn meadow? Or perhaps, in my unconscious, I believe in the power of touch, that I can magic away the wall by stroking it and reciting some baritone incantation.

It always ends the same way. I walk and walk, and the low mumble turns into a scream, and I fall on my knees and rhythmical beat my head against the door. No one comes. They know this behaviour, the acting out of despair, and they know now to ignore it. Not worth a stubbed out half-smoked cigarette or the effort of shouting at me. I'm just not worth the trouble.

I feel the welling up of long dry tears. They create a sense of pressure behind my eyes, but no wetness, no release. They are imprisoned tears and I can't let them out.

Rashid stays quiet. He has his own moments of despair, more often than mine in fact. He knows what it's like, that there's nothing he can say that will make a difference. I have to go through it. He has to watch in empathetic silence. We used to apologise to each other for these outbursts, as though they were rude or embarrassing. Now, we say nothing. They are just accepted as part of our life here.

Time passes. The mood changes. I don't know how much time has passed, and there's no point in consulting my watch. The sort of time I'm talking about has nothing to do with chromatic time. This is time you feel. It's more like the time you experience waiting for a bus or on the phone waiting to be put through to the next available 'agent' or, as a child, waking up far too early on Christmas morning and longing for dawn.

It is time we have to fill.

Eleven in the morning. It might be a little earlier. The sun is not at its highest. Rashid has suggested that we play our game, or rather that he would like me to play it.

It takes me a few minutes to find my story. Then Holly steps into the bar at the British Film Institute and it's crowded and noisy, with too few tables. The queue for drinks is three deep.

She has heels on. She loves heels. These are green.

I can see her from where I stand, at the window overlooking the National Theatre. It's odd seeing someone you know at a distance. She is unaware of me. She looks angry. Impatient perhaps, not angry. It enhances her sexuality. She's trying to get to the long, oval bar. Her body is taut, tensed to move. I want her.

This is how it should have been, how I once fantasised it would have developed.

'You are very passionate today,' Rashid remarks.

Perhaps I have offended him. I promised to temper what I say about Holly, the sex stuff, but it's the first time I have seen her clearly in several days.

She orders a large white wine, which costs her seven pounds, and as she is in the process of handing over her card, I call out 'Edelweiss', from the back of the queue. The woman behind the bar is irritated, but she serves the beer, and Holly weaves her way with the drinks through a knot of six or seven people to reach me.

'You can get the next lot!'

I seem to lean through ninety degrees to give her a peck on the cheek.

'Word got round!'

Rashid steps into my story.

'What does this mean?' he asks. 'Word got round?'

I explain that she visited this bar when it first opened and there was scarcely anyone there. So, like everyone else who tried the place in that opening week, she told all her friends how wonderful and empty it was.

Now, there are no unoccupied tables. So we lean on a stretch of the bar where they keep a variety of breads and olives and small white dishes filled with oil.

'What is this British Film Institute?' Rashid asks.

'It's a cinema. A movie house.'

'What is the movie you are seeing?'

'*Three Colours Blue*. Made in '93, by a Polish director called Kieslowski. It's in French. I'm trying to please Holly by going to see a foreign movie. To prove I'm not a complete philistine.'

'Who's in it?'

'Juliette Binoche.'

'I've not heard of her.'

'Beautiful woman.'

'Why is it called *Three Colours Blue*?'

'It's part of a trilogy: blue, white and red, the colours of the French flag, and each film explores one of the ideals of the Revolution. Liberty, Equality, Fraternity. This one's freedom.'

'Is that why you are imagining this story, Steve? It's about freedom.'

'Maybe.'

We enter the theatre at 7.30.

The grey of autumn, lonely buildings in the French countryside, unresolved feelings of grief: Holly loves it.

'And you, Steve?' Rashid asks.

'It's okay.'

'Is Juliette Binoche in all three?' Rashid asks.

'No, sadly. Just the first.'

'That is a pity.'

We have moved. Holly and I are walking along a wide paved embankment, the Houses of Parliament lit up in the distance, on the far side of the river. There is so much space, so much sky. Infinity of these.

I look over to Rashid, trapped here, hugging his knees in our cell.

'And you, Rashid? Who's in your story?'

'I have no story.'

'Not even your grandmother?'

'I can see no one.'

'You must be able to see someone. Try, Rashid. That's how we play.'

'I can see Holly. You have given me such a picture. I can see *her*. But no one of my own. I'm sorry.'

It's Rashid's turn to crave open space. He has had enough. He is convinced that the visit we had from the Great Man, with his kara-kul, was no more than a sham, intended to mess with our emotions and stir up false hope. He's even more sure than he was that we will not be released and that, one day, we will be killed. He says he has no alternative but to try to escape. I'm reassured that he feels fit again. It's futile talking to him about the risks because his mind's made up. In my view, his only prospect of escaping is if we work together, so I have offered to help him. We both know that the chances are that only one of us will get away. The decision is hard, but I am in no doubt that Rashid is desperate. His need is greater than mine. His faith is less than mine. However, if we're given the opportunity to make a break for it together, I will of course take it.

We have one point in the week when we can do it. We have been told we must take thirty minutes' regular exercise in the garden at the rear. My hope is that this is preparatory to our release. If not, it will nonetheless do us good, and it's the only time when the two of us will be together and outside this room. From now on, we are to be escorted through the outer office and along the corridor to the door that exits onto the yard. When we were first ordered to exercise, two guards accompanied us and observed us throughout the half hour. But now that we have persuaded them that we can behave as they would like, just one of them takes playground duty. He watches us complacently and sometimes wanders off to the far end of the garden to smoke a cigarette. At that point, he is a good twenty metres from the door in the garden wall, which Rashid knows leads out onto an empty square. The door is locked, but the wooden cross-struts would provide good ledges or footholds for anyone trying to climb up. From the upper strut, it must be less than a metre to the top of the wall.

The guard is approaching our room.

'Good luck!'

Rashid smiles, and then we shake hands before the door is unlocked.

As we walk towards the garden, I am hoping that none of our nervousness is visible to the guard. I feel it's running over my body like sweat. I have been under fire, but this bid for freedom rattles me in a much more aggressive and personal way. Fortunately, it is not Guard One on duty. He would talk to us, which would only make our fear more apparent.

We step through the door into the open air. I don't suppose my father, when he performed at the White House, felt any more ecstatic or terrified than I do at this very moment. It wipes out reason. I feel filled with determination that Rashid will get away.

We take our time and walk together around the garden. We keep to the pavement and talk quietly, trying to impress on the guard that this is a normal exercise period, nothing out of the ordinary. For perhaps ten minutes or so, he remains close to us, but eventually he sidles off to the other end and lights up.

My job is to distract him. He speaks no English, so I can't depend on conversation. Somehow I must make him turn away, if only for a few seconds. I pat Rashid quickly on the shoulder and start to make my way up the garden.

The guard is surprised. He drops his cigarette and grinds it out. He's staring directly at me, suspicious.

'I have a problem with my knee.'

He doesn't understand, and shrugs to tell me so.

'I'm worried it might be infected.'

He's clearly puzzled, but he seems to think I am mad rather than devious.

'Look!'

I bend to show him my injured knee, hoping he will follow my move. He hesitates. Then he leans forward to see what it is I'm talking about. I can hear the scrabbling at the other end of the garden. I daren't turn, but I know it's the sound of Rashid's feet struggling for a foothold. The guard hears it too. He pushes me aside and I fall onto the pavement. Rashid has one leg over the wall, clear blue sky above him. The guard is running over the small patch of grass and pulling out his gun. Rashid jumps. He's out, away. The guard searches his pockets for his keys. Time is against him. These are vital minutes in which Rashid is running, finding I hope a place to hide.

I hear the lock turn. The guard opens the door and steps out. Everything falls silent.

It has been four hours now, and every hour that passes is another that Rashid is free. That's how I see it. I have decided that if he avoids being captured for six hours, he will have got away. I don't know why I have settled on six, but I'm convinced. Six hours of freedom will mean that he's eluded all their efforts to find him.

The afternoon has been exceptionally warm, especiall

February. My chest and back are wet with sweat and I feel a kind of clammy weight pressing on me. My face is on fire. It seems to burn from inside out. I wish I could sleep.

I am searching for hope, wherever I can find it. There are places I associate with hope, places where humanity has comforted me. In the tight heat, transfixed by fear for Rashid, I want to play our game. Again. To escape into the kind of fantasy that has sustained us here. I want to leap through the walls of our cell and join Holly and Tim. We'll slide across white ice behind Somerset House, drink blue cocktails at the Hilton, buy bright fruit 'n' veg in Borough Market, anything that fills my mind with colour and joy.

But I'm not in London, but Salisbury, and not with Holly or Tim.

With my father. In the cathedral. 6 The Close. Odd that a cathedral has an address with a number.

We are seated in the choir stalls. It is evensong. He says it will calm me down.

Choral music invariably rises. Naturally. It ascends to the cathedral roof. The roof is so high I can hardly see all the way to it. Slim columns of grey stone, pale and perfect, reaching up to narrow arches.

My neck aches, from leaning backwards to look up, but there is a thrill to being caught up in the music, overtaken by it. It is the purest sound you'll ever hear, as pure as a mountain burn.

John Taverner, he explains. Sixteenth century.

They sing in perfect unison, voices tied to one another, twined within each other, overlapping, sewn together. The song flows from them and around them and above them, filling this vast space with harmony.

I am here near to tears.

'Pull yourself together,' he says, harshly.

How exquisitely wrong he is to say that. Doesn't he realise these are tears to be pitied, ironic tears, contrasting the abject and the sublime, the cell that is my life and the cathedral that is the game?

The music courses through me, but I still feel the damp shreds of my shirt on my back, the grit under my palms. I still smell the fetor of daily sweat and excreta, still hear the hard steel of doors slammed shut.

The music envelops me, but it can't save me, not any more.

The time has come and gone for our daily meal. Nothing has been said, but I take it this is my punishment for my part in Rashid's escape. If I only suffer a few hunger pains, I shall count myself lucky. I was expecting a severe beating. That may be yet to come, of course.

There are three flies buzzing in the ceiling. They seem to chase each other from one corner to another, random and ineffectual flights that expend huge effort and are regardless of the heat. I can't understand them. They make no sense. They irritate me with their insistent noise and skittishness.

Every time I hear voices in the outer office I am rigid with fear. The voices are agitated. I don't know what they're saying, but they sound impatient with each other. I fear they may take it out on me, their frustration with not catching Rashid. Or, worse, I fear they already have him and are discussing what to do, what brutal and degrading act to commit. At any minute, the door may burst open and they'll throw him in, beaten and bloody.

I try to read. *Time* magazine hasn't a weak article, but in my present state, not one of them engages me. I started reading piece about the Dead Sea Scrolls, about a scholar in Ame who doubts that they were written by the Essenes, a first century Jewish sect who lived in the desert. The article is passionately argued, but I'm thinking: who cares? I mean, there's a man running through the streets in fear of his life, and there's this scholar, Baumann, in Chicago or some such place, worrying about things that happened two thousand years ago. And his stuff is so important it makes *Time* magazine. Rashid could be shot dead in the time it takes me to read the article and no one would give a damn or write a word.

I don't get it. I don't understand how the world decides its priorities. It seems to me lives are cheap until they're history and then they may become special. Everyone tries to work out what the game plan was, how they came to die, the events that led up to it I mean, and what the purpose was. People think that's important to know. Hundreds of years later. Who cares?

I was the one who kept asking for reading matter, and now I can't read any of it.

Maybe it'll be different tomorrow. I'll probably feel different. My concentration will be better.

It's all so slow, waiting for a result that may never be announced. Nothing happening would be a result, wouldn't it? Nothing fucking happening here would mean that Rashid really had got away. Fucking marvellous.

I'd like him to pop in, just for a moment, and say 'I did it. I got away. See ya, Steve.'

I've often thought I'd have gone mad in here without Rashid. I've never been much of a one for my own company. I don't mind t for a bit, after a long day on duty with the lads. Under those cumstances, I quite enjoy being alone. I'll grab a coke from the ze, pull out a CD, relax. That's fine. But after an hour or two,

I've had enough and I'm glad to be back to work or down the mess for a chat and a bite to eat.

Strangely enough, I think I coped better with being on my own when I was younger. Not true of most things. Generally, I deal with life in a far more organised and reasonable way than I used to. But solitude, when I was seventeen, seemed to fit with the unhappiness I felt there was in my life. I had friends I saw. I saw them a lot. But I kind of retreated into myself at the same time and I didn't let on half of what I was thinking. I kept so much to myself. I kept it for when I was alone in my bedroom. I suppose teenagers are like that, but I had a bad case of it.

Five hours. Is that all? Five fucking hours. I feel I've been rattling around in my head for days. Thousands of thoughts and they occupied just sixty minutes. I will go fucking mad. I'm telling you.

It's getting dark. I have the usual sense that the light outside has faded and gone, and the temperature has definitely dropped. The sweat on my chest and back is now a cold damp. It feels colder than normal. That clear blue sky Rashid jumped into has left no cloud cover to hold in the warmth. I'll need all my newspapers tonight and I'll probably swipe Rashid's as well.

I'm not religious. That is to say, I am not a churchgoer. But I can't stop myself praying. It's more than hoping, more than that superstitious thing of throwing a can at the bin and promising yourself a win on the lottery if you get it in. No, what's shaping in my mind is a prayer. I'm asking you. What do I mean? God? Okay, I'm asking you, God, to save Rashid, to help him get away from these bastards. Let him run like the wind. Let him fly through the crowds and the streets like a bird. Let him be reunited, safely, with his wife and children. Let him find happiness.

6

2003

Over the following days they hoped that they would hear from Stephen, but there was nothing. Cara telephoned their local hospitals, the two in the area that had A&Es, but neither had a record of a 'Stephen Padgett' or of anyone fitting his description. Their GP, Paul Denning, hadn't been approached either.

Every now and again, Edward phoned Tim, whose anxiety increased with each conversation they had. Edward tried to reassure him by reminding him that it was only a matter of days since Twig had last seen Stephen and he was alive and reasonably well then. He didn't mention the possibility that he'd become ill, not sure himself that half-clothed men deep into drugs could be relied upon.

It was difficult to work. Cara now had the discipline of rehearsals to attend and she seemed, he felt, to go off happily enough to them, even with some enthusiasm. The part of Mary was a big break for her, which made it hardly surprising that her excitement occasionally got in the way of her worry.

He walked into the kitchen and yanked a bottle of Sancerre from the fridge door.

There were some consolations, in the garden but chiefly in sic, music for pleasure, MFP. The letters were so evocative, Id label on which he'd recorded many a time when he was young and cheap to hire. Did it still exist? You could buy a Tchaikovsky symphony or a Berlioz, usually the biggies, for fourteen and six. Nothing.

He took a swig of wine.

Why, in God's name, had Stephen done this? Why now? Why at *this* moment, when Edward's diary had never been more crowded, when his career was at its zenith, striking its top notes? There was even talk of dates in America, this coming autumn, concerts in New York, Washington and San Francisco.

It was, of course, characteristically, selfish. One interpretation of Stephen's behaviour over the years was that he enjoyed the thrill of deviancy, the fast pulse of not knowing whether he would get caught. The other was that it could all be reduced to attention-seeking, a personality flaw that ran right through his family. He'd seen it in Cara's mother, and Cara had identified it long ago in her grandmother, a refusal to allow conversation, the preoccupations of the family, ever to stray from *self* for more than a few minutes. Stephen had bathed in the limelight when he was a small child, the day to day celebration of his life, his mother's apparently unending surprise and delight. Did he do no wrong? Or did his infant charm mask any wrongdoing?

At any rate, Edward and Cara thought they were blessed.

Stephen's friend, Andy, called one morning to say that he thought he'd seen Stephen coming out of a house on Wordsworth Avenue, near the town centre in Petersfield. He couldn't remember the number, but he was sure that it had a green door and a satellite dish. Cara wanted to know why Andy hadn't gone up to Stephen, spoken to him. Andy couldn't explain.

'Perhaps I shouldn't go to rehearsal?' Cara said. She stood in the hall, her satchel of music and a book to read on the train on her arm, ready to take a taxi to the station.

The question struck him as rhetorical.

'No, no,' he said. 'I'm sure he won't be there. Silly for you to miss rehearsals. You go.'

She kissed him peremptorily on the cheek and shut the door behind her. He caught the sound of the rain as she stepped outside.

He contemplated waking Twig, who was asleep upstairs. She would want to come with him if she knew what he was doing, but he wasn't at all sure he wanted her with him. It might be better, calmer, if he went alone. He would leave her a note on the kitchen table.

Wordsworth Avenue turned out to be a long and busy road connecting the high street in Petersfield to the ring road. There must have been three hundred houses of differing periods and architectures flanking the two wide, tree-lined pavements. Edward drove up and down, mindful of green doors and satellite dishes, but on the look-out, above all, for any houses that were run down, less cared for, their paint chipped, a window boarded up. He'd driven the length of the road three or four times before he was convinced that there were no such properties. Everything looked neat and prosperous on Wordsworth Avenue.

At the far end, the ring road end, there was a row of shops and spaces to park your car. He left the Volvo next to an old Peugeot, took an umbrella out of his boot and started to walk back down the street. As he walked, he realised that he'd been aking the big, and probably wholly wrong, assumption that because Andy had seen Stephen coming out of a house, Stephen must be living there. But he could well have been visiting. Perhaps he knew people who owned expensive places. Perhaps he had well-to-do friends.

There was a satellite dish on every second or third house. He had yet to find a green door.

The umbrella provided little protection. The rain slashed his face and streamed off the bottom of his coat onto the thighs of his trousers. Within minutes, he felt soaked through, wet cloth clinging to his legs like a poultice. He walked on, not thinking about his discomfort, hoping that he wasn't wasting his time.

He could very easily have missed what appeared to be the only green door on Wordsworth Avenue, at the town end, a matter of seconds from the high street. Without entirely being aware of doing so, he'd dismissed it before he'd properly seen it, firstly because there was no satellite dish attached to the house and, more obviously, because of a large sign staked into a terrace near the front wall that said 'The Petersfield Clinic'.

He'd walked straight past it, but then something, a different sense, took him back. The clinic, whatever it was, did indeed have a green door. The satellite dish was to be found on the house next door, but if he'd been passing in a car, Andy could be forgiven for confusing the two. It was odd, though, that he'd not noticed, or failed to mention, the large sign.

At the door, Edward hesitated. He wasn't sure quite what he should ask, how he should put it. If Stephen had been to the clinic, his visit would have been confidential. He might also have used a false name.

He entered the building and went up to the reception, still uncertain what to say.

'I...'

'Do you have an appointment?'

She was one of three receptionists, blonde, with a high-necked rust jumper and red-framed glasses with small lenses. She seemed to sit behind a wall of light oak and computers.

'No, I don't have an appointment. I wanted to ask about my son.'

'Is he a patient here?'

'I don't really know.'

'What's his name?'

'Stephen Padgett. He's nineteen.'

'What is it you want to know, Mr Padgett?'

A fair question to ask. What did he want to know? Put simply, it would be that Stephen was alive and well and contactable at the following address...

'It's actually a rather personal matter.'

'Would you like to see one of the doctors?'

'I'm anxious about him, you see.'

'Perhaps the Practice Manager could help. Take a seat and she'll be out to see you shortly.'

He felt fobbed off. He hadn't been able to explain himself quickly and succinctly, so she'd become impatient. She'd pass him on to the Practice Manager because she was paid to deal with problem clients, and receptionists weren't.

It was a quiet part of the morning. Only two people were in the waiting room, an elderly man who coughed continuously and a young woman, scarcely more than a teenager, with a baby in her arms. Her name was called over the tannoy as Edward ᴀt down. He thought about Twig.

The waiting room looked new. There were smart, wooden

chairs with blue cushions, which showed few signs of wear. A glass-topped table with today's newspapers spread over it ran the length of a leather sofa. Watercolours of rocky landscapes - Cornwall, he guessed – hung on the walls and a digital radio relayed Classic FM to the waiting patients.

He picked up the *Times* and thumbed through the pages. It read like an almanac, an anthology of statistics and speculation, trying to explain, on one hand, why the vast majority of computers had not gone haywire, against all prediction, at the turn of the millennium and, on the other, to predict why Al Gore would succeed Bill Clinton at the White House, rather than George W. Bush.

The radio announced Bach's cantata, *Was mir behegt, ist nur die muntre Jagd*, famous, the presenter said, for the ever-charming 'Sheep May Safely Graze'. Famous not like Mick Jagger or Clinton, but as a Christmas carol was famous, lightly buried in the shared culture, retrievable in sentimental moments. He thought about his tour. Would the Americans demand grazing sheep? Would the same compromise have to be made if he wished to sing what he regarded as his 'signature' Bach?

The Practice Manager proved to be a friendly, middle-aged woman, who popped her head around the door of her office and, puppet-like, called out 'Mr Padgett?'. She smiled, welcomingly.

They sat facing each other across a small table.

'I'm Helen Cadbury.'

She moved a vase of lilies and her opened laptop away from the centre of the desk to give her an uninterrupted view of Edward.

'I'm not a doctor,' she said.

'No, I understand that.'

'I gather you want to know whether your son – Stephen, isn't it? – recently visited the clinic?'

'That's right.'

'That information is, of course, confidential.'

Helen Cadbury leaned against the back of her chair, as though she'd said all that was required.

'I do appreciate that,' Edward said. 'Perhaps I should explain. My son. Stephen. He was living at home and then he left, suddenly. We have no idea where he's gone, whether he's alright. We simply want to establish that he's okay.'

'He's not contacted you?'

'No. Well, not for some weeks.'

Helen Cadbury turned to her laptop, entered a few letters and numbers, and studied the screen in front of her.

'What made you think he might have come here?'

'He was seen leaving here. By a friend.'

She appeared to scroll down several pages before finding what she was looking for.

'I take it, from what you're doing there, that he was here,' Edward said.

She paused on the keyboard and stared across the table.

'You said so yourself. His friend saw him. You said he was seen leaving here.'

'Yes. But he might have been mistaken. We'd just like to know.'

The click of the keys began again.

He thought about Twig, back at the house, reading his note and no doubt wondering what she was to do with herself while Edward was away. Although his concern, ethically, should be entirely focused on her, on her pregnancy and how she was to lead her life from now on, there had been something about the tall lad, in his shorts, which had left him with the fear that Stephen might be seriously ill. Why had he run out after them? All he'd had to say was that Stephen had mentioned that he was 'sick'. But he'd clearly thought it was important, something that Edward and Cara, and Twig, ought to know.

'Sick' was such an unhelpful epithet. Did he mean 'flu? Had he over-dosed?

'I don't think we were much help to him,' Helen Cadbury said.

He thought he heard Debussy, but it might be Satie. It was a confusion he'd made all his professional life. Piano, in the waiting room, muffled by Helen Cadbury's partition walls. He'd made a fool of himself several times over it, in pub quizzes, shouting out the answers to *University Challenge*.

'I probably shouldn't tell you, but we referred him to a dependency clinic just up the road.'

'For drugs?'

The Practice Manager was surprised, caught off her guard. She spoke without thinking.

'Not for drugs, Mr Padgett. Your son's problem isn't drugs. It's drink. Alcohol.'

It was like swimming in a river when it's in spate, searching the banks for overhanging trees, anything to grab hold of and pull you out of the racing flow. He could not make sense of it. He walked back to the car slowly, scarcely aware of the rain, and when he found the Volvo parked at the shops, he sat in it for a long time.

When had he seen Stephen drunk? No, that wasn't the

right question. Every father had seen his teenage son drunk from time to time. He'd seen Tim drunk. Didn't make him an alcoholic.

Stephen must have been drunk at The Rock the day he'd given him notice to quit. He'd reacted angrily, out of control, and Edward had wondered whether he'd taken some drug. But when else? In France? A few times.

Surely alcoholics were conspicuous, unable to conceal their habit. They slurred their words, left bottles about the place, fell over. They had red faces and they forgot about the routines of conventional appearance. Their clothes were stained. Their hair was long and unwashed.

None of this fitted Stephen, who was fit and attractive, and always well turned-out, according to the anti-style of his mates. But what did he know? He drank too much himself. The stack of empty bottles he took to re-cycling every week was testimony enough to that.

What was different about Stephen?

She hadn't meant it to happen. At least, she was almost sure that she hadn't, and certainly not in this way.

She looked across the bed at his naked back. It was hairier than Edward's, with outcrops of short, dark hair approximating to the shape of his shoulder blades. In principle, she disliked hairy backs, but they'd found themselves naked in front of each other before she'd given it a thought.

The sex had been good, neither perfunctory nor tediously long. He'd attended to her body, explored her, and she'd found it exciting. He had an experienced eagerness about him, which appealed.

Afterwards, he'd flung his arms out and said, 'That was fantastic'. Within five minutes, he was deeply asleep, hints of whistling in his out breaths.

They'd rehearsed from ten until two, a long session, but Cara had been keen to sing as much of the part as she could, to get an idea of Mary's development through the piece, her drama. The others had shown signs of needing their lunch by about one, and Karl, mindful of the need not to over-exert, had released them.

'Shall we go from *The Arrival in Saïs*?' he suggested. 'I'll mark Joseph.'

Her voice seemed to improve, now that they were alone. She hit each note with a vibrancy and precision that was like a form of happiness she'd never experienced before. She was singing for him, of course, proving her worth, the rightness of his decision to cast her. He stood not ten feet from her, in his baggy black trousers and worn-out black corduroy jacket, and appeared unmoved. He counted and he sang Joseph's part, and yet he scarcely looked at her. He must be listening, she thought. Everything depends on listening.

After an hour, he'd heard enough.

'Shall we have lunch?'

Before she could answer, he'd explained that his flat was a matter of yards away, just around the corner in Bow Street. He had pasta, fresh basil and tomatoes, garlic, and a Saint Véran cooling in the fridge that was not to be missed.

'Wonderful!' Cara found herself saying.

Had she realised what was in his mind, even as he invited her? It had registered earlier, when they became aware that they were left alone, together in that large rehearsal room, that the mood had changed, that they were conscious of each other in a new and heightened way. Had it struck her then that he might have 'plans' for her?

It was a Regency building, with a polished, winding banister up to the third floor. They climbed in silence, he ahead of her. She noticed the bald circles where the elbows of his jacket had leaned too many times on a lectern and the soft tread of his leather shoes on the amber carpet. For a heavy man, he carried his weight well, with elegance.

Every sound was as memorable and distinct to her as Berlioz's manuscript. She heard the lock of his front door trip as he turned the key and the door glided open, brushing a mat with the word 'Wilkommen' printed on it in black capitals. He opened the fridge and the Saint Véran knocked another bottle next to it as he took it out. She heard him open a drawer and the clatter of cutlery, the squeak of the cork rising in the neck until it sprang out with that unmistakeable pop, which never failed to produce a smile.

He handed her a glass and they drank. His face couldn't have been more than a foot from hers.

'Are you hungry?' he said.

He was looking straight into her eyes, then he kissed her mouth, firmly, holding her tight to him. Whatever reservations she'd had moments before vanished. She wasn't even thinking now.

Cara took the phone call from Edward as she was leaving Karl's flat. Edward was, of course, the last person she wanted to hear from, reminding her far too abruptly of her life at home, of what she'd done, of her missing son. She pushed the centre button to accept the call, but felt, as she did it, a powerful sense of nemesis, a sense that what Edward had to tell her would be a punishment for her unfaithfulness.

'The good news is that he's still somewhere in the Petersfield area.'

'And the bad?'

'He has a drinking problem.'

Edward allowed the shock of it to sink in before trying to explain any more.

'Drinking?' Cara said. 'We never thought of drink.'

'No.'

'It's such a surprise.'

'Yes,' Edward said, 'though given our own habits, it hardly should be.'

'No.'

It was like stepping off a carousel, or perhaps a waltzer, at a funfair and re-discovering ordinary life again. However much you had been flung around, your body pinioned against the back seat, the sense of speed rushing through you, once it stopped, once your fragile legs began to work again and you lifted yourself from the car and started to walk away from the ride, it was, almost in an instant, a memory. She tried to hold on to the details, to the sounds and sensations, but they were going, taking their place in the past, even as she overcame her reluctance to speak to Edward.

'How do you know this?' she asked.

'The house with the green door turned out to be a doctors' clinic. He went to see them.'

'They told you?'

'Not so much of the detail, but enough.'

'And?'

'They referred him to a rehab clinic in town.'

'Have you been there?'

'Not yet.'

'Why not? Have you called them?'

'No.' Edward's voice changed. 'Just hang on a minute, Cara. I've done as much as I could in the time I had. They weren't exactly keen to talk to me at the clinic, you know.'

'Yes, yes, I'm sorry.'

A small apology, easily said, for being insensitive. She wondered whether she would find herself, at some distant time, making a much more significant apology for that day and with far less chance of its acceptance. As yet, she had no idea when, and if, that apology would be necessary or for how much, or to be accurate, how many times.

'What are you going to do?'

'I was rather hoping you would take over from here. I've got rehearsals. I should really catch a train at four.'

'I'm sorry, Edward, but I've got rehearsals too.'

She wanted to run back into the building, race back up the stairs to his flat, be in bed with him again.

'Can't you duck them? This is important, you know.'

His tone was hurt, rather obviously so. It protested that he had spent the entire morning trying to find their son and, at least, securing some valuable information about him. What had she done? Gone off to sing, enjoy herself. It was her turn.

'I…'

'What is the rehearsal anyway?' he demanded. 'I thought you said you'd be through by lunchtime.'

'I'll come home.'

'Well, which is it? Is there a rehearsal or not?'

'I'll come home.'

She closed the top of her mobile to end the conversation, the interrogation to which she had no truthful answers.

If she ran to the tube, she could make the 3.55.

They had not discussed what, if anything, they should tell Timothy. It would be an appalling shock for him. Even though he had been, in every conventional sense, the higher achiever, he'd always looked up to his brother. Tim admired Stephen for being everything he wasn't: an outlaw, unintimidated by the need to succeed.

Drinkers, on the other hand, were difficult to squeeze into the category of hero. There were Richard Burton, W C Fields, Dylan Thomas, Malcolm Lowry. Some of the old movie actors and writers could pull it off, at least until it began to show on screen, until the papers began to take more than a passing interest. Then every stumble was a news item.

Perhaps it wouldn't be a shock for him. It was conceivable that Tim already knew. Perhaps he'd been keeping it a secret from them.

Either way, they would have to talk soon.

The train swept through outer London suburbs and appeared to burst into the Hampshire countryside as if a border had been crossed into a new state. The trees and fields hung in a gloom of cloud and imminent night, and headlights coursed up and down the hills like the warm glow of sound waves crossing continents or the vacancies of space. Despite the dismal thought that there was nothing about home to look forward to, she felt comforted by the prospect.

Part of her could not accept that what Edward had said was true. She searched her memory and simply could not find the evidence. Why would Stephen want to drink? Whenever he'd been offered wine with a meal – something she and Edward had begun to do when he was fifteen, on the principle that temperate drinking, with food and in company, would introduce him to a civilised way to drink alcohol and might stick – he'd declined it, politely, not openly wishing to dampen their own enjoyment, but for all that with a persistent hint of disapproval. Both sons believed their parents drank too much.

How would he have started?

Back at the cottage, she found the name of the rehab clinic and telephoned. The woman at the other end was adamant that no information could be given out regarding patients.

'I simply want to find out whether my son *is* one of your patients.'

'That too would be confidential.'

Cara thought about driving over there, but the likelihood was that she'd have no more success face to face. It was scarcely credible that a mother could be so thoroughly excluded from her son's life. Why did all the right, the power, lie with them, with the clinic and with Stephen? Didn't she have rights too?

It felt like stalemate. Half way through the day they'd appeared to make some progress: a recent sighting and an explanation, however hard to believe, for his behaviour. But now that it was dark and the clinic closed, they could go no further. There were no useful leads to where Stephen might be living, no clues to what his state of health might be. Was he getting help?

On an impulse, she rang Timothy's school and left a message asking him to ring her. She would invite him down for the weekend. If he could escape the clutches of school not too late on the Friday afternoon, he could meet her at the rehearsal rooms and they'd travel on to Hampshire from there. She looked forward to it. Timothy, at least, seemed to be so far problem-free.

He rang soon after eight.

'Anything wrong?'

'No, darling, nothing. I was thinking you might like to come home this weekend.'

'Can't. Rugby.'

'Couldn't you get out of it, sweetheart? Your father and I would love to see you.'

'Is anything the matter, Mum? Have you heard from Steve?'

Cara realised that she was on the verge of crying and that Tim must be able to hear it in her voice. She couldn't imagine why she felt this way. Was it disappointment? Worry?

'I'm fine, darling, really, and no, we haven't heard anything.'

'I could pretend to be sick.'

'I don't want you to have to lie to anyone.'

'It wouldn't be a lie. I'm feeling pretty rough as it is. Everyone's got colds and flu here. They wouldn't be surprised if I went down with it.'

'Do they let you go home if you're ill?'

''Course.'

That seemed to settle it. Timothy would develop a nasty cough over the next forty-eight hours, at the end of which he would declare himself unfit for the school match on Saturday. Then he'd ask for a weekend exeat, explaining that his parents were particularly keen for him to have his illness at home.

Cara felt more delighted than she'd expected. She left Edward a message on his mobile, telling him that Tim would be joining them on Friday evening and that he should keep the weekend free of commitments.

The mood at home would be different. Tim would be there by now, providing his own brand of resentful, teenage anxiety.

He put on the car radio, punched the button for Radio 3 and recognized Berlioz at once. Colin Davis conducting the London Symphony Orchestra and Chorus. Not *L'Enfance du Christ* – that would have been too much of a coincidence – but the *Requiem*, the start of it. Dark, brooding violin, alone in the dark, then voices, male voices, marching through a dense, dark, pine forest, soon joined by other voices, female, moving more swiftly, grim, without hope.

Edward felt tempted to turn around and drive back to London. He allowed himself to fantasise about a night without worry, of fun, dare he say it. A number of the singers at the rehearsal were planning to meet up for an Indian meal at a place in Kensington. They'd invited him. He'd said he had to get back because of his son, but they'd be happy if he suddenly turned up. The thought of some Tandoori dish, nan bread and a pint of lager appealed, made him feel seriously hungry. He could get drunk, crash out on someone's sitting room sofa.

But it was, of course, just fantasy, nothing more. A symphonic fantasy.

Insistent mournful voices, hard rhythms, like the wind-screen wipers.

He turned into the drive shortly before eight. There were ts on in the kitchen, and in Twig's room above it, but apparently nowhere else in the house. He imagined Twig alone, possibly tearful, unprepared to listen any longer to Tim's unrelenting scorn down below. Oh, wasn't it just great to be home!

He parked up, grabbed his coat from the back seat and pulled it over his head, then ran through the rain.

To his surprise, there was not a row in the kitchen. Cara was by herself, peeling potatoes in the sink.

'Where's Tim?'

'In the loo,' Cara replied, taken aback by his urgency. 'Don't you say hello anymore?'

'Sorry.'

He went over, put his arms around her and kissed her cheek.

'How's he been?'

'Tim? Fine. We've been talking.'

Cara wiped her face with her arm and started to drop the peeled potatoes into a pan of water.

'And he's alright?'

'Seems to be. He's upset, of course, but I don't think it's as much of a surprise for him as it was for us.'

'I did wonder. And Twig?'

'Watching a video in her room. She said she was tired.'

'Fine. Drink?'

He was already at the fridge, cutting the metal cap from the bottleneck.

'I've been resisting,' Cara said. 'I felt guilty.'

'Nonsense.'

He placed two glasses on the dresser and half filled them with white wine.

'It's not our fault, this.'

'And whose fault do you think it is exactly, Dad?'

Tim was standing in the doorway, hands in his pockets.

'Hello, Tim.'

Edward went to embrace him, but Tim backed away.

'Whose fault?'

'Do we have to blame someone?'

'It sounds to me as if you already have. Sounds to me like you think it's all Steve's fault.'

He hung back in the door, apparently reluctant to enter the room.

'You knew about it? At least, I assume you did. We didn't, you see.'

'I knew a bit. I'd seen him drunk a few times.'

'Why don't you sit down, have a beer. We can talk about this.'

'I don't want a beer.'

He said it with such scorn, as if to suggest that they were re-enacting a scene with Stephen, one of the early scenes, in which he'd started to acquire a taste for alcohol. Is that how Tim saw it? Did he think that Edward's hospitality, his occasional offer of a beer or a glass of wine with Sunday lunch, was the cause of Stephen's problem?

Tim had sat down at the table. It was laid for supper, four place settings, four wine glasses, tumblers for water, if desired. Tim turned a fork round in his hand.

'He didn't believe you cared about him,' he said.

Cara stopped what she was doing and laughed.

'Don't be ridiculous, Timothy! We couldn't have given more time to trying to keep that boy on the straight and narrow.'

'That's my point.'

'What point?' Edward demanded. 'I don't understand. Talk sense.'

'That's all you were concerned about. Trying to make him behave. You didn't want to know why he did the things he did.'

'That's simply not true.'

Edward began to feel agitated. He wasn't sure whether it was anger at the unreasonableness of what Tim was saying or the pain of realising how distorted Stephen's perspective had sometimes been.

'He never really adapted to school,' Cara said. 'I tried to socialise him when he was small. He went to nurseries. I invited all the neighbours' children round, but frankly the truth was he wasn't happy if he wasn't the centre of attention.'

Tim looked up, incredulous.

'Did it not occur to you to ask why that was?'

'It wasn't for want of loving him, if that's what you're getting at,' Cara said.

'Sure.'

'What do you mean by that?'

'You know.'

'No, I don't. What do you mean by that?'

Tim refused to reply.

'What did you mean?'

Edward had had enough. He felt the need of fresh air. He stepped out of the back door and immediately felt a cold wind on his face. The rain had eased away in the half hour or so he'd been home and the sky was now a deep, navy blue and almost cloudless. He walked across the gravel to the Volvo and opene the passenger door to retrieve the papers he'd left on the se

He slipped them into a pocket in his jacket, closed the door again and locked the car.

Their voices were audible, but he couldn't make out a single word. What he heard was human, angry, hurt as well, condemning and protesting. He could tell all that from the different tones, the rise and fall of shouting, the cadences of the row. He didn't need to hear intelligible words to understand what was going on. Their voices at a distance were like shadow puppets, intonation mimicking their meaning.

It was really too cold to stay outside. He'd begun to shiver. Going back in, though, would mean taking part. As soon as he stepped into the kitchen, the conversation, if that was what you could call it, would swing towards him. It might come in the form of an accusation, or they might demand that he give them his opinion, his version of events. Either way, he would be fallible.

He might have remained in the courtyard a little longer, but the telephone rang, and he thought he should be the one to answer it. It might break the spell of anger and reproach. He went in, crossed the room to the corner where the kettle stood on a stand next to a water filter and the phone was attached to the wall above. He picked it up.

'Dad!'

'Stephen?'

'I need help.'

'Where are you?'

'I need your help really badly, Dad. You've got to come and get me. Help me! Help me, Dad! Help me, please.'

7

March 2014

Night. Middler night.
  Here, I am alone. Now.
 No Rashid. Where is he? Where-is-he?
 Werrizzee?
 Stutterering. Jabbera. Jab-berra.
 Extras. Extra letters...words.
 Cold.
 I.
 Splittiting headerache.
 I want. I want it.

This is now, but it reminds me...Time shadows away.

...of the clinic, years ago. I hated Dad for that.

For seventy-two hours, he couldn't help me, couldn't reach me. They put me in an isolation room, a box that was warm, well-aired and soft. The floor was soft. The walls were soft. At least, that's how I remember it.

 A toilet stood in one corner of this soft room.

 I'd fought them. Kicked. Shouted. Screamed more like. I punched one in the face, got a grip on his ear, yanked away. I damn near tore it off. All they had to do was give me a drink and

I'd stop. I kept telling them. Would they give me a drink? Would they hell! No. No. No.

So I ended up in The Soft Room.

I yelled.

Get me out of here!

I shouted until I could shout no more. I kicked the door. In bare feet.

Dad! Help me!

My stomach turned. I felt deeply sick, right in the sponge of my stomach, turning revolutions that sent shots of burning vomit into my throat. I found the toilet in the corner and emptied myself into it.

I knew it was the drink, the absence of drink. The vomit was sour and pale, all acid and gall, hosing from inside.

The liquid stopped, but the pumping continued, a mechanical retching, convulsing me, the pain growing with each spasm. I could scarcely breathe.

Please God!

Is this punishment? Is there a moral force that rules the body and punishes it for its abuses? Am I condemned? For how long?

Dad!

Eventually, I slept.

The second day was the same, and the third.

Then, it eased.

The chill of the night and the heat of the day are getting to me. Since Rashid's escape, I have developed a head cold. I sneeze and drip and shiver uncontrollably. This is the second day I have been denied food and water. It seems like every few seconds that my stomach clenches. I try to breathe slowly to relieve the pain.

We were taught breathing techniques to alleviate the pain from wounds. I thought I'd give them a try. It's all Yoga nonsense, and I don't suppose it would work if you had half your thigh blown off, but I'd hope here it might have some effect. The trouble is I can't breathe. My nose is so blocked, it's pointless trying.

It makes you laugh.

The door opened a moment ago and something was thrown into the room. The bolt slid, a hand appeared and then convulsed, a spasm of movement that released a brown ball through the dusty afternoon air. The hand went as quickly as it had come.

On the floor, sitting on its own patch of dirty concrete, is a disc of bread.

This is the first food I have been allowed since Rashid escaped. The guards, perhaps persuaded by Guard One, have decided to keep me alive. Their heated exchanges in the outer office have continued, and someone has raised the thought, I assume, that I may be more valuable to them kicking than stiff. Perhaps they too fear punishment if I were to die.

The bread is stale and gritty. I have to resist the urge to cram it in and swallow it whole, to puts its mass in my stomach as quickly as possible, to fill the gap, like tar pushed into every nook and crevice of a pothole.

Instead, I eat with a magisterial slowness. My teeth pull away individual crumbs and I relish the bulk of bread that remains. I love the burring it makes on my lips, the intensity of flavour as I let it rest on my tongue. When I lift my tongue and move the morsel into my throat, it is like no sensation I can remember. The novelty of it is engrossing. My throat is parchment dry and the crumbs stick to the walls as they try to go down. I feel as if I am gorging myself.

I want to scream.

Rashid's absence is excruciating. I have not adapted. Instead, I pretend he is still here, secreted in the darkness a few metres from me, listening patiently. When it's necessary, I speak aloud to him.

'Oh wait, I did hit a girl's legs a few times with a stick when I was about nine. Does that count? It was jealousy, I think. I was jealous that Tim was friends with her, and I wasn't. She was pretty. I didn't understand at the time, but I suppose it was the beginning of sex. Just came out as frustration and violence. I thought I didn't like girls. I think I was angry with myself for finding her attractive. Does that make sense?'

Of course, it wasn't a *girl*. It was Holly.

'Then I went and screwed her life up again by getting her pregnant. But I loved her, Rashid. I love Holly. Twig you know her as.'

It matters little whether it makes sense or not. This is not the first time I've examined that episode from my past. I've always felt ashamed of it, so it returns to me again and again. I go over it, following them through the woods, squirming at the moment I first hit her. Why? Why do it? I have convinced myself it was sexual. It's preferable to any other theory, to the idea that I might have been cruel, to the idea that I had no compassion.

We argued a lot in the house. I was in trouble all the time. Often it wasn't because of what I'd done, but because I lied about it. I was a really good liar. I don't mean that they never found me out. They did. Frequently. But the way I thought was that if I lie now, I'll put off any punishment for a few hours, maybe a few days, and it's just possible this time that they won't discover the truth, and I'll get away with it. That's how I thought when I was young. What I didn't grasp was that my parents were getting used to the idea that I lied, and so it got to the point when they didn't believe anything I said. I could be telling them the truth and I could see it in their eyes: they wanted to believe me, to trust their son, but there'd been so much lying they'd just lost faith and so they'd nod and pretend to accept what I said, but it was obvious they didn't. It used to drive me mad. We'd have whole new rows about the fact that I was telling the truth now, and they doubted every word I said.

I stopped talking to them. I kept everything to myself. I suppose I was about fifteen when I started doing that. I'd discuss things with my friends. They knew what I was up to. But when Mum and Dad asked, I'd brush them off. I'd say something deliberately vague and they'd usually back off because they didn't want another argument. I think they worried and I made them feel pretty desperate.

Had a baby with. Is that what you call it? Is that the phrase to describe the biggest mistake in my life? And I don't just mean getting Twig pregnant. That was an everyday failing. Lots of people make the same stupid, impulsive decision and take the risk, once. We didn't take precautions, as they call it, once. But that wasn't the biggest mistake. It was what I did afterwards, how I treated her once the baby was coming.

'I kicked her out, Rashid! In the rain.'

I want him to respond. I want him to judge me. But he's not here. He can't pass judgement. Or perhaps he did, days ago, weeks ago, and didn't say.

'Do you see? I kicked that poor, pregnant kid out into a dark, cold, rainy night. Do you see?'

I deserve to be in a prison and fed on shit food and never see daylight. Perhaps I should be tortured. Who knows? I should have been punished like this years ago.

The worst of it is that I can't understand why I was like that. I don't recognize myself in that teenager.

It's hot in the room, must be mid-afternoon, when it can turn sultry and heavy. I feel the sweat stream down my chest and the ribbons of my shirt cling to my back. It's like a shower curtain. The heat blurs thought. I'm wiping the sweat from my eyes and it's as if I'm cleansing my mind. For a few moments, there is clarity, then more sweat, then blur again. I have this constant sense of pressure on me to tell my story, another chapter of it, tell it to a vacant space. I wish Rashid to be here. He must listen to the bits I've previously censored.

I suppose I was just what you'd call depressed. I never know what that means. Do you, Rashid? We all feel deeply unhappy at times, don't we? But I guess I was worse than that. I was drinking more than I should and it was affecting my behaviour. You're very wise avoiding the stuff, Rashid. It does terrible things to you. I didn't know what to do with my life, but at the same time I didn't like any of the options. I was in a bad place, as they say.

But I had a woman who loved me.

It sounds so simple. The cloud is swept away and the sun bursts through.

Yes, you're right, Rashid. You'd think I'd value that, wouldn't you? But do you know, I couldn't have cared less. I enjoyed the sex, sure, but a loving relationship? Forget it. I wasn't callous. I just didn't think it was worth it. I'd got it firmly in my mind that, when it came down to it, I was a bad guy. But instead of making me humble, it made me angry, and I started to lash out – at anyone else who was around.

I don't mean 'anyone', do I? Even as I say it, I know that I am ⸱ thinking of friends like Andy, or Tim. I am entirely fixed on one person. Twig. She's the one I imagine when I say the words *lash out*. No one else. She's there, in my head, wearing that thin dress and those senseless high heels I loved so much.

She lost the baby. I'm sorry, I mean *we*. We lost the baby. Or perhaps I mean I lost it for her. I shoved her out in the rain, and I don't know exactly what caused it. She fell? I don't know. She caught a cold. Something happened. But if I hadn't made her leave the house and walk all that way in the rain, she'd have been okay. I know it. The baby would have been okay.

No? Well, what do you know about it, Rashid? I feel pretty sure. I was so preoccupied with me that I didn't really register she'd been taken to hospital. I couldn't think straight, and people were telling me Twig was unwell and she might lose the child, and I didn't get it.

Through a glass pane, on a hospital ward. I walked up the corridor and explained who I was and asked if I could see her. They told me to wait, and I watched a nurse go into her room. She must have been asleep because the nurse touched her shoulder and was obviously trying to rouse her. Then she bent down to Twig's face and said something and I could see, through the window, that she just shook her head.

She didn't want to see me, Rashid. She'd had enough. Hardly surprising. She told the nurse she blamed me for everything. She never wanted to see me again.

I was such a mess. I was leaning against a wall in a hospital corridor, pissed out of my head. It can't have been what I was expecting, or I wouldn't have gone to the hospital in the first place, but I don't remember feeling anything when I was turned away. I just caught the bus and went away. I guess what I understood was that she'd stopped loving me and that was right. Fair, somehow. Why should she? I deserved what I got.

The door to our cell has burst open, and Guard One lobs two bottles of water in my direction. The mood has changed again and I find I am surprisingly sleepy.

'Rashid.'

His name shapes my mouth, scarcely above a whisper. I'm calling to him, wherever he is.

'Rashid! Do you hear me? Do you want to know how the story goes on? How it ends?'

Wherever he is.

'She died a few days later. Our baby took her. Can you believe that, Rashid? After all I've told you? After the games we played? Holly died. I just lied about her. In Battersea. The fucking BFI. Lies. Because I so much wanted them to be true.'

Shall I make up another, Rashid? Another scene for our game? Another lie? The one I'd have given my life's blood to be true, to come true.

I will.

We're at a party, Rashid. Tim's. She's walking over to me, a glass of wine in her hand. She looks confident, older. I glance around to see if there's somewhere I can go, somewhere I can hide.

But there's nowhere, and she's on me.

I flail for words.

'How are you now?'

I blurt it out and realise too late that the 'now' gives context, the past.

'I'm fine, Steve,' she says. 'I've survived.'

She's smiling, friendly. How can she find it in her? I treated ~ so fucking badly, so cruelly, and here she is tolerating me, apparently kind, perhaps forgiving. I stand in front of her, a trained soldier, and I feel I could cry.

'I don't know how you can bear to be in my company.'

'It was a long time ago, Steve,' she says. 'We were young.'

'We? You were never to blame. You never did anything wrong, not once. It was all my fault. I was a bastard.'

'You were messed up.'

I sense the slightest touch and look down. Her hand is resting against my arm, her long fingers folded around the sleeve of my jacket. They stay there for only a moment and are gone.

Is she pardoning me, Rashid? Is this a benediction? I've lived ten years under a pall of guilt and self-loathing, and by accident here I am before the bar. The Bar of the World! Bar! How ironic is that, Rashid! But it's the only bar that matters now. I'm before the one judge who can absolve me, who can decide whether or not there's anything in me still worth respecting, still worth loving.

I touch her hand.

'Can you forgive me?'

She puts her glass down and looks up.

'I can forgive, Steve, but not forget.'

Aren't those beautiful words, Rashid? Just beautiful.

Day dawns. There are feet outside the room, more than one man. Two, I would guess. They walk across the office floor and stop at my door. Without intending to, I am holding my breath.

I feel I must crawl away from the door. My knee has begun to throb. It has largely healed, but there remains some swelling around the joint and I can't kneel on it without considerable pain. I manage to shuffle only a few steps when the door opens.

Today, I am given bread again, this time with humous in a

plastic cup and a bottle of water. Things are looking up. The feet walk away. There is silence.

Night falls.

Rashid has not uttered a word since he was returned to the room. He lies on his side, not in his old place on the far side of the window slit, but closer to me, within touching distance. His breathing is irregular and when it catches, I know that bolts of pain have ripped through one or other of his many injuries.

He drags himself over the couple of feet of concrete that separate us and I offer my arm to him and hug him to me. His body is skeletal. Nothing is said, but I am sure that these are the only moments of hope surviving in Rashid's life. He has been treated so brutally that it is only in the physical affection I can give him that he finds a reason for living. It is all that is left of love.

Sleep comes fitfully and with many spasms of pain. Set apart from me, perhaps as little as two metres, he is too frightened to sleep. In my arms, he feels safe. He trusts me to protect him, should the door burst open and the guards appear.

I have urged him to take a shower. I know he would feel better, a bit better, if he washed the clotted blood from his hair and face, and sponged his body clean of the grime and sweat of his last few days. But they have broken him. He has no interest in standing or sitting or talking. It is as much as he can do to crawl away from me to piss in the bucket.

Sometimes he doesn't even manage that.

He saved me. Dad always makes fun of me when I say that. He says that I saved myself. He's afraid of what he calls 'being sentimental'. Grand emotion he can cope with. Tosca. *The St Matthew Passion*.

They're fine. He'll weep through those. But an intimate moment of thanks? Not on your life. That kills him, makes him squirm.

It wasn't just the clinic. The clinical care was essential, of course. I couldn't have got through without it. They gave me rules and drugs for the pain and substitutes. That's the thing. They made me focus on other ways of living. These days I can strip down an old motorbike and fish a salmon river. I couldn't do those before. They require skills and concentration, and the pleasure can be bright, like a flame. It has no taste, but there's the same secret moment of bliss I got from drink. It's so refined, so distilled, it's like it's been squeezed out of something bigger.

Not just the clinic.

He stood by me. God, if he were here, he'd hate the cliché. But it's true. When I was residential, for those three months, he visited every day. Even if he had rehearsals or a concert, he'd find half an hour to drop by. He'd sit by the bed and he'd look at me. At that stage, I didn't have much control. I had long periods of feeling frozen to the bone and I'd shake under that ugly yellow blanket. I shouted at him and told him to fuck off. He'd try to hold my hand and I'd pull away. He'd try again and I'd continue to pull back, time after time, until I didn't and I let it rest there on the blanket and he squeezed it and he stroked my fingers with his other hand and I found that relaxing.

None of this was expected. If I'd shouted at him all day every day in that clinic, it would only just have paid him back for the shouting he'd done over the years. He used to frighten me. I'd be ten and I'd have done something or told a lie and he knew it. There'd be this look in his eye and I'd have a split second to make a run for it before he came thundering after me. He says now it was all show, but at the time I thought he'd kill me. He really scared me.

He scared me inside and he made me feel bad.

Why in hell should he have cared about me in that clinic? I was a pathetic drunk, no good to anyone. He could have walked away, and no one would have blamed him, least of all me.

Something must have made me think otherwise or I wouldn't have rung. I've often thought about that call. Why did I pray Dad would pick up? Mum had always been the kind one, the one who forgave. Dad did all the yelling. But when I lifted up the receiver, scarcely able to stand in that old red phone box, I wanted my father.

'Rashid.'

It's mid-afternoon, warm but not stifling, tolerable if you remain still, except that I am seated cross-legged and with Rashid's head resting on my thigh. My impression is that he's been asleep for over an hour, but time is elastic in confinement and it's hard to tell. It might be a lot less. I measure it by my discomfort. I am desperate to stretch out my legs and walk around. A patch of sweat, the size of Rashid's head, has formed on my upper thigh and it has begun to stream down towards my groin. My leg muscles ache from inactivity and Rashid's weight. If I don't move soon, I think my brain will burst.

'Rashid.' I try to whisper his name, whilst keen for him to hear. 'I need to get up. Rashid?'

I ought to be able to persuade myself that his need is greater than mine, that I should subdue my feelings of distress and pain in order to give him the reassurance and intimacy he wants from me. Generally, I do.

In this heat, it's never pleasant to have his body so close. He smells of what he's been through. I can't describe it. There is old blood, certainly, rank sweat, a hint of urine, but I believe I can also pick up fear. What does fear actually smell like? I can't find the words. Perhaps some wine connoisseur could, but I can't. I just know it. I've smelt it on the men, when we've found ourselves alone on a dark street, multiple alleyways to left and right, and flat roofs above us. Men can be in full control of themselves, carry out exactly what they're trained to do, and still smell of fear.

There is sweat in Rashid's hair and where it pools around his wounds, it might be mistaken for fresh blood. The humidity and filth of this room have slowed the process of healing, but I'm sure the cuts to his head should have scabbed over by now. I don't know that he could be said to be on the mend. There may be internal injuries which I ...which he is unaware of.

I can take it no longer. I'd hoped to wake Rashid so that he could move himself, but he's not responding, so I'll have to move him myself.

I take his head in my hands, supporting it on either side. The size of it, if not the weight, is so reminiscent of a football I can't help imagining one, the way a goalie holds it before a drop kick. There is something appallingly familiar about this shape as I hold it in my fingers. It's a shape from my youth, from childhood security, from a time of fun and hope, and – is this right - winning?

I can't coax him awake. He is thin and vulnerable. His bones protrude in his shoulders and at his elbows and down the length of his shins. He can't have eaten in days and yet his weight is so extreme I can't manoeuvre him away. I am obviously weak too. I have to slide myself from under him while suspending his head, like a goalie, in mid-air. I feel a sense of immense relief once I am no longer supporting him. Cool air seems to spread across my thighs and chill the sweat as it dries.

I lower his head towards the floor. It is a task that calls for infinite care and I do it with the concentration of a new father holding his babe for the first time in a maternity ward.

There is no word, no breath caught in pain, no form of protest at all. It makes me wonder how long I have sat, denying the truth, with Rashid's head at rest in my lap.

Time is elastic in confinement, but I know that I have been whispering his name for quite a while now.

I have to escape. There is no question about it. I have to think and not be distracted. With Rashid gone, it's clear that they are prepared to murder, and it'll only be a matter of hours or days before they turn their attention to me. I have seen too much of what they do.

They removed Rashid's corpse early yesterday morning. I was ready to remonstrate with them, but as it turned out, they treated his broken body with great sensitivity. Perhaps they are afraid of the dead, of their power. They certainly showed more respect to Rashid dead than alive.

I suppose it's a relief that he's gone. In this way. The smell of fear had continued throughout the night, and as his body went cold, he seemed to bring down the temperature of the room. I started to shiver and pulled on my shredded shirt and shoved the copy of *Time* magazine into it, to create another layer between my chest and the cold. Then I gathered up all the remains of newspapers and tried to fill my shirt with those too, and when I couldn't push any more in, I wrapped them around me as best I could.

I want that handle on the wall, the one that I fantasised about. pull it down and the wall will swing away and I'll step out into throng of the square. I found myself staring at the wall only a

252

moment ago, as if by some miracle there might be such a handle and I'd missed it. The hope for it seems to excuse me from devising a rational plan of escape.

The guards have been more generous since Rashid's death. I don't know whether it's their idea of politeness or what. Perhaps they never thought it would go this far. Perhaps they expected Rashid to recover from the torture and the beatings. Anyway, I am the beneficiary of this remorse, if that is what it is. I have returned to my usual gourmet diet and I have regular deliveries of water, more than I need frankly. They provide these things in a friendly and courteous manner. Service with a smile.

I hear them chatting in the outer office. They sound less anxious, less angry. They don't shout in the way they did at the time of Rashid's escape. Sometimes they laugh. I even heard singing. The smell of their burning tobacco drifts into my room. Faint and invisible as it is, I try to inhale it. If I can share their smoke, I can share in the life outside. It tastes of freedom, intoxicating as a joss stick or a thurible in church.

It's interesting to consider if this more relaxed view of me will lead to less vigilance and give me the vital moment of inattention I will undoubtedly need. You could argue that they're likely to watch my every move in view of what has happened with Rashid. Equally, they may think that I have been so intimidated by Rashid's death that an attempted escape is unlikely. I think I must put this to the test, a dry run before the real attempt.

Several days pass before I am allowed to shower again. This is m fault almost entirely. I have complained so often about the bre shower attachment and the insanitary state of the cubic⌐

the guards formed the impression that I would rather not bother. Guard One said, weeks ago, that they hoped to have it repaired soon, but since nothing has been done, he and the others seem to have taken the view that the shower is unusable.

When my meal is delivered, I try to explain. Without Rashid, speech is futile. I make gestures with my hands, my fingers splayed out above my head like the lines of water descending from a shower rose. Guard One barks out words that mean nothing to me and I begin to laugh. It's like a parody of 'Charades'. Guard One, yet again, takes offence. He thinks I am mocking him and he slams the door as he leaves.

All the same, the message has got through and another guard has brought me a fresh towel and a bar of soap, and he is proposing to escort me through the office and along the corridor to the shower. I thank him, making sure that I smile and incline my head a little in the way they like you to.

The shower room has deteriorated even further in the two weeks since I was last permitted to use it. Not only has nothing been repaired, but the weight of the loose shower head has brought down half a dozen tiles from the back wall of the cubicle. They lie in the shower tray, broken into a number of pieces, like gambling chips. As I clear them to one side, my eye is suddenly painful. Something has flashed and the light has dazzled me. At first, I have no notion what it might be. The fluorescent tube in the ceiling is functioning fine and doesn't flicker, and the chrome of the shower attachment is so corroded and dull that it has long ceased to reflect any light.

It is only when I have swept out the final ceramic crumbs from tray that I realise what I've been seeing. There is a hole in the ehind the cubicle and as I moved my head around, sorting out the tiles, my eyes were passing across it. The flash, as I called it, is in fact bright daylight, made intermittent by my movements. Just the idea of it is thrilling, a view of the outside unmediated by the guards. I switch on the shower in case I start to yell with the joy of it.

The hard, lukewarm water hammers against my skin. I have been longing for this opportunity, but I am entirely focused on the hole. I think it has disturbed the cockroaches. I haven't seen one. It's quite possible the sunlight has forced them to move. Their putrid smell is far less evident; it might even have gone, but my memory hangs on to it and won't give it up easily.

I soak my face and hair and body in the shower. If I stretch out, I can push my arm through the gap left by the fallen tiles and touch the edges of the hole in the back wall. The sensation is gloriously illicit. I am trying not to let my imagination run riot, but I am sure I can feel the heat of the sun on the tips of my fingers. I stretch my arm as far as I can and I am practically snatching a fistful of warm air.

It's vital that no one other than me knows about this. The guards never clean the shower room, but there is a danger that, after weeks of inaction, some repair man may turn up to fix the shower head and the tiling. I can do nothing to prevent that happening, but I may be able to conceal the hole. Some of the wall tiles are intact and, thank God, I can balance them against the brickwork in such a way that the hole disappears. Any casual observer would think the cubicle was simply in a bad state, with tiles that were about to slip. It must have looked roughly like this a week ago.

A small hole can become a larger one. I will have one cha▪ Once I have broken through the wall, there will be no going I could make my break now, but I feel I should prepare. ▪

and trousers are in the room, and I have hidden the trainers there. I hesitate to leave the shower, with the risk that the hole might be discovered, but I think it's probably alright to. I have to force myself to step out of the cubicle.

As I am escorted back, the guard appears unaware that anything has changed. I struggle to conceal my excitement, my ecstasy, but if I am giving any signs away, I guess he will think I am feeling refreshed from the shower, glad to be clean again.

The next twenty-four hours pass in anticipation, panic really. I pace the room, trying to imagine what might be beyond the shower wall and what I will have to do to escape. I am worried that, if it comes to it, I'll not have the stamina to outrun the guards. I'll be out of breath in a couple of hundred metres and whilst my legs seem firm enough as I walk the short distances to and from the shower room or around this cell, I'm sure I have lost a lot of muscle over the last few months, and that will tell if I have to run continuously through the streets or on open road or whatever it is that lies in wait for me out there.

It's not surprising that I am unable to sleep or eat. Guard One brought me a kind of soup and some pitta bread with humous and olives, but my stomach felt full and resistant. It's possible I'll feel able to eat later.

I break the seal on the bottle cap and sip the water he brought me. It tastes unusually sweet and cool. My teeth feel sensitive. As I savour it in my mouth, churning it around my teeth and gums, there is a hint of pain, oversensitivity, that passes like cloud across sun. I am tasting something new, and it's exhilarating. I am only conscious that this bottled water is delivered from the world, a world I am about to join.

There is no possibility of bringing forward the time of my shower. They would not agree to it and it would, in any case, risk arousing their suspicions if I asked for a change.

It would help if I could sleep, if only for a few hours. I try lying down, try to calm my mind, to quell the feverish need to move my limbs, to get going. Every minute is agony. The room is strangely silent. My restlessness makes the rats and insects, who usually come out in the dark, afraid. They keep themselves to themselves.

The noises from the outer office are magnified. I'm used to sudden bursts of laughter, footsteps, the scrape of chairs on a concrete floor, the burr of TV. But this clash of sounds reminds me of a waterfall. I don't know what the word is. A cacophony? It is so loud it is on the edge of pain. The room is alive with a sense of something pouring in. For a moment, I am frightened it might be gas.

But the idea of the waterfall is comforting, a high green cascade exploding out of rocks and pine trees a hundred metres above me, too vast to take it all in. I have to bow my head to follow the water as it hurtles down and pounds the rockpool below, so deafening I can hardly hear my own thoughts. They break up and run away in my head before I can grab them and turn them into words, scattering like pebbles or stones pushed in all directions by the sheer force of the water.

What was it Dad used to say about the sea? Always is all everywhere.

The sound of the waterfall excites me.

I must lie down.

I long to see a waterfall.

It's light now, or near to. I can see my hands in front of me. The walls have shape and intersect with the ceiling and floor. An animal has shot out of view.

This building does not wake like a home or a hotel. There are no shouted greetings or good mornings, no sound of newly running basins or baths, no pipes groaning as hot water rushes through them, no feet on the stairs, no aromas of bacon or toast. Such noise as there is comes from the outer office, where there's a change of guards about this time. There are two smells associated with this hour: burning cigarettes and burnt coffee. The coffee is like too much salt on my tongue. It may not be good, but I thirst for it. I yearn for the taste of it, a taste that would be overwhelming, I suspect, to match the enormity of the aroma.

I have not had a drop of coffee since I've been here. I don't even remember what it tastes like.

The bolt has shot. A guard is in the doorway. He has a short stick in his hands. He strikes his palm with it, once. It has a menacing solidity about it.

He seems to enjoy my uncertainty. He knows that I am wondering what he plans to do with the stick and that I am terrified he will hit me with it.

He gestures with the stick, and it's clear that I am to follow him into the corridor beyond the office. My guess is that he will take me to the shower, so I must be ready. I slip on my trainers, pick up my trousers and sling them over my shoulder. If he is at all surprised or concerned by this, the guard shows no sign of it. I imagine they are complacent now, sure that, after Rashid's death, I won't attempt anything.

We walk down the corridor, he in front, me behind. No one

appears. The other guards must be elsewhere in the building, on another floor perhaps. So far, I am blessed by the gods. This guard is, I know, lazy. I can see it in the way he walks. Once I am in the shower room, he will leave me to it and slope off for a cigarette.

He opens the door and allows me to pass through. Then he closes the door behind me and locks it.

I stand absolutely still, as still as I can hold myself, waiting for the sound of his footsteps.

There! He has turned away. His footsteps recede from me.

Nothing has been touched. The three tiles I pushed over the hole have stayed in position. I imagine no one has visited the room since I had my last shower. The guards have their own facilities and no one bothers to clean anything I use.

I turn on the taps and lift out the first of the loose tiles and place it carefully on the floor next to the shower tray. The hole is there, exactly as I remember it. I have now to make it large enough for me to get through. The hole is, of course, visible from the outside and as it gets bigger, it will be increasingly obvious to any passers-by in the garden. I must work quickly.

The tiles have been badly done and the grouting has fallen out in several places, so I have no trouble removing them from the back wall. The breezeblocks are no better. I'm sure, if I tried, I could push the wall down, but that would be noisy and conspicuous. Instead, I use my fingers to pick at the powdery cement around them and then pull cautiously at each block until it is loosened and ready to remove. Within a few minutes, I have taken out a dozen of these blocks and stacked them in the shower tray. It seems to me that I have worked swiftly and, I think, silently. The hole looks as if it is now large enough for me to squeeze through.

The sharp edges of the remaining breezeblocks catch my shoulders and snag my hips, but I manage to climb out. The sunshine hits my face like a guard's flashlight. I squint and shade my eyes as best I can. In front of me is a patch of dusty ground, the grass, then a wall and the gate.

I sprint across the yard. Despite everything I vowed, nothing is planned or thought out. I swing myself up on the gate and drop down on the far side. There is a square and a road out of it. Someone has started shouting behind me.

I run.

8

April 2014

They were woken by rapid knocking at the front door. Someone had taken the brass gavel and swung it hard against the scoop of the lion's mouth, three times at least, possibly four.

'What in God's name?'

Edward turned towards the clock on the bedside table.

'What time is it?'

Cara rolled on her shoulder. If she'd heard the knocking, she'd ignored it.

'It's seven fifteen!'

'Probably post.'

'It's practically dark. They don't deliver post until after eight. It sounds like there's a gang of workmen out there.'

'You'd better go.'

He searched the wall for the light switch, but failed to find it. One of those crazed, half-asleep thoughts occurred to him that it might have moved. He was half way down the stairs, pausing at the turn, making sure he gripped the banister before taking another step, when a voice called out from the driveway.

'Mr Padgett?'

He hesitated. Not the post. They didn't shout at doo· They put red cards through the letterbox.

'Mr Padgett!'

'I'm coming. Just a minute.'

He walked quickly through the kitchen. The window in the passage beyond was ablaze with hurtful white light. What in God's name? He took down his Barbour from the coat rack and slung it over his shoulders. Police? A dawn raid? He slid the bolts and turned the latch and flung the door open.

'Mr Padgett?'

Edward found himself squinting in bright light. He shielded his eyes while they adjusted. He had a sense of five or six people spread out over the gravel and the lawn. In front of him a young man in a sheepskin jacket was speaking into a microphone. Over his shoulder, another man repositioned the camera on his shoulder and swung away from the reporter and took two steps towards Edward.

'Gary Lawrence, Meridian News, Mr Padgett. I was wondering what your reaction was to the news that your son may still be alive...?'

'What?'

It had been eight months, months of merciless anxiety and despair, illuminated by flashes of false hope, as no doubt this would prove to be. For months there had been no news, no indication that the search was getting anywhere, no evidence of life or of death.

'How do you know this?' Edward demanded.

He felt embarrassed by his appearance, humiliated by his ignorance of whatever it was these news people knew. He pulled the Barbour on and tried to zip it up.

'You didn't know?'

The young man was clearly surprised.

'No.'

'We heard it from the MOD. A press release. You haven't seen it?'

'No.' He struggled with the zip. 'Look, it's seven in the morning. What is this?'

'We'd just like to hear your reaction to the news.'

'To what news?'

Gary was face to face with him, the microphone hovering at Edward's chest.

'The army has found the place where they believe Steve was held. It was abandoned. No sign of him. They think Steve got away.'

He started to shake. He felt the cold of the morning, a draught on his back, and he shuddered. He thought he might choke. Steve! What right had Gary Lawrence to talk about *Steve?*

'If my son…'

He sensed Cara behind him. Her hand touched the sleeve of his coat.

'Is it true?' she said, quietly.

'Mrs Padgett?'

Gary nodded to the cameraman and the two of them stepped past Edward to confront Cara.

'I don't think my wife…'

'It's alright, Edward,' Cara said, and she turned to the camera, ignoring Gary's attempts to get her to speak to him. 'If my son is alive…' She spoke directly into the lens. 'If Stephen has escaped his jailors and is alive somewhere, we thank God. It's what we have been waiting and hoping for all these months. We just pray he will be safely returned to us very soon.'

Gary appeared dissatisfied.

'It must be quite an emotional moment for you...?'

He wanted something less controlled, a gobbet of emotion for the morning bulletin.

'Do you think,' he said, 'you've been well treated by the MOD and the Foreign Office?'

'I have nothing further to say,' Cara said. 'Thank you very much.'

She turned to go. Gary and his cameraman would have followed her into the house, but Edward stepped across and barred their way.

'Thank you,' he said. 'That will be all.'

'One more question, Mr Padgett...'

As he closed the front door on them, Edward caught the last of Gary's question and the words *chances of survival*. He re-locked the bolts and went to find Cara in the kitchen.

'Why weren't we informed?'

'How should I know?'

She stood at the sink, filling the kettle. Her hands were trembling and the water spilt over them. Edward put his arm around her and kissed her cheek.

'Do you think it's true?' she asked.

'I've no idea. I'll ring as soon as they're open.'

'It'd be too cruel if it's not, wouldn't it?'

'We've been here before.'

She took the kettle away from the tap and plugged it in at the wall.

'Are they still out there?'

'I have to catch a train in an hour. They'd better be gone then.'

He lifted the window blind and looked out. It was just

about light now, a watery sun trying to burn through the pale cloud. Gary Lawrence had his back to the house and appeared to be speaking to the camera. He would be summarising, Edward thought, reminding his audience of the long period of waiting and wondering that the Padgett family had endured. Was that agonising uncertainty about to end? Edward could almost hear Gary Lawrence saying the words, stirring the viewers' compassion. Would it end happily with Steve Padgett's safe return or in tragedy? Either way, the next few days would be crucial.

Perhaps he was being unkind to Mr Lawrence. He probably wouldn't speculate. That was -- what did they call it? - editorialising. Gary's job was to report the facts and, given the opportunity, to elicit comment. Nothing further was required of him. If he did have any thoughts about Stephen's chances of survival, he was obliged to keep them to himself. It was for others to imagine the final outcome. That's why he'd kept thrusting his microphone into their faces, desperate for some keen expression of hope or fear, or love.

God knows, they'd had their share of hope and fear. Every morning had been a new engagement with the possibility that another day might bring news of his release or the discovery of his body. There were, of course, gradations of happiness and horror between the two, but it was the extremes that seized his imagination, and Cara's. Alive or dead? That was the issue. Nothing else seemed to matter. They had no time for gradations.

Later, when Gary Lawrence and his crew jumped into thei[r] van and drove off, he lifted the blind and crossed the kitch[en] to his study. He would phone from there. It might be bett[er]

Cara couldn't overhear or, for that matter, interrupt.

'We thought you knew.'

He had rung Stephen's regimental headquarters, which in the past had proved the most reliable source of information on any developments.

'How would I?'

The staff captain he'd been referred to hesitated.

'We assumed the Ministry would have told you before issuing the PR. It was embargoed until six this morning.'

'They didn't,' Edward said.

'No. I appreciate that. I can only apologise on our behalf, and there's no question they should have contacted you and Mrs Padgett.'

At first, someone from the regiment had made a point of telephoning - or emailing them – once a week. They might not have had much to report, but they wanted to emphasise to Edward and Cara that everything that could be done to find Stephen was being done.

That routine stopped after about five or six weeks. The calls and e-mails suddenly reduced to one a month, and quite soon not even that. The office continued to be helpful and precise whenever Edward rang up, but the army had ceased to have anything to say. Once Stephen had been missing for three months, the search for him was discontinued, and Edward was told that locating his son would now depend on intelligence from local people, a tip-off about something out of the ordinary, unusual comings and goings at a house or a factory or farm. That would be how they found him. The officer would conclude by reassuring him that they remained extremely confident that Stephen would be rescued.

'Is it true?' Edward asked.

'Is what true, sir?'

'That they found the place where he was held, and he'd escaped?'

'Well, it's certainly true that Stephen wasn't there.'

'How do you know that he ever was?'

'They found ropes and leg chains. Someone had obviously been kept there, possibly more than one person. And there were copies of *Time* magazine, I believe. Stephen is the only British serviceman unaccounted for. They put two and two together.'

'*Time* magazine is American.'

'Yes, sir.'

Edward switched off the handset. He began slowly gathering up the manuscript and the notes he would need for his rehearsal. Then he placed them neatly in the centre section of his briefcase, slid a pencil into the holster provided for pens and closed the case. The lock made a discreet click as he pressed it. After the noise of the television people, the noise of his anxiety using the phone, he felt, to his surprise, quite calm. The room was silent. The leather of the briefcase felt soft on his fingertips.

It was an unlooked for quiet. He went upstairs to shower.

I found a cave on the hillside shortly before dark. It reeked of some kind of animal, and the floor was rough with bits of jagged rock and bone, but I was glad of the shelter. I had been walking, sometimes running, throughout the day, in fierce heat, but as eve approached, the temperature dropped and I started to t might be forced to stay out on a freezing hill all night.

The cave is cold too. I miss the newspapers Rashid and I used to wear as blankets. Not that they'd have been much use here. The wind that blows in at the cavemouth is inescapable. I've retreated to the back, but am still conscious of a cruel blast snapping at the walls.

I try to make myself comfortable. The rocks stick into me in whatever position I try to lie. The choice seems to be whether I take the pain in my back, my buttocks or my legs. I thought I might be able to sit against the back wall, but in the dark I'd failed to realise that it was wet. A thin stream of very cold water runs down inside, probably from the roof. I trace it with my hands as far I can reach, balking at the icy chill it gives my fingers. There must be a crack or hole lower down the wall, through which the stream exits because I can find no evidence of it pooling on the floor. If there were, it would make drinking easier. I am taking a risk, of course. God knows what the origins of the stream are, but needs must. I haven't drunk all day and am feeling the effects of dehydration. My head and throat ache, and I feel a kind of sleepy and mildly hallucinatory torpor in the making.

I resist licking the rockface, but by craning my head around and pushing myself under a low overhang, I am able to catch a rain of drips on my tongue. As I swallow, the icy water splashes on my eyes and nose. It is like burying my face in snow. I shudder.

I'm staying alive by doing this. I might be deluding myself, but the water tastes clean and fresh, uncontaminated by dead ∙nimals or disease. The restorative effect is surprisingly imme-∙te. I'm hungry, but with each drop I drink, I begin to relish my ∙dom for the first time since I swung up and over the wall ∙nded in the square. Whatever happens in the next few hours and days, I shall have no regrets. I doubt that I will ever find myself a prisoner again in the room where Rashid died. I have at least escaped that.

My feelings of invigoration are quickly followed by a deep tiredness. I'd been kept going by a combination of fear and sheer determination. As I passed through the town – it had been a village really – I encountered no one. The streets were deserted. Even the small market area had been abandoned in the mid-afternoon heat. I felt ashamed doing it, but I knew I needed new clothes. My rag of a shirt was a giveaway. I snatched trousers and a baggy shirt from one of the stalls and ran on.

Once I was out of the town, the terrain was an open expanse of plain, treeless scrub if you like. There was no cover to speak of and not a building in sight. What worked to my advantage was that the road, which led towards the mountains, was actually a track and clearly little used. In the three or four hours I stayed with it, I didn't see a single vehicle. This was reassuring not only because I was anxious not to have to explain myself but also because it suggested the road would be safe and not threaded with mines, improvised explosive devices, IEDs as we call them.

The track eventually petered out, and I had then to decide whether I carried on in the same broad direction, up into the hills, which were by then both ahead and to my right. Although there might be people in the hills, I reasoned that I would be no less exposed tramping across the open plain. At least on the higher ground, there were contours and corners, opportunities to hide, to observe rather than be observed.

Between six and seven the sun began to set. The temperature had been falling for some while and I realised I would have to somewhere to pass the ten or so hours of darkness. The nothing apart from bare rock and soft marl and thin scrub. My rudimentary trousers, pantoons, now have a light patina of camel coloured dust. It clung to the palms of my hands as I climbed or steadied myself against a ledge.

The cave took me an hour to reach and it was dark.

I am awoken by dripping. It is a harsh, unwelcome sound that makes me shudder and turn over, unthinkingly, on my rock bed. I yelp with pain as jagged stones pierce my shoulder.

The drips have replaced the stream. A combination of factors far above, perhaps hundreds of metres beyond where I lie, turns this stream on and off like a tap. The sun may dry it up where it rises or something melts and redirects its course. Whatever the cause, there is no longer a constant supply of fresh running water.

I am hungry and cold and thirsty.

I try unsuccessfully to catch drips on my tongue. Their frequency is irregular and, newly awoken, I make hopeless estimates of when the next drip will fall. The few that touch my lips and tongue exacerbate my thirst. I can barely swallow.

In captivity, the mornings were times of thirst. The guards were invariably slow about bringing us anything to eat or drink. There was, however, the guarantee - or perhaps likelihood is more accurate – that we would receive our bottles of water eventually. I rarely doubted that we would. Rashid did, but I didn't. I always believed it was in their interests to keep us alive, or at least I did until Rashid died. Before they killed him, I was sure that we were useless to them dead or sick. In that, I was wrong, if only in applying a logic, an argument from self-interest, to circumstances and ole that were irrational and volatile.

on't know when I shall next be able to drink water properly.

I have to move on. Presumably, there will be other caves and other streams. Staying in one place, especially in these lonely and outlaw hills, would be a mistake. I have no language to explain myself and despite having lost my uniform, I am self-evidently what I am: a white westerner. I might claim to be an engineer or someone working with an NGO, but why would anyone ask or have the patience to listen? It's easier to shoot me.

The light in the cavemouth is raw and bright. It forecasts a hot day. I must get going before the burn of the sun becomes too much to bear.

I have no idea where I am. Instinctively, I recognize the need to keep on the move, but that is very different from having any sense of where I'm going. My memory is that my captors didn't drive very far after they pulled me into their vehicle outside Rashid's house, but equally it is possible that I fell asleep, from fear and exhaustion, or they knocked me unconscious. I simply can't remember.

Nor does it matter. Not now. The terrain is uniform and unfamiliar. I have no compass or other means of taking a useful bearing. Of course, the sun having gone and returned, I have now fixed east and west, but without a recognizable starting point, it is impossible to orientate myself. I have decided that I must find a river and follow it. It is inconceivable that I won't encounter some kind of habitation if I do that, though I am well aware that it could be hostile.

I must also find food. There will be crops in the valley, irrigated by the river.

I scramble down the hillside, setting off a fall of rocks that crackles like applause as it bounces down the gradient. I bring myself unsteadily to a stop and look around, anxious that other ea̶ may have heard the rockfall and decided to investigate its cau̶

I make myself stay there for three or four minutes, watching the rocks settle, scanning the hill. There is no one. The landscape above and below me is empty.

The heat rises rapidly here. It was quite cool as I left the cave, but now it's hot. The sky is cloudless. The sun is ablaze inside the blue. I can feel my skin burning. I have no means of protecting it. Perhaps I would have been better advised to travel later on in the afternoon, in the couple of hours before sunset. But I felt I couldn't afford to remain where I was or to travel so little. I have no idea how far I have to go. Two hours a day might drag out my journey for a dangerously long time.

My descent is slow and awkward. I have hit an area of scree and the winter ice has split the rocks into boulders the size of footballs. I have to step carefully on them and between them to avoid falling or twisting my ankles. After weeks in which I spent entire days sitting or lying in my prison room, I feel my muscles are being tested to their limits. The pressure on my knees is frightening.

At last, I get to the bottom, from where the valley floor stretches out, flat and hazy for as far as the eye can see. There might be people in the distance. I can't quite make them out. They'd be working the land. They could be a mile away. My eyesight isn't good enough to tell.

If I can see them, they can probably see me. At the moment, I don't have the confidence to approach. Until I have a better idea of where I am and, therefore, who the people are who live in this region and what their politics might be, I think it's wise to avoid contact. There is a green mist around where they're working, which suggests there are crops in the soil.

I have decided to make a broad circuit around them, as if they were the centre of a circle and I the circumference. I will maintain the same distance from them, the same radius, as I make my way around. It's as good a plan as any.

I walked for about an hour and realised I couldn't go on much further. I was wilting in the heat and light-headed from hunger. I came to a field, a patch of ground that was probably no bigger than my parents' garden in Hampshire. It was lush with a green crop. As I bent down and tore up a handful of leaves, I recognized the smell. It was spinach. I crammed the leaves into my mouth. They were dusty, but the fresh, almost meaty taste was unmistakeable. How long was it since I'd last eaten spinach? Years possibly. It might have been caviar or bacon and eggs or roast pork with crackling or a goulash with dumplings. It was delicious. I couldn't have found a better food. Every time I swallowed I just knew I was not only being fed and filled, but nourished. I could feel my strength returning, spreading through my body like an intravenous drug.

The field was bordered by a thin stand of trees, a dozen in all. I tore up more of the spinach plant and went to sit under a tree, taking care to position myself so that I was no longer in direct sunlight.

The coolness of it was astonishing. I hadn't appreciated how hot the sun on my face had become. Its absence made me shudder. I wiped the sweat from my forehead with my arm and chewed the spinach leaves. If I closed my eyes, I could pretend they actually were some sort of meat. My mouth was full. The leaves clung to my teeth and snagged between them. I couldr have cared less. It was pure joy to have found such good fc to be eating again.

I looked back across the field. Although it wasn't large, there were dozens of plants. I would take what I thought I could carry.

In the distance, two hundred metres maybe, I can see a reasonably well-made road. It divides fields of wheat and barley, and must connect two towns to be of this calibre of construction. Whichever way I walk, I'll come to a population centre eventually.

I approach the road slowly, not at all sure whether I should go left or right, south-west or north-east. This will be the first time I've travelled by road. Until now I have depended on farm tracks and worn paths, or I've found my way around grape orchards or the edges of huge fields planted with poppies. The road will make the going easier, but there are risks that go along with that. I'll be more exposed.

For some while I've been watching the road from my track and I've not seen any signs of traffic, but there's bound to be at some point. If this a road used by the army, and given the construction, it seems likely it is, there could be IEDs. We'd sweep it before sending any troops down it.

Perhaps the road would be better avoided. I had made up my mind to find a river and follow it, but I've yet to come on one. It could be days before I do.

I should wait. The barley is tall enough for me to hide in it. I flatten the stems in a small area and sit down and watch the road.

Every time I stop for a few minutes I realise how tired and hot I am. The sweat streams from my hair. It dribbles around my ears and down my neck into my collar. My forehead is glossy with it and I am constantly wiping my eyes, my chest, under my arms, y waist: everywhere is overrun and saturated. It's impossible to rid of the sweat. It irritates me, as an insect buzzing around ritates after a while.

The road is silent. All I can hear are the insects and the slow motion of the barley, which detects hints of breeze I am scarcely aware of. The ears occasionally dip and nod, as if they were tipping me off about something that is about to happen. But nothing does. The road bakes in the heat. I sit cross-legged in the barley and I begin to doze and forget.

Cara stood at the attic window and looked up into the weak, grey light above the Velux. The wind whipped the branch of a neighbour's tree and it fell across her view fitfully, dipping and rearing away, like a rodeo steer. The morning was lively, the rainclouds scudding. There was an energy about the weather, which she loved.

She hadn't played *L'Enfance du Christ* for years, nine or ten at least, not since Karl. In some ways, it felt like she was learning the part from scratch and she was aware of procrastinating before every day's rehearsal. She made coffee, flicked through the newspaper, switched on Radio 4, all displacement activities that put off the evil moment of study and practice. On really bad days she made a phone call and that could delay her work for up to half an hour.

She picked up the score and turned the pages. Somehow, the part looked more daunting than it had the last time. She had discovered new problems in it, moments of awkwardness in her breathing or in the phraseology that hadn't occurred to her before. Of course, in the first performance, she'd had nothing to lose, or so it seemed today. Karl had buoyed h up, instilled confidence in her where there had been n and she'd stepped onto the stage, nervous and excited, and wanting to do well. Had that gone, or was it that the expectations of her were now so high? She wasn't the person she'd been ten years ago. She had a long list of concerts behind her, a number of well reviewed recordings, and a full diary. Unlike then, people knew what to anticipate when Cara gave her Blessed Virgin Mary.

Anthony Burgess, his biographer said, had been close to tears. He'd cried out, *sotto voce*, 'What it is to be a mother!' Did he know? She seemed to remember reading that he and his wife had also had trouble with their son. He, too, had spent sleepless nights wondering where he was, what was to be his final outcome.

She was, though, less neurotic than she had been. When they'd heard about Stephen's disappearance, her sense of loss had robbed her of any coherence or calm. It had the vehemence of bereavement. She could not put from her mind the idea that he was dead, that he'd been shot on patrol or captured and, in some hideous way, killed. The panic that being at a distance induced, unable to establish what had occurred and where he was, anything, wore her down like a disease.

She cried as well because of what had happened to the family over the years. Tim, the son who should comfort her now, resented her, always had. She knew it, whilst having little idea how she might manage it. He was convinced that she loved Steve more than him, always had done, and nothing that she said, no gesture she made, seemed to dent his conviction. Perhaps that was the lot of the second-born, to feel the one grievance for which no reparation could be made: the grievance need of all children bar the first child, that there had never a moment they could call their own, a moment when they had the sole attention of the mother, her undivided love, the sense of being magical.

She had struggled to be fair, not because her love was, as Tim alleged, diminished by her second baby, but because Steve was always the more demanding. She loved the two boys as they might be the earth's poles, both compelling to explore, presenting unique challenges, but only superficially similar in character. She wanted to get to know them equally. With Tim, it was simpler. He had an easy manner, did what he was asked, without resentment. He enjoyed dressing up to go to a restaurant or to meet his grandfather. A day out with Tim didn't have to entail a tantrum. Stephen had a steely shine in his eyes, which said 'You know I'm going to take this to the bitter end'. There was no purpose to his disobedience, or none that Cara could find. It was a power struggle. To Tim, it must have appeared that despite the shouting and the anger, the runs through the house, the slammed doors and eventual tears, Cara's involvement with Steve was more intense. They made up elaborately, with long, gripping hugs and soft words of repentance. By contrast, the affection Tim received must have seemed bland. Perhaps he wondered whether Steve planned it that way.

What did surprise her was that Tim appeared never to have displayed any resentment towards Stephen. On the contrary, he admired his brother. He would hide in his room whilst the house vibrated to the clamour of rows and hysteria, but he didn't blame Steve. It was, perhaps, an aspect of his cleverness.

He could be so abrasive with her. She could not understand why he persisted in treating her, not with open hostility, b coolly, as if he knew how much affection she would like exact quantity of it, and deliberately withheld thirty pe

277

so that she was left always wanting more. Perhaps the carnations were more calculated in that sense than she'd imagined.

It was, of course, a kind of pay-back. No doubt he felt the love he withheld was equal to the maternal care he was convinced he'd lacked as a child. Tim's mind was nothing if not precise. He measured out emotion mathematically, rather like J.S.B., and he made every kiss, every touch, every soft word reverberate.

But the reason that she couldn't enjoy Tim's company now was less to do with Stephen, and all to do with the sense she had that he made her feel 'unforgiven'. She could cope with scanty affection. She was used to that. But the lasting sense of being 'unclean' she could barely tolerate.

And this last disapproval went back to the moment when he'd found out about that silly business with Karl all those years ago. How long had it lasted? A month at most. Why couldn't he forget it? She was sure Edward had also known, or at least suspected, and he seemed to have come to terms with it. Quite rightly. It was only a fling, after all. Unimportant. Tim should grow up.

As she said it, she recognized in the tone of her voice that Tim had a point. Perhaps she had always loved Stephen more. Now that there was news of him, alive, she wasn't sure how to react. She told herself that she ought to know how to deal with it. She had waited before. She had had to learn how to cope with a silent telephone, and a fearful and uncontrollable imagination. She had put up with the breezy assurances of friends who, she knew, privately assumed the worst. She had struggled with guilt. Stephen's failings, the conscious and delib- hurt he had caused her as a boy, left her ashamed of those moments when, at one and the same time, she saw in herself a mother who loved her son and one who was in the creative act of separation. His disappearance as a teenager had given a physical expression to what was already going on, and later, when he joined the army, they had learnt how to live apart. But now was different, wasn't it? Should she feel joy? Or was that too rash, too incautious, given the fragments of information they'd been given?

Harry Miles had turned out to be a tonic in producers' clothing. When they were planning the first recording, for the Spring, Harry had told Edward that this was 'the first note in the scale'. There would be others.

'You reckon?' Edward said.

'I do. You've had a rough patch, Edward. But that's all it is. I hear your voice. It's matured, but it's as beautiful as ever. We're going to do some good work together.'

Much to Cara's annoyance, Edward had refused to take seriously the idea that the disc would happen. For over a month, he'd expected the recording dates to slip, all sorts of excuses being made for the re-scheduling until they were eventually cancelled and the whole project abandoned.

Abbey Road was newly in leaf in April. He walked amongst the tourists thronging about the legendary crossing. A lad about Steve's age stood poised at the kerb, his arm extended, his mobile steadying for a selfie. A young man, standing on the edge of a pavement. It always brought back the same memorie

Was he alive? Had they really found the place he was he Questions he couldn't answer, like the thousand others tha crowded his thoughts over the last few months.

He'd reached the studio with half an hour to spare. They'd agreed on a compilation of Bach, pieces his name was associated with. He'd done the work, giving time to reinterpreting the parts and rehearsing their new versions thoroughly. People, Harry said, would appreciate the fresh approach.

'They know your signature stuff,' he said. 'But if we give it a twist, make it brighter, twenty-first century, they'll love it.'

BWV208 had been a sticking point, as it always was. Edward had argued that 'the twist' had already been added. *Sheep May Safely Graze* was conventionally sung by a soprano. When Edward recorded it, eyebrows were raised in the musical world. Critics had been shocked, then surprised and eventually delighted. What more was there to do with it?

'Take the flutes out?' Harry suggested.

'Boring.'

'Unaccompanied?'

'Don't be ridiculous, Harry.'

Nonetheless, it stayed on the list. They would no doubt discover the 'twist' to give it, *Sheep* for the twenty-first century, as Harry put it, in the course of recording.

Harry had reserved the small studio and hired a quintet. They were due to start at eleven. Edward realised that he was nervous. He felt he shouldn't be. These were the pieces he'd sung all his life, but the interval without work had sapped his confidence and, in any case, it was clear that Harry Miles had very high expectations. He might even have entertained the idea of making money.

Harry was to play continuo and conduct from the keyboard. Edward had requested that they begin with the wretched *Sheep*. Had to be done, then it were better done quickly.

The light above the studio door switched from green to red. *Good luck!* He heard Stephen's voice. Just then. Stephen wishing him success. Harry's arm went up. The flutes were poised at their players' lips. Fifteen seconds of intro, then he came in. He adjusted his headphones.

Schafe können sicher weiden...

It was like opening an old diary. Time swept up and thrown away. He hadn't sung it professionally for three or four years, and when he'd been rehearsing it at home, he'd felt no more than a mild regret about his agreement with Harry. But now, with the opening line, he was there, in the dazzle of the chandeliers, in the pool of light that encircled the impromptu stage, bathing in the goodwill and applause of Washington's elite with a simple shepherd's song about good governance. No wonder Clinton had insisted on it. A political point decked in bucolic innocence. He never missed a shot.

Wo Regenten wohl regieren,
Kann man Ruh' und Friede spüren
Und was Länder glücklich macht

'Very good! Very good indeed!'

Harry was on his feet, his arms raised up, as if he were celebrating mass.

'That had a wonderful rhythm to it, Edward. You know, how sometimes the German doesn't quite flow. But you got it. Well done!'

'Thank you.'

'We'll go again. From the top.'

Go again? He could not understand why producers swathe a singer in praise and congratulation and then announced need for another take. In all his years of studio work, i never made sense that a performance was excellent, but had to be improved. Harry would no doubt splice together bits of the numerous sessions they were about to embark on, but he was unconvinced that made for the best production. As the singer, he could always tell what came from where, or thought he could.

Peace & Rest, Steve. Come out of there alive, my dear son.

Harry was counting them in.

They were expected to be at Abbey Road for three days. Edward had thought they might manage with two, but Harry had argued that whilst the material was extremely familiar to Edward, the musicians only knew a few of the pieces and not all of them knew the same ones. Besides for an hour's CD, they'd had to find a large number of songs. We'll take it a step at a time, he explained. Edward suspected he was nervous, too, and that the extra time he'd booked was a sign of his anxiety.

Patiently, as a good shepherd watches his sheep safely grazing, we wait and hear the silence and hope that no disaster occurs, that no beast rushes at us out of the dark wood, no harbinger of death sends up his signal in the black night sky.

Where rulers govern well
We may feel peace and rest
And what makes countries happy.

I wake suddenly. I have fallen back into the barley, but the noise of the vehicle must have shocked me awake. I try to sit up, hoping might catch sight of what it was that went by, but my legs have e dead and I'm too late. It's passed. I struggle onto my knees and to the edge of the road. There is nothing in either direction.

I want to recall the noise. Was it a truck? I think I can hear it again. It sounds like a truck, a truck with a cab and a flat bed in the rear. It's the most likely vehicle to pass through here. I'm sure of it.

It's obvious that I have been asleep for several hours. The sun, sunk behind the hills, emits a wide orange glow. Dusk is approaching. I have now to worry about where I am going to spend the night. It was stupid to fall asleep. I should have resisted. I'm now a considerable distance from the hills and their sheltering caves. I have no choice but to take my chances on the road and hope to find somewhere out of the cold. Sleeping was really stupid.

I am now in the worst of circumstances. God knows, if I'd wanted to travel along this road, I should have done it in daylight, when at least there was a chance of seeing a disturbance on the surface or a device in the gutter. Travelling in the semi-darkness is frightening, and within the hour I shall be able to see nothing at all ahead of me except the lights of any unwelcome oncoming traffic.

I keep walking. Each step runs more risk. It's ironical that I might have been safer locked up in that room. I try not to think in that way. After Rashid's death, it could well just have been a matter of time. Freedom, on the other hand, is opportunity.

Behind me the glow of the sun is fading, languishing in the blues and greys and purples that float across the hilltops. As I look down the road, the sky is dark like iron, ready for night.

I suppose that I'd been walking for about an hour. It was black as pitch and very cold. I began to see flashes of light high up and several miles away, accompanied shortly after by the crump c shells. The flashes arched in both directions, an exchange of f At this distance, there seemed to be nothing frightening abc

The sky lit up, flaring for an instant. Then the sound that followed came softly, as though the target was cushioned.

I caught glimpses of my hands and legs, swinging forwards, mechanically, going on. I tried to forget the cold and to imagine that the more I willed my body on, the warmer it would get. I stepped up my pace. I would march my way out of discomfort, heat myself up by means of sheer determination and effort.

Every muscle hurt. I thought my knee would give way at one point. Ahead, the fighting continued, an aerial display, a *son-et-lumière*; it might be an ancient castle telling the story of its long history to a thousand tourists ranged on wooden benches erected on scaffolding that afternoon. I knew what it was, but if you didn't, it was beautiful, a pyrotechnic entertainment. It could have been a royal wedding.

I couldn't believe I was having these thoughts. They were surreal. I needed shelter urgently. I needed to get off this road. Yet my mind was full of fireworks and parties, things that belonged to a life elsewhere, a life back in England that I had left behind. It was almost as if I was juggling what was in front of me to transport myself home. If I could find no comfort on the road, perhaps it could be found in my imagination.

Yea, into the Valley of Death.

That was what they'd have assumed back home: that I was dead. What else could they think? They'd have hung on to hope for as long as they could, geeing each other up whenever anyone began to doubt. How many months did optimism survive in those circumstances, when there was no news, no evidence to follow ?? Two? Three? Not this long, that was sure.

So they would have begun to adapt, to create a life in which ceased to play an active part. To begin with, it would hurt like hell, all the more for being finality without closure. No body flown back to Brize Norton on a Hercules. No funeral. Just absence.

There is a house further along the road. I'm certain of it. I saw it in a shellburst. It appeared suddenly, a squat grey concrete box to the left of the road, a couple of hundred metres away. In the few seconds I had to take it in, I registered a flat roof, a television aerial or wires for a telephone – not sure which – and the fact that the main door seemed to be missing, blown out or perhaps beaten in by soldiers or looters. There might have been half a dozen other properties of a similar kind behind it.

This, I have convinced myself, will be my shelter for the night.

The front door has gone, taken away for firewood, I imagine. I was right about the adjacent houses. They shed a stray, weak light in my direction, enough for me to see that there are fragments of what might be a couple of broken tables scattered over the floor just beyond the entrance. I have to pick my way amongst them. It reminds me of the scree on the hillside.

I step over a table leg and try to make out the rest of the room. It would appear that once the house was abandoned, people came in and stole whatever furniture took their fancy. The broken tables stacked in the doorway are probably a source of firewood, just like the door.

The house has two rooms: one for living in, I imagine, another for sleeping. At the rear of the larger room, I find a tap. It would probably have had a basin beneath it, but that has been torn from the wall as part of the general ransacking that followed the owner departure or death.

I don't expect anything to come of it, but I turn the ta

feel it shudder and jump in my hand. A rapid ticking sound follows, like a mad clock, and I can hear the water rushing through a pipe somewhere. The tap begins to vibrate and jump again. Then water comes out of it, in irregular brown spurts. I cup my hands underneath and ladle the water into my mouth and splash it over my face. It is still lukewarm from the heat of the day. I feel myself trembling in the abundance of it. How can one throw away something so precious as this? It gushes now and splatters about the floor and wets my feet. There is no shortage. It flows like a mountain stream. I would shout with joy if I could.

I have several handfuls of spinach leaves in my pockets, squashed in as tightly as I could so that I can carry as much of it as possible. I take out some of them and begin to eat. The spinach has that same raw taste of something strong and earthy. I cup my hands again and scoop up water and drink it in large gulps. This is a feast. I find I am ravenous for the spinach.

I should switch the tap off. It suddenly occurs to me that the noise of the splashing on bare concrete could be audible beyond the house and attract attention, which is the last thing I want. The building should continue to look and sound empty and abandoned. I must keep up appearances.

Now that I have eaten and drunk, I must sort out somewhere to sleep. The shelter the house provides is very welcome, but it's not exactly warm. The wind blows in at the door and through the vacant window spaces. My best option is to jam myself into a corner and pull the broken bits of table around me. Any material, however fragmentary, that I can put between my body and the ‍ is a thermal gain. The tables are noisy and awkward to move. ‍ shift them quietly, but have only moderate success. As I separate them, they clatter and insist on falling over. Gravity is a curse I can do without.

Eventually, I manage to arrange them around me. Most of one tabletop survives and, placed on its side towards the door, it serves quite well as a windbreak. I try and crouch down behind it. Should any passers-by happen to look in, I should with luck be invisible, though whether I'll be as quiet as I should is another matter.

Frankly, it is too cold to sleep. I manage to dose, and I have a sense that I am at least resting. Travelling by day in the heat was exhausting and, in retrospect, it was not so foolish to sleep in the barley field. I probably needed it and my strategy from now on should be perhaps to grab sleep as and when I safely can. There is no guarantee that I will find shelter every night and, if I do, it may be difficult, as it is tonight, to do more than snooze from time to time.

What was the joke Tim and I had when all hell broke loose in the house and Dad was on the rampage after me? *Could be worse*, Tim would say. He always made me laugh when he said that. He had such a straight face, as if it was a philosopher's analysis. Stoicism. He probably learnt about it when he got to Oxford.

Clever kid, Tim. He had a knack for siding with me and never quite alienating our parents. I suppose that's why he does what he does. He couldn't be a high-flying civil servant without a certain amount of tact.

Christ! It's bloody freezing! I'd make a fire, but that'll bring everyone from a mile around, curious to know what's happening in the abandoned house. I have to be better organised. I need to find shelter that's remote and where I can light a fire if I need to.

I reckon Tim will have been the last to give up hope. He'll have stuck it out when Mum and Dad were on the verge of caving. When they started saying 'After all this time, Tim. He can't survived all this time', Tim would be shouting 'No! He's out there! We have to believe that. He's out there somewhere. If he'd died, they'd have found his body. I'm sure.'

I'm wildly projecting, of course, imposing on Tim hypothetical conversations I'm desperate for him to have had. The logic I give him in those exchanges is mine, a soldier with experience of the region, not a civil servant's, not the perspective from Whitehall or Hampshire. Would he think as I do? No news is good news.

He couldn't help forgiving me. Is that a reason for keeping someone alive in your mind? You forgive him, you say everything's alright, you can come home now, so you want to see it through. You want to act out the forgiving. To the forgiven.

Tim was the one who defended me. Even when he knew that I was slipping off the wagon again and taking the occasional drop, he told Dad I was determined. He could never have known the effect that had. He made me feel ashamed. I felt ashamed that my little brother felt he had to lie to our father, to keep him believing in me. I used to sit on my bed at four in the morning, sodden, and quietly cry about the shame and how weak I was. I'd wipe my eyes and my mouth and half the time I didn't know if the wet was tears or booze. If Dad had woken, if he'd had to go to the loo, he'd have passed my door and he'd have heard me. I dreaded it. All it would take was for him to open my bedroom door and that'd be it. He'd see me with a bottle of cider or cheap vodka. Sitting on the bed, crying about the shame and the sorry of it. Always the sorry.

But it never happened. He must have been a good sleeper.

s light again, but it remains cold as night. The sun has yet to rise. e are people in the vicinity of the house. I have been listening to their movements for the last ten minutes or so. I would guess there are three of them, and from the occasional metallic noises I've picked up, they are probably armed. I think I have heard a gun being swung onto a shoulder.

They talk in whispers. I strain to hear what they say, but it's futile. They are too far away and no doubt speak a language I won't understand.

So far they haven't entered the house, but I fear it is only a matter of time. They are either here to investigate the village or they are meeting others of their kind and this house is their rendezvous.

One of them has moved. I can see him through the window opening, or at least his head and shoulders. He has his back to me and the bright light silhouettes him. I can see enough to know that he's probably Taliban. He wears a dark topey, and when he turns to speak, I catch a glimpse of his long, shapeless beard.

He jokes with someone standing nearby. The two of them laugh. Fear makes me hate him. I hate his easy laughter.

They are waiting for something or someone.

His face is at the window. He peers in. Crouched down, I have a restricted view through the broken wood and the light is so fierce behind him that I can make out nothing of his features or the expression he has. He moves his head and I realise that he is searching the room, scanning it for anything useful or suspicious. I realise I have held my breath. The light favours him. It leaves him in the dark and falls in my direction. It splashes over me, liberally and lavishly. The tabletop obscures most of me, but I am theoretically visible through the struts around it. If he knew to look, if he chose to, he could see my legs.

He is staring directly at me. It is only a matter of time. Already, I sense a cramp building up in one of my calves and I'm desperate t be able to straighten it. Holding my head and torso in this hunched position is claustrophobic. I can scarcely breathe.

We play a game of poker. Will I show my hand before he shows his? It is only a matter of time. One of us must win. I struggle to keep Tim's motto in my head. *Could be worse.* Really? Nothing springs to mind.

He has turned and walked away. Has he decided there's nothing of interest in the house or is he about to come in? I raise my hand as much as I dare, try to ease the multiple pains in my neck, back and feet. I push my legs out through the broken wood, risking that he may at any moment reappear at the window. But I have no choice. If I don't stretch, I shall find myself groaning or crying out in pain, and give myself away anyway.

I quickly pull my legs back in. A fragment of conversation was all the forewarning I got, but it was enough, and now two men, dressed in black and carrying Kalashnikovs, step into the house. They hang back at the entrance to my room. One kicks a pan or cup, which must have been lying on the floor. It flies across the room and clatters as it hits the tabletop.

I am sure this has nothing to do with my presence. It was a fit of anger or not even that. Idleness perhaps. They have no idea that I am hiding here, and for as long as they keep chatting, they will not hear my shallow breathing. The time since they arrived and began to look around the building seems to have been inordinately long, but I imagine it amounts to no more than twenty minutes. They must go soon, surely? They clearly have no purpose here. The house is of no interest to them. It is merely a place to meet others.

They are leaving, only to step outside, but at least we are no longer in the same space. Perhaps they were stepping out of the sun. There is now a perceptible warmth entering the room as the sun gains height and the heat of the day rises rapidly.

I think I hear a truck in the distance. No question. A vehicle of some sort is rattling down a track behind the house. I sense it breaking and the driver changes gear as he pulls out onto the main road and swings round to the front. There are sounds of greeting. Shouts go up. The doors of the truck's cab are opened, one then another. There is more shouting and clambering. Things are being thrown into the truck. Men are climbing on board. The truck's engine throttles up.

They have gone.

If you can hear me, Tim, things could be worse.

Now that the building is full of light, I can see what has been left here. I have no intention of staying long, but it's as well to check out whether there is anything useful I can take with me. I'm not optimistic. The house has been stripped of whatever the neighbours fancied, and the militias would have taken whatever raw materials remained. Their war effort is a form of recycling.

I have, though, found an old sack in the corner of the smaller room. I wished I'd been aware of it before. It would have made an invaluable blanket or I could have torn a hole in the bottom and worn it as a nightshirt. I shall take it with me, but first I must open it and feel around inside for food. It might once have had flour or grain. It's pretty well empty, but not quite. In the seams are a few dried beans. I try to collect them, but they run away from my fingers and I'm forced to take them out one by one. They are hard when I first bite into them, but they soften quickly in my mouth, melted by saliva. Their taste has almost disappeared except for a vague saltiness. I chew on a dozen or so and rummage in the sack for more. This is breakfast, and I'm glad of the change from the spinach. Variety is all in a good diet, and I am happy to keep my pocketful of spinach leaves for lunch.

When I have exhausted the supply of beans, I run the tap for a few seconds. By the tabletop is the metal cup that one of the men kicked. I rinse it in tapwater, then fill it and drink it. I repeat this twice more. If only there were some receptacle with a stop or a cap I could fill, I could take some water with me.

After searching both rooms, I am almost convinced that there is nothing suitable when I discover a small rug thrown into a corner. As I roll it out on the floor, I can see that it must once have been a beautiful object with an intricate geometric pattern in reds and blues and blacks, but it is filthy and damaged. I happen to glance back at where it used to lie and spot a small plastic bottle with its screwcap still in place.

I fill the bottle at the tap and tuck it into the waistband of my trousers. I think about taking the cup as well, but decide against it. It would further encumber me. My pockets remain full of spinach leaves. I have the sack to carry. There is no room nor necessity for a cup.

I stand back from the doorway, hesitating to go out. The ground immediately outside the house is white with fierce light. I don't have to step into it to know that it is now hot as hell. There will be people around, despite the heat, and I have no choice but to pass among them. I have some protection in my clothes. With my cap and beard, dressed in baggy trousers, I'm hoping I might pass for local, as long as no one looks too closely.

I will leave the town as soon as I can.

The grass sparkled. The day had the warmth of summer, certainly of June. A simple sunshine glanced off the branches and the opening leaves and caught the specks of moisture in the grass.

Edward made for the river and the clump of apple trees close to the bank. He held his gardening gloves in one hand, a couple of supermarket bags in the other.

The grass felt soft and yielding under his boots. He picked up some broken twigs, which must have come down in the night. As he dropped them into one of the bags, they smacked against the plastic and he was reminded of something. He thought for a moment that it was to do with the windfalls he usually collected in the autumn, but he then realised that the memory was of bags, other plastic bags, years ago when he'd driven out on a wet, black night and spotted Stephen lying on the side of the road, clutching a plastic supermarket bag, just like these.

He'd rung in the middle of the night. When Edward answered the phone, he'd screamed, unintelligibly at first, terrified and naked screams, asking for help and not finding the words. Edward had never heard anything like it before and hoped he wouldn't again. He was listening to his son's fear.

When Stephen eventually began to make sense, he was saying: 'I need your help really bad, Dad. You've got to come and get me. Help me! Help me, Dad! Help me, please!'

After that the line had died. Edward suspected that Stephen had passed out or collapsed. There were snatches of crazed air and a dead thud before he lost contact altogether.

He was drunk and unconscious when Edward found him. He parked the Volvo some way down the road and walked the rest, not wishing to alarm him, though it became clear as he eased him onto his back that he wouldn't have noticed a military convoy if it had rolled past.

Edward knelt down by his son and spoke quietly to him. He stank of alcohol.

'It's Dad, Stephen. Can you hear me, ol' son. It's Dad. I've come to help you.'

His face appeared to be grazed, as if he'd been hit or had fallen and scraped his chin against a wall.

Edward bent down and kissed his cheek. Then he stood and placing himself at Stephen's feet, he took both his hands and lifted him. Once he was up, he shifted his support under Stephen's arms and hugged him to his chest. Part of him would have stayed like that. Part of him wanted to do no more than hug him and kiss his bruised face and, as he knew he eventually would, cry, cry because he had his son back and he was alive, and cry because of the desolate state he was in.

But it was raining and it was cold, and Stephen needed warmth and food and fresh clothes more than he needed affection. Edward swung his arms over his shoulders and dragged and carried him the hundred metres to the car. Then he opened a rear door and, as carefully as he could, he manoeuvred Stephen's limp body onto the back seat.

When they arrived home, he managed to move Stephen from the car into the house. For a grown man, he weighed next to nothing, but it was drunken and sodden weight and offered no cooperation.

Cara had been waiting for over three hours. She struggled with her tears as Edward brought him in and laid him on the sofa in his study. She held back from touching him, afraid that with the slightest contact, she would break down.

'We need to get him out of those wet clothes.'

Stephen was beginning to come round, slurring his words.

'You should have left me, Dad.'

Edward had been about to go into the kitchen.

'I'll boil a kettle,' he told Cara.

'Can you get him some dry clothes first.'

'Yes, of course.'

'And a couple of towels.'

'You should have left me. I've done such bad things.'

'Quickly, Edward.'

'I've done such bad things, Mum.'

'We can talk about that later, Stephen. What we need to do now is make you warm and dry, and put some decent food into you. That's what you need. I don't suppose you've eaten properly for days.'

'Bad things, Mum. You don't want to know me.'

'I'll be the judge of that.'

It took him a few days to recover. He had 'flu and that was accompanied by a succession of minor complaints like sore throats and stomach upsets. Twig had stayed over one night, but he hadn't been aware of her. She wanted to reassure herself that he was going to be alright, but she decided it would be better if she were not around when he was well again. Her mother appeared to take her back readily enough and Cara was surprised when, after a fortnight or so, she'd heard nothing further from her. Cara couldn't blame her, but at the same time she hadn't expected that Twig would simply step out of their lives.

Stephen said very little about the weeks he'd been away. He didn't ask about Twig, though Cara had made it clear to him that Twig had stayed with them and that they knew about the baby. Stephen made no attempt to contact her, and Edward didn't feel it was right to encourage him to. Difficult as it was for Cara to acknowledge, Twig was probably better off without her son.

He accepted Edward's and Cara's offer to pay for rehab, and went off without complaint. When Edward visited, at least in the early days, he raged and spat, and resisted all Edward's efforts to calm him.

He was eventually allowed home for a weekend. Tim came back from school and they knocked a football around in the garden. They avoided going out to the pub or to see friends they had in the village, just in case Stephen was tempted, and instead they went on long walks in the woods and played chess together, things they had done as kids.

Edward had locked away their stock of whisky and white wine.

'He's doing okay,' Tim told him.

'Yes,' Edward replied, and he looked carefully at Tim, trying to work out how much his younger son knew. Then he said: 'He's got a long way to go, you know.'

'Sure. I appreciate that. All the same.'

'I'm not underrating what Stephen's achieved, Tim. I'm just saying his condition can be deceptive. People can appear to recover quite quickly, but deep down nothing's changed. That takes time.'

Tim was angered by that. He felt that his father hadn't given Stephen enough credit for trying.

When exactly Edward had realised Cara was having an affair wasn't entirely clear to him. He'd suspected that she was, at least, flirting with another man for some while. He couldn't say why he'd done it, but he'd looked at her mobile and found messages that were innocent enough in themselves, but paid off with five kisses, which seemed somehow unnecessary. *See you there. Xxxxx.* That sort of thing.

They were performing artists, opera singers and musicians, given to extravagance and physical displays of affection.

All the same.

Cara would leave her phone on charge overnight. He wasn't sleeping well, so he would go to bed later than she did. He remembered standing in the kitchen and staring at her phone sitting by the kettle, challenging himself not to look at it. Occasionally, he resisted and later found it difficult to sleep. More often, he would pick it up and study her recent messages. She was clever, he had to admit. She regularly cleared the Inbox, so that there was no evidence of any loving tributes she'd received. But she was more careless when it came to the Sent file. There he found a series of texts to the same mobile number. None of them were passionate or sexual; they were, if anything, more intimate than that. In one she'd written *You know you love it* and signed off with a 'C' and an incontinent number of kisses. He couldn't be bothered to count them.

C xxxxxxxxxxxxxx

On the occasions he found messages like this, it was even more difficult to sleep.

He tried to work out what it was that hurt him. God knows, he'd dreamed of sex with dozens of women. He wasn't sure that the desire hadn't increased with age, and there had been what he termed 'close encounters', moments when his friendship with a woman, usually another singer, might have developed into an affair and then, without either acknowledging that a decision had been made, it hadn't. There had been an intensity, a renewal of feelings he associated with being young, a joy perhaps that wained, gave way to what he liked to think was good sense. Was it? Had he missed out? Was he simply too timid to take the risk?

Cara's texts made him angry as well as hurt. They imposed a sense of prurience, a sense of peering into whatever the secrets were that she and her lover shared. It was like watching coition on the page, on a screen. Above all, it tore up the contract, didn't it? The contract that they were, to each other, the closest friend, lover, confidante, support that they had, was no longer intact or true. She had another, with whom she shared, to whom she gave, in whose ear she whispered, and that man, whoever he was, had been chosen instead of Edward.

He'd thought about confronting her, accusing her of having an affair, but what seemed to him like hard evidence he knew she could dismiss as mere flirtation. He couldn't even prove it was a man.

Gradually, he came to recognize that there were other symptoms of her infidelity. In retrospect, he realised that he could pretty well pinpoint the start of the affair to a particular week, when they had made love on the night of Valentine's Day and from then on their lovemaking had never been the same again. Cara attributed it to the menopause. She apologised and said she hoped the feelings would come back in due course. When he pressed her, she became irritable, even defensive.

'We are getting older, Edward,' she said.

Not in one week, he wanted to say, but he resisted. What was the point? He couldn't make her want him. He couldn't force her to be excited and sexually urgent, and it wasn't as if she had entirely given up on him. They continued to make love, but in a way that was desultory and without passion. They were regular as clockwork, every Sunday morning. He began to think of it as Cara covering her tracks.

All this time he knew that his weakness for conjecture was spinning out of control and sending him quietly mad. Idle speculation was like a virus that was taking him over. He wanted proof. However awful the truth was, he wanted to face it. He took to examining her phone twice, sometimes three times a day, and the evidence was always of the same kind, troubling but indefinite.

He began to hunt through the drawers of her desk, the pockets of her clothes, her handbags, hoping to find the unequivocal letter that put a name and an unfaithful emotion together. He found nothing. Either she was very good or he was creating a fantasy of self-torment that, if he didn't stop, would destroy their marriage.

Eventually, though, he did find, not exactly what he was looking for, but something tangible. Cara was in London, rehearsing. She'd taken her laptop in her backpack and left behind the satchel in which she usually kept it.

He went through the pockets, and in the large section at the back of the satchel was a printed out copy of an e-mail. It was from a hotel about forty miles away and addressed to Cara, but at an e-mail address he didn't recognize. The text of it was confirming her reservation for a room for two people on a date about a month earlier. He read it carefully. He wanted to be sure that it stated that the room was for two, not that it was a double room. That's what it said. A room for two.

It was an e-mail, but it seemed to Edward like an adulterous love letter. He wanted to tear it up, burn it, but he held back because it was the only proof he'd found. He tried to remember what Cara was supposed to be doing on the date of the booking. Nothing stood out. He went to the calendar they had hung up in the kitchen and flipped it back to the previous month. Against the day, it said 'Cara to London'. Nothing more. She could have been doing anything.

He didn't know whether to cry or to shout. All he could think about was the young woman he'd married, Cara beautiful in pink, on the terrace of a hotel in the Loire, laughing, just the two of them. They sat there with their cigarettes and their Sancerre and they were, as he saw them then, happy.

What now? What were they now? Did she want a divorce?

Sadness. That was all. After an hour or so, sadness was what he felt more than anything, deep down sadness, as if a fatal and irrevocable decision had been taken or some natural disaster had occurred, sweeping a family to their deaths, drowning them in fast, brown floodwater. Silly. Stupid. He wanted to know why, when it was avoidable. She could have had her own 'close encounter', like his, and walked away. But instead she had done something irreversible.

He said nothing. For two weeks, he said nothing and tried to allow his thoughts to settle, so that whatever course of action he eventually took would be the right one, thought through, sensible. The problem was his mood swings, which got in the way of any sensible decision. In his mind, he cried out for Cara, craving the return of their relationship to what it had been. But then the 'evidence' worked on him: the texts, the log of her calls sent and received, which he continued to monitor regularly, and the e-mail from the hotel.

It was an anger he couldn't remember experiencing before, engaging as it did his pride, his love, his hurt, his sense of her ability to secure the desire of another and enjoy it. When he felt that anger, he could have stabbed out the eyes of the innocent and burnt down the villages of the poor. There was no controlling it.

As it was, in the end, he did nothing. At the moment when he could have struck, when the iron was hot, when the evidence of the e-mail was recent and in his hand, he turned aside and decided he would not confront her. He kept asking himself whether this was simply weak, yet a further sign that he was afraid to live on his own, even if the price of cohabitation was disloyalty. But the answer he came back with was that his choice was not rooted in fear, but common sense. The affair would not last. If it had had the momentum or pragmatism to be sustainable, the evidence would have been, he argued, less ambiguous. Her absences would have been longer and more frequent, less guarded perhaps. No, Cara's affair had all the hallmarks of a spree. She would come back to him.

But there was a price for his silence. He knew that too. A little part of his heart went cold.

Why then try to preserve a relationship that has lost some of its meaning and value? Why remain with someone to whom your feelings have hardened? These were questions he found impossible to answer. He loved Cara. That he didn't doubt. He cared about her and wanted his marriage to continue. If he had his way, they would live out their days together. In that sense, he wanted to forgive her and, in due time, this affair of hers, whatever it was, however briefly it lasted, would fade away and take its place in the past in much the same way that the poor decisions they'd made about Stephen as a boy had receded and become no more than indistinct regrets.

He couldn't just forgive and forget, though. Cara had done what she'd done. She'd been unfaithful. He thought to begin with that what he was worrying about was a sense that she felt less for him, but it was the other way around. As he turned aside, he closed a part of himself to her and on the night he'd been expecting, the night after the *Mass in D Minor* in Salisbury Cathedral, when the adoring, adulatory Fiona offered him her body, he happily took it.

9

The rain had started two days earlier. They had a brief respite on the second evening, then it came on again overnight. They heard it pelting against their bedroom window from early morning. Cara turned over and laid her head on Edward's shoulder. He felt the warmth of her body the full length of his side. He pulled her in close and kissed her forehead.

'Couldn't I just ring in sick?' she said.

'They can't do much without you.'

'Does that mean you're going to make me go?'

He laughed and kissed her again, and she released herself and reluctantly got up from bed and went to the bathroom. He heard her switch on the shower and the dull thud of the cubicle door shutting behind her.

The rain drilled against the panes, and slewed out of the gutters above them. The forecast was for rain all day and throughout the weekend. BBC Radio seemed to think it might not ease up until the middle of the following week.

By eight she'd gone, driven off to the station in the Volvo. He planned to have a leisurely lunch and then, in the afternoon, he thought he might read or watch football. Tim was due anytime after six and he was expecting Cara to get back shortly after that. The day ahead looked attractive and undemanding. He was unusually cheerful, he realised.

They were rehearsing in Duke Street again, which she loved. The pleasure she took in singing was somehow intensified by the high ceilings and the elegant Regency windows overlooking the Selfridge Hotel. The weather in London was better than Hampshire's. She was so glad she'd made the effort to come up. Sunlight streamed into the room and everyone looked as though they were there for a party.

'You look happy,' Fiona remarked.

'It was raining cats and dogs at home. I thought it'd be the same in London.' She paused. 'The fact is that it's not the weather that has really bucked me up. It's the news about Stephen.'

'Which is?'

'Oh, maybe it didn't make the national news. It was all over our local programme. They think they've found where he was held. The army think.'

'And?'

'And he wasn't there. They're hoping he escaped.'

'What do you think?'

'I don't know, Fiona. I change from day to day. But today's a good day!'

Cara shrugged her shoulders as if to imply that she knew it was an insubstantial reason to be in such openly high spirits, but it was the best she could do.

'Let's hope Jakob's in one of his better moods, then,' Fiona said. 'I'd hate for him to bring you down.'

'I'm not as thin-skinned as all that.'

'No? I guess things have gone well for you.'

Cara was surprised. If she wasn't mistaken, the remark was catty.

'What do you mean?'

'Nothing,' Fiona said, and she changed the subject. 'I saw Harry last night. Harry Miles. He said the recordings with Edward have been going brilliantly. That's good, isn't it? I think they've been fantastic. Has Edward said anything?'

'He may have done.' Cara couldn't shake off the suspicion that Fiona thought she'd not deserved the success she'd had. 'I think he's very pleased with how it's going.'

'Great. I'm really glad they got together.'

'Of course, we have you to thank for that.'

'Just the messenger.'

Jakob appeared in the room and marched up to the piano. He apologised for his lateness. He looked flustered and when he took off his black trilby, Cara could see that he was sweating. His forehead shone in the morning sunshine.

They began with the scene in Bethlehem. Mary cradles her baby son and, somewhat incredibly, encourages him to feed strands of grass to the sheep grazing around the stable. She is then joined by Joseph and, in what Cara thought one of the most beautiful duets in the piece, they urge Jesus on, adding flower petals to the grass, apparently to the increasing delight of the sheep. It was all slightly ridiculous and a touch heavy-handed in its prescience. Was Jesus a good shepherd before he could walk?

She sang well, immersed in the beauty of it. Jakob seemed pleased with her and most of his notes were for William. Joseph, he felt, was a little behind Mary throughout.

She realised that the reason she felt hurt by Fiona's comment was because it echoed, or might echo, everything that Tim accused her of. Tim attributed her success to her affair with Karl

Rouse. He would never say it, of course, but that was what he believed. Put bluntly, she'd slept her way to the top.

It wasn't true. She might have had a few breaks as a result of her fling, but it wasn't the foundation, or even the catalyst, of her career. She would have liked to have had it out with Tim, made him say exactly what it was that he found dishonest about her. But he shied away whenever she tried. When he thought she wasn't aware, he would stare at her. She sensed the criticism, the hint of a sneer. Sometimes she'd round on him and bark: 'What is it, Tim? What's on your mind?' He always said the same. 'Nothing,' he'd say, and then he would add: 'Nothing you'd understand.'

They took a ten minute break. She avoided Fiona, not she hoped rudely, but she just wanted a few minutes on her own. It was probably not a sensible thing to do, not on a day when she felt optimistic about Stephen. Dwelling on the problem with Tim dragged her down. It was intractable, and it provoked in her a deep sense of injustice. He exaggerated what she'd done and tried to find in her single indiscretion the whole of her personality, the nature of her being, whereas the truth was that it had been the exception to the rule. If she examined the rest of her life, the affair with Karl seemed anomalous.

There were occasions when she felt she'd rather not see Tim. He would be there tonight, when she got home, settled in with his father, whisky on the go or the fine bottle of Sancerre he invariably brought as a gift for Edward. She resented it. This cosiness, the wine, the imputations, the cruelty of it. She might now have only one son, and he denied her his love.

'Everyone!'

Jakob's assistant was calling them all back to the rehearsal. '*Choir of Angels*. From the top.'

There were dozens of people on the main street. This, it turned out, was the hour for shopping. The market stalls and canopied shop fronts were raucous with trade and argument and laughter. Women in twos and threes sauntered between the fruits and vegetables, their burkas as colourful as the produce.

I kept my head down and walked quickly. I thought if I had a sense of purpose, I was less likely to attract attention. I tried not to look around me, but those few seconds of warning before someone pounces or raises the alarm are precious, so I couldn't stop myself glancing left and right from time to time, trying to get a sense of whether or not I was being observed.

The heat made me nervous. I was sure the sweat pouring down my face made me different, conspicuous, but I was two thirds of the way down the street and nothing had so far happened. There were men on low benches who looked up as I passed, but they quickly forgot me, more absorbed in their talk and coffee and hookahs.

The air was heavy with the aromas of tobacco and spices and the produce of the market. Despite my state of panic, I found it wonderful, beautiful even. War happens in greys and reds and blacks. The only colours are fire and blood. The colours of the market made you forget. I was tempted to pause and enjoy it for a moment, but I'd been fortunate so far. There was no point in pushing my luck. I needed to get away from people and the risk of discovery.

I pressed on down the main street. Once I was clear of the market and the street cafés, I came to a crossroads. Ahead of me the road continued through low rise housing and there were parked cars and trucks. Off to the left, though, an empty road led straight out to open countryside. Such buildings as there were had windowless walls and very few entrances. I would be quickly beyond them.

Luck continued to run my way. Leaning against one of the featureless walls was a bicycle. I walked the few metres down the street, took hold of the handlebars and swung the bike round to point out of town. I had a quick look back to the crossroads. A truck rattled across the junction, speeding away from the market. I draped the sack over the bike's saddle and climbed on to it and started to pedal. No one shouted or screamed. There was no sound of a mustering lynch mob taking to their feet after me. Someone would miss the bike and I felt sorry about that, but for me it could make the difference between life and death.

Within a few minutes I was riding between fields of maize and poppies. It was a great feeling.

I was travelling three to four times faster than I would otherwise have done. In the vicinity of the town, the roads were better constructed and the surfaces reasonably intact. I had no trouble avoiding the ruts and holes and within an hour I'd probably covered fifteen kilometres. The heat prevented me from cycling any faster and I had to make frequent stops for a slug of water, rationing myself to a single mouthful at a time. Even doing this, by the end of that hour the bottle was half drunk.

I was now on the far side of the town, heading in the direction of the shelling I'd seen the previous night. On one level, it seemed madness to be making my way towards a battleground and the danger of being caught up in an exchange of fire. But on the other, without a map or compass or the language skills to ask anyone for help, this was the only way I could imagine contacting the lads. Somehow, I told myself, I would find the engagement and work out which was my side.

The traffic got heavier than I was expecting, probably because the market was over. There were cars and several large trucks in both directions. I bent my head down as they passed, as if with the effort of pedalling, and their drivers ignored me. I was just another poor guy on a bike.

I was more concerned when a motorcycle came up alongside and the biker started shouting at me. I couldn't understand. He was pointing behind me, at something behind the saddle or the back wheel. When he realised he was getting nowhere, he patted his head to indicate that I was obviously an idiot, and accelerated off.

Moments later it became clear what he was getting at. The bike sank under me. Then I skidded and fell off and rolled into the ditch at the side of the road.

I lay in the dry mud and stones for what seemed like quite a while. Several vehicles passed by without stopping. The stones pressed into my back and hurt, but I knew there was a more serious problem with my right ankle. I was reluctant to get up and discover what it was. The pain was sharp and racking. I was pretty certain that I couldn't have broken it, but a sprain was all too possible. What I'd most dreaded was the possibility of disabling myself. I'd always said that I had a fair chance of survival and rescue as long as I managed to keep going.

The sun tortured my face. I could feel my skin burning. It couldn't be long before it caught fire. As much to avert my head as confront the injury to my ankle, I raised myself to a sitting position and looked at my foot. There was nothing to see, no blood or deformation. That much was good. I tried to kneel, but that hurt too much. The alternative was to drag myself backwards up the side of the ditch, using my hands for leverage and shuffling on my arse.

I glanced at the bike. The rear tyre was flat and had torn itself from the rim of the wheel. It didn't look like something I could repair. The motorcyclist must have seen that the tyre was soft and was trying to warn me before it got worse.

I needed to establish whether I could stand. I turned myself over and gasped for breath as my chest thudded on the roadside. I forced myself onto my knees. With my foot at forty-five degrees, the pressure on my ankle was excruciating. I dragged my good leg forward under me and tried to put all my weight on that side. Cautiously, I pushed down on my hands, leaned on my left foot and began to stand. Once I was up, I moved my right foot forward and transferred my weight as carefully as I could. I thought I would faint from the pain. It bolted through my ankle. I felt a surge of adrenolin rush through every part of me. There was pain in my head, pain in my eyes. I made the next step, moving my left foot forward. The pain eased, miraculously. It was as if I'd been taken from heaven to hell and back again. I could breathe. I could think.

The wrecked bicycle lay next to me. I bent down and grabbed the sack and flung it into the field. Then I struggled to lift the bicycle. I got it off the ground, and using both arms, swung it round and dropped it into the ditch, where it wouldn't be visible to passers-by.

Two facts were evident. One, I wouldn't be able to walk until the swelling had died down. Two, I couldn't stay where I was. Somehow, I had to get away from the road and allow my ankle the time to recover.

With difficulty, I lowered myself onto my knees and then to a position sitting on the bank. From there I managed to slide down into the ditch. I manoeuvred myself onto my knees again and started to crawl amongst the poppies in the field, trying not to crush them, so that my path through them wouldn't be obvious.

I used the sack as a mat to protect my knees. I could move if I lifted my left foot first, placed it ahead of me and then dragged my right leg behind. I was surprised by how much effort it involved rearranging the sack, hauling my own body weight forward and overcoming the pain that came with all that.

I stopped and took a slug of water from the bottle. I had about a third of it left.

When I'd forced my way about five or six metres into the poppies, I allowed myself a rest. I slumped down and lay on my back and the sun scorched my face again. My forehead was greasy with sweat. My beard felt damp and it itched like mad.

I tried not to think too hard about what I was going to do next. The priority was to rest my ankle and get fit enough to walk. It was just a sprain. Once the inflammation died down, I'd be fine.

I was lying on a bed of pink petals. The poppy heads must have shed them a matter of hours earlier, or at most a day. They looked very fresh and still had moisture in them. I grabbed a handful and squeezed them. I felt the moisture in my fingers. They were fleshy and new, signalling the harvest. When I tried to throw them away, they clung on like wet flour or pastry. I couldn't shake them off. I smelt my fingers. Nothing. I had beautiful pink flower petals in my hands and they smelt of nothing at all.

I began to wish I'd landed in a pistachio field or a vineyard, somewhere that produced food I could eat.

Eventually, I slept.

He switched on Radio 3 and sat down at his desk. Tippett. Not his period. He couldn't get on with it. Too many odd changes. It was as if Tippett had been afraid of logical sequence. He'd develop something quite beautiful and then jump away from it into an entirely new and discordant piece, unrelated to the first.

The music made him restless and he went over to the French window. Rainwater splashed down the windows from the gutter above, which was overwhelmed by the volume of water falling into it. Edward knew it was clogged, like the other gutters, and that he should have cleared them of leaves weeks ago, but like most postponable jobs, he'd thought about it and then forgotten and then remembered on a day when it wasn't practical, either because it was raining again or he hadn't the time.

But it wasn't the choked gutter that now alarmed him. At the bottom of the garden, where it met the river, the water level had risen to the point that the river was spilling onto the lawn. There were, so far, only scattered pools, and the water lapped lazily across the grass, but it would get worse, he had no doubt. Within a few hours, he estimated, the river would flood the whole garden.

He put on wellington boots and his Barbour and walked out to the bank and the bench where he used to sit with the boys and watch the river's flow. The river was the brown of milk chocolate and thick with the accumulated silt it was carrying. The water was racing now. It looked swollen and weighed down with riverbank debris it had picked up and run away with. He watched a dead fish sweep past, a perch. It was closely followed by a sodden and broken pallet, which circled around on itself as it flew by. The river seemed to be overwhelmed, in a state of hurry and panic, as if it could not quite deal with its own grandiose energy.

It sped past Edward's garden as if the last thing it could be bothered with was diverting its flow to take over an acre of Hampshire lawn.

But the pools at his feet said otherwise. The river spilled across the lower lawn and the small vegetable patch. He'd never before known the river so high, the lawn so saturated.

The rain had been relentless all morning. It had prevented him from taking his Saturday stroll down to the village to buy a newspaper and a pint at The Rock. He didn't mind too much. Tim would probably bring *The Guardian* with him and if he was so desperate for a drink, there was always wine in the fridge.

He pulled up the hood of his Barbour and went to find a spade. There wasn't much he could do to prevent a flood, but building up the bank might help.

He fetched the spade from the garage and then began to take soil from the flowerbeds close to the house, gradually filling the wheelbarrow. Then he walked the barrow down to the river and emptied it at one end of the frontage. After a dozen barrows of soil, he'd constructed a low wall twenty feet across. They might be lucky. For the river to rise another few inches would take a while and in that time the rain might have begun to ease.

He worked on, slowly building up the defensive wall. Behind the garage, he had a pile of bricks, left over when they had the terrace laid in front of the French windows. He lobbed the old yellow bricks into the wheelbarrow and carted them down to the river. He then wedged them into the face of the mud wall, reinforcing its base. When the bricks were used up, he found a couple of broken fencing panels and drove those into the soft ground in front of the wall. It was all flimsy and easily breeched, but anything that gained the house a few extra minutes might save it.

This had been a long time coming. He'd thought about it whenever the river had been high and there had been flooding in the village. He'd watched the television news pictures of coastal villages in Cornwall devastated by flash floods. One, he remembered, had only just begun to recover when a second torrent wiped away most of the reconstruction and revetting carried out after the first. He'd seen children passed hand to hand into rescue boats and women up to their knees in brown water, throwing ruined rugs and cushions into a skip.

It had made him think that it was only a matter of time before a flood hit his own house.

Those pictures had prompted him to order a couple of hundred sandbags. They were delivered to his door the next day and he stacked them along the back wall of the garage. Cara didn't know. He hadn't told her. She'd have laughed and said that he was being melodramatic. She'd seen the same television bulletins and she'd felt for those people and how their houses had been wrecked in the course of an afternoon. But she didn't think it could happen in Hampshire.

He stepped across the terrace and through the side door into the garage. Then he piled some of the sandbags in the barrow and wheeled them to the French windows. He stood back on the lawn and studied the house. The front was slightly higher and would probably be protected by the rising ground. At the back most of the windows had a metre of bricks under them. They would be safe enough. But the doors onto the terrace were vulnerable He watched the rain splashing on the paving and bouncing against them. He felt cold.

He put down a first layer of the grey sandbags, twenty of them, across the full width of the terrace. Then he returned to the garage and brought back more bags, and placed them in a second course, staggered so that the joins of the bags on the lower course were covered by the bags above them, like a built wall.

It was tiring. He felt it in his back, lower down, at his waist. Every time he bent down, he expected his back to go into spasm.

He managed to put down three layers of sandbagging, but then felt too exhausted to go on. Perhaps he would add more later. The wall of bags was impressive and substantial by comparison with what he'd done by the river. The heavy rain had begun to darken the grey cloth, which made the bags look heavy and immovable. They might not be waterproof, but he was sure they would hold back the kind of slow flood likely to creep up the garden later in the day.

Inside, he hung his coat on a hook on the back of the kitchen door and pulled off his boots. The coat dripped on the doormat. The house felt cold.

He put on the kettle and opened the post. It was almost entirely bills and mail-outs from companies selling shirts or wine or pizza. He threw the flyers in the plastic bin they used for recycling and filled the caffetière with boiling water. He watched the rain beating out patterns of drops on the windows. A day which had begun happily enough now seemed to him to have turned grim and full of apprehension. He thought about the river and wondered how long it would be before it broke through to the house.

How long have I been out? An hour or two? Three? Although the sun is still high, it strikes my face at a different angle. I feel a chill run through me, but it is momentary, part of adjusting to being awake after deep sleep.

There is a great deal of pain in my ankle. My sleep obliterated all that anxiety and I woke up having entirely forgotten that I'd injured myself. Now the memory of it returns, the realisation, and with that the pain.

I gently bend my right leg up towards me and, very tentatively, I touch the ankle. The pain is nasty, like an open wound, but not intolerable. I lower my leg and try to roll over on to my front. The effort winds me and it is several minutes before I can attempt the next manoeuvre.

I prop myself up on my elbows, then draw my left leg under me so that I can put my weight on my left knee. At this point, I hesitate. So far, it's cost me a good deal of effort, but not much pain. Trying to get on all-fours will, I know, be excruciating.

But it has to be done.

I pull my right leg through and kneel. The pain is curiously pure and unvarying. It doesn't grow or decrease or come in waves. It simply is. I know I can put up with it. I have to go through it. I lift my leg and place the foot down and shift all my weight to it and stand.

The sweat rains down my face. I am in agony. But I know it. I know this is as bad as it will get, and if that is so, I can survive it. I can tolerate the intolerable. I start to walk. The poppies cave away. Each step is an ordeal of pain and trembling, but I manage to convince myself not only that I can take it, but that it's going to get easier. With each step, I am continuing a process of walking off the pain.

That's what I believe.

I reach the road, claw my way up the bank and start to walk along the tarmac.

I have cut down from the road and am making for the river. I spotted it a few metres back. The sun glanced across it and there was a flash of light on the surface of the water. I just caught a glimpse of it through the tall grass. I'll be glad to get away from the road. I have been lucky so far. I've not seen a single vehicle since I left the poppy field. But that can't last, and if I'm hobbling along, it's bound to attract attention. Someone will slow down, if only out of kindness, and take a proper look at me.

Progress has been very slow, as I'd expected. I've probably covered no more than half a kilometre. I need to disappear, get somewhere where I can have another rest and let my ankle recuperate. It's swollen up all over again and is as bad as when I first sprained it. The river will be soothing.

It's as much as I can manage to reach the riverbank, and I fall to my knees and lean down and cup the water to my mouth with my hands. It is delicious and freezing cold, a taste of the mountains, and I don't much care if there's a goat's carcase snagged in a tree root two kilometres upstream. I drink until I can swallow no more of it. This is Elysium.

In the river, my ankle is pain-free. The flow is fast and the vivid cold serves as anaesthetic. I can't feel my foot. It's as if it's been cut away. I have sensation down to my knee, but not below it.

The immediate task is to regain my equilibrium, and to neutralise or reduce the pain to a point at which I can think straight.

Fortunately, this part of the river can't be seen from the road. Behind me are tall grasses and a wheat field and for as long as I am sitting like this, crouched down, I am invisible to passing traffic.

The ground on the other side of the river is more open, but it rises quickly to the mountains, where there are cart tracks and goat trails, but nothing navigable by a vehicle. I might be noticed by a shepherd on a hill path, or even by a gunman, but at this distance I'm sure I'd be mistaken for a local man taking a drink and bathing his feet. To that extent, I'm safe. But the sun's declining and I can sense the temperature beginning to turn and fall. There's no shelter here. I have my sack, but that will give little or no protection once night falls and the wind picks up.

This is the worst position I could have put myself in, what army training teaches you to avoid, being out on a bare hillside at night in freezing conditions. If I call out, if I shout, it's doubtful anyone would hear me. I'm too far from the road. I must try and limp or crawl my way back. Whatever it takes, I must get back to the road and hope that I can flag someone down. Does that make sense? I'm not sure. I know the cold here. On patrol, I've come across the bodies of people caught out in it. As they were dying, they struck an attitude, limbs flung out, like branches half torn from trees.

That's how death often appears in these mountains.

The forecast didn't change over the next few hours. He listened to local radio just before the hour, every hour, and the presenters always said the same, with a cheery resignation he found irritating. Rain and more rain, they said. They didn't seem to realise how much damage was about to occur. Perhaps their homes weren't threatened.

Around four he sat down in the armchair in his study with a bottle of malt whisky and a book about the wines of the Loire. He leant across and retuned the radio, relieved when he heard Bach and not some modern nonsense.

Outside, the sky was black with rain and the trees swayed violently in the wind. When he glanced at the purples and browns and the golden sun in a photograph on his desk of Saumur in early autumn, it made him want to laugh.

The malt was good. Islay. He took it with a splash, as the experts recommended, enough to release the aromas and specify the flavour. He picked up the scent of heather as he sipped it and let the cool liquid stay in his mouth for a moment. He thought there were hints of caramel as he swallowed. It was very good.

The plastic gutters above the terrace had ceased to channel water away for some time. Water now fell out of them in a curtain. It gave the French windows a smoky mist that began to obscure the garden.

He knew the river had yet to rise to the critical height. It was in the process of doing so, adding to itself with each minute of rain.

He drank his whisky, waiting, finding himself thinking about Stephen.

They had not had any word from the army for several days, not since the fiasco over the MOD press release. Cara said they'd been abandoned. She thought Stephen's C.O. had given up hope of his recovery and had taken the view that the family should be left to draw its own conclusions and start the process of grieving. It angered her because she had not given up. Stephen could be hiding in the hills. Anywhere. It might be no more than an instinct, but she believed that Stephen was alive.

Edward agreed with her. At least, he always said that he agreed with her. There seemed little point in not doing so. It upset her if he so much as intimated that she was alone, that everyone else had accepted that Stephen would not return. In the early days, months ago now, his assent had been tacit and that had not been good enough, nowhere near good enough. She had railed at him. He was either with her or against her. He had to choose. It was like signing up to a campaign.

He peered through the mist at the river wall and thought he might have seen water spill over the top. It was brief, a wave and it was gone. But he was almost certain he'd seen it.

It had been the same with e-mails. For a time, they received short and rather formal reports on searches that had been conducted and how they had failed to locate Stephen or to secure any intelligence about his whereabouts. Then these communiqués dried up too. Edward discontinued his daily routine of switching on his computer before breakfast to look at his messages, and quite soon he was only consulting his Inbox every few days. He didn't expect any work to come in that way. As far as he knew, there was nothing in prospect apart from another recording with Harry Miles in December, and if there were anything new, Derek would ring. He was an old-fashioned agent in that way. He hated computers and mobiles.

His glass was empty. He reached out for the bottle and dragged it over.

His bloody fault Stephen was in the army at all. All his bloody fault! He could have prevented it, but they'd come up against a brick wall, hadn't they? What was Stephen to do? After he'd recovered, got his life back together, there was a yawning chasm. The question that had been put off and put off could no longer be put off. What was Stephen going to do with his life? They had to come up with an answer. There was no point in procrastinating further. If they didn't have an answer soon, Stephen would simply slip back into his old, bad ways. Or that was Edward's fear anyway.

He had mentioned the army almost as a joke. He'd seen one of the recruitment ads on television, with its promise of adventure, and it popped out one supper time as if it were the most ridiculous idea anyone could come up with. Failing everything else, what about the army? The last refuge of a scoundrel kind of thing. Cara had laughed. She'd realised Edward had intended it as a joke.

But the boys had looked at each other. Suddenly, it was something for them to discuss. They'd spotted the kernel of a plan in it and they needed to talk it through. Stephen even said, as he was leaving the room, that he thought his father might have hit on something.

He and Cara were so shocked that they didn't speak for several minutes and when the boys returned and Stephen said that he was going to apply, it was as if they had passed from ludicrous suggestion to confirmed career plan without any steps in between.

But Edward knew that he could have prevented it. If he'd wanted to. He didn't try, that was the truth of it, didn't even pause to assess it. It was a good idea because it was something as opposed to nothing, practical, dare he say – attainable?

He topped up his glass and walked over to the French

windows and waited out the sodden afternoon. The wind had picked up again. The trees swayed up and down like a crowd fleeing for the exit after someone has shouted 'Fire!'. They were bent so far he thought they might snap or be torn up by the roots. They were being tortured by a wind more powerful than they.

It occurred to him that he might now be drunk and displaying a slight weakness for anthropomorphism.

The rain came on as Tim joined the M3. It had been dry in west London throughout the morning and early afternoon and the sky had given no indication that a downpour was on the way. He turned up the windscreen wipers. They swept away the pelting rain as well as they could, blading bucketsful to left and right, and just about coping. He noticed that the traffic was slowing down in all three lanes.

He expected to have an hour or two with his father before his mother arrived. That, at least, was welcome. He'd offered to collect his mother from her rehearsal and drive her down, but she'd declined, saying it would be easier for both of them if she took the train. It was a relief when she said it.

Dad wouldn't talk much. If there'd been anything to report about Steve, he'd have passed it on immediately. No, they'd pass the time discussing Tim's job, the paucity of bookings in his father's diary, this year's apple crop. Sometimes, he felt his father sounded bitter, but it was difficult to pinpoint a reason for it and he always denied it if Tim asked him. Perhaps it was old age. Perhaps that's what six decades did to you. Whenever Tim hinted that Edward might be depressed, or more often *slightly down* would be the phrase he used, his father became unnaturally cheerful and suggested another drink or going for a walk or a tour round the garden, anything that relieved the awkwardness of the face to face encounter. Dad wanted to appear to be in control, successful. If he let the mask slip, he'd be frantic to put it back in place, to re-establish the proprieties of the father-son relationship as he saw them

He did wonder whether Edward was simply waiting for someone to give him permission to retire. As a freelance, there was no fixed end to his career, no letter announcing that he was sixty or sixty-five and must leave his job and draw his pension. He could go on for as long as someone was prepared to hire him. Now that not many people were prepared, he might like to be told to stop, to be given an exeat and sunny days and a deckchair with Bach's entire oeuvre and a pallet of white wine.

The radio was advising motorists to expect exceptionally heavy downpours throughout the southern region. They gave a warning that driving conditions could be hazardous.

At that moment, every vehicle in front of him came to a halt. Their red brake lights had a bright diffused glow as if he were seeing them not through rain but a smear of Vaseline. It further contributed to a curiously cocooned feeling he had, brought on by the weight of the rain.

The vehicles edged forward. They were probably advancing at the rate of no more than a car's length every minute or so. As he waited between opportunities to move, Tim glanced at his fellow drivers. He noticed one man beating his steering wheel with his hands, but it was impossible to tell whether he was in a fury about the delay or listening to rock music. All Tim could hear was the hammering of the rain on his car roof and the neurotic thrash of the windscreen wipers.

They had waited so long, hadn't they? They had waited while the army offered reassurance and plans of action. They had waited when there were reports of sightings and they had waited patiently while they were told that everything had been done that could have been done.

But now, it struck him, they waited in silence, all the more painful and frustrating for there having been a hint that Steve might be alive and free. It was the kind of silence in which he imagined that there were voices speaking to him in whispers, but they were so quiet they were inaudible. He knew what they were saying, though. Had he been able to make them out, they would have said 'Move on' and 'You know he's gone. Stop pretending.' And 'It's time to get on with your life.'

These were the voices he would rather not hear because he feared that they were his own. He would have liked to prove them wrong, to google the earth and show them the spot where Steve was, captive again maybe, but alive. That's the evidence, he would have liked to have said, to silence the silent voices.

His lane was crawling forward, sloping past drivers on either side, who regarded him, he thought, with disbelief and resentment. He quite quickly picked up speed and then the whole motorway appeared to be up and running again. The road was shiny with a greasy membrane and thin sprays jetted up from the wet tyres. Life on the M3 seemed to be returning to something approaching normal.

The sun is just perceptible, a stringless balloon of orange light skirting the top of a far hill. The shadows are very long now and the river has darkened.

I caught sight of him about half an hour ago. At first, I thought it was a sheep or a goat, grazing on the riverbank. Then I realised that he was making steady progress along the line of the river, heading for the road in a way that no animal would do.

I'd made so little headway myself that I might just as well not have bothered. Once I'd taken my foot out of the river, I tried to stand, but it was impossible. The pain was too severe. I had no choice but to crawl, and that too entailed intense spasms of pain. Every time I drew my right leg forward, it felt like a dead weight. My foot dragged in the grass and put pressure on the ankle. I felt I could weep with pain.

He's probably only a few hundred metres away. He has a grey cap and a matching tunic. I can't begin to guess his age, except that the speed at which he travels across the landscape suggests that he can't be old.

The river, just below me, is dark and fast. I feel dizzy. Perhaps I have a fever coming on. I am apprehensive about this young man's approach. It's not exactly fear. He doesn't appear to be carrying a weapon and his determined stride suggests that he has yet to see me. Oddly, it crosses my mind that I may pass out before he reaches me.

Cara had said goodbye to Fiona shortly after the rehearsal finished at four. They were the last to leave. They slammed the door shut behind them, hurried down the stairs and out onto Duke Street. They walked arm in arm to the tube.

'That was fantastic,' Fiona said.

'Jakob seemed pleased, didn't he? Are you catching a train?'

'No, I've got shopping to do. I'll see you next week.'

They kissed, and Cara went down the steps into the Underground and took the Jubilee line to Waterloo. She felt good about herself. A rehearsal wasn't a performance, of course, and they had some way to go before they would be of a standard to appear before the public, but given her nervousness about the high expectations Jakob, and indeed the rest of the cast, had of her, she was immensely relieved, both that she had sung as well as she thought she could and that people had liked what she'd done.

She was on a train to Hampshire by five and looking forward to the evening. Tim would be his usual difficult self, but the rehearsal had made her confident and with a couple of glasses of wine in her, she wouldn't mind any of his looks or jibes.

The rain whipped the windows of the train, leaving wet ribbons trailing across them like scars. She looked out on the transitory countryside. The sheep and horses were pitiful, she thought, but perhaps they didn't mind. Everyone near her was reading or chatting softly. She'd deliberately reserved a seat in one of the Quiet Carriages, hoping to avoid people with mobiles and MP3s and badly designed earphones. Nonetheless, there was a girl in her teens at the far end and Cara could hear a faint, percussive hiss from her direction.

She thought then about Fiona. She'd sometimes wondered whether Fiona had had a thing for Edward. She'd always been a good friend and they'd had a lot of fun together, in so far as their considerable age difference allowed. When Fiona had first enquired about Edward's work, Cara had been embarrassed, not wanting to divulge that he had little or none and was very depressed about it. But it had later occurred to her that what Fiona was interested in was not the state of Edward's career, but Edward himself. She liked him, admired him, and Harry Miles, it had turned out, was not merely an opportunity for Edward to return to the recording studio; it was also an opportunity for Fiona to spend time with Edward.

Would she mind? After what had happened with Karl, it would seem hypocritical, wouldn't it, to object? She suspected that Edward would have no interest in someone as young as Fiona, but you couldn't always tell. He'd said nothing about her, or rather he'd mentioned that he'd bumped into her a couple of times at rehearsals and at Abbey Road. There had been no hint of enthusiasm in his voice, no attempt to conceal an attraction. The likelihood was that she'd been briefly infatuated and Edward hadn't even noticed. That would be typical of him. She smiled at the thought.

She was still smiling as the train pulled in.

Edward was sitting in his study, with his face in a crystal tumbler of whisky, when he heard Tim's car on the gravel outside. He didn't immediately get up. He thought about it, and then calculated that it would take Tim a few minutes to unload his bag and lock the car. He needn't make a move to the door until Tim knocked.

He sipped the whisky, as little as he could, which was the way to drink when already very drunk. Very good whisky, this. Islay.

The knocking, he felt, had gone on for rather longer than it should and someone should have answered the door by now.

Cara should have answered it.

But Cara wasn't around, was she?

'I thought you were going to leave me out here all night,' Tim said.

He handed Edward a wine bottle. Edward leaned back to read the label and nearly dropped it.

'Very nice. Thank you.'

'Usual stuff. Always reliable. Can I come in, do you think? You're kind of in the way.'

'Sorry.'

Edward sidled off to the fridge and put the Sancerre on a shelf on its side.

'Are you okay?' Tim asked. In the short distance between his car and the house, the torrential rain had drenched him. He put down his case and shrugged his coat off his shoulders. Edward not having offered to take it from him, he hung it alongside the Barbour and followed Edward to the study.

'Drink?'

'Dad! Are you okay?'

'Fine, thank you. Very well.'

Tim was struck by an odd smell as he walked in.

'For Christ's sake, Dad! There's water coming in under the French windows. You're pissed, aren't you? You didn't notice.'

'I'm sorry?'

Tim examined the shallow pool that had accumulated on the parquet floor inside the garden door. It was dirty, like dishwater, and the green carpet had begun to draw it in. It had a dark patch, like a vast jigsaw piece, black with seeped water.

'What are we going to do?'

'I put some sandbags down to prevent it.'

'I can see that, Dad, but they haven't been entirely successful, have they? Are there any more?'

'I expect so. A few,' Edward said. He sat down rather heavily and picked up his whisky.

'Well, where are they?'

Tim was shouting now.

'Have a drink, Tim. Stop fussing. It's only a little water.'

Tim marched over and snatched the glass away from him.

'You've had enough, Dad. Really. You're pissed. Where are the sandbags? Your house is flooding.'

Edward looked up at him, hurt. He said:

'In the garage.'

It would be a waste of time asking for Edward's help, so he grabbed his coat and went out into the dark wet alone. What in God's name had his father been doing? He hadn't seen him as drunk as this in years, if ever. Surely he couldn't have been drinking all day? After all, he had managed to erect some kind of sandbag defence on the terrace and, as Tim crossed the garden, the light from the house allowed him to pick out a similar structure down by the river. The stench of the floodwater was almost overpowering. Parts of the lawn had disappeared under a foot of water, which was presumably continuing to rise. He suspected it had not long crept over the step of the terrace and soaked through the wall of sandbags, but given another hour the study would be flooded.

He hurried over to the garage and found the remaining bags stacked in a corner. He was surprised how heavy they were when he tried to lift three at a time and had to settle for two. Building those walls must have exhausted his father. Not the ideal job for a man with a history of heart failure. But then, he had had no choice. He had to do something.

Tim carried the bags into the house and laid them under the windows. There didn't seem to be much point in attempting to clear up the water that was already there. It would be quickly soaked up by the sand.

He arranged the bags so that they were snug against the crack at the base of the doors. Then he went outside to fetch more.

Edward had finished his drink. He considered re-filling it, but decided not to, and placed the glass, with studied care, on his desk. He caught sight of the time and the thought occurred to him that he would have expected Cara to be home by now. It had gone seven.

Tim came back several times with sandbags, which he gradually built up into a low wall. Edward thought it all had a touch of the Blitz about it, pictures he'd seen as a child.

'Do sit down and have a drink, Tim,' he said. 'You seem to be working awfully hard, and you've driven all the way from London. You must be worn out.'

'Just a few more, Dad.'

Edward smelt the river in his room. The smell had an earthiness to it and a hint of waste, like the municipal dump. It was an outdoors smell, out of place amongst books and musical scores and Radio 3 and single malts. He wanted to laugh. The incongruity tickled him.

'There we are.' Tim was back in his chair. 'That's the lot. If those don't hold back the water, we've nothing else.'

'That's the spirit!'

'The garden's flooded, you know that?'

'Doesn't surprise me. Doesn't surprise me one bit. The

river's been swelling up all day.'

'Well, you've a foot of water on the lawn.'

'Doesn't surprise me. A big, fat, swollen river. Strong, brown god.'

Edward laughed. He stood up and went to his desk. 'Drink?'

Tim came over to join him.

'I think you've had enough.'

'You don't think your old Dad can be the judge of that?'

'Not really, no.'

Edward wasn't going to insist. He sat down whilst Tim went to the kitchen and poured himself a glass of wine from the fridge.

'It's a sad day when a son doesn't trust his father's judgement,' Edward said when he returned.

'I do trust your judgement, Dad. I just think you've had one too many and now might be the time to stop.'

'I haven't been drinking all day, you know.'

'I know that.'

'You should leave me to make my own decisions.'

Had he shaved? Tim couldn't quite tell.

'Is anything wrong?' he asked.

'No, why should there be?'

Edward looked directly at him, his eyes defiant, if a little squiffy.

'It's only that you don't normally behave like this. You're not someone who gets drunk.'

'I'm bored.'

'That's no excuse.'

'No?'

'Not really. You're a man with plenty to occupy him. You read. You listen to music. You walk. You garden.'

'Not today.'

'No, well, perhaps not today. But the point is you're pretty self-reliant, Dad.'

'Am I? I wonder sometimes. Go on, Tim. For goodness sake. Let me have a drink.'

'It's your choice. I can't stop you.'

Edward didn't hesitate. He took the whisky bottle from the desk and started to pour himself a large measure.

'Is it work?' Tim asked.

Edward drank. Then he became thoughtful. He looked towards the French windows and the wall of sandbags and smiled.

'I don't know what it's about, Tim. I apologise. I am just having a down day.'

'As long as there's nothing bothering you. A longer running problem, I mean?'

Edward turned to him, but said nothing.

'Sorry. Of course, I know there's Steve. I hadn't forgotten, you know. But that's something we all live with, isn't it? It's not peculiar to you.'

'Do you remember when Stephen was recovering, he used to sit in that chair you're sitting in now and talk and talk. It was supposed to be part of his therapy. Instead of tucking himself away somewhere and drinking, he was told he must talk. Talk to me, you, your mother, all of us, whoever was around at the time. We went along with it, didn't we? Because we were advised that it would help. He said some terrible things, you know, Tim.'

'I know, Dad. I was there.'

'Not all the time. You didn't hear everything.'

'A lot of the time I was there. And, yes, he said some horrible things. But he had a right to. His childhood and teen years were shit.'

'Whose fault was that?'

Tim shrugged and drank his wine.

'Well, whose was it, Tim?'

'I don't know, Dad. It's hard to say.'

'What exactly is hard to say? You think I treated him badly, don't you?'

Tim thought about leaving the room. This was not the time, with his father drunk, to recriminate.

'I think you treated each other badly.'

Edward had his glass to his face. He snorted into it.

'Very diplomatic. Very civil service. Balliol, was it?'

Tim ignored him.

'He was a shit a lot of the time,' Edward said.

'So were you!'

It was too late. He'd said it. He hadn't meant to, but the combination of the jibe about diplomacy and his instinct to protect Steve had made it, he realised, inevitable.

'Sorry,' he added. 'That's not fair.'

Edward swigged his drink.

'No, Tim, I'm sure it's entirely fair. I chased the bugger around the house and probably terrified him, the little mite. You wouldn't do it to a cat!'

'Why couldn't you appreciate that all he wanted was for you and Mum to think well of him, think he was a success, a person who achieved things, who was worthwhile knowing?'

'We did.'

'Well, you didn't show it.'

'Yes, we did!'

'Not so he saw it.'

'I can't comment on that.'

'Nor me.'

The phone was ringing. Neither of them seemed to want to move to answer it. Edward kept expecting the answerphone to take over, but the ringing continued. He started to get up.

'It's okay, Dad.'

Tim hurried across the room.

She'd been on the verge of terminating the call when she heard Tim at the other end.

'Darling, it's Mum. I need your help. The river's flooded and my car's stalled and I'm stuck. I can't get it started. Can you and Dad come?'

'Of course, Mum. Are you alright?'

'I'm fine, darling.' She tried to keep any hint of fear or panic out of her voice. 'But you'd better come as quickly as you can.'

'Where exactly are you?'

'By the bridge. Our side of it.'

'We'll be there straightaway.'

They're only five minutes away, she thought. It'll be fine. The floodwater had breeched the driver's and passenger doors, and when she put on the interior light, she could see that there were now several inches of water on the floor by the pedals. She'd raised her feet and tried to rest them on the gearbox mounting.

The light went out, and she realised the electrics must be soaked. There would be no chance of starting the car again.

She'd tried opening the door, but the weight of water against it had made that impossible. This was such a silly mistake, and the rain showed no sign of easing.

The journey from the station had been straightforward. It was largely downhill and although there was a good deal of water around, it was running off the surface of the road into the ditches on either side, and the little traffic there was around appeared to pass up and down without difficulty.

She'd come to the t-junction in the village and turned left towards the river and the bridge without a second thought. It hadn't even occurred to her that the river might have burst its banks. In fact, she was on the brow of the bridge before she realised there was anything wrong. Ahead was what looked like a lake, lying across the road and in the flanking fields. In the dark it was hard to see how deep it was. She put the car headlights on full beam and noticed that there was a ripple agitating the water, which meant that it was still rising.

She could so easily have reversed up and driven back into the village, but she wanted to be home, and she'd been through floods of this kind before. The river quite often flooded this part of the road when there was heavy rain. Edward always advised second gear, slow but sure, and in a couple of minutes she'd be on the far side, after which the road was invariably clear.

Cara let in the clutch and edged forward down the narrow back of the bridge and into the flood. For five or six metres the water was shallow and the Volvo pressed on through it. Then it stalled. She knew that what lay in front of her was deeper. It was somehow obvious from the colour of the water in the headlights and from the submerged fence posts. But when she tried the engine and it started, she still made up her mind to go on.

Within a matter of seconds, it seemed, the car had stalled again and the floodwater had begun to fill up the footwells. She pulled at the door handle and leant her weight against it, but it wouldn't budge. She was determined not to allow herself to be frightened. That would only get in the way of being practical. She needed to think. What would Edward do? He would sit tight and wait for the engine to recover, and try it again, and once she'd got it going, she had to press on, second gear, slow but sure, through the flood.

She waited, then turned the ignition key. It wasn't even like a flat battery, that tired sound of a motor endeavouring to start and failing. There was simply no response at all. She heard the click of the key in the ignition lock and that was it. The starter motor was completely dead.

Then the headlights failed. It was suddenly very dark. The rain hammered hard on the roof.

Now, she was frightened. She tried the driver's door again, pushing as hard as she could. It didn't move. Then she pushed the button to open her window. Nothing happened. It was the same with the sunroof.

She reached for her mobile and dialled the home number. It rang and rang.

He is shouting. I can't understand. I shake my head and point at my ankle. I squeeze my eyes and contort my face, trying to convey to him the idea of pain.

What remains of the sun is behind him. His dark silhouette

lours over me, and as he shouts, he moves about and the sun flashes and blinds me.

I can't explain, and the less I understand what he says, the more he shouts, as if he might yell sense into me. I think he realises that I can't walk, but he's presumably puzzled by my presence here, a white man stranded in a remote field. He bends down to me and roughly pushes me over so that I lie on my front. Then he pulls me back. Is he looking for signs of injury? My clothes must confuse him. Does he think I'm a spy?

It occurs to me to show him my dog tags. I tug them out of my shirt and point to them. He pauses for a moment, shouts at me again, and stretches out his hand to touch them. This man is my age or younger. He has a strong but lined face, and he looks worried. He fingers the dog tags. It's going through his mind that finding a soldier puts him in danger. He is probably cursing himself that he didn't take another route home.

He snaps the dog tags. A shot of astonishingly sharp pain whips across the back of my neck. What does he want? Are they a trophy? I can scarcely breathe. I am just waiting for him to pull out a knife.

Then he laughs. He laughs and, for what seems a long time, he can't stop himself laughing. His face is a sinuous pattern of laughter lines. His eyes are suddenly bright. He leans down and gestures to me that I should give him a high-five. Our hands clap together. We are suddenly the best of friends. He says several things, rapidly, but makes no attempt to show me what he means.

I feel his strength as he kneels and braces my shoulder with his arm. He is laughing. He lifts me to my feet and when I squirm with pain, he pulls my weight onto his shoulders. He laughs, discoloured amber teeth in a black beard. In this way, I can hobble in short bursts and we begin to make our way slowly towards the road.

Tim had managed to persuade his father to come with him. To begin with, Edward had protested and wanted to know what all the fuss was about, but once he'd left the house and had rain in his eyes and cold air on his face, he sobered up. Tim threw a torch into the boot and checked that his tow rope was still there.

They drove in silence. There were no cars on the road. The wipers struggled to clear the windscreen. From time to time, they stumbled across areas of minor flooding, which forced Tim to slow down. The trees swung out violently from the hedgerows. One had blown down on the north side of the village and branches of it stuck out into the road. Tim drove round them. He'd thought for a moment that he ought to stop and clear them to the side, but his mother's need seemed greater.

Edward said 'Oh my God!' when they reached her.

As they came down the hill, it was obvious that the Volvo was submerged in nearly a metre of floodwater. In the headlights they could see the upper part of the bonnet and the water appeared not to have yet reached the height of the windows. Tim could just make out his mother perched behind the steering wheel. When she waved, it seemed to him inappropriate somehow, ridiculous, like cracking jokes at a funeral.

He drove as close as he dared, taking his car to the very edge of the flood, but well short of the deeper water.

'What do we do now?' Tim said.

'We get her out of there,' his father said. 'That's what we do.'

He seemed to have lost all trace of being drunk, and when he jumped from the car into the pouring rain, Tim thought he looked like a man with the energy of someone twenty years younger. He watched his father in the headlights, wading forward, and felt strangely unable to move himself, frozen at the wheel.

Edward pushed through the water. It was astonishingly cold and rose quickly to his waist. He was shocked by both the weight of it against his body, resisting every step he tried to take, and the temperature of it. His legs and feet felt numb. He'd nearly reached Cara, but there seemed to be no sign of Tim following him. He looked back into the glare of the headlights. Tim was nowhere to be seen.

Cara smiled and shrugged her shoulders, as if to say this was all a stupid mistake, like getting a puncture or running out of petrol.

'Can you open the window?' he shouted.

He could barely hear her reply. The dogged downpour and the noise of the wind scooping up the floodwater screened all other sound. He couldn't hear his own voice, let alone Cara's.

She was squatting on the driver's seat, her legs underwater. She would be chilled through. He wondered how near to hypothermia she might be.

He got his hands onto the door handle and pulled. He knew it was futile and the cold of the water was almost unbearable. They had to get Cara out. The water was still rising and was now pouring into the car through the vents on the bonnet, where it met the windscreen. Suddenly, the water level in the cabin was up around Cara's waist.

Edward looked back to the road. He couldn't understand it. Tim was simply leaning on his car, taking it all in, watching him struggle to save his mother. Edward called out to him.

'Aren't you going to help?'

Tim appeared to shout back, his hands cupped around his mouth, but the only word Edward made out was *police*. He must be suggesting that they phone the emergency services. It was too late for that.

He tried to make Cara hear him by pressing his face against the glass.

'I'm just going to talk to Tim. To *Tim!*'

He pointed and Cara seemed to get the message.

Edward turned and forced his legs forward through the heavy floodwater. It took him for ever, he felt, to wade the four or five metres to where Tim was standing.

'We have to get her out of there.'

'Shall I ring 999?'

'There isn't time. She'll have drowned before they get here.'

'So what do we do?'

Edward was surprised. He would have expected his intellectually able son, the civil servant, the organiser and administrator, the planner and policy maker, to take more of a lead, but it was as if the crisis had stripped him of his years and experience. He looked to his father to solve the problem.

'I have a tow rope,' Tim said.

'It'll snap. The Volvo's too much of a tank for your car. We'll have to break in. See if you've got something that would smash the sunroof.'

Tim backed up his car and swung it round so that the lights pointed towards the ditch and the field beyond. Edward, in the meantime, took the torch and started to search the hedgerows. Cara would have been plunged into darkness again when Tim moved his car. She would be frightened, he thought, and probably wondering what they were doing and why he hadn't returned to her.

His head ached from all the bloody whisky he'd drunk. What the hell did he think he was doing, getting that drunk? It had been a kind of idleness. He'd got drunk because the bottle was there and there didn't seem to be any compelling reason not to. But he was paying the price, by God!

'Dad! Over here!'

Edward went to join Tim at the back of his car. He had the boot open and was looking at the scissor jack, part of the emergency kit for dealing with punctures.

'Heavy enough?'

'Worth a try,' Edward said.

Tim dragged the jack out of the car's tool bag and the two men walked back into the flood and waded out to the Volvo. The water had reached Cara's chest. She looked relieved to see them. Edward thought he saw her say 'Help me!' as he approached the car.

'Can you climb up on the bonnet, Tim? It's the only way you'll swing that thing.'

Edward took the jack from him whilst he struggled to find a foothold on the bumper and lever himself up. The bonnet was slippery and he had difficulty crawling over it. The water had reached the windscreen, but once he was standing, it barely covered his feet.

Edward passed the jack up to him, water swelling around his waist. The cold and pressure of it were shocking. He tried to explain to Cara that she needed to move into the back seat. He brought his fist hard down on the sunroof to make her understand. She jumped and looked alarmed, and then realised. It was hard, though, for her to change her position. She was clearly frozen through and extremely tired. As she forced herself to climb through the narrow gap between the front seats, she lost her balance and fell in the water. She kept her head up, but by the time she'd manoeuvred herself into the back, her clothes were soaked and she was wet up to her neck.

Tim slammed the jack down. The sunroof cracked in a dozen places, but held. He tugged the jack out of the glass and adjusting his weight so that he wouldn't slip on the bonnet, he brought it down a second time, hard. This time the roof shattered and parts of it fell in. A large piece of glass dropped into the water swilling around the passenger seat. Tim swung again, aiming for another part of the roof, which gave way as he hit it. There was now a hole the size of a suitcase. He worked the jack around the edges of it. Fragments of glass splintered and disappeared inside the car. They could now communicate with Cara.

'Mum! You need to get into the front now.'

Her face was level with the water, and she was wary of the glass shards floating towards her. She spat out the water that lapped at her mouth and made an attempt to move forward. She was so cold she couldn't feel her arms or her legs. They were like pieces of driftwood she was pushing into place.

Tim and Edward were both shouting words of encouragement. She wanted to give up. The effort seemed enormous.

But she had to make it. For their sakes as well as her own. She got herself between the front seats and dragged one leg forward and planted it firmly on the driver's seat. She pushed down as hard as she could and at the same time pulled her other leg through, and stood up.

She nearly cried when the rain hit her face and she felt the cold air of the wind behind it. Tim bent down and kissed her. His lips felt warm and hard on her cheek.

'Just one last effort, Mum. You're nearly there. You've got to get your feet up on the seat backs and push up.'

'Where do I put my hands?'

It was an absurdly simple question and she was worried she would tear her skin on the jagged edges of the smashed sunroof.

'You give them to me,' Tim said, and he offered to hold her hands in his while he pulled her up.

She stepped through the gap and as he helped her over the bonnet to the front of the car, he squeezed her arm.

Edward was there to hand her down. He took her in his arms and held her.

'You stink of whisky!' she said. 'No way to greet a girl after she's nearly drowned.'

When the phone rang, the three of them were standing in the kitchen, soaked to the skin, their clothes dripping on the red tiles. Cara felt close to tears. She watched Tim while he took off his coat and she wondered whether there had been some kind of reconciliation, whether the act of helping her out of the car, when she might well have drowned, had found in him some of the love he had felt for her as a little boy. He gave no sign of it and when he threw his wet coat on the floor, she found herself shouting at him.

'Can't you hang it up!' she yelled.

He turned to her with a look of real shock. She had taken him aback, and she thought he was about to shout at her in return when she started to cry, suddenly and uncontrollably.

She had expected that the tears would come, but the moment they did was still a surprise and when he took her in his arms, she pressed her face into his shoulder and didn't even try to hold back.

'It's okay, Mum,' Tim said. 'It'll be okay.'

She caught sight of Edward over Tim's shoulder, and he smiled at her. He appeared awkward, as if Tim comforting her left him with nothing to do.

'I'd better check on those windows,' he said. 'See how much water's coming into the study.'

She felt Tim's movement above her as he twisted his head to speak.

'Isn't anyone going to answer the phone?'

She saw Edward hesitate. That same awkwardness seemed to paralyse him, as if he were afraid of the phone and the message it might have for him. He looked directly at her. She could see in his eyes that she was meant to understand. She, of all people, should know why he failed to act and she realised that he believed, from some deep intuition, that this was the call they had been dreading.

She watched him take up the handset and extend the aerial. He spoke so quietly she could scarcely make out his words.

'Hello,' he said. 'Edward Padgett speaking.'

Afterwards he couldn't explain why, when he'd heard his voice, the words *just walking dully along* had come into his mind. He wasn't sure, but he thought they might be lines from a poem by Auden. Perhaps there had been a setting which he'd sung and part of it had been laid down, like sediment, in his memory.

'Is it you?' he asked, to be sure.

'Stephen?' Cara called out. 'Is it Stephen?'

'It's me, Dad.'

For several moments he couldn't say anything. He didn't know whether it was his drunkenness or the flood of relief.

'I'm safe, Dad, and I'm fine now.'

We may feel peace and rest and what makes countries happy.

'Thank God,' Edward said.

'I know, Dad, I know. We'll be together very soon.'

Together very soon.

'I'll be home in a few days.'

Words he'd been hearing in dreams, off-guard, half asleep fictions, in which all the anxieties of the last months were put to rest in a single phrase. They were holy words. They had the comfort of religion, the sense of an ending. They were the most welcome words he had heard in his entire life.

'Are you there, Dad?'

'Yes, I'm here, Stephen, and I will see you very soon.'

He said no more and passed the handset to Cara.

'Stephen? Is that you? Oh Stephen, Stephen.'

She kept saying his name, over and over again, until she believed that it was real.

The end

ACKNOWLEDGEMENTS

Firstly, I want to thank James Essinger for accepting *Prodigal* for publication and Charlotte Mouncey for capturing the essence of the book so skilfully in her cover design. I'd also like to take this opportunity to express my huge thanks to the friends and family who have read and commented on *Prodigal* through its various stages of development: Honor Clerk, David Crane, Richard Morris, Christopher Nicholson, Genevieve Waterhouse and Thomas Waterhouse. For their continuing support and advice over many years, I owe my lasting gratitude to Richard Kerridge and my wonderful wife, Tessa.